Praise for *The Sixth Lamentation*

'This is a first novel, and although incredibly complex, a wonderful one ... The engrossing essence of this novel is the morality of the individual. And then – a rarity in English-language literature since 1945 and astonishing for a writer of William Brodick's generation – there are throughout the book superb descriptions of events, people and their mindsets in occupied France which are entirely familiar to me from the two years I spent there in the 1940s' Gitta Sereney, *The Times*

'Utterly convincing. It has the merits of a work of art . . . a remarkable first novel' Allan Massie, *The Scotsman*

'Such a combination of narrative mastery, psychological insight and moral vision suggests a John le Carré in the making' Francis King, *Telegraph*

'A remarkable novel' John Dugdale, *Sunday Times*

'A highly intelligent first novel . . . an original exploration of law, theology and the past' *Sunday Telegraph*

'A summary cannot do justice to the intricacies of this novel . . . this is a thriller with intellect, a sensitive treatment of war crimes trials, and something of a love story to boot' *Good Book Guide*

'Brodick keeps the story going at a cracking pace, flitting back and forth between its various elements, characters and eras with timing so expert the reader is compelled to keep turning the pages' *Time Out*

'Brodick writes well about age and memory, buried pasts and the consequence of opening them up' *Guardian*

'The story is beautifully written and constructed, yet easy to read and completely compelling. An excellent book from this debut author' *New Books Magazine*

'The seriousness of the subject matter might easily have been compromised by the requirements of the thriller genre. But Brodick strikes the balance well, largely because of the skill with which he portrays Agnes and her wartime love affairs, which are crucial to the story' *Literary Re*

'An engrossing story of courage and suspense' *Evening Herald*

'[Brodrick] writes with a wisdom and poignancy that makes this a compelling novel' *Sunday Herald*

'*The Sixth Lamentation* is a tightly plotted story of love, betrayal and conscience – and the long shadows left behind by war' *Irish Independent*

'A haunting and compelling story which lingers in the mind long after the last page has been turned. This enthralled reader went back to the beginning to read it again' *The Oldie*

'A deeply thoughtful first novel' *Church of England Newsletter*

'With an unexpected twist at the end, this is a great first novel which I thoroughly enjoyed. A superb tale of intrigue and courage. With well defined characters this is a book that should not be missed by anyone who loves a good read' *Lowestoft Journal*

'A riveting story of retribution stretching over several generations' *RTE Guide*

'A wonderfully strong and moving novel, which lingers in one's mind for ages . . . brilliantly observed' *Publishing News*

'A tense, sophisticated, wholly convincing novel of suspense . . . a remarkable debut' Michael Holroyd

'A wonderful book. It has a timeless quality and really should go on to become a classic. It reminds me of the early works of John le Carré, but captures much more acutely the internal workings of ordinary people, and shows how, just by bumping into each other, they can be utterly transformed, and go on to extraordinarily brave and cowardly acts' Paul Britton, author of *The Jigsaw Man*

'It's indeed rare to find such a masterful blending of sharp suspense and literary resonance . . . Brodrick has produced a truly compelling novel' Jeffery Deaver, author of *The Stone Monkey*

'*The Sixth Lamentation* is a meticulously plotted, cat's cradle of a mystery with the interwoven stories pulled as taut as a piano-wire. William Brodrick has written the first of what I hope will be a series of especially literate thrillers' Martha Grimes

The Sixth Lamentation

William Brodrick

ABACUS

ABACUS

Published in Great Britain in 2003 by Little, Brown
This edition published by Abacus in 2008
Reprinted 2010, 2012, 2013

A CIP catalogue record for this book
is available from the British Library.

ISBN 978-0-349-12113-0

Typeset in Bembo by Palimpsest Book Production Limited,
Grangemouth, Stirlingshire
Printed and bound in Great Britain by
Clays Ltd, St Ives plc

Papers used by Abacus are from well-managed forests
and other responsible sources.

MIX
Paper from
responsible sources
FSC
www.fsc.org FSC® C104740

Abacus
An imprint of
Little, Brown Book Group
100 Victoria Embankment
London EC4Y 0DY

An Hachette UK Company
www.hachette.co.uk

www.littlebrown.co.uk

For my mother

For my mother

Acknowledgements

Generally speaking, debts are disagreeable things, especially those that endure. One kind, however, is a pleasant exception. I extend my warm gratitude to Ursula Mackenzie who helped me to produce the book I wanted to write as opposed to the one I had written; to Pamela Dorman for insightful analysis and championing this novel in the United States; to Araminta Whitley and Celia Hayley, both of whom have brought me to where I now am; to Nicki Kennedy and Sam Edenborough for ploughing foreign fields on my behalf. I'm grateful to Joanne Coen for her patience and scrupulous attention to detail in preparing the text for publication. While I dislike general expressions of thanks, that is the only way I can encompass the many individuals at Little, Brown Book Group and Penguin Putnam who have worked on this novel with unstinting dedication: I'm grateful to you all.

I reserve a particular word of thanks for Sarah Hannigan who encouraged me to write and helped me discover the way I wanted to do it. I also thank: Penny Moreland (who pushed me from doubt to confidence), Austin Donohoe (who urged me to take the risk), Paulinus Barnes (for sound advice), James Hawks (who told me to get on with it); Damien Charnock (who politely remarked upon the prevalence of sentences without verbs); Nick Rowe (who suggested including a list of principal characters); my family (for their part in shaping who I am, and for always smiling upon my endeavours); and my Chambers (for accommodating the peculiarities of someone who is writing a novel). I am grateful to the following for help with specific enquiries: William Clegg QC; Michael Walsh (Archivist, Heythrop College, University of London); Dr E. Rozanne Elder (Director, Institute of Cistercian Studies, Western Michigan University); Inspector Barbara Thompson (Suffolk Constabulary); Ian Fry and John 'Archie' Weeks (Old Bailey). I am responsible for any errors of interpretation that may arise from what I was told.

I reserve a special paragraph for Anne. Constant selfless support (all manner, in all weather) and solitary childcare (three of them) combined to mark out the space that made the writing of this book possible. No formal words of thanks can do her justice or reflect what I would like to say.

We both thank the community whose quiet presence graces the valley where this novel was begun and completed.

Principal Characters

This novel deals with three generations: those living in Paris during the Occupation, their children, and their offspring: old age, middle age and youth. Each is a bearer of memory, actual or transmitted. It is hoped the following table will furnish some assistance in holding in mind a number of characters and their place in the narrative.

The family of Agnes Embleton (née Aubret)
Freddie (father of Lucy)
Lucy

Characters mentioned in Agnes' journal recounting the resistance activity of The Round Table:
Father Rochet (parish priest, co-founder of The Round Table with Madame Klein)
Madam Klein (a Jewish widow, guardian of Agnes)
Jacques Fougères (operational leader of The Round Table)
Victor Brionne (childhood friend of Agnes and Jacques)
Franz Snyman (a Jewish refugee)
Eduard Schwermann (a Nazi Officer)

Monks at Notre Dame des Moineaux:

Father Morel (the Prior)

Father Pleyon (a member of The Round Table; successor
 to Father Morel)

Father Chambray (librarian who leaves the monastery after
 the war)

The family of Victor Brionne:

Robert

Other characters:

Father Anslem (a monk of Larkwood Priory)

Salomon Lachaise (a Jewish survivor, saved by The Round Table)

Max Schwermann (grandson of Eduard Schwermann)

Pascal Fougères (descendant of Jacques Fougères)

'L'Occupation'

April's tiny hands once captured Paris,
As you once captured me: infant Trojan
Fingers gently peeled away my resistance
To your charms. It was an epiphany;
I saw waving palms, rising dust, and yes,
I even heard the stones cry out your name,
   Agnes.

And then the light fell short.
I made a pact with the Devil when the
'Spring Wind' came, when Priam's son lay bleeding
On the ground. As morning broke the scattered
Stones whispered 'God, what have you done?' and yes,
I betrayed you both. Can you forgive me,
   Agnes?
(August, 1942)

Translated from the French by Father Anselm Duffy
Feast of Saint Agnes
Larkwood Priory, 21st January 1998

Part One

'Now is the time for the burning of the leaves'
(Laurence Binyon, 'The Burning of the Leaves', 1942)

First Prologue

1

April 1995.

'"Night and day I've lived among the tombs, cutting myself on stones",' replied Agnes quietly, searching her memory.

Doctor Scott's eyes narrowed slightly. His East Lothian vowels had lilted over diagnosis and prognosis, gently breaking the news while Agnes gazed at a gleaming spring daffodil behind his head, rising alone from a rogue plant pot balanced on a shelf – a present from a patient, perhaps, or free with lots of petrol. Soon it would topple and fall.

She forgot the flower when those old words, unbidden, rumbled from her mouth. Agnes couldn't place where they came from. Was it something Father Rochet had said, worse for wear, back in the forties? Something she'd read? It didn't matter. They were hers now, coming like a gift to name the past: an autobiography.

Agnes glanced at her doctor. He was a nice fellow, at home with neurological catastrophe but less sure of himself with mangled quotation. He looked over-troubled on her account and she was touched by his confusion.

'Do you mean to tell me that, after all I've been through, I'm going to die from a disease that will stop me talking?'

'I'm afraid so.'

3

'That's not fair, Doctor.' Agnes rose from her seat, still wearing her coat and holding her handbag.

'Let me get you a taxi.'

'No, no, I'd rather walk, thank you. While I can.'

'Of course.'

He followed Agnes to the door and, turning, she said, 'I'm not ready yet, Doctor.'

'No, I'm sure you're not. But who ever is?'

Agnes breathed in deeply. A sudden unexpected relief turned her stomach, rising then sinking away. She closed her eyes. Now she could go home, for good, to Arthur – and, funnily enough, to the knights of The Round Table. She'd never noticed that before.

Agnes had known there was something wrong when her speech became trapped in a slow drawl as if she'd had too much gin. She let it be. And then she started tripping in the street. She let that be. Like so many times before, Agnes only acted when pushed. She'd made an appointment to see a doctor only after Freddie had snapped.

They were walking through Cavendish Square towards the Wigmore Hall. A fine spray of March rain floated out of the night, softly lit from high windows and streetlamps. Freddie was a few impatient steps ahead and Agnes, trying to keep up, stumbled and fell, cutting her nose and splintering her glasses. Tears welled as she reached for her frames, not from pain, but because she knew Freddie's embarrassment was greater than hers.

'Mother, get up, please. Are you all right?'

Agnes pulled herself to her feet, helped by a passer-by. She wiped her hands upon her coat as Freddie produced a neatly

4

folded handkerchief. His exasperation spilled over. 'Look, if something's wrong, see a doctor. You won't say anything to me. Perhaps you'll say something to him. But for God's sake,' he blurted out, 'stop this bloody performance.'

Agnes knew he would berate himself for hurting her, as she berated herself for failing him. Neither of them spoke again, save to put in place essential courtesies.

'No, you first, really.'

'Thank you, Freddie.'

'A programme?'

'I don't think so.'

Agnes felt unaccountably tired by the interval so he took her home. She saw Doctor Scott within the week and he made the referral. She saw a consultant. The results came back. Doctor Scott had given her a call, and now she knew.

Leaving the doctor to a mother of five, Agnes ambled to her beloved home by the Thames where tall houses were cut from their gardens by a lane that ran to Hogarth's tomb. Here was her refuge, among brindled masonry and odd round windows with the copper glint of light on old glass. On the way she passed a troop of children holding hands and singing, the teachers front and back armed with clipboards. Piercing voices dislodged stones in her memory, stirring sediment. Frowning heavily, she thought again of Madame Klein and Father Rochet, Jacques and Victor and Paris and . . . all that.

No green shoots of forgetfulness had grown. The memory remained freshly cut, known only to Arthur. And now she was to die, without any resolution of the past, with no memorial to the others. But how could it be otherwise?

Turning the corner past the newsagent, she came into view

of the river. The breeze played upon the water, tousling a small boy pulling oars out of time. She slowed, caught short by the resilient disappointment that always struck like a sudden cramp when Agnes paid homage to brute circumstance.

'Loose ends are only tied up in books,' she said quietly, and she pushed aside, probably for the last time, the lingering, irrational hope that her life might yet be repaired by a caring author. Agnes stopped and laughed. She turned, walked back to the newsagent, and bought two school notebooks.

2

Freddie and Susan drove over from Kensington that evening, and Lucy took the tube from Brixton.

It was like a set piece of bad theatre: Freddie standing by the bay window, Susan fiddling with the kettle flex and Lucy, their daughter, the unacknowledged go-between, sitting slightly tensed in an armchair opposite Agnes, who was reluctantly centre stage.

'It's called motor neurone disease.'

No one said anything immediately. Freddie continued to avert his eyes. Lucy watched her mother keeping still, the flex suspended in her hands.

'Gran, did he say anything else?' Lucy asked tentatively.

'Yes. He expects it to advance on the quick side. At some point I won't be able to walk or talk, but I never did . . .'

Freddie walked across the room and knelt by Agnes' chair. He put his head on her lap and Agnes, a mother again, stroked his hair. Susan cried. Agnes wasn't sure if it was for her or the sight of Freddie undone. It didn't matter. Agnes continued '. . . I never did say much anyway, did I?'

After a cup of tea, Freddie and Susan left. There'd been a surprising ease between them all and Freddie had said he'd come back tomorrow night. It felt like a family. Lucy stayed on.

Joined by familiar silence, they sat at the scrubbed kitchen table preparing a mound of green beans, nipping the tips between their nails. Eight minutes later they curled up with bowls upon their knees, sucking butter from the prongs of their forks.

Agnes didn't watch television very often but she did that night. After Lucy had left she waited with the volume off for something interesting to appear. Images flickered on the screen, throwing stark shadows across the walls, lighting her face and blacking it out.

The telephone rang. It was Lucy, checking up on her. As she put the receiver down, Agnes' attention was suddenly seized by a grainy black and white newsreel of those elegant avenues she'd known so well, the slender trees and the sweep of the river. It was Paris before the war, almost sixty years ago.

'No, it's not,' she said, looking for the remote control. 'It's the Occupation. All those damned flags.' *Merde! Where is it?*

When she glanced back at the screen, she saw him and lost her breath – a handsome youth in sepia, with thick, sensual lips, for all the world a reliable prefect. Agnes froze, her eyes locked on the flamboyant uniform. 'My God, it's him. It must be him,' she whispered. Then she saw a sombre monk shaking his head. The item must have ended.

Agnes did not move for an hour. Then, purposefully, she opened the drawer of her bureau and took out one of the school notebooks she'd bought that morning. Not the first time, Agnes was struck by that puzzling confluence of events which

7

passed for chance: that she should decide to commit the past to paper on the day circumstance seemed to be forcing it out into the open.

Chapter One

1

'Sanctuary.'

'My bottom!'

'Honestly.'

The Prior, Father Andrew, was fond of diluting harsher well-known expressions for monastic use, but the sentiment remained largely the same. He was an unconverted Glaswegian tamed by excessive education, but shades of the street fighter were apt to break out when grappling with the more unusual community problems.

'It was abolished ages ago. He can't be serious.'

'Well, he is,' said Anselm.

'When did he come out with that one?'

'This morning, when Wilf asked him to leave.'

The Prior scowled. 'I suppose he declined to oblige?'

'Yes. And he told Wilf there's nowhere he can go.'

The two monks were sitting on a wooden bench on the south transept lawn of the Old Abbey ruin. It was Anselm's favourite spot at Larkwood. Facing them, on the South Walk cloister wall, were the remnants of the night stairs from the now vanished dorter. Anselm liked to sit here and muse upon his thirteenth-century ancestors, cowled and silent, making their way down for the night hours. The lawn, eaten by moss, spread away, undulating towards the enclosure fencing and beyond that to the bluebell path which led to the convent. It was a sharp morning. The Prior had just come back from a trip to London, having managed to miss the main item on all news bulletins. He'd returned home to find a gaggle of reporters and television crews camped on his doorstep.

'Give it to me again, in order,' said the Prior. He always insisted upon accurate chronologies.

'The story broke in a local newspaper of all places. By the time the nationals got to his home he was here, claiming the protection of the Church.'

'What did Wilf say?'

'Words to the effect that the police wouldn't pay any heed to Clement III.'

'Who was Clement III?'

'The Pope who granted the Order the right of sanctuary.'

'Trust Wilf to know that.' Disconcerted, he added, 'How did you know?'

'I had to ask as well.'

'That's all right then.' He returned to his mental listing. 'Go on, then what?'

'Wilf rang the police. The first I knew about anything was when the media were at the gates. I had a few words with them, batting back daft questions.'

Father Andrew examined his nails, flicking his thumb upon each finger. 'But why claim sanctuary? Where did he get the idea from?'

Anselm shifted uncomfortably. He would answer that question at the right moment, not now. It was one of the first lessons Anselm had learned after he'd placed himself subject to Holy Obedience: there's a time and a place for honesty, and it is the

10

privilege of the servant to choose the moment of abasement with his master.

The Prior stood and paced the ground, his arms concealed beneath his scapular. He said, 'We are on the two horns of one dilemma.'

'Indeed.'

They looked at each other, silently acknowledging the delicacy of the situation. The Prior spoke for them both.

'If he goes, there'll be international coverage of an old man protesting his innocence being handed over to the police; if he stays we'll be damned for supporting a Nazi. Either way, to lapse into the vernacular, we're shafted.'

'Succinctly put.'

The Prior leaned on a sill beneath an open arcade in the south transept wall, reflectively brushing loose lichen with the back of his hand. Anselm joined him.

'Father, I think one horn is shorter than the other and more comfortably straddled.'

'Go on.'

'The sooner he leaves the better. Otherwise we risk protracted public fascination with why he came here in the first place.'

With a tilt of the head the Prior drew Anselm away, leading him towards the stile gate and the bluebell path. 'I'm going to find out what the sisters think. They had a Chapter this morning.'

As they walked through the grass, wet with dew, Anselm pursued his point. 'If he's forced to go now, any uproar will be short-lived. And there is an explanation we can give in the future if we get hammered for throwing an innocent man on to the street.'

'Which is?'

11

'This is a monastery, not a remand home for the elderly.'
Anselm was pleased with the phrase. It was pithy and rounded:
a good sound bite . . . prepared earlier.

The Prior nodded, mildly unimpressed. Anselm persevered,
eyeing the Prior as he'd often eyed judges in another life when
trying to read their minds.

'The alternative is the other, longer horn. If he moves in,
and that's what it will amount to, we're in trouble. There could
be a trial.' Anselm paused. 'Nothing we say will convince anyone
that we're not on his side.'

They reached the stile and the Prior climbed over on to the
path, gathering his black habit under one arm, the white scapular
thrown over one shoulder. Anselm sensed him drifting away,
chasing private thoughts. 'We'll find out more tomorrow night.
Detective Superintendent Milby's coming at six. I'd like you
and Wilf to be there. Then we'll have a Special Chapter. Let
everyone know, will you?'

'Yes, of course.'

Anselm watched Father Andrew disappear along the path,
across a haze of blue and purple, his habit swaying in the breeze,
his head bowed.

Anselm had met Detective Superintendent Milby several times
in the past. In those days Milby had been a foot soldier with
the drugs squad. He'd had long hair and dressed in jeans, but
had still managed to look like a policeman. Anselm had been
a hack at the London Bar and their meetings had been limited
to the pro-forma cross-examination about stitching up and
excessive violence. Like all policemen familiar with the courts,

Milby had taken it in his stride. That was well over ten years ago and they'd both moved on since then.

Leaning against the stile gate, Anselm could almost smell the heavy scent of floor wax from his old chambers, and hear again the raucous laughter of competing voices in the coffee room. He smiled to himself, winsomely.

When Anselm left the Bar it caused a minor sensation, not least because it was such a wonderful Robing Room yarn. Since it was endemic to the profession to treat such things with private gravity and public levity, Anselm only heard the lowered voices of shared empathy: 'Tell me, old son, is it true? You're off to a monastery? I can say this to you; we've all got secret longings. The job's not everything . . .'

Anselm had knocked up ten years' call but, unknown to his colleagues, had never fully settled into harness. There was a restlessness that started to grow shortly after he became a tenant. Imperceptibly, he began to feel out of place, as if in a foreign land. There was another language, rarely spoken, and he wanted to learn it. Determined attempts to live a 'normal' life as a professional man floundered at regular but unpredictable intervals. He could be waiting for a taxi or heading off to court, doing anything ordinary, and he would suddenly feel curiously alienated from his surroundings. It was a sort of homesickness, usually mild, and occasionally acute. He later called these attacks by stealth 'promptings'. All Anselm knew at the time was that they were vaguely religious in origin. He responded by purchasing various translations of the Bible and books on prayer, as if the answer to the puzzle lay somewhere between the pages. On one occasion he left a bookshop having ordered a thirty-eight volume edition of the *Early Church Fathers*. They remained

13

as they came, in three cardboard boxes strapped with tape which he stacked in the corner of his living room and used as an inelegant resting place for coffee cups and take-away detritus. Anselm would then recover and continue his life at the Bar until ambushed by another God-ward impulse. It was a sort of guerrilla war for which he was always unprepared and ill-equipped. And all the while his book collection became larger, more comprehensive and unread. Eventually he stopped buying books. He realised one day while looking through a wide-angle lens that he wanted to become a monk.

It was a slightly odd experience. On leaving the Court of Appeal one late November afternoon, he was stopped in his tracks by a Chinese tourist who never ceased to smile. Several gesticulations later Anselm stood beneath the portal arch of the Royal Courts of Justice looking into the camera of a total stranger.

Suddenly he felt the urge to put the record straight, to say: 'Look, you're mistaken. I'm not who or what you think I am; I'm a fraud.' This happy man from a faraway place had pushed an internal door ajar and Anselm knew at once what was on the other side. He set off down the steps with incomprehensible protestations ringing in his ears – from himself and from the tourist who'd inadvertently nudged him away from the Bar. Taking the bus to Victoria, Anselm walked past the bookshop and into Westminster Cathedral, where he sat down beneath the dark interlocking bricks of the nave and prayed. It was to be the only moment of near certainty in Anselm's subsequent religious life. The jostling between doubt and perseverance was to come later. But at that time he understood, at last, what the underlying problem had been. It had been Larkwood Priory all along.

14

Chapter Two

1

Lucy Embleton made a stab at the washing-up and then took the tube to Brixton, knowing her grandmother would do them again. They'd cleaned out all the beans and even squabbled over the cold ones lying limp in the sieve. It was macabre, for Agnes would soon be gone, and eating had suddenly become a singularly futile activity. Waving goodbye, Lucy sensed every gesture now had another meaning that each of them would recognise, but never articulate, shaped by the torpid proximity of death. Her spirits sank into a chilling silence: a part of her past was almost complete and she'd never even understood it.

Lucy was twenty-five years old and had spent a large proportion of that time trying to understand her family's winning ways. She had never been able to locate any particular moment of crisis within the family history that might account for the present entanglement. It was more of a cumulative happening constructed out of tiny, otherwise insignificant building blocks tightly pressed together and cemented over time. As a child she asked penetrating questions borne of innocence; she guarded the answers with such care that, when she was older, confidences rained upon her – but never from Agnes or Arthur. Lucy became the one in whom the different facets of the past had been consigned, as if she was the one to bring them all together. And from that privileged position she conclud~d that if there was a simple explanation for what her father called 'the mess', it lay in the war years.

The received history was as follows: Agnes was half French, half English, and had lived in Paris during the Occupation. She was there when the black shroud from burning oil reserves hung over the city. She saw the German troops taking photos of 'La Marseillaise' on the Arc de Triomphe. She heard the thin, high voice of Marshal Pétain say he made a gift of himself to France, that he would seek an armistice with Hitler. About this period she was able to talk. It was the time after that had to be handled carefully, if at all. As a child, Lucy was small enough to inch under the fencing with her curiosity, moving from one month to the next, into the following years. But always the details from her grandmother became sparer, begrudging; her mood increasingly unsettled, her replies sharper, until Lucy learned she was approaching the place of shadows where she could go no further: where, as Freddie once spat out to his burning shame, Agnes became 'La Muette': the dumb one.

Of course the family knew what lay beyond the wire. A town and a village: Auschwitz and Ravensbrück. As to the why and wherefore, that was a mystery. Susan often said that only Grandpa Arthur knew where she'd been and why, but Lucy, as usual, moved as close to the line as possible trying to find out.

'No, I was never in the Resistance,' Agnes said wearily to one of Lucy's unremitting schoolgirl questions.

'Did you know anyone who was?'

'Yes, I did.'

'So you were involved with them?'

'Not really. I was just on the edge.'

16

'Were they brave?'

'Very brave.'

'So you must have edged towards bravery?'

Agnes became very still, distracted. 'We were all so young, so very young.'

'So you did do something?' pressed Lucy, eating chocolate.

'Nothing much to write home about. Now, stop your questions.'

That was usually where the probing ceased. But this time Lucy chanced her arm, pushed into the place of shadows: 'You can't have a big secret and not tell us what happened.'

Agnes gave a low animal growl through bared teeth. 'Enough.'

It was Lucy's first experience of atavistic fear. She became scared of her own grandmother. For Freddie, who was sitting in the corner, watching over a collapsed newspaper, it was simply another example of his mother's hopelessly introspective temperament. But Lucy, aged fourteen, still possessed the awesome non-rational percipience of childhood, and was young enough to be acutely sensitive to something neither she nor anyone else could name or know. It was that which made her shrink instinctively back: a smell on the wind.

So the reason for arrest and what had happened during two and a half years of incarceration lay out of reach. The narrative trail resumed, through Lucy's persistence, at the moment of Agnes' release, as if nothing had gone before: 'A Russian soldier stood gawping at me. He was no more than a boy, and his gun looked like a battered toy. He couldn't say anything. I couldn't speak. I was standing with children on either side. He cried. We just watched him. Eventually he said in English, "You're free now."'

Agnes wearily passed a blue-veined hand through her grey

17

hair, rearranging a silver clip, and added, 'I got out of Babylon, but there was no Zion. No promised land.'

'What's that, Gran?' Lucy enquired, puzzled.

'Just an old song about homesickness. And hope.'

'By Boney M?'

'A psalm.'

It was an opaque exchange, and all the more peculiar because Agnes was not a religious woman.

After the war Agnes returned to Paris where she met Captain Arthur Embleton in a hospital. They were married within two months, staying on in France for the next couple of years, during which time they had twins: Freddie and Elodie. After leaving the army Grandpa Arthur brought the family back to a suburban existence in north London. He became a solicitor in a large London firm and their life was superficially comfortable and predictable, except for those who knew otherwise. After Lucy's unnerving exchange with her grandmother, Freddie told Lucy about his own inexplicable childhood memories.

At times Agnes was captivating and extrovert, Freddie explained, but could suddenly and for no apparent reason become swamped by abstraction. It was as if the apparatus of her personality shut down, like a vast generator losing its source of power. The life in her would drain away until all the lights blinked and flickered before going out. And then she was gone, even though she was still in the same room, and everyone else was left adrift and awkward, trying to make contact across the space left by her absence.

This was the kind of thing Grandpa Arthur called 'a tactical withdrawal from the field of conflict', which was his thin attempt to joke with the children. But it also named a truth. Ordinary life was a battle for Agnes. Lucy's father also remembered those frightening moments: when Agnes suddenly froze, as if gripped by vertigo, shaking and sweating, holding on to the rim of the sink, the edge of a table, the back of a chair, until talked down by Grandpa Arthur.

Later, when Lucy's relationship with her father became more complicated, her mother passed on a little more history so that Lucy might better understand the man she had ceased to know in a simple way.

'Try to understand your father,' Susan said appealingly. 'It wasn't easy for him as a child, even though Grandpa did his best.'

Grandpa Arthur, she said, had tried to provide some consistency for Freddie and Elodie, giving them what he thought was a warm English upbringing, with lots of Gilbert and Sullivan, *Wisden* annuals (which Elodie loved) and regular tea at four o'clock. But he could not completely protect them. Where Agnes had been approachable and inviting one day, Freddie in particular would run towards her the next only to find her withdrawn. There had been one little incident that Freddie had never forgotten:

'Mum, look what Alex gave me. It's Excalibur. The sword pulled from a stone.'

Freddie held out the plastic brand with both hands, holding tight, just in case anyone actually tried to take it. Agnes slowed for a moment, but carried on peeling carrots.

'Mum, look, it's Excalibur. Alex gave it to me.'

Agnes continued roughly peeling off the skins, aware that Freddie was at her side, unaware he held out the toy he no longer wanted.

And Susan continued: 'You see, it wasn't easy for your father. It wasn't that bad for Elodie.'

'Why?' Lucy asked, and was granted more history.

Part of the problem for Freddie was that Elodie did not need Agnes like he did. Ironically, that made relations between mother and daughter moderately relaxed. Elodie drew water from another well. She naturally gravitated towards her father, with their shared love of cricket, leaving Freddie behind, resentful. Batting averages held nothing for him and he vainly searched for something he could bring to his mother, but she gave no lead. So he found himself unable to reach his mother and jealous of his sister. When they grew up and left home, the distance between siblings was weakly bridged by Christmas cards and awkward phone calls, the most memorable of which was when Elodie rang to say she had cancer. Freddie didn't know what to say and to his horror said nothing of consequence. He groped for the language they had once shared as children but that was long gone. He asked questions but could not remove the note of polite enquiry. He said goodbye as if nothing had really happened. The illness took its time, drawing Elodie down despite treatments, prescribed and otherwise. Curiously, as Freddie heard the details of decline he felt the need to talk to her. He rang spontaneously, often in the middle of the day, without knowing what he would say. More often than not conversation flowed easily, and something began to grow. He paid a few visits, always arranging another. And then Elodie died, sedated and beyond the comfort of her family, aged thirty-two. He blamed himself for having become a stranger. And, somehow, Freddie blamed Agnes.

And Susan said to Lucy, 'So you see, it hasn't been that easy for your father.'

Lucy could remember her father still trying hard, despite his confusion. Grandpa Arthur had always said, proudly, that Agnes was a jolly good musician. So her father bought a piano. But Agnes never played it. He bought various records, but Agnes never listened to them. In that conventional period of family calm, after Sunday lunch, the piano and records became a silent accusation. The lid had not been lifted; the records were still wrapped in cellophane. It was Lucy who first pressed the keys and introduced 'Chopsticks' to the house. It was Lucy who scratched Fauré's 'Romance sans parole', anxious because of the simmering *politesse* among the grown-ups. The scratching was a symbolic mishap, because the second of those three little piano pieces was her grandmother's favourite melody. That was why Freddie bought it.

It seemed to Lucy – not surprisingly – that her father's attempts to reach his mother became more deliberate and dutiful, his need constrained by a thin skin of self-protection. And yet, simultaneously, as Agnes grew older her oscillations in mood were replaced by a more moderate inaccessibility. But by then it seemed to be too late for Freddie. He could not slough the skin. Lucy's memory of Grandpa Arthur at this time was of a tired man, endlessly patient and exquisitely gentle with Agnes but a man who had learned to live more or less alone. He died quietly in his sleep one day, after a sudden stroke, as if he had slipped out of the back door in his slippers, unnoticed.

Agnes was strangely composed until the funeral, when her grief broke out like a flood. Then it sank away like a stone beneath flattened water. However, she refused to stay in the family home and sold up within two months, moving to a spacious flat in Hammersmith, by the river.

The loss of Grandpa Arthur left Freddie bereft. And Agnes, of all people, could not help him. The remaining links between them began to fragment, and Freddie's anger at his mother began to break out. He snapped at her more frequently, his outbursts becoming less of a protest and more of an accusation: for being his reluctant mother.

2

Even as Lucy received and experienced the living history of her family she understood that her father's problems had juddered wholesale into Susan, and embrangled her own most formative years.

What should have been a playground for a child had turned out to be more of a No Man's Land, strewn with adult debris. As she'd tried to romp around she'd snagged herself on unseen obstacles, until she'd learned by experience to locate and map out the specific danger spots between all her relations. By the age of fifteen Lucy had acquired the ability to move among her family with the supreme ease of a sophisticated adult. She became the deft one, prodding people away from plotted minefields. She seemed wise.

It was this shining characteristic that led her father to speak so unguardedly, and her mother to say more by way of further explanation. They didn't mean any harm, but they said enough to take, inadvertently, the glow off Lucy's innocence. Only Agnes and Grandpa Arthur left her alone.

So, it was not surprising that, after Grandpa Arthur died, Agnes and Lucy were imperceptibly drawn to one another, without effort, decision or the swapping of inner wounds. They grew to enjoy each other's company, neither of them placing demands upon the other. There was no weighted expectation. Long periods of silence could be shared, punctuated by clipped, comfortable conversation. It was obvious to anyone else in the same room that there was an alliance of sorts between them. But this only triggered a jealousy within her father that he could not bring himself to acknowledge, but could not stop himself from expressing, even when something far more serious was at stake. As he did when Lucy announced she was leaving home to live with a man:

'A man?'

'Yes.'

'Could you be more specific?'

'Tallish . . .'

'Don't be cheeky to your father,' said her mother, flushed.

'Have I met him?' he pursued.

'No. But Gran has.'

'*Gran* has?' said her father, incredulous, and lowered his head.

'Only once, Freddie, by accident,' said Agnes apologetically from her chair by the fire.

'He's called Darren and he's thirty-seven.'

'But you're only twenty,' Susan said, pale and desperate, smoothing her blouse. 'Darren, you say?'

Her father collected his coat and left the room, saying, 'Lucy, I'm going home. You can tell *me* as much as you see fit when you feel like it. Or maybe Gran can tell me next Sunday.'

He apologised profusely that evening for his petulance, by which time he'd got to grips with the anxiety that really troubled him. At the time of her announcement Lucy had recently dropped out of Cambridge, after winning a scholarship at King's to read Economics. It had been more of a triumph for Freddie than for her – she had made it to the same college to read the same subject as he had done. It was just marvellous . . . even though Lucy's interest lay in literature, not the science of wealth

23

distribution. When Lucy left university at the end of her first year, her father entered a sort of mourning. So did Lucy; she wore black and dyed her hair. For a short while she attacked the structure of Capital by drawing Income Support. Her father spoke to his old college – the place was open for the next academic year. But she found a job as a finance clerk for a small company that manufactured pine chairs. Pine chairs? Freddie cried. Yes, and a few tables. Oh my God, he said. Her mother bought a rocker. And then, at a party, Lucy met Darren, who had a lively interest in Lenin. He was the only person she knew who'd read the lambent phrases of Joseph Schumpeter. He introduced her to the vast, liberating plain of Other People's Misery but he quarried his authority from Lucy's lack of self-esteem. Age and force of manner overwhelmed her innate, cultured sophistication and she became a disciple. The large house called Home fell under the heavy sword of ideological scrutiny. She moved out. There was little Freddie could say. Her mother cried and cried.

The most interesting aspect of this episode was that Agnes didn't like Darren either. But she knew instinctively that it had to run its course. As a consequence, while Lucy knew Darren she kept visiting her grandmother; she rarely went home. That was the thing about Agnes, and in it lay a mystery: while she was inaccessible to 'normal' people the route was left open for 'outsiders'; like the bag-lady she frequently met in the park; like Lucy, in a way.

Then, long after Darren had left the scene, Lucy turned up at Chiswick Mall, Agnes' home, while her father was listening to the cricket (he'd lately discovered its secret joys, but only after the other two 'had been bowled out').

'Dad, I've got a place to read English at King's College.'

24

'Cambridge?' he said, alight.

'No, London.'

He smiled broadly. At least it had the same name as his alma mater. Susan baked a cake. And Agnes, the person who had always been there, to whom there was never a homecoming, pretended nothing had happened.

In leaving the cut and thrust of chair sales and becoming an undergraduate, Lucy entered another sort of No Man's Land that was not altogether unattractive. She had made no lasting friendships in the office and her new youthful companions at King's were broadly interested in drinking and running through the preliminary stages of an emotional crisis that would probably flower in the second year. This was familiar, uninviting territory. And so, in her first year studying English, aged twenty-five, Lucy found herself between a life she had left behind and a future that was yet to find a shape.

Lucy did retain, however, a small link with her past. It presented itself one morning when she was walking down High Holborn. Among the bobbing heads she caught sight of blonde hair and a stare of enquiry that turned rapidly into recognition. It was Cathy Glenton, a girl Lucy had known at Cambridge. She was one of the few people with whom Lucy had found any affinity. Their mutual attraction appeared to lie in sheer difference. Cathy was effortlessly brilliant and endowed with generalised talent, more like a machine that smoothly went to work on any activity she cared to assume. Between hot-air ballooning and acting in the drama club she discharged high marks in all her papers. She ate what she liked without putting on weight. She had it all, including a sublime boyfriend called Vincent. Even misfortune seemed toothless before Cathy's exuberance. Shortly into her first year she had had an accident in a drunken bicycle race, striking a pot-hole on a narrow bridge over Hobson's Brook, flying off her bike and landing on the railings, cutting her hands and face. She had been left with an almost insignificant scar, more of a twisting in the skin, situated upon her left cheek. For anyone else such an outcome would have teetered on the edge of psychological importance. But not for Cathy. She couldn't have cared less. When Lucy met her in High Holborn she noted the subtle presence of pink foundation, something Cathy had never used, and wondered why it should be needed now. After the preliminaries and the truncated histories, Lucy said, 'Still ballooning?'

'Nope.'

'Acting?'

'Nope.'

'How's Vincent?'

'Gone with the wind.'

'Oh.'

'Just work. Nothing but bloody work. And Turkish baths for pleasure.'

'Turkish baths?'

'Every week,' she laughed.

Cathy had gone into advertising, thinking up clever ways to persuade people that they wanted what they didn't really need. 'I'm a sorcerer,' she said. They exchanged numbers and thereafter each of them lurched for the phone every once in a while. They met, had a laugh and parted without planning another meeting, which somehow felt right. For different reasons they were both alone, crossing different fields.

26

Lucy stepped out into the cool night air and made her way to her flat in Acre Lane, trying yet again to move around the various bits of history which put together properly might give a coherent explanation for her family's broken ways. There was the war; the camps; a swift marriage; and the mystery that was Agnes. How did they all fit together? Was there something else? God alone knew.

Lucy's persisting regret was that things could so easily have been different for everyone: Agnes needn't have been lost to those around her; Grandpa Arthur needn't have sacrificed himself so much; Freddie needn't have felt rejected; Susan needn't have been run down by someone else's past; and Lucy could have had a childhood, at least for a while. They had all, to a greater or lesser extent, been unnecessarily damaged. Looking at the workings of the world and all therein, it seemed to Lucy that everything had been put together quite nicely at some point in the past, only now it didn't work very well. And no one knew why. But now that her gran was dying, explanations were of no consequence. If there was one, only Agnes knew it, and maybe it was better she take it with her.

When she got to her flat, Lucy switched on the television and drew the curtains, shutting out the night. On impulse she rang her grandmother, just as the news was about to begin.

'Are you all right?'

'Of course I am. Don't worry.'

'Are you frightened?' It was a personal question, the sort she'd never asked before.

The answer came smoothly: 'No. There's not much more in this life to be scared about, is there?'

'I suppose not. Goodnight, Gran.'

'Goodnight, Lucy.'

Lucy watched the news with interest. She thought the monk handled the silly question about complicity rather well.

Chapter Three

Brother Sylvester, the Gatekeeper, escorted Detective Superintendent Robert Milby and Detective Inspector Madeleine Armstrong into the parlour at the main entrance of the Priory. At ninety-three years of age Sylvester's memory was now best equipped to deal with his youth, the subsequent decades having become somewhat indistinct. His mind was often somewhere else, and most visitors were treated to forays into his past without the need for any particular enquiry.

'You'll be going back to Martlesham tonight, Detective Superintendent?'

'No, no, I've got to go on to London. No rest for the wicked.'

'Yes, there is,' said Brother Sylvester. He leaned upon the open door, in contemplation of a distant glimmering. 'The last time I was in London was with Baden-Powell . . .'

'Brother, thank you.' The Prior's words were firm, with an undertone of familiar entreaty. Brother Sylvester, a little startled, reluctantly withdrew.

The Prior, Anselm and Wilf were seated at a large table. Milby had changed a great deal since Anselm had last seen him. The days of flinging drug suppliers over the bonnets of their cars had ended and, through promotion, he had eased himself into a suit and a certain studied gravitas. As he sat down, Milby announced: 'This is a matter for the Metropolitan Police, but

29

conduct of the enquiry will be shared with us because the subject is in our area.' He raised a large hand towards his colleague. 'Detective Inspector Armstrong will be handling our involvement.'

Anselm regarded her pensively. Her manner suggested self-containment, separation. Short jet-black hair made her stand out sharply from her surroundings, like an etching. Long eyelashes, also black, moved slowly as she scanned a sheaf of notes that lay on the table.

Milby said, 'Madeleine, would you explain what's come to light.'

She nodded at Father Andrew, as if he were the one who had invited her contribution. Her voice was even, controlled, with a slightly hard edge.

'His name is Eduard Walter Schwermann. It seems he was a low-ranking SS officer based in Paris during the war. He's incriminated in the deportation of thousands of Jews to the death camps.'

Father Andrew sat with his hands joined, only the fingertips touching, a characteristic gesture known by Anselm to mean intense, troubled concentration.

'He was captured in January 1945, disguised as a priest and with transit papers for England.'

'A priest?' repeated the Prior.

'I'm afraid so. He was recognised on a train and subsequently arrested. At that point he appears to have informed the military police that he was travelling with someone else, a Frenchman named Victor Brionne. He too was arrested. Both men had false identities. Both were interviewed by a Captain Lawson. Both were released and their passage into this country went ahead.'

30

The Prior frowned. 'Why were they released?'

'We haven't the faintest idea. I'll be talking to the inter-viewing officer in a few days' time. He's now a Labour Peer. Back then he was a captain in Military Intelligence.'

'Who provided the false identities, the travel papers?'

'We don't know. But the fact that Schwermann was caught dressed as a priest might suggest an ecclesiastical connection.'

'And then again,' interjected the Prior logically, not defen-sively, 'it might not. There may be a diplomatic link, though I can't imagine why or how.' The Prior drew a hand across his tight lips.

'Of course. The strange thing is' – her manner altered suddenly, becoming warmer, less analytical – 'that the false iden-tities appear not to have been recorded. It is as though they were let into the country and the trail to finding them was quietly brushed away.'

'By Captain Lawson?'

'So it seems.'

A reflective pause ensued, until Anselm said, 'So what happened for the next fifty years?'

'Nothing, until Pascal Fougères, a young Frenchman and foreign correspondent for *Le Monde*, found a declassified memo in the United States setting out the information I've just given you. It turns out he has a personal interest, because Schwermann was responsible for the deportation of his great-uncle, Jacques Fougères. Apparently he's a Resistance hero.'

'So what did he do?' asked Anselm.

'He wrote an article – this is about a year and a half ago – alleging that two war criminals had found a safe haven in Britain. It caused a big splash on the Continent, but only a ripple over here. And then another peculiar thing happened. Fougères

31

received an anonymous letter giving him the name under which Schwermann had escaped: Nightingale.'

'The number of people who knew that can't be very large,' said Father Andrew pensively.

'No, but Fougères hasn't pursued that angle. I have to say I find that puzzling. Anyway, what he did do was contact Jewish and former Resistance organisations in France. They quietly started putting together the case against Schwermann—'

'And Brionne?'

'No, not against him, which is even more puzzling. When they had the outline of a case they presented it to the Home Office. Somehow Schwermann found out before we could arrest him and the next thing we know he's here, claiming sanctuary.'

She glanced at Detective Superintendent Milby who added quickly, with a studious frown, 'We find that a little odd, sanctuary.'

'A right granted by Clement III. It has no legal force,' Father Andrew said dismissively.

Anselm caught Wilf's eye – he had been an historian in the world – and read astonishment at the hidden erudition of his Prior.

'But what gave him that idea?' asked DI Armstrong.

'Father Anselm will enlighten you.'

Anselm recounted to the police officers what he had told his Prior the previous night just before Compline, when the Great Silence would fall on Larkwood and the chances of reproach were least likely to blossom. On the day of Schwermann's arrival Anselm had been on the afternoon confessions. No one had come. When he'd left the confessional there had been only one other person in the nave, an old man sitting at the back, as still as a painted figure in a frieze. As Anselm had walked past he'd suddenly moved, grabbing Anselm's habit, saying, 'Father, what does a man do when the world has turned against him?'

Anselm had paused, disconcerted by the tight grip on his clothing rather than the question posed. It was one of those ponderous enquiries, he'd thought, which is the lot of the monk to answer.

'In the old days,' he'd replied, pulling at the cloth, 'you'd claim "sanctuary", the protection of the Church, if the accusation was unjust.'

'And would you be safe?'

'Oh yes.'

'Truly?'

'I promise you.'

'Thank you,' the old man had said, with a quiet calm that Anselm had later recognised as the threshold of decision. At the time he had simply walked away reflecting carelessly on the eccentricities of the faithful and the curious things that troubled them.

'Therefore,' Anselm said to Milby and DI Armstrong, 'I fear he took words lightly spoken as an invitation.'

Father Andrew turned to Brother Wilfred and said, 'Now is a good time to tell us what happened next.'

Wilf was the sort of gentle, reflective man who could not talk to the police without feeling as if he had committed a crime. Nervously, he said, 'I was talking to Brother Sylvester at reception about a news item I'd just heard to the effect that a local man accused of wartime atrocities had vanished from his home. Then in he walks and says, calmly as you like, he's claiming sanctuary. I told him it had been abolished. I asked him to leave and he refused, so off I went to call the police.'

'And then,' said Father Andrew, musing, 'the troops of Midian arrived at our gates with their panoply of cameras.' He waited for a response, his silver eyebrows slightly raised.

The Detective Superintendent said, 'The Press. They're always one step ahead.'

'Indeed,' said Father Andrew dryly. 'What happens now?'

'There will be an investigation, and then we'll review the evidence,' informed DI Armstrong.

'That isn't quite what I meant,' said Father Andrew gently. 'I meant how do you propose to remove him?'

DI Armstrong looked at her superior officer with, to Anselm's judgment, a hardening of expression. Milby leaned across the table in a sort of sprawl. In a confiding way he said, 'We've given that some thought. If at all possible, we think he should stay here, as a short-term measure at least, if only for his own protection.'

'Detective Superintendent, this is a monastery, not a remand home for the elderly.' The words were strangely familiar to Anselm.

'I appreciate that, but—'

'And our first duty is to our common life.'

'Of course—'

'And we have the peculiar sensation of having been deliberately compromised.'

Springing unforeseen from pliable courtesy, the accusation stung the Detective Superintendent. From Anselm's point of view there followed that delicious silence upon which he had often dined in the past. The embarrassment of the police is every defence barrister's illicit pleasure and years of committed monastic life had done nothing to diminish his appetite. And, curiously, on this occasion it seemed the delight, ill-suppressed, was shared by DI Armstrong.

34

Unconvincingly, but ready for a tussle, Milby said, 'I'm not sure I follow you.'

Father Andrew smiled benignly. He never engaged in useless arguments. In the absence of an admission where one was required he abruptly closed a conversation down. It was a powerful, unnerving tool. Returning to his former gentility, he said, 'I'll let you know our position a week from today.' He turned his attention to DI Armstrong – 'I'm very grateful for all you have told us.'

The meeting over, Anselm walked the police officers to the courtyard in front of Larkwood. The gravel crunched underfoot as the question came from the Detective Superintendent: 'Haven't we met before?'

'Yes. I used to be at the Bar. I'm sure we had a few courtroom squabbles. I moved on.'

He laughed and said, 'Well, you did the right thing. Wish I'd become a monk.' He slumped in the back of an unmarked car and slammed the door.

DI Armstrong seemed to hesitate. She glanced around as if not wanting to leave and said, 'This is a lovely place. Goodnight, Father.'

Anselm returned to the parlour to join Father Andrew and Brother Wilfred. Brother Sylvester had shuffled into the room and was laying out a selection of leaflets on the sideboard. He said:

'When Wilf told that chap sanctuary had been abolished, he said he'd done it before.' He continued arranging neat piles of pink and green paper.

'What?' said Father Andrew quietly.

'After Wilf left to find Anselm, he said he'd done it before, a long time ago.'

The Priory bell rang ponderously, slow, deep chimes echoing around Larkwood, calling the brothers to prayer. Sylvester turned obediently to get himself ready – 'I'm off. Don't want to be late.' – and slipped out of the room, leaving the other monks to digest the implications of his words.

'I'm glad he kept that to himself,' said the Prior judiciously. So was Anselm. He was thinking ahead, catching sight of a shifting shadow. 'Why here? Why come to us?'

'Good question,' said the Prior pensively. The ringing had come to a close. A busy shuffling of feet came from the cloister. 'Come on. Time for quiet.'

Anselm entered the long dark nave and found his place in the choir. Sylvester's space behind him was empty. He would, as usual, be late. Leaning against his stall and leafing through his Psalter, Anselm smiled to himself about the Prior – his sally about Clement III and the remand home remark. Father Andrew always listened carefully to everyone with whom he spoke, and used what he heard at some future point as if it was fresh to his mind. Like the Lord, he reaped a harvest from fields he had not sown. He mulled over how it was that the Prior was so sure the police had informed the Press, and had done so in order to force Larkwood to keep their guest. Someone, of course, must have told him.

36

Chapter Four

1

It was the stone in his shoe, lodged inadvertently when Anselm visited Larkwood Priory on a school retreat at the age of eighteen. He only signed up to avoid yet another geography trip, plodding in the rain over that wretched limestone pavement near Malham Tarn. But an extravagant claim on a vocations leaflet caught his eye (laid on a table by a monk who said he'd met Baden-Powell):

'We can't promise happiness,
But if God has called you to be here
You will taste a peace this world cannot give.'

Throughout the years that followed, the words slunk into his mind and out again – not when he was restless but when he was content. The contingent pledge became a goad, an unwanted invitation that reminded him of what he most wanted to forget.

The loss of peace – for that is what it was – had trodden an unknown path. When beset by the dogmatic turbulence of adolescence Anselm turned to Proust. Seeing his life in epic form, he subjected his past to a minute psychological investigation. He easily identified the events that had sent ripples into the present: the death of his mother whom he had hardly known; the nineteenth-century formality of his father; the paradoxical but defining insecurity that arises from being wedged between two older brothers and two younger sisters; the welcome nuance of banishment to a French boarding school for part of his secondary education. Anselm concluded that he, alone among men, was in grave need of internal repair.

When he joined the chambers of Roderick Kemble QC, fondly known as Roddy, and had a few run-ins with some of the more difficult members of the profession, he learned that he wasn't in that bad a shape after all. Roddy was a red, round and joyous man, loved and bled over profusely by all who knew him. While he was one of the most outstanding advocates of his generation it was compassion that truly set him apart. His one theme of consolation was habitually volunteered when drunk: 'None of us get here without being broken to pieces along the way, old son. None of us know why. So let's just bear with one another.' And, lunging for a bottle, he would say, 'Now, bring on the fatted calf.'

The dislocation that beset Anselm in his maturity, however, was of a wholly different order and could only be assuaged by long periods of solitude and . . . prayer: an activity that took him beyond himself, but which collapsed the moment he thought about what he was doing – like falling off a bicycle. And, picking himself up again, he remembered those frightful words on the leaflet. He began to wonder, on a purely theoretical basis, whether for some people (but not him) monastic life was the only way of finding contentment.

He went back to Larkwood out of curiosity, attending an occasional Office and having tea in the village. He visited the Priory more often, dreading the return to London, but without wanting to stay in Suffolk. On the fateful day he met the tourist at the Court of Appeal, Anselm recognised that in brushing against this other life he had sustained a fine wound on the

38

memory, causing a longing, a homesickness that would not let him settle in any place other than the source of injury. And so, Anselm began his return to Larkwood. After two years of visiting, and being politely discouraged (in accordance with The Rule), he became a postulant. He left behind a baffled family. He was thirty-four.

Anselm's first surprise on entering religious life was to discover the monastery contained ordinary human beings alarmingly similar to one or two villains he had represented at the criminal Bar. He had thought only the prison system could withstand the outrageous behaviour of its members. But the same was true of Larkwood, where, unlike enforced incarceration, each individual had promised to live a life of ongoing conversion. Thankfully, Brother Bruno performed an important act of mercy on the day of Anselm's arrival. He briskly punctured whatever reasonable expectations Anselm might have entertained about a life of wholesome tranquillity.

Bruno had been a Tyneside docker for thirty years and brought to monastic life a playful candour that generated various maxims – most of which were only quoted to be discounted. 'I think there's something you ought to know,' he confided, having been introduced to Anselm five minutes earlier. 'You'll find out as you go along, the good guys always leave and only the so and sos remain.'

Time passed with a peculiar swiftness known only to those who live subject to the rhythm of monastic life. The chant, the ancient regularity and the silence mysteriously brought together the fragments of Anselm's past and gave him a sense of completeness – but only for the first few months. That turned out to be a glimpse of who he might become, rather than who he was. Within a year the pieces shattered again, falling back to where they had been before he'd become a postulant. He understood what agnostic Roddy had told him when he'd left the Bar: that being a monk had nothing to do with putting the bits back together. And he learned the meaning of another Bruno aphorism: 'Nobody stays for the reasons they came.' The liturgical cycle rolled up the years. Some very pleasant chaps returned to the world. But Anselm stayed put, abandoning any pretence of being one of the good guys, or of searching for peace through internal reconstruction. And sometimes, in that half-sleep savoured last thing at night and first thing in the morning, Anselm began to wonder how much of it had been choice, and how much unwitting cooperation.

Larkwood's life became Anselm's. The Priory supported itself through bookbinding, ceramics and the production of apple juice – along with a now legendary cider of a particularly vigorous character. Anselm learned the balanced crafts of labour, rest and prayer. After twelve years of monastic life the elements of living a fulfilled life were broadly in position. A planetary motion of doubt, certainty, joy, anguish, loneliness and boredom, each on their own trajectory, encircled an evolving contentment. And very, very occasionally, when he wasn't looking, the Lord of the Dance brushed past.

2

The man from the Home Office turned up the day after Milby's visit and before the community meeting. Fortunate timing that, thought Anselm. He didn't get the chance to share this reflection with Authority, however, because Father Andrew, in the days following the arrival of Schwermann, had withdrawn from corridor and cloister and only emerged to growl his way through Office and tell the morning Chapter who was coming.

His name was Wilson, apparently. Peering through a window in the bursar's office, Anselm saw the black Jaguar creep across the Priory forecourt. The mandarin emerged in a chalk pin-stripe of the deepest blue, his hair a laundry white, each strand obedient to its place in life. He extended a pale hand graciously to Father Andrew, as if it was a Royal visit, his faint smile conveying shyness, a remote fragility masked by exquisite courtesy.

Precisely what Mr Wilson said was revealed that evening. Community meetings, like gatherings in Chambers, were notorious for bringing out everyone's worst qualities. For a group of men capable of savage argument over nothing in particular, the prospects of a sensible discussion on modified asylum for a war criminal were not promising. But on this occasion there was a surprising display of common sense.

The monks silently took their seats in Chapter, side by side around the circling wall. All eyes fell on Father Andrew's stern face. A single candle burned brightly on a plinth beside him. From where Anselm sat, the tiny flickering danced upon the Prior's narrow glasses, lighting his eyes with fire.

'I'll be brief. The Home Office has asked us to provide this man with a short-term refuge. You already know what he was, and what he's alleged to have done. He must be accommodated away from the public eye, and be protected. He can't go home. Transfer to prison is considered inappropriate.' Father Andrew had anticipated most of the questions and answered them mechanically in brief succession. 'An expedited investigation has already commenced. No charges were brought after the war and it's thought unlikely any could be brought now.

41

He's never been in hiding from the British authorities. Our involvement is nothing more than a matter of convenience. Costs sustained by the Priory will be met, and the police will deal with any protesters. A personal protection officer will stay with the man himself. He should be off our hands in three months. That's it. The question is this: does he stay or go?' He surveyed the room gravely, waiting for a response, and then dutifully checked himself. 'Oh yes, Lord Thingummy-Other, a Catholic peer, humbly endorses the government's request.'

'Do you mean Lord Crompton?' purred Father Michael with deferential enthusiasm.

'I'm sorry, I didn't note the name,' said Father Andrew brusquely.

'What do the sisters think?' asked Anselm, realigning the debate but relishing the way Father Andrew had batted down Michael's impulse for social climbing.

'That he should leave.'

There was a general murmur of assent.

Father Jerome, a muscular chap troubled by occasional asthma and the only member of the community ever to have been imprisoned, named the problem. 'Leaving aside any assurances, he's come here for protection. Claiming sanctuary's all about holy innocence, an appeal to God for higher justice. We can't give that. And if he doesn't deserve it we're in for big trouble. In this world and the next.'

'Nonsense,' snapped Father Michael. 'If he's rejected this way and that because of a false accusation, then he should stay. His own appeal is backed by the Establishment. How the world chooses to interpret our cooperation is neither here nor there. Appearances count for nothing.' And by way of retort he added, 'I know exactly what the Trotskyites among you think, but I

42

happen to know Lord Crompton has a distinguished war record. He knew Mother Teresa. An assurance from him can be trusted.'

And so it went on. Only two monks kept silent: Father Anselm, who was biding his time, and a recently professed Brother, the youngest member of the community.

'Benedict, what do you think?' asked the Prior warmly.

The young monk stood, as was the custom, and looked uncertainly around him. 'I'm afraid I don't have an opinion. Just questions,' he faltered.

'Go on.'

'If he's innocent, why the false name?'

'A good question.'

'Why come here?'

'Another good question.'

'Why wasn't he indicted after the war?'

'I don't know.'

'Against expectation, if there is a trial, what happens then?'

'As Father Jerome has rightly pointed out, we're in trouble, especially if he's convicted.'

Brother Benedict scratched the shaved hair behind his ear. 'That's all I can think of for the time being.'

'Thank you very much,' said Father Andrew, leaning back. 'Jerome and Benedict have kindly demonstrated the nature of the problem facing the community.' A reflective silence spread across the gathered monks. Now, thought Anselm, was the time for his planned contribution. He coughed, and stood. The Prior nodded.

Anselm held back from advocating any one course of action. Instead he donned the mantle of impartial adviser, reaming off an impressive summary of issues, neatly numbered, with recommendations depending on the view taken of other points raised.

43

It was all very professional and implicitly based on lofty experience of these difficult matters: sound advice from a man who knew the ropes. To the trained eye, Anselm feared he would be found out by his brothers – that he was angling to be involved in the handling of the Schwermann case.

'Thank you, Anselm,' said the Prior. 'And thanks to you all. Now, time for quiet.'

Father Andrew said a brief prayer and extinguished the candle between his fingers. The meeting was over. And, having listened to all, the outcome was for the Prior alone to decide.

The Papal Nuncio came to Larkwood the following day – yet another unexpected visitor demanding to see Father Andrew. Not some hobbledehoy, exclaimed Father Michael, but the top brass, you know. Precisely what the Nuncio had to say was not disclosed but word went round that Rome must have leaned on the Prior to throw Schwermann out.

And so it was the week drew to a close. Anselm stayed up late, waiting for *Sailing By* on Radio 4, and mused lightly on the curious sequence of events. In four days, four driven horsemen from different quarters had galloped across the hearth: the fugitive, the sheriff, the Queen's good servant and, last of all, a Prince of the Church. But as he drifted off to sleep to the consolation of the shipping forecast with warnings of gales at Tyne and Dogger, he was gripped by a darker thought, and suddenly woke. Their coming had the mark of a grand reunion.

Chapter Five

Lucy propped herself up in bed and laid the manila envelope carefully on her knees. Agnes had given it to her that afternoon and Lucy had nearly cried. The soft clunking of Grandpa Arthur's wall clock grew louder, as if he were coming, as if he would take off his hat and coat and sit down.

In the three months that had passed since Agnes had told the family about her illness, the tight pattern of relating, built up over so many years, had begun to fall apart, threatening something more significant, like the one or two loose rocks that topple down a scree. Freddie came to visit his mother more frequently, tussling with the old awkwardness he preferred to avoid; Susan's spirits rose as she saw the coming together of separate worlds – not just that of her husband and mother-in-law but also their daughter. As Lucy recognised, she had once been the small hub in a wheel where everyone else's long spindles found a meeting place: that arrangement had splintered a while ago, but now, with the news that Agnes would soon die, a strange re-ordering of things was under way. As with all great changes, there was a constant: Lucy came frequently with market vegetables in brown paper bags.

The subtle transformation was not restricted to the inner workings of Lucy and her parents. Agnes, too, was on the move. Arriving unannounced one afternoon, Lucy found a pile of

45

newspapers in the hall. Surreptitiously she leafed through them: two or three bore the same date and cuttings had been taken. As she realigned the pile, puzzled, Lucy halted, suddenly identifying the subtle difference in ambiance that had struck her as soon as she opened the door, but which she had not been able to name: the radio was on. She crept into the kitchen. Grandpa Arthur's Roberts had been retrieved from some forgotten place and now stood upon the windowsill by the sink. Agnes was twisting the dial, grumbling about modern music.

On another day Lucy rushed into the sitting room chasing a stray cat that had formed an unreciprocated attachment to Agnes but who, out of mercy, had been granted a tenancy. The beast escaped through the window. Turning to go, Lucy caught the tiny twinkle of a red light. She scanned the familiar room as though she were a traveller in a foreign land: the record player was on; the piano lid was open . . . there was music on the rest. Lucy glanced at the title: 'Romance sans parole, No. 2' by Fauré, her grandmother's favourite melody. All at once Lucy saw Agnes, alone, when she knew no one would call, her long fingers finding their way across the keys.

As for Agnes, she was slower, more measured in her movements, and when she walked from one room to another she held out her slender arms like a ballet dancer, touching objects lightly as she passed – sometimes it was only the leaf of a plant – as if dispensing blessings.

'I don't need to, but I like to feel something on either side,' explained Agnes.

She was losing her balance.

On a muggy afternoon in early July Lucy rang Cathy Glenton and arranged a night out. Then she went to Chiswick Mall, resolved to touch upon what her father called 'the real issue'. She stood over the piano, playing 'Chopsticks' slowly, with two fingers, her heart in her mouth. 'Gran, you're going to need specialist help.'

'*Please*, anything but *that*,' Agnes pleaded.

'I'm sorry, but it's true. Someone has to tell you.'

'I mean that tune. For God's sake, stop it.'

'I've played it every time I've—'

'Believe me, I've listened!' said Agnes impatiently. There was an uneasy pause.

Lucy bit her lip. 'I meant what I said, you—'

'Yes, yes, yes, I know. Don't worry. I'm all right for now. And anyway, there's always Wilma.'

Lucy gaped and almost exclaimed: a bag-lady . . . I thought you just met in the park . . .

Agnes swiftly shut down any objections. 'Wilma's a very interesting person. She used to be in the theatre. Did a lot of Rep. I'll introduce you.' She smoothed a pleat on her skirt. 'She's my friend, Lucy. Don't shut her out.'

'Of course not,' said Lucy uncertainly. Before she could draw her thoughts together, Agnes continued, with assumed cheerfulness, 'Anyway, enough of that. Let's have a cup of tea.'

They moved awkwardly into the kitchen.

'There's always some rubbish on about now,' said Agnes, moving towards the radio, touching a chair . . . and then a counter . . . and then the sink. She turned the control. Suddenly there was a sort of explosion. An orchestra was involved . . . and a jazz band. And someone, thought Lucy, listening carefully . . . is hitting a biscuit tin of broken glass.

'*Post-modern*, you know,' said Agnes, nodding gravely, ignoring the tension between them.

47

Lucy made the tea and they sat nursing their mugs, their eyes frequently meeting. Lucy was going to raise the subject of professional help again whether Agnes liked it or not. But the glances from her grandmother made it clear she would not budge, she would make her own arrangements. And, as if providing a soundtrack to a silent film, an out-of-tune jazz band fought with an orchestra while someone had a whale of a time with a hammer.

Lucy chose her moment when a languid, knowing voice ushered in the news at five o'clock. But Agnes outflanked her with a newfound passion for current affairs. She sat forward with a convincing display of concentration. The swift volley of headlines between broadcasters began but Agnes dismissed each new story with a pout before the introductions ended. After a few minutes, she signalled with her head to turn it off. A clatter of falling plates echoed from the dining room.

'That blasted cat.'

'Sounds *post-modern* to me,' said Lucy, nodding gravely.

Agnes rose to investigate, touching a lamp-stand, a chair and the door on her way. She wasn't going to discuss the need for help any more that day.

Lucy was getting ready to leave when Agnes handed over the key to her Morris Minor, bought by Grandpa Arthur in 1963. She'd named it Duchess.

'It's no use to me any more.'

'But Gran—'

'Take her. I've arranged the insurance. But treat her gently. She's a tired old bird.'

Before Lucy could find words of thanks, Agnes produced a manila envelope. She said, 'There's a notebook inside. I want you to read it. But say nothing of what you learn. Not to anyone.'

'What's it about?'

'You'll find out.'

Lucy frowned.

'Don't worry,' said Agnes. 'I just want you to know more . . . about me' – she hesitated, embarrassed – 'before I die.'

These last words fell on Lucy like a sword. Her composure slumped and, with rising tears, she turned quickly to go. By the vestibule door she caught her foot on a pile of newspapers. Lucy stared at them, as if they might speak.

'The answer's in the notebook,' said Agnes, looking aside. 'Don't cry for me, please don't cry.'

As Lucy turned the ignition she looked back to wave and saw Agnes with one hand on the doorframe. Her face was drawn and she looked terribly small and alone. Something had drained out of her.

Cathy opened the door to her flat in Pimlico later that evening before Lucy could even ring the bell.

'I'm just getting ready,' said Cathy. 'Fancy a meal out?'

'No, thanks.'

They walked into a sitting room of astounding chaos, clothes thrown everywhere, junk mail scattered like discarded handouts after a demonstration. The walls were covered with posters from various exhibitions.

'A drink?'

'No . . .'

Cathy flopped on to a sofa and said: 'What's wrong?'

The fact that they rarely saw each other somehow set Lucy free to say what she had said to no one else: 'My grandmother's

49

going to die from a disease I'd never heard of until now. It attacks your body but leaves the mind alone. In full throttle you just lie there unable to move or talk, blinking at the ceiling. You feel as if you're going to choke to death but it doesn't happen. That's where you stay, right on the edge of dying, but you remain alive.'

'Motor neurone disease,' said Cathy, sitting up.

'Yes. How do you know?'

'I read an article.'

Lucy sat on the edge of an armchair and shrugged. 'It's just ordinary life showing its colours.' She didn't want to talk about it any more, and said so.

Cathy thought for a moment and said, 'I've a good idea.' She left the room and came back with a pack of cards. 'Let's play Rummy.'

'I don't know the rules.'

'Any other game?'

'No.'

Cathy pondered the scale of ignorance. 'You must know Snap.'

They moved to the dining table and started laying down the cards, flip, flap, flip, flap, their concentration fixed on whatever turned up, waiting for a match.

'Do you ever think about the past?' asked Lucy.

Flip, flap.

'Never.'

Flip, flap.

'Why?'

Flip, flap.

'It's dead.'

Lucy paused, eyeing the Queen of Spades. 'Do you really mean that?'

'No.'

Flip, flap.

'Then why . . .'

'Because it's already won.'

Flip, flap, flip, flap.

Lucy threw her hand across the table and said, 'I've changed my mind. Let's have a meal . . . and a drink . . . what do you think?'

'I'll just put on a subtle, enhancing cream,' said Cathy, reaching for a make-up bag. 'You can help me think up a slogan to flog a critical illness insurance policy.'

They had a good time talking about death and money, parting in the knowledge it would be months before the phone next rang. Lucy went home clutching the envelope, thinking of her grandmother who seemed now to pervade each waking moment, each conversation. She climbed into bed with the distinctive loneliness that only arises between members of the same family. Agnes was breaking away and there was no time to adjust. She had begun her departure and an awkward goodbye was under way. She was like one of those rare desert plants, apparently lifeless but opening petals just before death under the heat of the sun. It was late, so late in the coming. Cathy was right. The past had won.

Lucy pressed the quilt into the folds of her body and pulled out a school notebook from the envelope. Grandpa Arthur's old wall clock struck midnight.

2

Throughout the week following Larkwood's four extraordinary visitors, Anselm lingered in the cloister after every Office on some unconvincing pretext, hoping the Prior would take him to one side – to confide or seek guidance. But he did not. On the sixth day the Prior informed the community of his decision at the usual morning Chapter, after the customary reading of an excerpt from The Rule.

'As you know,' he said, 'I received a visit from the Papal Nuncio. It has been strongly suggested by Rome that I permit Schwermann to remain here while the police carry out their investigation.' He glanced around the vaulted chamber. 'Rome's suggestions are even more loaded than mine. The view I hold is that they wouldn't take an interest unless it touched on wider implications – matters I may not fully appreciate. Accordingly I have decided he can stay.' With characteristic brevity he made the necessary appointments. 'He will be housed in the Old Foundry. Security arrangements are in the hands of the police and the Home Office. Brother Wilfred will be the daily point of contact on all matters relating to Schwermann. Brother Edmund will handle all enquiries from the media. That's it.'

Anselm bridled. He had waited with the anticipation of certainty for his name to be mentioned. He thought, angrily: that's it? I'm the lawyer . . . I know Milby . . . I speak bloody good French.

The Chapter moved swiftly on to deal with a dispute about the work rota.

Anselm continued to wrangle. Edmund? He doesn't speak to anyone in the monastery, never mind the world . . . how can he handle an investigative journalist? Wilf? He's timid to the point of paralysis . . .

The Chapter ended: the monks filed out to their cells for the time allotted to Lectio Divina; the Prior did the same; and Anselm stood in the cloister smarting at the rejection.

Over the next few weeks the lawyers came and the Press made their enquiries. Wilf apprehensively led the first group to the Old Foundry by the lake but never let his curiosity off the leash. Edmund gave interviews to the second lot but told them nothing of significance, not even about the monastic life. As a consequence, no one in the Priory or the outside world gleaned any information other than that which had already been released. In recognising this outcome, Anselm beheld the astuteness of his Prior.

Anselm only saw Schwermann once, while taking a walk by the lake after his afternoon session in the bottling plant. The elderly fugitive was sitting on a stool, painting. The brush flashed across the paper while he urbanely chatted to his personal protection officer. The weeks turned to months and still Schwermann did not leave. The investigation continued and the Prior became increasingly brittle. But he did not confide in Anselm about what the Priory should do if it transpired allowing Schwermann to stay had been a mistake. There were difficult issues to handle, involving Rome, the Home Office and the media. Anselm wanted to remonstrate. The Prior was deliberately wasting the skills he had to offer. Anselm's mind teemed with exhortations from scripture and the *Early Church Fathers* (which he'd eventually read) to the effect that lights should not be put under bushels, talents shouldn't be buried in fields, a monk should be given work suited to his powers and capabilities, and so on. However, Anselm was also obedient and said nothing to the Prior; and the Prior did what he knew was wise and said nothing to Anselm – until the day Anselm had a devastating encounter with a stranger by the lake; the day the fax came from Rome.

Chapter Six

Grandpa Arthur's old wall clock struck midnight. The German bullet had probably been a stray, but it came through an open window, tore past Grandpa Arthur's head just as he took off his helmet and smashed into the central glass panel of the wall-mounted wooden clock. The pendulum swung out of the way and back again, as if nothing had happened. The dull clunk of the ticking continued softly, as before, while Captain Embleton lay shaking on the ground, wetting himself like a baby.

Grandpa Arthur had always said there was a moral in there about Providence, but he didn't know what it was. He brought the clock home with its missing panel and hole in the back and never let it wind down. It was a sort of companion, holding time to a measured tempo and giving assurance that troubled times always pass. It had only stopped once: the day after he died. That was when Lucy had burst into tears, and Agnes had simply said: 'The pendulum's stopped swinging.' She never wound it up again.

When Lucy left home after the row with her parents, Agnes gave her the clock, saying, 'Here's an old friend. Wind him up every morning, like Arthur did.' It had sprung to life at the first turn of the key. It was as though Grandpa was nearby, out of sight.

Lucy smiled at the front cover of the school notebook. From old habit and the embedded obedience of a diligent pupil,

54

Agnes had carefully printed her name along the dotted line, ready for her work to be handed in and marked. The text was in pencil, with a crafted yet fluid hand, the kind that used to be taught by severe masters and perfected in detention. There were no corrections. The swift strokes imperceptibly became a voice, and Lucy could hear Agnes speaking to her in a way she never had before. She read without pausing to rest. Grandpa Arthur's wall clock ticked and softly chimed the half-hours. The night traffic rolled on, like the distant moan of the sea. The pendulum swung and the tiny bells trembled, as if stirred from sleep.

Lucy put the notebook to one side. She was unable to move. Her eyes swam out of focus. Eventually she stumbled into the kitchen. From behind the microwave she fished out a packet of Camel, bought the same day Darren had left her to go back to the wife and kids she hadn't known about. She'd thrown them unopened across the room when she'd got back from the corner shop. Lucy lit up her first cigarette on the gas cooker, singeing her eyebrows. Sitting on the floor of the living room with a side plate for an ashtray, she smoked and grimaced, calmed by the sudden punch of nicotine.

In reading her grandmother's story a kaleidoscope had turned, and almost everything Lucy knew about Agnes had tumbled out of place and fallen into a new configuration. Memories of peculiar things her grandmother had said and done in the past, making sense now, burst across her mind. Like that shopping trip after Christmas to the Army and Navy store in Victoria Street. They'd walked across the piazza facing Westminster Cathedral as the sound of the choir had filtered through the open doors. Agnes had suddenly turned and gone inside. She'd sat at the back for something like half an hour. Mosaics had glittered in the distance, and a boy's voice had spiralled between pillars that rose to hold the darkness overhead. As they were leaving Agnes had said cheerlessly, 'The Feast of the Holy Innocents.'

'What's that, Gran?'

'The remembering of a great slaughter. After the birth of Christ, King Herod wanted him killed. He didn't know where he was so he ordered the massacre of all children under the age of two.'

'How many was that?'

'Two thousand.'

'What about the one they were after?'

'Warned beforehand, by an angel. The family escaped.'

'Why not warn all the others?'

'A very good question.'

Lucy looked at her gran enquiringly. 'How do you know all that?'

'A decent education.'

'Do you believe any of that stuff? God, angels, three wise men?'

Agnes hadn't replied immediately. She'd slipped her moorings, as she was prone to do when loosened by an unspoken memory. 'Sometimes I think it's homesickness. But you can't get back.'

Lucy hadn't taken the matter further, but Agnes' remarks had stayed in her mind. Now she understood.

During her third cigarette, lolling but seasick on rising waves, she ran for the toilet and vomited. Lucy faced the mirror. She studied her black hair, the colourless oval face, the translucent skin, those dark lashes that always got her into trouble. She was a stranger to herself.

56

Lucy made a large mug of tea with two heaped teaspoons of sugar, to help swallow the unpalatable. Her mind turned bitterly to Schwermann, who lay protected in a monastery, and to Victor Brionne, the man of fine words, the collaborator who'd betrayed Agnes. But how did he get away after the war? Who on earth could have wanted to help a man deaf to the cries of children?

She poured the tea down the sink and made her way back to bed, knowing that a different person would see the morning. Her old self had closed her eyes for ever. Lucy glanced at the notebook lying open on the floor. What has happened, she thought, in my growing up that I can read such things and not even cry?

Chapter Seven

The first notebook of Agnes Embleton.

3rd April 1995.

Dear Lucy,
I have just seen the face of the man who took away my
life, on the very day Doctor Scott said I was going to die.
I sensed that months ago, when the voices and faces of
my youth came back, like rooks coming home. I should
have known Schwermann would turn up as well.

I would have liked to talk to you about me, and my
childhood friends, but I'm not able. Soon I'll be gone and
I do not want their memory to go with me. The time
has come for you to know everything.

10th April.

I've often wondered why the path of my life diverged
from what I hoped for, and sent me on track for what I
got. But there's no point in seeking explanations. There
are no 'might have beens'. So I look to London, and my
birth in March 1919.

My father was French and came to England in 1913
to work in a bank. He met my mother, who was Jewish,

at a work function. She was the daughter of a regional manager. Within the year they were married, and then I came along. They used to say I was the second great blessing of their life. The first was to have escaped the war. My earliest memories are of playing upon Hampstead Heath, threading daisies, half understanding conversations about 'The Great War'. Most of the people we knew had suffered loss, and even now the names of those terrible battles conjure up a strange remembrance of warm summer days and other people's grief. You see, by some miracle (as my father used to say), the war had passed us by while touching all around us. And so I grew up feeling protected, as if God had carefully placed us beyond catastrophe. Until my mother died on 17th August 1929.

From that day my father wanted to go back to France, away from every reminder of her. I wasn't surprised because England had never become his home. He was always making comparisons, which showed he saw things from the outside. Even the milk was better in France. He began to tell me wonderful things about Paris, and I would go to sleep seeing bridges, a shining river and tables in the street lit by thousands of candles. We set sail in early 1931.

I suppose he wasn't to know. He thought he would simply move back into his old bank. But those were hard times and no positions were available. I know that now. At the time I presumed we had landed on our feet. We lived in a nice flat, I did well at school and I wanted for nothing.

I was especially good at the piano and my father bought me a monstrous upright for Christmas. Each week I went to see Madame Klein, my teacher, and each week I came home vowing never to see her again. She was a Jewish widow who lived in a magnificent apartment opposite Parc Monceau. My father told me she was one of the best piano teachers in Paris, and had once been a concert performer. That's as maybe, I thought. Because every Saturday afternoon I climbed those stairs dreading the scowl that never left her face. I hated every second. I said she couldn't even play. For she nursed her right hand and only touched the keys with her left. My father laughed and sent me back each week. I have never written her name down before, and doing so makes me pause. I see her now as I saw her then, dressed in black silk with a vast coiffure of silver hair. She looks at me over quite useless glasses that seem to be part of her nose, her eyes impossible to read.

Anyway, back to my father. I never thought to ask where he worked, or how he could afford lessons from such a lady. But I came to recognise he was troubled, despite all his efforts to conceal it from me. Children may not know which questions to ask but they already sense the answers. He started scratching his arms, practically scraping the skin off. Before long it was all over his body. He joked it was the lice. So I started itching, and together we'd scratch and scratch, laughing. One morning he said casually he had to go and see the doctor. I was fifteen so that would be roughly 1934. I came back from a school camp three days later and, to my surprise, was met by a young nun who brought me to a hospital. She kept glancing at me when she thought I was looking the other way. My last memory of my father is that day, sleeping in a white room with a high ceiling, dressed in a white gown beneath white sheets, and a smell of strong disinfectant. The nun stayed with me, trying to hold my hand. A doctor came in and said my father had widespread cancer, and there was nothing they could do. I was left alone, me on a chair, my father asleep in a bed.

When I turned to go there was a priest standing behind me. He was short and badly shaven, with bags under his eyes. His name was Father Rochet.

12th April.

Father Rochet. He had known my father from school-days and would frequently drop by, usually when I was going out. He always looked as if he'd slept badly. I had never spoken to him for long as he was a man of few words. But I saw him a great deal, going into the flats in and around where we lived, which I suppose was strange because it was not his parish. He was a great one for carrying something under his coat. I used to think it was a bottle, though I know better now. My father said he was always getting into trouble with his bishop, which Father Rochet thought very funny. Anyway, there he was, behind me in the hospital, looking as if he'd just got out of bed. I followed him into the corridor. Everything had been arranged, he said. I was to go with him and he would take me to the house of a friend. We would talk about my future another time.

Father Rochet took me in his car. Neither of us spoke. It was a black night and the rain was so heavy I could not recognise any streets or buildings. I remember watching the windscreen wipers and wondering how they worked.

The water falling in sheets across the glass. Eventually we arrived. I opened the door and saw what I least expected or wanted: Parc Monceau.

Up those stairs I went, dripping everywhere. By now I was crying. When the door opened, Madame Klein scowled and shook her head. 'For heaven's sake, stop soaking the floor.' Those were her first words.

My father died that night.

Father Rochet came to see me after the funeral. Again he hadn't shaved properly, and this time I could have sworn he smelled ever so slightly of stale wine, which distracted me from taking on board what he said. It was my father's wish that I now live with Madame Klein. He had seen to all the finances.

And so I believed family resources had sustained me in the past and would do so in the future. I didn't realise they were both feeding me a story to save my dignity.

I wasn't to know Father Rochet had introduced my father to Madame Klein when we first arrived in Paris; I wasn't to know my father went out each day in a suit, then changed and earned his living cleaning floors. I wasn't to know that Madame Klein was our landlady; that she had waived the rent from the outset; that she had given the piano to my father; that my lessons were free; that both of them were what some call saints.

13th April.

Madame Klein was the most extraordinary woman I have ever known. She must have been in her early seventies when I came to live with her. At first I thought maybe I

62

was there to act as a nurse. Far from it. She was too busy to want any help.

Her husband had died about ten years earlier. He'd been a gifted violinist, and his death had come without any warning while performing on stage. From what she said it was rather like Tommy Cooper. He made an amusing aside, and then dropped down. Everyone laughed, including Madame Klein. They'd never had children, and extended family were out of reach and touch. So she found herself alone. She told me the first few years were the worst, and getting worse. And then she had an accident.

Madame Klein was an atrocious driver, always banging into things. On this day, for once, it was not her fault. A van collided into the side of her car, breaking her right wrist. She never played the piano professionally again. However, the van had been driven by a young woman who worked for a Jewish children's welfare organisation, 'Oeuvre de Secours Aux Enfants' (OSE). Its headquarters had moved from Berlin to Paris in the early thirties, after the Nazis came to power. It became Madame Klein's life, just when she thought she had nothing to live for.

You have to understand what it was like then. Thousands of refugees had flooded into France, with children separated from their parents. You've seen something similar on the news. It still goes on. Then, as now, people did what they could. So Madame Klein was out each day, doing I don't know what. It was not something she talked about. But she often took her husband's violin.

On some evenings there were meetings with friends she'd made through OSE. I was never present. But the

63

same men and women came. To my child's eye they were always dressed in black and arrived in a long shuffling line after dark. They gathered in the salon, with its low lights and drawn curtains. I thought it was terribly exciting. And I was desperate to know what they talked about. So I started listening at the door.

You'll find, Lucy, as you get older you start seeing yourself from the outside. Particularly your childhood. You'll see a child enacting her part innocently, while you watch, knowing what is going to happen, unable to intervene. As for me, the need to intervene, if I could have done, comes later. For now I can see myself in my nightie, with bare feet, bent over by a great white door with beautiful shining brass handles. I'm trying to breathe as quietly as I can, looking through the keyhole at those gesticulating arms and solemn faces.

They never seemed to converse. It was always an argument, even when they agreed. What was going to happen next? That is what they fought over. Were they on the verge of the greatest pogrom they had ever known? And what was to be done? The killings had been under way since 1930. Within months of Hitler becoming Chancellor, there were camps. I remember one voice from the far side of the room say fearfully, 'If they've killed us in the street, they'll kill us in the camps.' And then a deep voice by the door spoke, so close to me I almost jumped back. It was Father Rochet. 'You are not safe in France. You're not safe anywhere.' There was the most dreadful silence after that. Through the keyhole I could just make out an old man with a stick propped between his legs. He still had his dark hat and coat on. I can't recall his name, but I've thought for years about his face, caught in the yellow lamplight. He had a look of recognition: this was an old, familiar warning.

When I heard a chair scrape, I ran upstairs. Sitting on the landing with my arms around my knees I would hear them all troop out, as if in rancour, and from the window see them disperse into the night, in twos and threes, often arm in arm.

In time, these meetings occurred more frequently. Events in Germany and France were followed closely. Some talked about emigration. There was no need, said others. The Germans have got us out of their hair, we're safe. Not yet, said Father Rochet.

He always stayed behind, Father Rochet, to confer in private with Madame Klein. I never found out what they talked about. Back by the keyhole, I only saw them huddled round a table, like mother and son, whispering. God knows why. No one was listening.

Chapter Eight

Vespers was not for another half hour so Anselm had gone for a secret roll-up. He strolled along the bluebell path and took a narrow track through the woods leading to a stretch of sand by the water's edge. Then he saw him through the laden branches and paused. Anselm guessed he was in his late fifties. He was a very small man with the smallest feet Anselm had ever seen. Whoever the stranger was, he kept perfectly still, like a sculptured memorial, silently looking over the lake.

'I suspect you and I are asking ourselves a similar question,' said the stranger without averting his gaze. His voice was disturbingly deep, like wet churning gravel; at once musical and melancholy.

Anselm stepped out of the shade. The stranger continued:

'You wonder why I am here. Just as I wonder why he is over there.'

Across the lake, just visible through the surrounding trees, shone the red tiling of the Old Foundry roof, where Schwermann had been accommodated.

'May I ask who you are, and what you are doing here?' said Anselm hesitantly, walking slowly to the stranger's side.

The man peered solemnly at Anselm through heavily framed glasses, his eyes enlarged and penetrating, and said, 'I've come to look upon the father of my grief.'

Anselm followed his gaze, confusion giving way to the first flutterings of fear.

'Don't worry,' said the stranger dispassionately, 'I'm not mad. But I do have a penchant for the telling phrase.' He smiled paternally. 'My name is Salomon Lachaise.'

Anselm took in the loose cardigan and galoshes, the profound relaxation in circumstances that should have produced embarrassment – he was, after all, a trespasser within the enclosure. Salomon Lachaise was like a man in his own drawing room, receiving a guest on a matter of grave importance. Speaking as much to himself as to Anselm, he said, 'Have you any idea how painful it is for me to stand here' – he gestured uncertainly across the water – 'knowing who sleeps over there?'

Anselm felt the slow flush of humiliation. Salomon Lachaise smiled sadly, drawing pipe and tobacco from his cardigan pocket. He began the endless ritual of packing with his thumb, drawing air and trailing match after match over the bowl. 'I'm sorry. It's an old rabbinic trick,' he said through a swirl of smoke. 'Posing the question to a man who cannot answer without discovering his own shame. Jesus did it quite a lot.'

Anselm was dumbstruck. Not expecting an answer, his interlocutor said, 'It's time for me to go. What's your name?'

'Father Anselm, but—'

'Saint Anselm of Canterbury? Now there's an interesting fellow. A man in search of God. But not that fond of . . .'

At that moment they heard twigs cracking underfoot and three figures emerged through the trees, one in front, two behind. Anselm took in the calm, concentrated glance of the police officer in his Marks & Spencer casuals, one hand inches away from a concealed weapon, but Salomon Lachaise stared beyond, through the branches, to a shape moving through the

67

shadows. A voice spoke lightly to a young man with his hands sunk deep in his pockets. Max, the grandson. He'd come every week since his grandfather had taken up residence in the Old Foundry.

Anselm shivered in the sun, alarmed by a sudden, dark prescience. A meeting of ways lay ahead: one of those rare instances where the past coagulates into the present.

Schwermann pushed aside some brambles with a stick and stepped into the open, looking up as if in a dream. His eyes rested lightly on Salomon Lachaise and then moved on to Anselm with a courteous nod. He smiled briefly, as if to a friend, saying, 'I haven't thanked you for your advice, Father.'

Anselm sickened.

'Sanctuary is not what I expected and more than I could have hoped for.'

They had not met since that unfortunate exchange at the back of the church. Anselm studied him afresh: didn't evil have a known face, angular and pinched? If so, this was not it. The eyes, awash with a dull black iris, lacked focus, and the slow, tired blinking suggested . . . suggested what? For the life of him Anselm could not tell whether this was the torpor of old age or the persisting trace of ruthlessness. He looked no different to the stooped parishioner who waved the collection plate.

'At least I can still paint.' Schwermann lifted his paintbox, like the Chancellor with his budget. 'These enchanting woods help me to forget.'

At that, Salomon Lachaise groaned through his teeth and stumbled forward towards Schwermann, falling on his knees right in front of him. The policeman's hand shot inside his jacket. With one great, savage movement, Salomon Lachaise tore open his shirt from top to bottom, both hands ripping the fabric apart, exclaiming in a loud voice, 'I am the son of the Sixth Lamentation.'

Schwermann stepped back, appalled, breathing heavily, the features of his face suddenly alive. 'Gott . . . mein Gott . . . help me!'

The policeman swiftly placed himself before Schwermann and ushered him back through the trees. The grandson, paralysed, fixed wide, flickering eyes upon the man on his knees – the bowed head, the extended arms – and then, as if abruptly woken, turned and ran.

In a moment they were alone to the sound of feet moving urgently through the woods. Late afternoon sunlight slipped through pleated branches on to their shoulders. A light wind idled over the surface of the lake, crumpling the reflections lying deep in the water. Salomon Lachaise did not move until Anselm lightly touched his shoulder. With help from the monk he stood up.

'Forgive me,' he muttered thickly.

'What on earth for?'

'I don't know.' He covered his upper body as one shamed, hunching over the bared skin. Anselm's arms were raised foolishly, as though he would start a Mass. He wanted to do something, anything, to touch with balm this astounding, wounded man who now, clasping himself, began to stumble along the path through the woods that Schwermann had taken. Anselm followed like a disciple.

After several minutes the stranger abruptly stepped off the track and made through the trees towards an old breach in the monastery wall, a hole that had never been repaired. Anselm thought, apprehensively, he knows his route: he's been here before. Upon impulse he asked, 'What brought you here?'

'I'm a Professor of History at the University of Zurich. A medievalist, but I like to keep my eye on the modern period.' He stepped carefully through the fallen stones towards a car parked on the verge. 'You see, with one or two notable exceptions, he sent my family to the ovens.' He patted pockets in turn, searching distractedly for keys. 'I only wanted to see his face but now . . . we've actually met. Believe it or not . . .' He sighed and held out his hand, letting his shirt fall open. 'Shalom aleichem, Anselm of Canterbury.'

The great bells of Larkwood sang over the trees, summoning Anselm to Vespers. Torn by the obligation to run and the desire to stay, Anselm said, 'Can we meet again?' He scrambled for a reason: 'Perhaps we could talk . . . go for a walk?' The idea of leisure rang a ridiculous note but Salomon Lachaise replied quickly, sincerely, 'I would like that very much.'

He climbed into his car, still dazed. Winding down the window he said, 'I'm staying in the village, at The Grange.' The engine rumbled into life and the car pulled away, never quite gathering speed but moving slowly out of sight.

After Vespers the monks shuffled in procession out of choir and into the cloister. In the shadow of a pillar stood Father Andrew, waiting for Anselm. With a gesture he led Anselm to his room. Behind a desk, his chin resting upon the backs of his hands joined in an arch, the Prior said, troubled:

'I've received a fax. Rome wants someone from the Priory to handle a particular matter on their behalf relating to our guest. I've recommended you. The flight has already been arranged.'

Anselm, instantly curious, said, 'Have they said anything else?'

'No.'

'Just a fax?' asked Anselm.

'Yes.'

Anselm's imagination perceived a nuance of irregularity which he tamed: 'That's odd.'

The Prior's arched hands dropped on to the desk. 'Indeed. I rang the Nuncio. Even he didn't know anything.' He eyed the telephone. 'You'd think he'd have been briefed. Very odd.'

Awake in bed that night, unable to sleep, Anselm barely thought of Rome. Instead he listened again to the words of the trespasser confronting the man in the woods, and he thought of the five lamentations of Jeremiah, each mourning the destruction of Jerusalem, each placing absolute trust in its sworn Protector. What then was the Sixth Lamentation: the tragedy of a people, or a personal testament? In asking the question, Anselm felt a sudden chill, like the passing of a ghost. He didn't want to know the answer. He closed his eyes and saw Salomon Lachaise upon his knees. Instantly Anselm prayed, wanting to cry but not quite knowing how to.

Chapter Nine

The first notebook of Agnes Embleton.

14th April 1995.

Of course, in the first weeks and months of my living with Madame Klein, I knew nothing of her past, nor what she did when she went out with her husband's violin.

On my first night I was sent to have a bath and packed off to bed. I thought she could not possibly know how I felt to have lost my father. I was wrong. She eased my way through routine and piano practice. Three times a day: when I got up, before I could think, after lunch before going back to school, and every evening. She sat by me or in the corner, groaning loudly at my mistakes. She had a string of pupils. None of them paid (I later found out) and she was horrible to them all. It was through music that I got to know her, not words. I've never been one for talking, maybe that's where it comes from. She used to say, 'Your ears are more important than your mouth.' And Father Rochet would add his bishop was of much the same opinion.

It was about a year later, 1935 or thereabouts, that Madame Klein started to host musical evenings every Sunday. The same people came each week. Those who had come by night, as my child's eye had seen them, returned, along with some others brought by Father Rochet. Six families from his parish and a couple of rather vocal atheists ('My strays,' he would say). It was the same with the Jewish group – some were devout believers, others weren't. The first evening was stilted to say the least but that gradually lessened as the weeks passed, as we all listened to the same music. We were an audience of families providing the performances ourselves. That is how I met Jacques and Victor.

15th April.

Jacques' father, Anton Fougères, was a great friend of Father Rochet. Anton played the piano with an enthusiasm unsupported by talent. His wife, Elizabeth, sang. She was quite good, actually. Apart from Jacques, they brought with them a man called Franz Snyman. He was a refugee, about Jacques' age, who had been introduced to them by Father Rochet. Originally Mr Snyman's family had come from South Africa, but business interests had taken them abroad. In three generations they had fled from Romania to Germany to France. He'd lost both parents along the way. His father had been killed in Kishinev. They'd moved to Gunzenhausen. His mother had been beaten to death in a campaign for 'Jew-free' villages. Aged fourteen, he had made his way to the Saar, where a non-Jew family friend had offered him a roof. Then the Saar became part of Germany, so off he'd moved again, coming to Paris on his own. Where he'd lodged with Mr and Mrs Fougères. He always dressed in a suit. Perhaps that is why we called

73

him 'Mr Snyman', rather than using his first name – it was a kind of affectionate, mischievous respect. He was a superb cellist and he and I played a lot of duets together. Jacques had an elder brother, Claude, who lived near the Swiss border. I don't recall much about him. All I know is that after the fall of France he became a vocal supporter of Vichy and Pétain. There's nothing so strange as families.

I must now turn to Victor. He's played an important part in my life. Victor's father, Georges, was married to Anton Fougères' second cousin. But there'd been an almighty row between Anton and Georges, and the two families hadn't spoken for years. The Fougères family were committed Republicans, whereas Georges was a Monarchist. Another member of the Brionnes had even been a 'Camelot du Roi'. They were a Royalist youth movement, and I'll tell you about them later for it touches on Victor. And, I suppose, Father Rochet. Suffice it to say, Anton Fougères disapproved and that was that. A major rift.

Victor, however, went to the same school as Jacques and they were best friends. He spent as much time at Jacques' house as he did at home. So Victor had to pull the wool over his parents' eyes whenever he went to visit the Fougères. He once said it was perfect training ground for a spy.

Same day.

In due course I found myself more with Jacques and Victor than anyone else at our musical evenings. They

74

sought me out and I began to expect it and to want it. Even then, at that early stage, I knew I was coming between them. It seems to be the role of a girl, to split the covenant between two boys. It often happens. But I was only sixteen and they were scarcely older. At that stage there were no choices to be made. Looking at things from their beginnings we were all innocent then, even Victor, making our clumsy way forward, away from childhood. We became a threesome and I lay upon a dais in the middle, fêted on either side. I led the pranks and they got into trouble on my behalf. My hair fell long over my shoulders and I would cast the whole lot to the wind, as if it was necessary. Victor once caught me on camera, in full swing, but I never saw the picture. I wonder what happened to it?

16th April.

These gatherings went on each week, right up to 1940. In the summer we would go on picnics, driven by Father Rochet in a roaring bus. The exhaust was held in place by an old coat-hanger. Madame Klein was not allowed behind the wheel. She'd sit towards the back, shouting at him to go down driveways into private gardens and houses, always with that violin on her lap. For her damaged hand could draw the bow. I see her now, standing by the Seine, somewhere between Poissy and Villennes, playing dreadfully to the river. To think, she was taken away, beaten and gassed. And I didn't even get the chance to say goodbye.

17th April.

I did very well at the piano and entered lots of competitions. Madame Klein, who never cried, wept every time I won. She said it was a complete catastrophe. When I gained a scholarship she made so much noise she was asked to leave the auditorium. So off I went to the Conservatoire in 1937. Madame Klein arranged a few classes under Yvonne Lefebure at the École Normale, where I played for Cortot, but he didn't think much of me. For what it's worth I didn't think much of him either, and neither did Madame Klein. Too many wrong notes. And it is those happy memories that bring me back to Jacques and Victor.

18th April.

Father Rochet once said, 'Those boys are sword and scabbard.' Jacques was short and slightly stooped, pressed in on himself by ideas, his dark eyes strangely timid for someone always ready for an argument. That was his problem really. By nature withdrawn, things he thought wrong dragged him outwards, uncomfortably, into the light. I always thought he was rather like a rabbit in the middle of the road: blinded by injustice and unable to back down. He said very little but his face disclosed the constant workings of his mind. I think that is what drew me to Jacques, the absence of words.

Now, imagine him with Victor standing like a general, his hands behind his back, firing off frivolities to whoever would listen, hooting playfully at Jacques' indignations. He winked a lot at the spectators. He was very careful with words and that rather sums him up. Beneath the badinage lay caution and a calculating brain. He always saw both sides of a problem and you never quite knew which side he was going to take. Sword and scabbard. Which was which?

Same day.

I'm not sure when the parting of the ways began. Perhaps it was the day Jacques' father called me 'Guenevere'. With that one word he named where we stood on the stage. One of the more unfortunate things about late adolescence is that you understand the part you're playing without being able to appreciate the likely consequences. You see, in a way I led Victor on, and I knew it. For anyone else this was just a part of growing up. But for me, the whole shebang got caught up with the war, when heroes were needed before their time and when my stumblings became the stuff of tragedy.

It wasn't me who made the choice that set us apart. It was Jacques. By then he was studying Classics at the Sorbonne. He turned up once 'by chance' at the Conservatoire and I showed him Chopin's death mask and a cast of Paganini's long pointed fingers. He said something about relics in Saint Eugene across the road. When I told Madame Klein that night about our meeting, her eyes narrowed and after a long pause she said, 'I think you should go for him,' and I said, 'Don't be ridiculous!' A week later I saw him at a recital when I hadn't said I was playing. Shortly afterwards, by an old bookstall where the shelves were fastened to the outside wall, he muttered,

'There's something I have to tell you.' But he couldn't get the words out. I had to put various suggestions to him. He shook his head mournfully after each one. Eventually he looked away from me and grimaced, 'I think I might be attached to you.' I felt nothing. But I woke the next morning with a fountain spurting from the pit of my stomach.

19th April.

Victor must have known, but he said nothing. Maybe because we never spelled it out he never took it seriously. Remember, words were very important to him. If something hadn't been reduced to language he didn't understand it. And, appropriately, writing that sentence reveals how careless I was. For Victor wrote poems for me and I should have taken him, of all people, at his word. They were lofty with plenty of classical allusions, making them sufficiently impersonal to be safe. I kept them in a book. I should have told him to stop, but I didn't. You see, on the face of it we were a trio, and I didn't want to cut Victor off. But lurking within that laudable sentiment was the truth – a reluctance to give up the attention he gave me. Against myself I encouraged him, ever so slightly, but I did it without really meaning it. It's called vanity.

I told Jacques that Victor was just showing off. Our failure to speak up became a sort of conspiracy of pleasure between us, in the secret kept from Victor who blindly carried on. I remember the three of us looking over the waters of Launette to the Isle of Poplars at Ermonville. Victor recited something about Euterpe's aching soul before Rousseau's empty tomb. Jacques and I listened, watching creamy clouds drift across the sky, making his words our own. But I knew Victor wrote them for me. Maybe Jacques did as well.

And there you have it. Jacques and I, and Victor soon to be disappointed. That was the beginning of the end.

Same day.

And all the while something else was under way. The weekly musical gatherings, the summer outings, had brought us all together and we grew up side by side. Through the keyhole, after everyone had gone one Sunday night, I could see them. Father Rochet finishing off the bottles. Madame Klein at the table, telling him not to drink too much. But each of them looking very pleased with themselves. Looking back, I can see it was the beginning of The Round Table. Father Rochet was calling together his knights for when the time was right.

Chapter Ten

1

Anselm's presence during that harrowing confrontation in the woods had established an understanding between him and Salomon Lachaise such that future relations could never be characterised by mere acquaintance. They had stood on the same burning ground. A few days later, just before his flight to Rome, Anselm knocked unannounced at the door of 'The Grange', a small B&B with a name plaque of heavy iron. He'd planned a walk deep within the monastic enclosure to The Hermitage, a shack by a stream where no one ever went except with the Prior's permission – which he had obtained. Salomon Lachaise emerged, smiling and expectant, and Anselm led him back to the Priory to a locked oak door in a high wall of Saxon flint.

The bent key was ancient and large and required both of Anselm's hands in the turning. The door swung open and they stepped through into the hungry silence of the fields. As with many hidden places in the grounds of a monastery, the fact that it was cut off produced in those who entered a surprising sensation of having been freed, set loose from a captivity they had barely recognised. With a light step they set off for The Hermitage in the distance.

'How long will you stay?'

'Until he goes.'

Anselm said, with feeling, 'It was most unfortunate that you should meet him in the way you did . . . without warning . . . or preparation.'

'I could never have prepared myself.' His relaxed face scanned the rolling fields, sunlight flashing upon his heavy glasses. 'Anyway, I always look for something to be grateful for.'

Anselm flinched at the notion of thanks. But Salomon Lachaise said, 'I am glad my mother was not there, to see him and to see me before him. It would have been . . .'The sentence vanished, not through emotion but because the right word did not exist.

Anselm asked, 'Does she know that you are here?'

'She died before he was exposed,' he replied evenly. 'I am also grateful for that.'

'Tell me about her,' said Anselm, tugging, he suspected, at the one significant thread of a seamless garment.

'In many ways I am here on her behalf. Her story will never be told. And neither will mine.'

Anselm understood that to be an imposing refusal, but Salomon Lachaise continued as though it had been a preface:

'Like so many others, the war told her who she was and who she wasn't. She thought she was a young Frenchwoman, a Parisian, with a sister, two brothers and the usual clutch of uncles and aunts . . . and, out of mind, a couple of estranged German grandparents she'd never known. There's always someone that everybody else isn't speaking to. Then France fell and the occupier told her she was Jewish – on account of the grandparents. She'd never seen a synagogue in her life.'

Anselm slowed, for Salomon Lachaise was keeping slightly back; but the small man maintained his position, almost out of sight, close to the shoulder of his guide. His deep voice came on the air, while Anselm could only see the empty fields, the wild abundance of the grass.

'My mother and I escaped to Switzerland with the help of a smuggling ring known as The Round Table. Then the border closed. The rest of the family were taken . . .'

Anselm said, to the breeze, 'Did she know anyone, where she settled?'

'No. Like all the others she lived waiting, waiting, waiting . . . during the war . . . after the war . . . until she died . . . in some sense always waiting. But no one else survived.'

The bare grass ran to a long line of trees, their tops hazy where the phosphorescence of the sky fell upon them. Diffuse sunlight picked out against the vague green a sloping wall of The Hermitage.

'Hitler, she liked to say, had been responsible for her conversion. Confronted with such evil, she said, there had to be a God. She crossed the border a believing Jew. There were many like her . . . alone, cut off, yet free . . . and there was help. She opened a kosher shop beneath a bridge . . . in a sort of cavern . . . the shelves were packed with mysteries last seen by Solomon. And yet . . . paradise? Not quite. The shop became a meeting place for those who'd got out, and all of them were looking for someone, hoping by a wild chance that they might turn up. My mother did what she could to help, refusing payment, wiping the slate clean, but most of all she simply listened. She never mentioned her own loss. Ever since, hope, for me, has not been about anticipation . . . but endurance. Like the food taken at Passover, from a very early age I was introduced to the bitter and the sweet.'

They reached The Hermitage. Salomon Lachaise stared at the parched silver timbers with wonder, as though they were part of the Holy City. Through age and want of repair the whole shack sloped to one side. A covered veranda fronted a stream that chattered between low banks towards a copse. Anselm said:

'We're allowed to come here for a few days at a time. There's tap water, a stove, a couple of chairs and a bed ... little else.'

They sat in the shade of the veranda, and Anselm asked, 'Did you ever find out anything about your family ... those you lost?'

'We only ever talked of them once,' said Salomon Lachaise. 'I asked, late one night when I was in bed. She said, "Get up and put your coat on." I did. Back we went to the shop. She pulled out a cardboard box of photographs and a menorah ... and there, by the dim light of eight candles, she gave me through tears the names for the faces ... then she put them back under the counter. That was as far as she could go.'

'She kept them in the shop?'

As if explaining what should not be uttered, he replied, 'She spent her waking life there, in that cavern.'

Anselm held in his mind the image of a woman, alone, the till counted, ready for home. She locks herself in, comes back, lights the candles and reaches for the box, that lid. Ah, thought Anselm ... that's why she turned the key ... to let her tears free. He said, 'So you never learned anything about them?'

'No. At first, I constructed lives for them. Later, I took refuge in learning. It was a most remarkable sensation that only left me as I got older, but I would read through the night as if those strangers of my blood were there in the room, inhabiting the shadows. That is how I reclaimed them for myself. And, with their help, I did well at school. It was said I had considerable promise.'

83

'That must have been a joy for your mother.'

'It was. But there was very little money around. I was expected to work in the shop, but then . . . my life changed.'

'What happened?' asked Anselm.

'Something extraordinary. At the beginning of the term I was due to leave school I was summoned to the headmaster's office. Sitting in his chair was a wiry fellow with a stiff, self-important manner – a lawyer, it turned out – who had come on his client's behalf to see me. His message was simple enough. He had received funds from "a survivor" to secure me a university education.'

Anselm, marvelling, said, 'Some would call that a blessing.'

'Indeed,' replied Salomon Lachaise with a numinous, inquisitive smile. 'So you would. My mother did the same. She spent the remainder of her days trawling over the names of all those she had helped, wondering who it might have been so she might thank them. She saw a door open before me, and in due course I passed through to a whole life, a whole universe I would never have otherwise known.'

'And your patron's identity remained a secret?'

'Yes.'

Salomon Lachaise explained that the lawyer had entrusted administration of the finances to a local solicitor of his choosing – insisting on separate representation in case a conflict of interest arose between his client and the young Lachaise.

'And that is how I met a wonderful man, Josef Bremer, who became something of a father to me. All my life he has been a source of advice and encouragement.'

'Incredible,' said Anselm. 'Whoever it was probably knew your mother, knew you, and just did it, forsaking recognition or repayment. It is the sort of thing that makes life worth living.'

'And worth the dying.'

Anselm had the strange sensation of something hot having passed him by. A trace was left behind, slightly acrid, like exhaust from an engine, but then it was gone, quickly dispersed by a breath of air. Salomon Lachaise said:

'I found my home in the art of the Middle Ages. It has brought me great joy . . . and pain . . . always the bitter and the sweet.'

Not entirely sure the true meaning of the words had reached him, Anselm thought of the rivalry of academics, known to surpass even that of children. Consolingly, he said, 'Like all homes.'

'And, no doubt, like all monasteries,' said Lachaise.

'Verily.' Automatically, insensitively, Anselm said, 'You remained alone?'

'Yes . . . although I nearly got married once . . .'

'What happened?'

After a thoughtful pause, Salomon Lachaise said, 'She ran off with the maths teacher.'

'Oh dear.'

They both looked at each other and burst into ringing laughter.

2

Evening light came with a faint chill. Together they retraced their steps through the fields, away from The Hermitage crouching by the stream. When they had gone a fair distance Salomon Lachaise stopped and turned, as though taking a mental snapshot of a place to hide.

Anselm said, 'I meant to say sorry for the fact that . . . he is here at all.'

85

'Thank you. I have to say your Prior must be singularly unconcerned about appearances.'

'He is, actually. But it wasn't his decision.'

'I see.'

Tact and a sudden disquiet prevented Anselm from disclosing that it had been the Vatican's proposal. He simply said, 'I know it looks bad.'

'Perhaps it is bad,' said Salomon Lachaise. 'For someone like me it could so easily belong with all the other springs of lamentation which, I am afraid, are not simple misunderstandings.'

'What do you mean?' asked Anselm apprehensively. Immediately he wished he'd let the matter pass.

'There are too many to mention . . . they run wildly, one into the other, from the first charge of deicide . . . to the expulsions of the Middle Ages . . . through to the complicated time of anguish, silence and diplomacy. In my own way I, too, have known these.'

It was the old agonising problem for Anselm. He was forever confronting the face of a church to which he belonged, many of whose features he did not wholly recognise. He said, 'I hope Larkwood offers you something different, another kind of spring.'

Salomon Lachaise, glancing over his shoulder, said, 'I have already discovered one, in a place I least expected to find it.'

They walked on, the light swiftly thinning, the mad swooping of distant birds suddenly ended, leaving the sky bare, unscored. The high monastery wall grew larger, a dam between great banks of trees.

Salomon Lachaise said, 'Do you know which great romance of literature emerges beside the pogroms of the Middle Ages as they erupted across Britain, France and the Rhineland?'

86

'I'm afraid not.'

'It is the poetry of the mystic king . . . Arthur, The Round Table and the Grail.'

'How strange.'

'It's as though the attacks upon the Jews and medieval chivalry belonged to the same cultural flowering. And then, fifty years ago, some genius set up a Round Table to save the Jews, to redeem its association with ancient hostility.'

Anselm, intrigued, glanced at his companion. Lachaise's head was lowered, his face dark as he said, 'Isn't it all the more tragic, then, that the person who broke it apart was—'

Anselm finished the complaint, to demonstrate his understanding, his profound regret, '—able to find refuge in the arms of the Church.'

Salomon Lachaise seemed not to have heard. They had reached the oak door in the wall. Anselm forced in the key and turned it heavily. They parted, promising to meet again, and Anselm felt the slow, piercing influx of shame: he had quite deliberately said nothing about his planned trip to Rome, which had imperceptibly come to present itself as something disagreeable. Unable to shake off the discomfort, he hurried back to the Priory. Climbing the spiral stone stairs to his room, it dawned on him that Salomon Lachaise had told him everything, and yet, with calculation, with regret, he had told him nothing.

Chapter Eleven

The first notebook of Agnes Embleton.

20th April.

How can I now think of my Jewish comrades as different from the rest of us? For we were one group. The fact is they had been hunted, we had not, and the hunt was still on. I suppose I too should have been scared, because I was, am, half Jewish. But my identity on that level was indistinct. The inks had run together. I discovered just how separate they were one morning when looking through Madame Klein's desk for a letter opener. I found a baptismal certificate in my name, one in my mother's, a marriage certificate for my parents, and a death certificate for my mother. A whole Christian history lived out in Normandy. I saw the scheming hand of Father Rochet, although I couldn't imagine how he'd done it. Pretending to be cross, I asked him, 'Why?' He grabbed me by each arm and the smell of stale wine hit me in the face. 'I hope to God you'll never need them,' he snapped. 'These are dark times, Agnes. If you doubt me, read widely. Read what others are thinking in the streets you walk.' That night he gave me Céline's *Bagatelles pour un massacre*. It described France as a woman raped by Jews, looking to

Hitler for liberation. For the first time in my life I did not feel safe.

The reports poured in from Germany. Jews banned from this, Jews banned from that. You might as well make your own list because everything was on it. And, of course, more camps. We knew it wasn't just regulations for the death toll went on and on, long before Kristallnacht, and long after. So the music drained out of our Sunday gatherings. There were too many questions to ask. 'Should we get out while there's still a chance?' 'How much will it cost?' 'What about so-and-so's grandmaman?' 'And her cousin, the one who's ill?' There were no easy answers. You must realise these people had either grown up in France or had fled from somewhere else. They'd had enough. They wanted to believe they were safe. That said, two families did jump and made it to Canada, but they left behind half their blood because of visa problems. That was a warning in its own right, for the doors of escape would soon close. We had a party for them and Mr Rozenwerg sang a Yiddish song of farewell. He was the old man I told you about, the one through the keyhole who understood Father Rochet's warning. After all these years I've remembered his name. I cannot think of that night without seeing the faces of those who stayed behind, trusting in better times when the endless partings would cease. That is my overwhelming feeling of those days, a gradual falling apart, of broken pieces being broken still further.

The Germans occupied the Sudetenland, and then invaded Czechoslovakia. Next, Poland. They were on the march. War was declared. That was when Father Rochet called the meeting.

21st April.

No one knew who else was coming. Each had been told it was secret, although in my case Madame Klein had already been informed. We all knew one another for we were the non-Jewish members of our Sunday gathering. By then we were all aged between twenty (me, the youngest) and twenty-three. I must name them: Jean, Cécile, Philippe, Tomas, Monique, Mélaine, Françoise, Alban, Thérèse, Mathilde, Jacques and, of course, Victor.

Same day.

We met in Father Rochet's presbytery on 1st November 1939. It was a large, yellowish room with a very high ceiling, and a single central light without a shade. The grate was empty, and you could smell the damp. There were no curtains. We were so cold that no one took their coat off. Yet Father Rochet didn't seem to notice.

He said he'd called us together to form a 'Round Table' of knights dedicated to chivalry. I remember thinking that he must have been drinking. But he was deadly sober. He said he'd always loved the stories of Arthur, the dream of a fairer world and the longing for the return of the King. I recall that distinctly. He said life is a great waiting. There was no King, as yet. So we had to struggle for the dream in the meantime.

Do what? asked Victor. Father Rochet said that if France fell the Nazis would move against the Jews in a matter of months. Many would not be able to escape. But we could make a small difference. The Round Table would smuggle children to safety. He could not tell us when or how or where or who else was involved. He just wanted to know if we would act as young parents, older brothers and sisters, taking a child from A to B.

We all looked at each other, huddled in the cold, sitting around a huge oval table. Father Rochet drew a circle in the air with his finger, bringing all of us in on his scheme. Everyone nodded. Including Victor, but he voiced some doubts.

I should tell you something else about Victor. He was an organiser. Very practical-minded. He was the one who'd arranged the picnics, getting everyone to the pick-up point on time, allocating different jobs and so on. He liked lists and crossing things off. After Father Rochet's little speech he said he didn't think the Germans would ever march along the streets of Paris. If they did then the survival of everyone would be through cooperation, not confrontation. Including the Jews. That would be the key, finding an accommodation. In due course that is precisely what Victor did, at the expense of everyone in that room.

As I recollect, Father Rochet replied that Victor would soon change his mind about cooperation when he felt a jackboot up his bottom.

22nd April.

I discovered the full explanation for The Round Table in two parts, one openly, the other at the keyhole.

First, I asked Father Rochet and he told me it was a private literary joke.

91

At the turn of the century a political movement called Action Française had been formed, dedicated to re-establishing the monarchy. It was an extreme right-wing organisation, attracting certain types of Royalists and Catholics. Its leadership and many members were notoriously anti-Semitic. Soon it had a youth movement called the Camelots du Roi and they entertained Paris by rioting in the streets with the Socialists.

So far, I understood it. Then he said this: he wanted to use the myth of Arthur from the Middle Ages to carry out his own small purge of history – the Christian persecution of the Jews. The Round Table, he said, would enact the chivalry denied to Jews in the past. I didn't understand what he meant at the time. Father Rochet was a learned man, always reading something, and he knew tracts of medieval verse off by heart.

But now the keyhole, which made a bit more sense.

Madame Klein asked the same question as me. Father Rochet replied that he was swinging a punch at his old Prior who had thrown him out. There had been a bitter election for the leader of the monastery and one of the candidates had had connections to Action Française. Father Rochet had made a stink about it, hoping to stop him getting elected. He'd failed. Shortly afterwards, Father Rochet had been shown the door.

For opposing him? asked Madame Klein. Wasn't there another reason?

There was a long pause, so I looked. Father Rochet had his face in his hands. I never heard the reply.

23rd April.

The Germans took Paris in June 1940. I'm afraid from now on my memory is all in pieces, some large, some small. Many of the simple day-to-day details have been blotted out, and not the things I'd rather forget. It has always been a curse of mine.

I have disconnected pictures in my head.

I am standing near the Gare Montparnasse. I don't know what I'm doing there. Thousands are queuing for the trains, desperate to get out. Gaunt, hot faces. Hordes of people burdened with everything of value they can carry, and children running wild. For months afterwards there were notices in the shops from mothers listing the names of their lost boys and girls, just like those 'Have you seen . . . ?' things in the newsagent describing missing pets. Name, age, colour of hair and so on.

Next I am standing at the gates of a park. This must be later on. It is deadly quiet. A pall of black smoke hangs over the city. An old gardener tells me, 'That's our boys. They've set fire to the oil reserves. We're on our own now.' The streets are empty. I remember thinking the buildings are like a wall of scenery, where maybe there is nothing behind the façades but planks of wood and trestles, holding up a front. Paris is hollow and if you knocked upon its dome with a hammer you'd only hear an echo. There are two dogs trotting down the Rue de la Bienfaisance, sniffing at the closed doors.

I don't remember the moment they came. But I can see those wretched flags everywhere, on almost every building. I am standing on the Champs-Elysées watching

93

a parade. They did that every day with a full military band. At some point they even landed a plane on the Place de la Concorde. They were great ones for letting you know they were there, the Germans. Hitler turned up at some point but I have no recollection of it whatsoever, which is gratifying.

At first they were extremely polite, which surprised everyone. And that's not all. I remember seeing a truck by one of the bridges, with soldiers leaning out of the back charming the girls with jokes and chocolate. With some success, I might add. I think it was Simone de Beauvoir who said now that they were here there were going to be lots of little Germans running around.

What else? A curfew, the hours sometimes changing. Shots in the night. Queuing endlessly for food. Everyone awfully hungry. Bicycles everywhere, because special permits were required to drive (Jacques' father got one because he was a doctor). People heaving cases along the pavement or using a wheelbarrow. That was daily life under the Germans.

I know it doesn't sound so bad to you, seeing the war as you must from its outcome. But for those of us who were there, the fall of Paris, the fall of France, was devastating. From the moment they came and soiled our streets the mourning began. I cannot tell you how dark those times seem to me. And all around the Germans were on holiday. That's another memory I have. I can see lots of young soldiers larking about, taking photographs of each other in front of the Arc de Triomphe. Some of them have an army-issue guidebook.

I think it is the frailty of time that brings people

94

together. When you don't know if you will even see the year out, and you've lost a great deal, you seize what happiness comes by. In those days, we all held on to each other in different ways. For Jacques and me there was a strange, satisfying desperation about our coming together, as if we were one step ahead of misfortune. One evening Madame Klein, trying to winkle an admission out of me, said, 'I expect you see rather a lot of young Fougères?' I said I did. She said, 'I suspect he rather likes you.' And I told her to stop it. She was a terrible schemer, that woman.

But then we both got a big surprise, way beyond her suspicions and my expectations. I became pregnant.

1st May.

My generation doesn't talk about this sort of thing. Things got out of hand. It only happened once but, as you will appreciate, that's all it takes.

Jacques displayed his Catholic entrails, as Father Rochet put it, offering to marry me within the week. As he spoke I all of a sudden saw him dressed in a respectable black uniform, safely behind the rail of a huge ship, throwing me one of those circular life rings. Standing over his shoulder was a severe captain, his eyes concealed by shadow. Then he was just earnest Jacques again, alone with me by the windmill in Montmartre. I said no, not yet. I've never been that good at giving explanations so I described my picture. He couldn't see what I was trying to say. I said, 'Give it time.'

Jacques' family were the best kind of Catholic – principles never interfered with practice. They welcomed me and our child for what we were – part of their fold. Madame Fougères was very pleased: she already had one grandchild from Claude, a boy named Etienne. One day, she said, they'd play together.

I suppose it was a very modern arrangement. I lived overlooking Parc Monceau and Jacques was a stone's throw away on the Boulevard de Courcelles. Our infant was happily tossed between the two households. So I think we would have married, eventually. In all that matters he was an utterly devoted father, but he clung to wilful ignorance when faced with the more unpleasant chores of parenting – like most men I have known (including Freddie).

Notwithstanding the 'Not yet' to marriage, I did agree to a baptism, if only because I wanted Father Rochet to place his hands upon my boy. All I remember about the ceremony is sticking my head around the parlour door afterwards and seeing him alone with my baby. I instantly thought of that story by Maupassant, 'Le Baptême', about the lonely priest caught crying over an infant. That was 21st April 1941.

I have said nothing about Victor. He found out about Jacques and me by chance. And it was ironic that he should stumble upon us in the way he did. I said in passing to Father Rochet that an anti-Semitic exhibition had just opened in Paris, 'Le Juif et la France'. He told me to keep well away from such filth. But Jacques and I decided to go anyway. On the day, Victor suggested going over to Saint-Germain-des-Prés to hobnob with the intellectuals solving the problems of France in a café. Jacques and I made our different excuses, met up secretly and headed off. Who did we meet at the exhibition? Victor. And for reasons best known to himself, Father Rochet had urged him to go.

After that I have only two or three other memories of Victor. When I told him I was pregnant, it was as though I had struck him across the face with the flat of my hand. I didn't see much of him from then on and neither did Jacques. He withdrew, as if betrayed, and only came forward to witness the consequences of his revenge. For come it did.

Chapter Twelve

1

Left to his own devices, Anselm would have preferred to walk – a long, irreverent ramble through the vineyards of France, blistering his feet on the Alps, drinking too much wine and then descending, light-headed and a boy again, through the landscape of frescoes on to Rome. Instead, he did as he was told and took the 12.15 p.m. flight from Heathrow to Fiumicino. He was to stay with a community of friars at San Giovanni's, an international house of studies incongruously situated between two restaurants near Santa Cecilia in Trastevere, beneath the Janiculum Hill. A priest would collect him.

Anselm was standing in the arrivals area in his long black habit, beginning to feel the heat, when he was greeted from behind by a back-slapping friar in cut-off shorts and a T-shirt:

'Hello there, I'm Brandon Conroy. But call me Con.'

He had the build of a shaven ox with hands like pit shovels. But the most startling feature was his eyes, china blue, elfin and glittering, deeply set beneath a brow of heavy bone.

'I knew it was you from your outfit,' said Conroy. 'Here, give us your bag,' and off he went, whistling, while Anselm trailed behind, all pores opening.

Conroy compressed himself into a flaming red Fiat Punto, with Anselm at his side, and took the autostrada to the city.

Crossing the *Grande Raccordo Anulare* and accelerating towards the west bank of the Tiber, Anselm sensed a gradual disintegration in conventional road positioning. A slanging match of horns, bewildered voices and Latin passion tumbled through the open window, while Conroy made various offensive hand signals to right and left. There seemed to be a wide digital vocabulary, the sophistication of which had completely escaped Anselm's well-informed schooldays. The whole mêlée was thrashed out under the blessed heat of the sun and a cloudless cobalt sky.

'Been here a month now and I'm beginning to get the hang of it,' said Conroy, his gesturing arm at rest on the doorsill. 'I thought Rio was bad, sure. But here you've got to play *to kill*. No arsing around, you know, or they'll have your *cojones* on pasta.'

Anselm didn't quite know how to respond. It wasn't the usual language of recreation at Larkwood. He kept a firm grip on the door handle while Conroy clattered on.

'I'm brushing up my theology. Then back to Paula and the kids.'

Paula? Kids? Anselm had to reply. He'd start with the children.

'Kids?'

'Yep.'

'How many?'

'Too many.' Conroy waved his first and little finger at a priest on a bike.

Anselm's eyes widened involuntarily. 'I see,' he observed, politely sympathetic but resolved now to make no further enquiry about Father Brandon Conroy's domestic arrangements. Each took a side-glance at the other.

'Loosen up, Father, I'm only having a laugh,' chuckled Conroy, his hands off the wheel while he scratched his shoulders. 'Street kids. The homeless. São Paulo. I've been at it thirty-five years.'

Anselm laughed. Small buttons flew off some carefully ironed garment of childhood restraint. He'd never met anyone like Conroy in his life, except perhaps Roddy: they both gave copiously from the wine of themselves. The Punto weaved its way into the narrow streets of Trastevere and Conroy, tired of rambling, turned to enquiry:

'Anyway, what brings you to Bernini's twisted columns?'

'My Prior received a fax asking me to attend a meeting at four o'clock tomorrow.'

'Sounds serious.'

'It is. We've just had a Nazi land on us claiming "sanctuary".'

'My arse.'

'Funnily enough, that's what my Prior said.'

'Really?' asked Conroy, surprised, gesturing in response to an attack of horns.

'Not in quite the same terms.'

'Thought not.'

They drove on. Conroy was thoughtful. He'd slowed down his driving and the roads were somehow all the quieter for it. He said, 'Who's your meeting with?'

'Cardinal Vincenzi.'

Conroy chewed his bottom lip. 'There's only one other higher than your man, and that's Himself.' The jester was no longer at the wheel. With the earnestness of experience he asked, 'But why you?'

'I used to be a lawyer and I speak French. Our visitor was based in Paris during the war. That's all I can think of.'

'Father, let me give you some advice, all right? I know this place.'

100

'What do you mean?'

'Let's just say I've had my little run-ins. If you're going to get dragged into Church politics, you're entering one of those tents at the circus packed with curved mirrors, twisting and pulling things out of shape. Be careful. Don't go by appearances. Nothing's what it seems here.'

The car came to an abrupt halt and they walked into San Giovanni's, Conroy restored to his former self, shouting out for peaches, Anselm trailing behind, subdued.

2

Beniamino Cardinal Vincenzi, the Vatican's Secretary of State, welcomed Anselm as if he were an old friend from whom he had been separated by cruel misfortune. He had a disarming warmth wholly Italian in its excess, which almost concealed his formal identity – that of a highly polished diplomat more familiar with crisis than tranquillity. He was short and round with dark olive skin, the burden of his office carried by gleaming eyes that lured condolence as he spoke. He drew Anselm to one of three elegant chairs forming an intimate triangle at the furthest end of the room. One chair was already occupied by a priest in a neat black soutane, a red sash draped across one knee. He was introduced as Monsignor Renaldi. Of paler skin than his master, he conveyed a similar warmth, its expression subdued by an air of professional competence. He had the happy sheen of a recently appointed Recorder. Anselm took his seat by a small, highly polished table with legs like a dancer on tiptoe. A green cardboard folder lay upon it. Bright sunshine flooded through graceful windows on to paintings of sober men dressed in scarlet. They watched with old, expressionless eyes, keeping their own secrets.

101

Cardinal Vincenzi said, 'Father, I must give you some delicate information, the sort that is never printed. What you are about to be told you must not repeat, save to your Prior. You must appreciate that with an institution like the Church one cannot always allow the complete truth to meet the stream of public enquiry. There's a place and a time. Occasionally that moment never arrives. It can be very difficult, keeping silent about what you know. That burden of silence will now be placed upon you.'

Monsignor Renaldi smiled at Anselm encouragingly, as though it were a burden that had its rewards.

The Cardinal said, 'I have sought your help because of the arrival of Eduard Schwermann at your Priory.'

Flattered and slightly inflated, Anselm nodded with self-conscious gravity.

'A great deal is already known about him, but we know a little bit more, something that would greatly compromise the Church if ever it were made public.' He was a man of expansive gestures, but his arms lay still, as if wearied. 'Monsignor Renaldi will explain.'

'Let me give you the stark outline of the problem we face.' The Monsignor spoke confidentially, like a calm doctor before a specialist operation. Anselm noted the reddish tint to the cheeks, a morning inflammation caused by shaving close enough to draw blood. 'Immediately after the fall of France, Eduard Schwermann was posted to Paris. He was only twenty-two. He served as an SS-Unterscharführer in the Jewish Affairs Service of the Gestapo and his duties involved supervising the deportation of Jews to the death camps. A French policeman of roughly the same age, Victor Brionne, was assigned to the same department. They were, shall we say, colleagues. So, we have

102

two young men, a low-ranking German officer and a collaborator, both involved in grave crimes against humanity.'

Monsignor Renaldi paused, widening his warm eyes slightly. 'Let me now take you from Paris to Notre-Dame des Moineaux, a Gilbertine Priory in Burgundy. It is at the centre of a smuggling operation to hide Jewish children, as a result of which its Prior, Father Morel, is shot against the monastery wall in July 1942.'

Anselm felt the burdened eyes of the Cardinal upon him. Monsignor Renaldi patiently smoothed an eyebrow with a delicate finger and continued, 'Now we come to our problem. We don't know what evidence has been presented to the police in England but *we* in Rome are certain of this: the Allied forces broke out of Normandy at the end of July 1944. The war was over. Schwermann and Brionne fled Paris together and arrived at Les Moineaux on the twentieth of August 1944. De Gaulle marched into Paris a week later. Both men lay concealed until December 1944. They left with forged identity papers. As far as we know, neither of them was seen again.'

A charged, heavy silence fell. Sensing an invitation to speak, Anselm said, 'That's inexplicable.'

'We have been thinking about these facts longer than you, but our conclusion is much the same,' replied the Cardinal.

'Are there any monks left from that time?'

Monsignor Renaldi said, 'Only one is alive, a Father Chambray, but he returned to the world shortly after the war. We've already approached him, but unfortunately he was not entirely cooperative.' Moving on rather too quickly he said, 'We are lucky enough, however, to have a report that was written by the Prior in early 1945.' He reached for the green folder on the table and withdrew several sheets of pale yellow paper.

103

'Before you read this,' he said, 'I want to say something about the author. It was written by Father Pleyon, a man who quietly acquired a great reputation for wisdom and holiness. He came from a distinguished family with extensive political and diplomatic connections and would in all probability have followed the path of his forefathers into government service had the Lord not called him to the hidden life. But as you no doubt know, certain lights cannot be concealed. He became a confessor to those who carried the responsibilities he might have borne, individuals who often have no guide competent enough to understand the peculiar problems that come with worldly authority. It was this man who became Prior after the execution of Father Morel, and it was this man who presided over the escape of the two men with whom we are now concerned.'

Monsignor Renaldi handed the papers to Anselm.

The report was addressed to the Prior General of the Gilbertine Order. A covering note showed it had been passed on to the Vatican, into the hands of Archbishop Alfredo Poli, Secretary of the Cipher, who had simply marked it: 'Noted'. Anselm turned to the front page. After the usual obeisance, Father Pleyon had described the events already reported to Anselm. The text went on:

The smuggling ring was called The Round Table and involved a former member of the community, Father Rochet, who had been based in Paris. This monk had left Les Moineaux in disgrace, although I do not think it necessary or relevant to disclose the circumstances of his departure. I beg your indulgence on this matter, for I would prefer to protect my brother monk's dignity by not formally recording the reason for his ignominious down-

104

fall. Prior to his departure I managed to secure a place-ment for him in a parish where I had connections, informing in advance a family known to me for many years named Fougères who, I was sure, would give him a warm welcome. I cannot be certain of this, but it seems that from their meeting was eventually to spring the smug-gling operation to which I have referred. As you are aware, France fell in June 1940. Father Rochet visited Les Moineaux in the October after a census of Jews had been ordered in Paris by the Nazis. He came with his proposal for The Round Table which was accepted by the then Prior, Father Morel. The function of the Priory was to hide the children in the orphanage run by our sister community and to provide false identity and travel docu-ments – the skills required to produce such things being possessed by two of our monks when they were in the world, one an artist, the other a printer.

In unknown circumstances The Round Table was trag-ically broken in July 1942 and Father Morel was shot. Fortunately the detachment of soldiers that came to carry out the execution did not search the convent. Had they done so they would have found several children whose passage to Switzerland was still under preparation. I became Prior and was holding that office when Schwermann and Brionne arrived in August 1944.

Anselm turned the page and read the last few sentences:

I used my connections to facilitate their escape to England with false identities. Schwermann was given the name Nightingale; Brionne was called Berkeley. The reason I took this grave step is complex, and I now set out a full explanation which, you will readily understand, treads upon matters of profound secrecy. Appearances were never perhaps as deceptive as that which I now disclose.

Anselm glanced down the page, scanning the empty lines.

Monsignor Renaldi said, 'While we are fortunate in having the report at all, we are not so fortunate in that Father Pleyon died before he could complete his revelation.'

'Not a good time to die,' Anselm said, handing the letter back to Monsignor Renaldi.

'That was our conclusion,' said Cardinal Vincenzi, settling his paternal gaze upon Anselm. 'No doubt you see our difficulty. We do not have an explanation that meets the facts.' Speaking fluidly, as though there was no time to pause, he went on, 'You may have heard about priests and prelates helping fleeing Nazis' – Anselm had, but it was so vague and so beyond his own experience of the Church that it lay on the fringes of relevance, almost as a fiction – 'and that is another problem on my desk, but you can forget all about that.' As if to wave away any possible connection, he added, 'At the time, the Church was very concerned about the advance of communism, and out of that fear some of our wayward sons assisted fascists on the run.' It was a local problem, his tone suggested. 'The institution forever has its prodigals. In due course I will have to answer for them.' He gave a worn, sour smile. 'But, as I say, you can forget that.'

Smoothly removing any hiatus for reflection, Monsignor Renaldi said, 'The unanswered question remains: why did this community hide these two young men? It is perhaps stating the obvious, but the only ones who need to escape are those with something to fear. That is our worry. And, in the absence of an explanation, we are forced to consider logic.'

The application of reason alone to such a problem struck Anselm as a particularly desperate measure. And somewhat unconvincing. But nothing had been hidden. They had told him all there was to know. Monsignor Renaldi said, 'I understand you were once a lawyer.'

'Yes, but not a particularly good one. My practice was restricted to hopeless cases, and they tended to stay that way.'

'Well,' said the Monsignor appealingly, half-amused, 'what do you make of this one?'

The question jarred with Anselm. It was an approach he used to follow at the Bar when trying to prompt an intelligent, obviously guilty crook into seeing sense; it often pulled them on side. However, the vulnerable look of Beniamino Cardinal Vincenzi, the man who presided over the Secretariat of State, a noble dicastery of the Roman Curia, banished such tawdry associations. Anselm wanted to help. He thought for a long while and then said, 'On the face of it, Father Pleyon must have thought that both men were blameless. But if that's the case, he must also have concluded that proof of innocence could never be made known to the public. Otherwise he would not have found it necessary to devise an escape strategy.'

Quietly and slowly, Cardinal Vincenzi said, 'But what if they were guilty? What then would you make of the assistance provided?'

Anselm scavenged for an innocent explanation. 'He must have known something of sufficient importance to outweigh whatever Schwermann and Brionne may have done.'

'Yes,' said the Cardinal, assuaged, 'they are the only possible explanations.'

107

'And,' added Anselm, gathering confidence, 'I would have thought Father Pleyon must have already known and trusted one or the other, otherwise he would not have taken the risk of facilitating their escape.'

Monsignor Renaldi and the Cardinal glanced at each other like two judges sitting in the Court of Appeal. They shared a look of agreement, acceptance of a submission they hadn't thought of. The case was won. Monsignor Renaldi said, 'If Schwermann is brought to trial the role of Les Moineaux is likely to become public knowledge. We need to know why Father Pleyon acted as he did.'

'Of course,' said Anselm, as though he, too, were encumbered.

'You may well know,' said the Monsignor, 'that those who tracked Schwermann down succeeded because someone disclosed the identity under which he had been hiding.'

Anselm nodded.

'We think that person might have been Victor Brionne. Apart from Father Chambray, no one else alive would know the name. This has given us some encouragement that he may be prepared to speak the truth, regardless of personal cost, if he can be found.'

The Cardinal spoke with an enticing note of solemn commissioning. 'Father, I would like you to track down Victor Brionne and discover what really happened in 1944.'

Monsignor Renaldi rose, urging Anselm to remain seated. Beneath the dull gaze of painted Cardinals he walked the length of the room to a large panelled door and slipped out. The Secretary of State brought his eyes on to Anselm. They contained concern and fear and, to Anselm's elevating satisfaction, gratitude.

*

Cardinal Vincenzi summoned Anselm with a wave of the hand to an open window overlooking the Vatican Gardens.

'I want you to understand the delicacy of the situation,' he said confidingly. 'These are difficult times for the Church. Relations with our Jewish brothers and sisters are especially fragile as we try to resolve nearly nineteen hundred years of shared hostility. A great deal has been achieved in the forty years since I was ordained. But the role of the Church before and during the war is a particular stumbling block, especially what is alleged against Pius XII.'

'Anguish, silence and diplomacy?' asked Anselm, suddenly thinking of Salomon Lachaise and the empty, hungry fields.

'The caution of the Pope was shared by the world,' the Cardinal replied simply. He looked over Rome, which was glistening under the sun, the heavy hum of business afar. 'You are fortunate, Father, in not having to negotiate the boundaries of responsibility. I'm afraid dealing with history has always been a trading activity of sorts. We are bidding for a manageable form of truth. It is a most delicate exercise, for I am trying to protect the future from the past.'

The Cardinal moved away from the window, taking Anselm paternally by the arm. 'Which brings me to the Schwermann case. In these difficult times the last thing the Church needs is a war crimes trial tearing open the wounds we are trying to close, and that is what I fear will happen if he reveals precisely who effected his escape in 1944. With your help I need to prepare myself for that eventuality.'

The Cardinal walked Anselm to the panelled door, his heavy hand upon his shoulder. He blessed him and said goodbye. As the door opened, Monsignor Renaldi appeared on the other side. Their steps echoed down high corridors and wide stairs until they reached a side door on to the world. Upon opening it, they were struck by a rush of heat. The Monsignor, squinting in the light, said offhandedly, 'I suppose if Berkeley can demonstrate Schwermann's innocence then all well and good. But if he can't – well, it would have been better, for everyone, if we'd left him alone. Don't you think?' He smiled confidentially and withdrew.

Anselm headed towards an iron gate protected by a guard in a preposterous uniform. He entered the street aware that an obligation had been placed upon him; not at all sure he knew whose had been the laying hand.

3

Conroy was seated at an old olive press, installed as a table beneath orange trees in the middle of San Giovanni's ornate fifteenth-century cloister. A large jug of wine and a bowl of peaches in water lay on the press. At Larkwood it would now be the Great Silence after Compline, but for Conroy it was time for 'a bit of a wag'.

'And there's plenty more where this little divil came from,' he said, nodding at the jug. 'A bit rough, mind.'

Anselm pulled up a chair and they sat opposite each other like card players in a cheap Western surrounded by shooting cicadas.

'Now, can you tell me what the holy men had to say?' asked Conroy.

'No.'

'Thought not,' he replied, gratified.

Anselm remembered Conroy's warning about mirrors

twisting things out of shape. He had been wrong, which was not altogether surprising. The likes of Conroy, while highly entertaining, were not disposed to understand the subtleties of high office and the demands it placed upon its servants.

Conroy held the jug in his hand, saying, 'There isn't much time, you know, so give me that glass. We were born to celebrate.' He poured, squinting at some private thought, and then, measuring his words carefully, said, 'If ever you want information above and beyond what the holy men have told you, let me know. I've got a pal or two in the library with very sticky fingers.'

Conroy dropped a peach in his glass.

Anselm shook his head. There was no need for any such thing. And then, with dismay, he heard himself say, 'As a matter of fact, I do.'

'Tell me, so.'

It was as though another person was talking and Anselm was being helplessly pulled along. He said, 'What is known about a French Priory, Notre-Dame des Moineaux?'

Anselm winced as he sipped savagely dry white wine. Conroy quaffed and said, 'I won't write that down, so.'

'No, please don't.'

'And I won't write down the answer either.'

'No, please don't.'

They looked at each other, conjoined by deceit.

'Have a peach,' said Conroy.

'I will,' said Anselm, laughing for no reason, ready to celebrate he didn't know what.

Then Conroy took off at a pace. 'Did I tell you the story about me and the Cardinal? No? My God, well, listen.'

Conroy filled his glass.

111

'After I got a clattering for my book, I was invited, *invited* I tell you, to share evening prayer with the Prince of the Sacred Congregation for the Defence of the Faith. Well, I made an awful hash of it. You know that antiphon for Lent, "Heal my soul for I have sinned against you"? Well, God forgive me, it came out wrong. As solemn as you like I spoonered the opening words, with *emphasis*, and Jasus, you should have seen his face.' Conroy was fishing in his glass, trying to grip his peach. 'It was gas, I can tell you.'

'What book did you get into trouble for?' asked Anselm, intrigued.

'You won't know it. I agreed to have it withdrawn. The clever boys behind the door weren't happy with my Christology. Too low.'

'I'd like to read it.'

'I burned every copy, thousands of 'em. But I'm thinking of writing another. Now, Father, your glass please, it's empty.'

Anselm was rapidly slipping out of his depth. These were Roddy's waters, not his. But by tomorrow night he'd be back in Larkwood obeying the bells, so he dived in with Conroy and swam for his very life.

Anselm woke between two and three in the morning, lying on the kitchen floor with a block of English cheddar in one hand and a potato peeler in the other. Conroy was nowhere to be seen. He could remember little of their conversation except for one exchange which seemed to bring them both to sobriety. Conroy had asked what Schwermann was supposed to have done, and Anselm had told him. Conroy's face had darkened and his features had contracted in pain. He'd played with his glass, rolling its slender stem between his thick, gentle fingers.

112

Very slowly he'd muttered, 'Once you've heard a child cry out to heaven for help, and go unanswered, nothing's ever the same again. Nothing. Even God changes.'

Chapter Thirteen

The first notebook of Agnes Embleton.

2nd May.

Father Rochet was right about the Germans. Within months of taking control a census of Jews was ordered. At the time I was pregnant, so this would be late 1940. Madame Klein and I had moved out of her apartment to a rental property she owned in the eleventh arrondissement. 'I do not want to be too conspicuous,' she said. But it was a strange thing to have done. For while she became just another face among the crowd – the crowd in question was unmistakably Jewish where, with all the others, she would easily be found. It was a poorish neighbourhood but many of her friends from our musical evenings lived there. I think she wanted to be with her people when the end came, for she knew I would be safe, come what may, as a 'Christian'.

Madame Klein obeyed the census. I did not. The first round-up followed a few months later, of foreign Jews. Shortly afterwards, every Jew had to hand in their wireless to the police. She did, and I didn't. Then there was a huge round-up in our area, lasting about a week. By the time they'd finished, all our friends from the music group

114

had gone. Do you remember Mr Rozenwerg? I saw him with two gendarmes. He walked calmly on to the bus wearing his prayer shawl and a wonderful big fur hat. Twice they came to our door. Twice they looked at my papers, nodded and told Madame Klein, my 'grandmother', not to bother looking for hers. Isn't that strange? She would not give herself up to them, but neither would she take any forged papers from Father Rochet. But that was Madame Klein. The net began to close, for the next orders were that Jews could not change their address and had to obey a curfew.

They knew where you lived and you couldn't get out. The whole rotten, stinking business was under way.

Then Father Rochet called together his knights.

3rd May.

My little boy was about ten months old. So that would be early 1942. It was the same group as last time. Except for Victor. Father Rochet had not spoken to him for months and someone said they'd seen him dressed as a policeman. Father Rochet nodded. Victor's family, apparently, were very pleased with him.

The Round Table was ready to operate. Acting alone or in pairs, our task was to collect children from a pick-up point and take them outside Paris where they would be hidden. Someone else would take over after that.

Jacques was the coordinator among ourselves. He would be the sole link with Father Rochet and would tell each person where and when to do 'a run', distributing any travel papers that might be needed. He was the natural choice because members of his family, based in Geneva, handled the other end of the escape route.

Father Rochet stressed that if caught, stay calm and blame him. 'All you have to do is say I told you the parents were ill, and I'd asked you to take the children to stay with a relative. Leave the rest to me.' I asked him wasn't he frightened of what they might do to him? 'No, no,' he laughed. 'I've lived among tombs all my life. I'm not scared of dying.' Afterwards, Jacques said that worried him because there was a weak streak in Father Rochet. He often smelled of wine, even though he was a priest. He was the sort who might well cave in under the pressure. 'Never,' I said.

I did several 'runs', my own boy on one arm, a little charge in the other. They passed without hitch or hindrance.

4th May.

About this time there was another order from on high. All Jews had to register the names of their children. That is what it was like. Every now and then there'd be a new requirement or regulation affecting the Jews. The next one was to wear a six-pointed star with 'Juif' printed across it. Jacques and some friends from the university decided to protest by wearing a star with their names on. Come to think of it, I think Jacques' said 'Catholique'. He was duly arrested. The memory of that day is bitter for many reasons.

Almost overnight, thousands of people suddenly became visible, separated from everyone else by a single piece of yellow cloth. I saw two girls, twins, walking hand in hand, dressed in the same clothes, and with sky-blue ribbons in their hair. Over their hearts, neatly sewn, were these yellow stars the size of my hand. I stopped on the pavement and watched them pass, dumbfounded.

That makes me think of Madame Klein, a week or so before the regulation came into force. She is sitting by a tall lamp-stand, glasses on the end of her nose, carefully sewing the yellow cloth on to her black dresses. She has three of them. I don't remember her going out any more. She took fresh air by the window, describing the statues of musicians in Parc Monceau, or the turns in the paths and the odd people she used to meet there.

Worried about Jacques after his arrest, I went to see Victor at Avenue Foch, hoping he could help. On the way I saw Father Rochet. He looked more dishevelled than usual and nipped down a side street. Anyway, Victor crawled from under his stone and I asked if Jacques was all right. He couldn't even bring himself to speak to me. He just stared back in a way that scared me and showed me the door.

A few days later I bumped into him on the Champs-Elysées. 'I know what you're up to,' he said. And he warned me to back off from the heroics. I suppose I should have seen it then, that he was capable of selling us all down the river. But it never entered my head. Instead, I did something which, I'm ashamed to say, I have often relived these past fifty years. I gave him a great big belt across the face. It was glorious.

13th May.

The end came on 14th July 1942, Bastille Day. I had been
given a 'run'. It was straightforward enough. I went to a
dummy social club, set up by OSE, and there I collected
a little boy. I met his mother. She was about my age but
very beautiful, with dark green eyes. Needless to say, she
was distraught. It was like a scene in a film about a sinking
ship. I am there, taking the boy who will survive, but with
no space left on the lifeboat. Anyway, the mother had no
papers, so the plan was I would leave my boy with her
and her son would come with me, relying on my papers
if we were stopped. Her last words to him were, 'I'll see
you very soon.'

I took the train from the Gare de Lyon to a village in
Burgundy. I was met by a monk who took me to a convent
with an orphanage. That was it. I took the next train back
to Paris.

I got to the social club in the middle of the afternoon.
They told me my boy had cried after I'd gone so I took
him straight home. Trudging up the stairs, I heard a low
cough from an open door. It was an old busybody who
lived on the first floor, Madame Vignot, who often
complained about the noise. She shook her head, pointing
up at the ceiling. I leaned in. She whispered that Madame
Klein had been taken away. She'd fought and they'd dragged
her down the stairs by her hair. Then three others had
come, half an hour ago. They were waiting upstairs. I asked
for a description and one of them was obviously Victor.
There was a German soldier and a nurse.

I walked out on to the landing. That was the turning

point in my life. Because I could have walked down the stairs, on to the street and out of Paris. But it was only Victor. He'd come to explain about Madame Klein, with the nurse. All my papers were in order. There was nothing to fear. The German just wanted to know why I was living with a Jew. Anyway, I hadn't seen Jacques, I couldn't just slip away. So I went up the stairs. It all happened very quickly, but in my mind it is painfully slow.

The German soldier was Eduard Schwermann. I had seen him once before, sitting with Victor in a café. Father Rochet had pointed them out to me. Well, Schwermann barked something. Victor asked for my papers; everything – birth certificate, baptism certificate, the lot. I passed them over. Another bark. He wanted my parents' papers. Shaking like a leaf, I dug them out of the cupboard. My boy started to cry. Schwermann didn't look at a single piece of paper, he just put them in his pocket. He barked again. 'Downstairs,' said Victor. Off we went. The nurse followed.

I was taken into the street and round a corner, where a couple of parked vehicles were waiting – a truck with some soldiers in the back and a car. Both engines started. The rest is a blur. As I was being pushed into the back of the truck Schwermann pulled my boy out of my arms and handed him to the woman. She ran to the car and it pulled away. I was dragged off my feet, kicking and screaming. I can't remember much after that.

21st May.

I don't know how long I was locked up in Paris, and I

119

don't know when I left. But I was taken to La Santé prison and later transferred to Auschwitz.

It was in that appalling place that I had a bit of luck. I'd been there about four or five months. Up at 3 a.m. Standing in the yard until 7 a.m. Then labouring till I dropped. Constant, indiscriminate beating. One afternoon, a group of French women arrived. About two hundred or so. They marched through the gates singing 'La Marseillaise'. They were political prisoners and their detention at the camp was later the subject of a complaint by some government or other. I didn't get to know them immediately because I got typhus. For ten months I was in quarantine, and that probably saved my life because I was pulled out of the Auschwitz regime just as I was losing the will to survive. For six months I lay in a bunk beside Collette Beaussart, a former journalist who'd been deported because of what she thought rather than anything she'd done. Every day we talked of the simple things we'd like to do if ever we were free. She wanted to make jam and I wanted to eat it. I can't remember what else we said, but the words formed a sort of ladder and I clung on to them, unable to move up but not slipping any further down. When I came out of quarantine, the French politicals were being moved to Ravensbrück the next day, in response to the protest. By some clerical error, or so I thought, my name was on the transfer list. In fact, Collette had told the camp officials I was one of their number.

We left Auschwitz in 1944 and I remained at Ravensbrück until it was liberated by the Russians. I worked like a slave in the Siemens factory, making telephone equipment. I thought it would never end. When it did, the Germans abandoned the camp, leaving a few of us behind to deal with the sick.

22nd May.

I have often wondered whether I should tell you about your past, never mind my own. But now the two are inextricably linked. I cannot give you partial truths. So, read these words slowly and understand that I hope not to hurt you. I'm telling you part of your own history and, however painful it might be, it is yours and no one else's.

I met a woman who had only just arrived in the camp. I could not understand her language, so I know nothing about her. Not even her name. I think she was Polish. She had two children and was gravely ill. Ravensbrück was a women's camp so I can only assume her husband, your grandfather, had been taken from his family at some time in the past.

You don't need words to express certain things, or to understand them. So I think, in what mattered, we made contact with one another. She knew she was dying. She knew her children would be left all alone. She knew I was the last person she'd ever speak to. Pleading sounds the same in any language, and she asked me to do something, over and over. I held both her hands, muttering helpless assurances in French. I knew she was begging me to look after her twins, Freddie and Elodie. And I knew she was comforted by my replies. She died while we were talking. Her hands lost their grip, as if she'd let go of a rope, and she fell back. I did not have a name for her, until you were born. I called her Lucy, after you. And you have grown to have her delicate, haunting features.

The rest you know. I returned to Paris with fifty or so other camp survivors. We were all terribly thin and a waxy grey-green colour, with brown rings under our eyes. As we lined up on the platform at Gare de l'Est, everyone stopped and stared in silence. They began 'La Marseillaise'. It was the most moving moment of my life. The last time I'd heard it was at Auschwitz.

While I was in hospital I met Grandpa Arthur, who was recovering from a broken foot. I found him talking to Freddie and Elodie. He introduced himself. Over the next few weeks I told him everything. From then on I didn't need to say any more. He understood. After that I knew I never wanted to leave him. I long to see him again.

When I was discharged I went to what was left of my home. Nothing remained of Madame Klein's life, or mine, or anyone I had known. I made enquiries and pieced together what I could. Victor betrayed us all. Each and every member of The Round Table had been arrested on the same day as me, mostly that afternoon, in one swoop. Jacques' family had managed to escape but he'd stayed behind. He must have waited for me in vain, for I did not come. He was arrested that night, in his own home.

I tried to keep my promise, to look after the children, but I failed. And I have never been able to forget the little boy who cried because I'd left him with strangers at the social club. Arthur helped me find out what had happened. My boy had been taken to an orphanage. All of the children were deported to Auschwitz in July 1942. The Red

Cross told me the obvious: no one with his name had survived. At least I spent some time in the place where he met his end. That has been a comfort.

Well, that is what happened, and that is why I am who I am. Do you remember reading out loud with Grandpa Arthur on Sunday afternoons, doing silly voices with serious plays? Do you recall King Lear, when he finally understands that his failures have cost him the lives of his children? He says, 'I am a man more sinned against than sinning.' Can you bring yourself to think that of me?

Part Two

'All burns! The reddest rose is a ghost;
Sparks whirl up, to expire in the mist . . .'
(Laurence Binyon, 'The Burning of the Leaves', 1942)

Second Prologue

'I shall be your amanuensis,' said Wilma with theatrical gravity.

Agnes nodded. It would be the only way, now that she could not write. 'There isn't much to say, but I'd like it set down.'

Ever since she had completed her notebook, Agnes had pored over that dreadful time, rehearsing the order in which things had happened. The act of committing herself to a narrative had lit the past with a new light. She saw new shapes and the hint of an outline she partly recognised.

Agnes opened the drawer of her bureau and took out the remaining school notebook she'd bought six months earlier. She gave it to Wilma, who settled herself down at the table.

'Start when you are ready,' said Wilma ceremoniously, pen poised.

Agnes closed her eyes, feeling her way. And then she began:

'"Night and day I have lived among the tombs", comma, "cutting myself on stones". Full stop.'

Wilma wrote slowly, in great swirls. 'I like that story.'

'What story?' asked Agnes sharply, wondering if this was a sign of things to come.

'The one about the poor chap in the hills. He was possessed by so many demons that no one could control him. He lived night and day, just as you said, among the tombs. Like we do.'

'Why do you like it?' enquired Agnes with feeling.

Wilma put down her pen. 'Because help eventually came,

after everyone had given up and when he was unable to ask for it.'

Agnes' memory flickered. 'What happened?'

'The Saviour sent the lot of them into a herd of pigs grazing on the fat of the land.'

'That's right,' remembered Agnes. 'The demons were called "Legion" because there were so many of them.' Father Rochet had likened them to the German army in France, just as the Roman legions had occupied Palestine.

'They charged over a cliff into a lake and drowned,' said Wilma with great satisfaction. 'And the poor young man was returned to his family.'

Oh yes, that's it, thought Agnes. Father Rochet had said there were plenty of pigs, but no cliff, and as yet, no Messiah. 'So we have to act while we wait,' he'd said.

'Did I say who this was addressed to?' breathed Agnes, weakened by a new, unexpected certainty.

'No.'

'Go back to the beginning then, please.' She closed her eyes, trying to conjure up an old friend.

'Dear—'

Chapter Fourteen

Alone at last in the first-floor sitting room overlooking the sea, the old man opened once more the letter from his wife, penned just before she died while he slept in a chair by her bed. She'd told him to read it every time the guilt threatened to overpower him.

My Dearest Victor

I've often watched you while you sleep. The bad times have even marked your peace. They've never really left you and I doubt if they ever will. But you must believe me: you acted for the best in the most difficult of times. I was right when I said all those years ago that sometimes there have to be secrets. What a relief it would be if a great wind would blow and sweep it all away! But that is not going to happen. For twenty-six years we've had each other and you could turn to me, and now, well, that is coming to an end. So this is what I have to say. Just look at Robert! Look at all his children! Look at them all! This is your testament. They only see the good man I married, even if the world comes to judge you one day out of hand. I know, and I bless the day I met you.

Your ever-loving
Squirrel

Pauline the squirrel: because she never threw anything out.

He folded the paper and put it back in his pocket diary. The words had no effect. They never had done. It wasn't that Victor didn't see the wonder of his family. He did. But each shining face was only a flickering candle against the endless shadow of slaughter he had known.

After his wife died Victor went on a binge. Not a single monumental blow-out but rather a gradual build-up of solitary chaotic sessions, a ritual that gathered pace and eventually left him flat on the floor almost every day. He learned what only the gravely fallen know: there's a sincerity to drinking, a bravery. It's not an escape – that's at the amateur level, carried out with newfound comrades, takeaways and taxis. It's the opposite. It's standing your ground, utterly alone, as the demons rise to dance and sneer.

In the end, Robert found out what was happening from the parish priest, Father Lacey, who found Victor slumped in a confessional. Victor hadn't eaten or washed for days. A meeting was called. Father Lacey said he knew of a good place, out in the country, but it was expensive. 'You'll have to face the grief, Dad,' Robert implored, and Father Lacey added knowingly, with a stare, 'along with your past'.

All the family helped, once they were allowed to visit. The professionals involved said Victor hadn't fully cooperated, implying he'd dodged about rather skilfully, but that he'd 'learned a lot about himself' and they'd been over various 'coping strategies'. And so Victor came back to 'normal life'. For most of the observers it was a matter of a grief under control, a man who'd found a way of living without his wife. Only Victor and his confessor, Father Lacey, knew of the demon legion sleeping out of sight.

Victor often returned to his wife's letter, hoping the recitation of the lines might yet have some effect, like the workings of a spell that only required a solemn, heartfelt incantation. But he didn't believe in magic. What about the fragile light of candles? Yes, he believed in those. He lit them every week in the side chapel for Robert. For – a gust of laughter suddenly burst through a door somewhere downstairs – Robert's wife, Maggie, and the grandchildren, all five of them, two boys and three girls, all 'grown and flown, to homes of their own', as Robert liked to say. Victor smiled. Two of them were married. Great-grandchildren had followed. The whole clan came to thirteen – a blessing of biblical proportions. Only, it wasn't that simple, was it? He caught his reflection in the mirror over the fireplace. Even when he smiled he couldn't hide that ineffable, intractable sadness. Why was it that, after all these years, whenever he looked in a mirror he thought of Agnes and Jacques, her long thick hair and his dark beseeching eyes? And why, oh why, did their shades always part, with a moan, leaving him with another remembrance that would not be staunched? How could it be that even now, in his mid-seventies, he could not see himself without seeing Eduard Schwermann? Was it any wonder he could not explain to the children why there were no mirrors in granddad's house?

Here, in Robert's home, there were many of them, unforgiving windows into his soul, and that of his accomplice. He said under his breath:

'Zwei Seelen wohnen, ach! in meiner Brust.'

As they sat round the crowded, laden dining table on the night of his arrival, conversation turned, as Victor had anticipated, to the Schwermann case. In order to protect Stephen, the eldest great-grandchild, key terms had to be spelled out. He'd reached the dreadful age of four where listening and repetition went mercilessly hand in hand.

'From all accounts he was a complete b-a-s-t-a-r-d,' said Francis, Robert's first son.

'He'll probably say they've got the wrong man,' someone chipped in. Other voices turned over the material they'd all heard and read:

'Oh no. Apparently there's no doubt that he was there.'

'Then what's he going to say? He's got to say something.'

'Didn't know what was going on, only obeying orders. It has to be one or the other.'

'That's always struck me as odd.'

'What has?'

'Well, where I work, even the cleaners get to know all the dirt.'

'That's an awful pun. Pass the chicken, please.'

'It's the same at our place. I don't know how they find out because no one admits to telling them. At the end of the day, you can't hide anything.'

'It's not chicken, it's soya.'

'And you'd think "doing as you're told" and "d-e-a-t-h c-a-m-p-s" don't really belong in the same sentence. Not unless you're mad.'

'And he's sane.'

'Either way you're right, Francis; he's a b-a-s-t-a-r-d.'

'What's that, Daddy?' asked Stephen with a curiosity that, from experience, would not be easily deflected.

'Nothing, son, nothing.'

'Daddy, what are you talking about?'

'A naughty man, that's all. Now eat up.'

The words nearly made Victor sick.

'But Daddy . . .'

Victor heard no more. Although he couldn't be sure, for he kept his eyes on his plate, he felt Robert's gaze upon him, talkative Robert, who for some reason kept out of the conversation.

That ordeal was last night, his reticence passed off as old age worn out further by the delayed train from London. Now he was alone in the sitting room, waiting. There was no need to make an arrangement. Soon he would come. Repeating snatches from his wife's letter, Victor walked over to the bay window of Robert's much-loved home, The Coach House at Cullercoats – a rambling pile of creaking rooms on a low cliff between Tynemouth and Whitley Bay, overlooking the old harbour. He could see the jagged black rocks collapsing over each other into the incoming tide, the great rush of metallic water, always cold, always bound to the sky, always seemingly inviting him to cross over, into the thin wisp of evening light where memory was left behind. Great fat gulls swooped under gusts of wind and then surrendered to the drift, floating high out of view.

God, bear me up, help me.

A fire, freshly made, crackled in the grate.

The door opened quietly. He heard the soft approach of familiar steps. A hand rested on his shoulder. Now was the time. He would have to speak of things he'd vowed never to say.

'Dad . . . ?'

'Yes, son?'

'Tell me what's troubling you.' He spoke almost in a whisper. 'Come on, I'm a grandfather, you know.'

Victor breathed deeply; his eyes scanned the silent, tumbling sea, the long threads of foam clinging on to light that vanished

133

on the shore. Robert remained by his side, as if he were a boy again, and together they faced the vast, brightening darkness.

'Son, I am not who you think I am. I am another man, someone I buried fifty years ago, after the war. Someone who, but for you, would have been better dead.'

No questions came. And, not seeing Robert or the confusion that must be clouding his eyes, Victor picked his way over all that might be said.

'My name was Brionne. I was a police officer seconded by chance to the Gestapo.'

Victor's attention shifted to Robert's hand. It was heavy upon him. *I beg you, don't take it away* . . .

'To some I was a collaborator . . . there was nothing I could do to stop . . .' Now that simply wasn't true, and he knew it. His voice trailed off. How much shall I say? If I go too far, I'll go over the edge. It will all come out. I can't . . . I can't do that.

Victor tried again. 'I worked as an assistant to a young German officer, Eduard Schwermann. He's the one who's claimed sanctuary in a monastery. You've read the papers . . . Francis talked of him last night.'

Victor lived each moment through that hand, his existence depending on the movement of someone else's fingers.

'Pascal Fougères, who found Schwermann, will almost certainly come looking for me . . .' Again, his voice faltered on the threshold of complete disclosure. 'Schwermann will also seek me out . . . I suspect there will be others . . . they'll all want me for the trial.'

Victor felt the grip of panic. He told himself: you'll be all right, you've already planned for this. When he left Les Moineaux he had a new identity; he was Victor Berkeley. But that name was known to Schwermann and the monks. So when Victor got to England he changed it again, to Brownlow. No one else knew. Again he said to the beating in his chest: you'll be all right . . . but don't wait around . . .

It was now completely dark outside. Tiny lights from fishing boats twinkled in the distance upon the hidden, brooding presence of the sea. The catch was out there somewhere in the deep, but they'd be found and decked by morning.

'Robert, I cannot tell you any more. Perhaps one day things might be different. But for now, if you can, trust me. Trust me as you've never trusted anyone before. Believe me,' Victor swallowed hard, reaching out for words that might slip through the gap between truth and deceit, 'it has been the curse of my life that I ever knew that man.'

Victor waited, his eyes closed, facing an abyss. Robert's hand lay still upon him.

'I have to hide,' he said simply. 'I have to go where no one would think of looking for me, until it's all over. Then I can bury Victor Brionne for the last time. And after that . . . I'll be your father again . . . the man you have known.' Tears filled his eyes, rising from a deep, ancient sorrow.

Robert's hand fell away.

After a long moment, Victor heard these words, quietly spoken: 'I don't know Brionne. As far as I'm concerned, he's still dead. He's not my father and never was. You are. You were and always will be.'

Tramping footsteps and voices mingled on the stairs. It was time for a game of Consequences before the crackling fire.

135

Chapter Fifteen

1

'I won't be going into hospital at all. I want to die here.'

'But you can't.'

'I can and I will. This is my home. This is where I'll die.'

Lucy sank her nails into her thighs, as if they were part of her father's neck. Susan fiddled with the buttons on her blouse. This was the inevitable confrontation between mother and son. They had all gathered at Chiswick Mall that afternoon, at Freddie's instigation, to deal with the question 'my mother won't face'.

Agnes walked deliberately across the room as if she had a pile of books on her head. She flopped confidently into her usual chair by the bay window.

'Mother, your legs are giving way more often, you—'

'I know.'

'—need a wheelchair—'

'I know.'

'Getting in and out will not be straightforward.'

'No.'

'You already need help with washing.'

'Freddie—'

'Before long, there are going to be problems with feeding, talking, moving—'

'Freddie,' said Agnes, her voice rising and the muscles on her face beginning to contort.

'The house will need cleaning, sheets washed, bedclothes changed—'

'Freddie—'

'—what about going to the toilet—'

'FREDDIEEeeeeeee!' Agnes' cry became a strange howl, rising and trailing off. She heaved with a sort of anguished laughter, tears gathering in her eyes, her thin hands shaking uncontrollably.

'Now look what you've done,' snapped Lucy, running towards her. Agnes waved her away, angrily, her mouth locked wide open.

Freddie pulled at his hair, saying sorry over and over again. Agnes was trying to say something by hand gesture, her head thrown back while she moaned.

Lucy could barely contain her anger. 'Just read this, will you? Go on, read it.' She reached over to the bureau and handed her father a piece of paper. Agnes had written an explanation:

Sometimes I laugh or cry or wail for no reason. Please ignore me while it lasts. It will stop soon. Thank you.

Lucy took the paper back. Agnes was quiet now. No one said anything. Susan made some tea.

Agnes sipped from old china, the tinkling saucer held beneath. The cup was so fragile that sunlight passed through its clay, tracing the outline of frail fingers on the other side.

'Freddie, don't worry. It's difficult for all of us. But I've made my mind up,' said Agnes kindly.

Freddie moved to speak. He was resolute, as if he too had made up his mind. He was going to press his point. Lucy felt a flash of anger and confusion. There was such a dreadful mix of motives and concerns. Yes, Agnes was going to deteriorate, and planning was necessary. But there was another powerful drive, and that was Freddie's reluctance, if not refusal, to become ensnared in day-in day-out nursing care. The illness was creeping up on all of them. Lucy could see her father's terror. He wasn't *capable* of giving Agnes what she needed, he could not carry the strain of intimate dependence on him. And now he was feeling rising desperation, shifting from right to left as if routes of escape were closing down. Lucy saw all this internal squirming, while her father sat stock-still on the settee, his hands on his knees as if for a school photograph. And she loathed it, in him and in herself.

'I won't need your help. None of you need worry about that.'

Freddie immediately spilled a lie: 'We're not *worried*, we *want* to help. It's just that we've got to be practical. All of us.'

'I've already planned everything, Freddie.'

No one knew what to say. The question they were all asking themselves didn't need to be asked. Agnes nodded at her tea cup, wanting more. 'And a chocolate finger, please, Lucy.' Freddie relaxed a little with the promise of relief. And, hating herself for it, so did Lucy.

'I've spoken to Social Services. As and when it becomes necessary, carers will come each day to help with washing and dressing. They'll provide appliances "subject to budget" and I can get all sorts of toys from the hospital or Trusts. There really is nothing to worry about.'

Susan was still fiddling with the buttons on her blouse when she spoke. 'I don't want you being cared for by strangers. It's not right. You need your family. I want to help, if you don't mind, I really do. I'll do anything you like – I can cook, clean up, I can . . . do anything . . . give me the chance, can't you?'

Agnes was visibly moved. Lucy had always felt Agnes valued Susan's confused attempts to establish normal relations with her mother-in-law. It cost her so much, and always without reward. Susan, like Lucy, wanted things to be different, and in her own way had kept on trying.

'Thank you, Susan, there's plenty of time, yet, for both of us. Of course you can help.'

Freddie, ashamed, ran for the line: 'But all this isn't enough, is it? I mean, it's not just about bits of help at certain times of the day. What about the nights? You're going to be needing' – Freddie hesitated, the corner flag was in view – 'twenty-four-hour-a-day assistance,' and then he dived, full length, 'from people who know what they're doing.'

He was pale. He'd finally said it. He'd said he couldn't and wouldn't become a nurse, or move in, or take Agnes to his own home.

'That's right, Freddie, and I've sorted it all out.'

For the second time, no one knew what to say. Lucy, incredulous, guessed immediately. The question fell out of Freddie's mouth: 'How? In what way?'

Agnes put down her saucer, and then the cup, and then the biscuit, saying, 'I've asked Wilma to move in.'

Freddie, rigid again, almost stopped breathing.

2

It seemed it was going to be a day of arguments. After her mother and father had left, Lucy urged Agnes to give a statement to the police.

'If I get involved,' replied Agnes, 'your father will have to know everything. I don't want that. His life with me has been

139

hard enough.' She spoke without a trace of self-pity. 'It would be too much to ask of him.'

'What would?'

'To understand me more than he understands himself.'

'But if he knew what was done to you, and how you saved him—'

'Lucy, you forget, I also failed him.' She raised a hand to stop any protestation. 'That can't be changed, even by forgiveness. I used to blame myself, but after I met Wilma I realised things couldn't have been otherwise. But that only makes the remorse all the more insupportable.' Her features became still and extraordinarily beautiful, like a rapt child at a pantomime, and she said, 'In a way, I lost Freddie as well. I could not bear to lose the little I have left.'

Agnes had a way of saying dreadful things with complete simplicity, as if she were commenting on the wallpaper. Unless one inhabited a similar inner landscape it was quite impossible to reply. Even Lucy came up against these awful flashes of tranquillity, where one would expect to find anguish, when she could only look upon her grandmother from a distance with a sort of shocked reverence.

Outside the window rain began to fall, bouncing off the pavement, gathering the litter, washing stray cuttings from tidy gardens, and Agnes, serene, reached for the newspaper by her side, saying, 'There's a documentary tonight on The Round Table.' She paused. 'One of the contributors is Pascal Fougères. I'm worried he might mention me . . . the family will not have forgotten . . .' Her eyes reached out to Lucy. 'You'll have to stay.'

'All right then, if I must.'

'You must.'

140

Lucy regarded her grandmother and became almost cold with apprehension. Impulsively, with sudden terror, she said, 'Does it make any difference to you?'

Agnes looked up, mildly surprised, and said, 'Of course it does.'

'No, Gran,' Lucy replied, squirming, prickling with intimacy, 'I mean, does it matter that I'm not your own blood?' She flushed hot; sweat tingled across her back and neck.

Agnes dropped the paper. With coruscating simplicity she said, 'It has made you utterly irreplaceable.'

The documentary had been constructed in such a way as to follow the steps of Pascal Fougères through a tragic moment in history. To her amazement, Lucy found her sensibilities dozing, sluggish, as she watched the footage of German soldiers surveying Paris with the lazy contentment of ownership. She could not rouse the naked fear they must have represented. Anodyne war films and comedies about silly Nazis had tamed them, even in Lucy's eyes.

The narrator described how Fougères, a foreign correspondent for *Le Monde*, had inadvertently come across a cryptic memo recently declassified in the United States. The document briefly reported the capture and release of a young German officer by British Intelligence. The journalist immediately recognised the name for it was Schwermann who had been responsible for the breaking of a Resistance network and the death of its leader – Pascal's great-uncle, Jacques. The viewer was taken back to the time of Occupation, when Jacques, with other students, formed The Round Table. On the day the Star of David had become compulsory apparel, Jacques had worn his own star, marked 'Catholique', outside the Gestapo offices on

141

Avenue Foch. He had been arrested and interned in Drancy for two weeks. But that had not discouraged the young protester.

'The Round Table continued with its work,' said Pascal, his face filling the screen, dark-eyed and pensive, 'but it was broken by Schwermann within the month. They were all deported. None survived.'

Schwermann escaped from France after the war and made his way to England, along with a Frenchman, Victor Brionne, who had been based in the same department of the Gestapo. They did so under false identities that had never been discovered. All this, and no more, was set out in the terse memo the young journalist had been fortunate enough to find. He publicised his findings, expecting a strong reaction throughout Great Britain. It caused a brief outcry somewhere on the third or fourth pages and then became yesterday's news. Attempts to trace Schwermann through official channels floundered. Meanwhile, back in France, a consortium of interested parties had been formed and the case against the fugitive Nazi was painstakingly constructed. The decisive breakthrough came when Pascal Fougères received a letter, anonymous and tantalisingly brief, disclosing the false name under which Schwermann was hiding: Nightingale.

The narrator, interviewing Fougères, asked about the Frenchman whose whereabouts were still unknown. Pascal replied, 'Victor was Jacques' best friend and, as with so many others, the war split them apart. He fled, I think, because he'd been trapped by circumstances. He was just an ordinary policeman but ended up at Avenue Foch.' He smiled, as if cracking a joke: 'I doubt whether it would have been a good idea to trade arguments with the Resistance after the Germans had gone.'

142

As for Schwermann, said the narrator with a level voice, he had found sanctuary in a monastery.

Lucy turned off the television. It was dark outside and the rain was still falling, lightly but interminably. She said, 'You weren't mentioned.'

'No.'

'I didn't realise Jacques had been the one who set up The Round Table.'

'That's not how I remember it.'

Lucy reflected further about Pascal Fougères. 'He's got no idea what Victor Brionne did to you and Jacques . . . and the others.'

'No,' replied Agnes, distracted. She smoothed a wrinkle in the fabric on the arm of her chair. Her eyes narrowed as if trying to make out a figure in the dark, half seen, familiar but receding from view.

'I wonder who wrote that letter . . . giving the name?'

'Yes, I wonder . . .' Agnes stared into the shadows, still calmly smoothing the material.

Chapter Sixteen

1

Finding the whereabouts of Father Louis Chambray (for he had never been laicised) was a relatively straightforward matter. While a Gilbertine monk like Anselm, he belonged to a different Province, a French strain, which had nonetheless been founded as a result of Henry VIII's delirious policy of closure that had removed the Gilbertines from English life. Remnants of the Order had sought refuge in Burgundy – mindful, perhaps, that its Dukes had once sold Joan of Arc to the English. Such courtesies promote lasting trust, a commodity the Gilbertines required if they were to survive. For whatever reason the characteristic double-houses (monks and nuns in separate buildings but joined for services on Sundays and feast days) thrived, notwithstanding the various anti-clerical movements that followed the feast of revolution two hundred years later. The French Order subsequently re-established an English presence at Larkwood Priory in the early 1920s. After that there was little contact between the two Provinces, not least because each house was self-governing. But historic familiarity and a sort of religious *entente cordiale* helped Anselm's purpose.

The French Gilbertines' motherhouse in Rome freely supplied Anselm with details about Father Chambray, as they had evidently done on an earlier occasion to an emissary from the Vatican. Chambray kept in contact with his Order once a year, sending a *Bonne Année* card to a Prior General he had never known. He'd gone, but that one slender tie remained.

'Why's he so popular all of a sudden?' asked the plump archivist, chewing one of his fingernails.

'Some ancient history, that's all,' replied Anselm.

'History is never ancient,' said the keeper of the books, blinking solemnly.

'Indeed,' said Anselm dryly. He wasn't altogether fond of inversions. They tended to sound good and mean very little. He thanked the young sage, placed the address in his pocket and wandered back to San Giovanni's. There was much to be done before returning to England.

Before directing his efforts to finding Victor Brionne, Anselm decided to follow the escape trail from Paris to Notre-Dame des Moineaux. Tracing history had its own poetic attraction, but geography and pride were the decisive factors: Chambray now lived in the capital, and since Anselm had to pass that way to reach the monastery he thought he might as well track down the one living survivor from the time. All the more so, coming to the pride, because Anselm considered himself particularly adept at handling individuals described as 'uncooperative'. It had been his hallmark at the Bar. Back at San Giovanni's, Anselm rang Father Andrew to explain matters and get the necessary permissions.

'While you've been away,' said the Prior, 'there's been a run of stories in the Press implying that we are sympathetic to Schwermann's predicament. Worse, there are heavy implications that the Church may have eased his passage out of France in the first place. Just wild guesses.'

'I'm afraid those guesses may not be that wild, but appearances aren't what they seem.'

A troubled pause crept over the line. 'Tell me everything when you get home.' The Prior's voice changed tone. 'Anselm, I want you to be careful. Remember, first and last you're a monk. Protect what you've become because it can easily fall apart if you're careless. In one sense you've left the world behind, so in all you have to do you should sense you don't quite belong. If you begin to feel you do belong, you're at risk. Remember what one of the desert fathers said. The house caved in not because it was struck by rain but because it was built on sand.'

Anselm packed his bags and slipped out, praying that Conroy would not emerge from his lair. By early evening he'd landed in Paris, taken the metro to Porte de la Chapelle and walked to Saint-Denis. Upon an impulse, Anselm made a casual enquiry at the Basilica. Yes, said a young priest, they knew Chambray well but he was in considerable ill-health. He'd been coming to daily Mass for thirty years and had never been to Communion once.

Anselm made the final two-minute walk to the flat, climbed four floors of rough concrete stairs and knocked firmly on the dull brown door. A small brass eyepiece stared back remorselessly. The lights on the landing were broken and thin streaks of grey daylight lay adrift upon the walls. Anselm heard a rattle from the other side, getting louder, as of air being pulled into thick lungs. An unseen cover scraped off the eyepiece. Anselm swallowed hard in the long, heaving interval that followed. The door opened slowly and smoothly.

In the gloom Anselm saw a shortish man, his wiry head pushed forward with a thick moustache falling over his mouth. All other features were indistinct, but Anselm was not really looking. His gaze had fixed upon the long knife.

146

'Good afternoon,' said Lucy.

Pascal Fougères nodded an acknowledgement with such a direct gaze that Lucy could have sworn he'd said something. He held out his hand with a smile. Lucy took it, suddenly self-conscious. While only twenty-eight, he seemed older. Relaxed in his body, as the French say, his energy spilled over in the swiftness of small gestures.

'Take a seat,' he said, pointing to a chair.

After watching the documentary on The Round Table, Lucy brooded upon the strange exoneration of Victor Brionne. A suspicion had grown that the Frenchman's artless ignorance was more of a subtle contrivance . . . which would be warmly received by Victor Brionne had he seen the programme. With growing conviction, like one who has found a footprint, Lucy checked the various newspaper cuttings retained by her grandmother. On too many occasions to be described as coincidence she perceived a clear agenda: the emasculation of Victor Brionne's past as a collaborator. With that understanding came the further critical insight that prompted Lucy to contact the producer of the programme. Her details were passed on to Pascal Fougères who promptly returned her call. They arranged to meet in Sibyl's Cave, a pub by the river at Putney Bridge, after Lucy had finished a morning tutorial.

Upon arrival Lucy instantly recognised Fougères sitting at the far end of a terrace, absorbed in a novel. He wore a striped shirt, the collar wide open without a tie, and a rather shapeless jacket that had once probably been green. One hand covered his mouth while his eyes squinted at the fluttering page.

'I've never been here before,' said Lucy.

'It's not just a pub,' he said, closing the book. His black hair fell forward, quite long, and extravagantly thick. Lucy suspected he cut it himself.

'Through there,' he continued, pointing towards the lounge, 'you can join any table you like and get involved in whatever debate is going on. No politics or religion, they're the only rules.'

At Pascal's suggestion they ordered lunch and came back to their table while it was being prepared. Lucy glanced across the river towards Hammersmith, towards Chiswick Mall, towards someone slipping away on the heavy pull of a late tide.

'Mine are peculiar circumstances,' she said. 'Unfortunately I can't tell you about my background because I'm protecting someone. Let's just say I have an interest in the fate of Eduard Schwermann. I know all about your great-uncle Jacques, Victor, Father Rochet, Madame Klein, The Round Table . . . Mr Snyman . . . all of it, not from the papers, not from books . . . but I can't say any more, because of a promise.'

Pascal's whole body tensed with interest. He looked at Lucy afresh, as if trying to recognise her.

'From what I have read,' continued Lucy, 'I suspect that through words of encouragement you are hoping Victor Brionne will come forward to be a witness at the trial.'

A light wind tousled Pascal's thick hair, pushing it over his eyes. 'No one is better placed to condemn Schwermann.'

Lucy grimaced at the admission. 'The reason I've asked to see you is to give you a warning. I know that if Brionne responds, for whatever reason – to make amends for his past, to offer consolation to your family, whatever – nothing he says can be relied upon.'

148

Pascal's brow contracted fleetingly, smoothed away by a deeper, contrary conviction. Lucy went further: 'Brionne will not say a word against Schwermann.'

'I know someone who thinks otherwise.'

'And I know someone else.' Calmly she watched his confidence falter. 'That is all I can say,' said Lucy with finality. 'Except for this: if Victor Brionne contacts you, persuade him to meet me, if only for a few minutes.'

'Why?'

'Because afterwards he will tell the truth about everything that happened.'

A waitress brought their lunch. Lucy picked up her knife and looked at Fougères expectantly. 'Well, will you help me, to help you, to help the rest?'

He glanced down at the knife in her hand, eyebrows raised: 'Is that a threat?'

3

Anselm could not take his eyes off the dull glint on the blade. One edge flashed as the shadow holding it stepped forward on to the landing. Chambray threw a swift, raking stare over Anselm's habit.

'What the hell do you want? I'm trying to eat.'

There was something in the brash confrontation that persuaded Anselm this was a performance, possibly concealing hidden warmth. More confident of his ground, Anselm ventured, 'I wondered if we might have a brief talk—'

'What about?' Chambray fired back. He did not budge. There was no invitation to come in. His chest rose and fell angrily.

Anselm faltered. He'd been very wrong. This was not the

149

harmless banter of an old soul in need of a playful ribbing. He pressed on, 'I understand you were once at Notre-Dame des—'

'I've already told the other lot. I'm not saying anything, to no one.'

Anselm seized on the distinction: 'I'm not really from the other lot,' he said alluringly.

'Then where are you from?' challenged Chambray, waving the blade impatiently and still not moving.

'My name is Father Anselm Duffy. I'm a Gilbertine monk, like you, from Larkwood Priory. It's a rather . . .'

Before Anselm could trot out some guidebook particulars, Chambray lumbered back through the doorway and turned around. With one hand on the door he flung it shut with a single savage movement. The unseen cover scraped off the brass eyepiece. Slower breathing hovered on the other side, not receding, while the two monks looked towards each other. After a long moment, Anselm retraced his steps to the evening light.

4

Pascal ate a plate of sausages and mustard while Lucy searched for the scallops that had given the salad its name. When they had all but finished, Pascal said, 'I'm going to talk openly . . . Perhaps I'm being rash, but I trust you.'

'Why?' asked Lucy, more inquisitive than gratified.

'Because you mentioned Mr Snyman. No one could know that name who did not have a link to the inner world of my family.'

'You are right.'

150

'And you can't tell me what it is?' he asked, mystified.

'One day ... soon, in fact.' Lucy thought of her grandmother and the swift, merciless approach of death. 'But not now.' She glanced instinctively over the river towards Hammersmith once more.

Pascal said, 'You're so sure about Victor that I don't know what to think. You see, I've got two good reasons as to why you are wrong.'

'And they are?' invited Lucy.

'First, Mr Snyman was a close friend of both Jacques and Victor—'

'I know.'

'He's still alive; I grew up with him and he has no doubt that Victor would condemn Schwermann if he was given half a chance. Victor's problem, of course, is that he was a collaborator. He can't speak out without being accused himself – which is why I am trying to reassure him.'

Lucy thought: he really has no idea at all that it was Victor Brionne who betrayed The Round Table. She said, 'And what's the second reason?'

'I have a feeling it was Victor who wrote to me, giving me the name Nightingale.'

Jolted, Lucy asked, 'Why?'

'Because the only other explanation is that it came from the individual or organisation that helped him escape in the first place. I don't see any reason why they should undermine what they did.'

'They could have regrets.'

'Possibly. But the letter was written to me, Jacques' own blood, and that suggests a personal motive.'

'But you wrote the article saying Brionne and Schwermann

151

had found refuge in Britain. You were the obvious person to contact.'

'Again, possibly you're right.' Pascal pouted doubt. 'It's far more likely that Victor arranged to have it posted from France to cover his tracks.'

Lucy pushed her salad to one side. She said, with polite impatience, 'I can't see that it matters. Let's suppose it was Brionne who wrote to you. It doesn't follow that he would give evidence against Schwermann in any trial.'

Pascal looked with dismay across the river, to Hammersmith, to the rough area where Lucy herself had gazed. 'That is why I will do what I can to arrange the meeting you want.'

As they left the veranda and passed the debating lounge Lucy noticed a man by the door with a shock of white hair and an amused, enquiring face, as if someone had just told him a wonderful joke. A moustache and beard, also white, suggested both Gandalf and Father Christmas: a dispenser of wisdom and toys. He gave Lucy a donnish nod as if she were welcome to join his class.

Outside, Lucy and Pascal shook hands and parted. She walked lightly to the Underground, more quickly than usual, thinking how agreeable it was to have found a place where you could argue for the hell of it and where people smiled at you for no good reason.

Chapter Seventeen

1

Anselm and the Prior of Notre-Dame des Moineaux strolled over neat lawns between graceful horse chestnuts to the memorial plaque on the medieval refectory wall. The Gilbertines had taken over an old Benedictine Abbey in the seventeenth century. And so it was that the same Rule had been read on the same spot for eight hundred years.

'This is where he was shot. We commemorate it every year.'

A small tablet of stone recorded the name of Prior Morel above an inscription taken from the Prologue to The Rule: We shall persevere in fidelity to his teaching in the monastery until death.

The Prior was a short, stocky man with a rounded back, as if his spine were strapped to a hidden tool of penance. He stood arched over his folded hands, solemn and still.

'It was a most simple operation,' said the Prior, taking Anselm by the arm and turning away. 'Children were brought here in twos or threes during the day and placed in the orphanage run by the nuns. We had our own printing press, turning out false identification papers, baptismal certificates and the like. The children would then move with couriers into the Occupied Zone and down to Switzerland, hopefully to be reunited with their parents at some point in the future. Frontier guides would take them over. As you know, it was tragically betrayed.'

'By someone unknown?'

'Yes. But whoever it was didn't know very much. When the Gestapo came, no searches were carried out. Not even the orphanage. They just shot the Prior.'

'Why were the children smuggled here on their own?' asked Anselm, dreading the answer.

'Adults are hard to hide, and easily found, and children were liable to give away their hiding place. But here in broad daylight, among others, their chance of survival was higher. That is one of the terrible things about this whole episode. The parents were desperate. They chose separation from their infants because they were certain it was only a matter of time before they themselves were arrested.'

'We've no idea, have we, Father?'

'None at all. And do you know what I find most moving? The knights of The Round Table were students. It was the young saving the still younger from the adults.'

They walked on, momentarily distracted by the growling engine of an old tractor.

'Unfortunately,' resumed the Prior, 'there's no one left from that time, so all we have are stories handed on by monks with unreliable memories.'

'Do you mind telling me?'

'Not at all. Come, we'll walk along part of the escape route. The railway line has gone but it's a pathway now. It is a place charged with the actions of the past.'

They left the Abbey grounds and took the lane to the abandoned station. On the flanks stood endless regiments of vines, thickly woven over low hills, touching the resplendent skies of Burgundy.

★

'One of the problems,' said the Prior, 'was that the smuggling operation relied completely on trust. All the knights knew each other. They knew this place. The risk of betrayal is nowhere more grave than at one shared table.'

'Can you tell me anything about Father Rochet?' asked Anselm.

'By all accounts he was a most gifted man – well read, with a passion for medieval literature – but his life here collapsed in disgrace.'

'How?'

'It has never been substantiated, but it was said he formed . . . shall we say, an attachment to a young girl in a nearby village. She died in childbirth and it was said Rochet was the father. The rumour was not entirely fanciful. He had apparently asked to be laicised, but he withdrew his application after the death. He was moved out to a parish in the city . . . a very broken man. He only came back to propose The Round Table. It is touching that he should later lose his life saving children.'

In that one dreadful sentence Anselm glimpsed an untold epic. He pursued the other questions he had prepared. 'How were Schwermann and Brionne known to the Priory in the first place?'

'They weren't. Both men arrived as complete strangers.'

'And yet they were concealed even after the execution of Father Morel,' said Anselm, with the hopeless puzzlement of one gathering scattered jigsaw pieces.

'And now we come to the most disturbing mystery of all.' The Prior recounted the oral history carefully, making sure the terms used were accurate. 'Father Pleyon, the Prior of the day, decided both men would be hidden. All he would say was that Schwermann had risked his life to save life.'

155

'Save life?'

'Yes.'

'How?'

'Only the Prior knew the answer to the riddle. But one thing is certain: whatever he was told persuaded him that Schwermann and Brionne should be spared. He never explained himself and died with his secret untold.'

Anselm looked down at the black sleepers sunk deep into the path, all that remained of the old railway line that had carried the children to Les Moineaux. He said, 'I assume the whole community knew about The Round Table – is that right?'

'There was no other way. Some of these children didn't speak French. They were German.'

'How many people would have known?' asked Anselm.

'About sixty. But if you're thinking one of them betrayed The Round Table, you're probably wrong. Remember, the Gestapo were ill-informed. If it was someone from here the children would have been found, and the nuns hiding them would have shared in the retribution.'

'I wasn't thinking anything of the sort,' lied Anselm.

'Well, I do, occasionally. So I wouldn't blame you.'

Their conversation turned to lighter things: the 'Ontological Argument', the shortage of vocations and the acting ability of Eric Cantona. Suddenly, the Prior changed subject:

'Father Anselm, you will appreciate the emergence of Schwermann has caused us considerable anxiety. This Priory is revered as a place that served the spirit of resistance. Every time an old man is exposed for crimes against humanity in France I shiver. Is it him? Is he going to point to us? We have no explanation to offer. And now it's happened. As soon as he

156

opens his mouth the Priory will be drowned. Memories of the Occupation are raw and great stones are still being turned over.' He paused, suddenly troubled. 'We've already had one visitor.'

'Who?' asked Anselm instinctively.

'A survivor, one of the children. He asked me a terrible question.'

'Yes?'

'He said, "Could it be that one of Herod's servants once rested within your walls?" I told him I didn't understand. Afterwards, I realised I should have said "No" . . . because my confusion was a sort of admission. He was a most unnerving man.'

Anselm pictured Salomon Lachaise posing a question to a man who could not answer without discovering his own shame. 'I've met him. He came to Larkwood.'

'Oh Lord . . . us, and then you . . . he must know everything.'

'I don't think so,' said Anselm uncertainly. 'He told me he was the son of the Sixth Lamentation.'

'After the Five of Jeremiah?'

'Yes . . . I think he meant the Holocaust.'

They walked in silence until the Prior said, 'I hope you find Victor Brionne, for the sake of my community and for the sake of Larkwood.' He stopped, surveying the treetops with shaded eyes. 'I think you should talk to Mère Hermance,' he said. 'She was here at the time. But be warned. She'll make you buy a box of biscuits.'

2

Cathy Glenton had persuaded Lucy to have a Turkish bath after a particularly tedious lecture on the demise of the novel.

'It's an awful place,' she said, 'run by two former wrestlers from Lancashire. A husband and wife team.'

'What do you do?' asked Lucy, horrified.

'There are three rooms, each getting hotter than the one before, and when you've sweated yourself silly you lie on a table and one of the wrestlers washes you down. Then you dive into a pool of freezing water.'

'It sounds like hell.'

'It is . . . but then comes paradise. You wrap yourself in a massive warm towel and lie on a couch for as long as you like eating bacon sandwiches and sipping hot, sweet tea. There's nothing like it this side of the grave.'

They were just about to leave Cathy's flat when Lucy's mobile rang. It was Pascal Fougères.

'Would you be interested in having a minor role in the preparation of the trial?'

'Pardon?' she replied, incredulous.

He went on, 'It's not much, believe me. I'm a sort of liaison officer between the lawyers here and those with an interest in the case back in France. It means I have small practical jobs to do for the prosecution. I'm sure you could help . . . with a stapler, or something. Look,' he hesitated, 'are you free now?'

'Yes,' said Lucy with muffled joy. She lowered the mobile and said, 'I'm really sorry, Cathy, but I'll have to cry off.'

Cathy nodded through her disappointment while Lucy sorted out a time and place with Pascal. When she'd finished, Cathy said, 'I hear the heavy tread of a man.'

'Not quite,' replied Lucy, acutely self-conscious.

'Name?'

'Pascal.'

'French?'

'Yes . . . but it's not like that.'

'I know. It never is.'

'Truly.'

'Does he have a spare friend interested in a beautiful mind?'

'I'll ask.'

An hour later Lucy met Pascal outside the National Portrait Gallery. Traffic swept behind them in surges, down into Trafalgar Square. Crowds, maddened by maps and itineraries, jostled on the pavement, looking for the next sight. Pascal took Lucy's hand and they stepped out of the bustle into the mute halls of captured faces. They walked from room to room watched by Audrey Hepburn, Paul McCartney and lots more. Talking in long snatches, they leaned towards each other, looking around.

'Are you still a journalist?' asked Lucy.

'Sort of. After I found that memo I gave up my job on *Le Monde*. They give me lots of freelance work so I survive. And you?'

'Student . . . second time round.'

'Pushy parents first time?'

'Sort of.' She thought of Darren, who'd made that specific judgement with hostility, noticing how from Pascal's mouth the question carried the promise of understanding. Without doubt the time would come when she would explain, but not now. She continued, 'Pascal, I've been thinking about our last conversation. I don't understand why you want Brionne so much for the trial. What about all the other evidence?'

Pascal said, ominously, 'This trial is going to be about what the victims remember as much as what Schwermann did.'

They left the gallery and joined the crowds walking round to Nelson's Column. The naval commander towered above them, safe, as they walked through a sea of fat, scratching pigeons.

159

'Do you ever wonder how Schwermann and Brionne got out of Paris in the first place?' asked Lucy.

'Frequently.'

'I mean, where did they go, and who would want to put them on the road with new names?'

'No one knows. One minute they're both at Avenue Foch, then four months later they're in the hands of British Intelligence with new identities and a story that got them into England. Sometimes I think of the Touvier case.'

'What's that?'

'Basically he was an old-school Catholic hidden for years after the war by his own kind.'

'A collaborator?'

'Yes. He was head of the Milice Intelligence Network for Savoy.'

'Protected by the Church?'

'It's more involved than that, but he was hidden in a monastery. So I do wonder in my wilder moments if the Church could have been involved . . . but it's so unlikely. Hiding a Frenchman, maybe, but an SS officer? That stretches even my imagination.'

He looked down at the demented scavenging of the birds and said, 'Are you hungry?'

Half and hour later they were eating at a small table in the crypt of St Martin-in-the-Fields.

'Funny place for a restaurant,' said Pascal.

3

The convent was situated half a kilometre from the Priory. The orphanage had long since closed and the school buildings were

160

now a diocesan youth centre. Anselm had seen it all before. Hordes of champing, over-sexed youths arriving in transit vans, closely supervised by impossibly confident chaplains and teachers, all of whom deserved the Croix de Guerre.

Mère Hermance had worked in the laundry during the war. She was lodged upon a wicker chair in the convent gift shop, recalling the good old days when religious life was hard. Anselm had to drag her towards the subject of his visit.

'Oh, yes, Father, it was a terrible time, terrible. I saw poor Prior Morel fall like a rag doll. I waited for him to get up. There were three children hiding in the orphanage.' She smiled, as only the very old can, intimating an acceptance of things that once could not be accepted.

'Do you remember the two men who stayed at the Abbey in 1944?' asked Anselm gently.

'I do, yes, but not much. In those days religious life was lived as it should be. You didn't talk to men unless you had to.'

Anselm nodded in firm agreement.

'I never spoke to either of them,' she said. 'We were told it was as secret as the confessional. We were used to that sort of thing. But I do remember one thing, Father—'

Mère Hermance broke off to answer the phone. The shop was open from three to five . . . the biscuits were handmade . . . by the young ones with nothing better to do . . . fifty francs . . . very well worth it . . . goodbye. She put the phone down and carried on as if no interruption had occurred: 'When I came here as a novice in 1937 there were thirty-nine sisters. The Prioress at the time was a dragon. Her father had been in the army and . . .'

Anselm listened patiently for ten minutes or so before he cracked and reminded her of what she had been about to say.

'Oh yes, that's right. He came to the orphanage almost every day.'

'Who did?' pressed Anselm.

'One of the young men we were hiding. He talked and played with four or five little German boys and girls. Those were the last Jewish children to come here. Their parents had fled Germany to France, only to be hunted all over again. They saved their children and then perished. He was a good fellow to visit those poor dears. One of them never spoke and had the deepest brown eyes you have ever seen.'

'Do you remember which one came?'

The phone rang again. The nun listened distractedly, once more delivering pat lines on the quality of biscuits and the weakness of the young. She put the receiver down. 'As I was saying, the Prioress was a dragon—'

'Mère Hermance, the young man, do you recall which one?'

She looked darkly into the past, into the presence of a banished fear. 'I think it was the German.'

Unfolding a large starched handkerchief, she wiped her eyes. 'It was a terrible time, Father, a terrible, terrible time.'

Chapter Eighteen

1

Agnes sat by the kitchen table, her hands limp upon her lap, palms open. Her head leaned forward slightly and to one side, as if in a trance of concentration. It was, of course, not quite that. Her posture was assuming a life of its own, pulling her body slowly down, with Agnes quietly tugging the other way, her blue eyes bright with resistance. She was still able to look after herself, but not for much longer – Agnes was tired by evening and soon the slumping would encompass the day. Freddie knew it but had no idea what to do, given Agnes' refusal to involve anyone skilled or trained in her care. By default, an interim system had emerged to which Agnes did not object. Each evening a member of the family took it in turns to drop by, to make sure everything was fine before she went to bed. And Agnes cooperated not because she required their help but because she knew they needed to come.

Sitting opposite her, Lucy tipped the green beans out of the bag and began the ritual of nipping and throwing, taking off the curled ends and putting the long remaining stems into the waiting pan. Agnes watched.

'What's he like?' asked Agnes, deadly calm, her eyes following the deft movements of Lucy's fingers.

'Older than me and younger than me at one and the same

time. The past means as much to him as the future, maybe more.'

'You've missed one,' said Agnes, pointing towards the pan with her head. Lucy retrieved the rogue. The soft clipping of her nails, the patter in the pan, the ticking of a clock in the hall suspended time's nimble passing. The moment lay open, unexplored, healing, inhabited by them alone. The stray cat, no longer stray but ensconced and enthroned, idled by, surveying his subjects with transcendent scorn.

'He's known Mr Snyman all his life.'

Lucy glanced over to Agnes and met in her eyes the question, the plea. Lucy turned away. She would not provide the answer . . . no, Pascal did not refer to you . . . I'm sorry, but he didn't seem to know that Jacques had had a son. Instead, Lucy said, 'Mr Snyman believes that Brionne would probably condemn Schwermann if he got the chance.'

'Does he?' asked Agnes, made alert. 'Are you sure?'

'Yes.'

From somewhere immeasurably cold she said, 'Maybe he's right.'

Stung by her grandmother's remark, Lucy pushed the pan across the table. Agnes lifted a wavering spoon of salt from a bowl and let the grains spill into the water.

Lucy said, 'I've a small role to play in the trial. I will be there on your behalf.' She would say nothing of her intention to confront Brionne with what she now knew and compel him to enter the courtroom. Her grandmother would discover that in the happening.

Agnes nodded, unblinking, her mouth sloping to one side. It was a smile, against the will of failing muscle and the tiny, dying engines of the nerves. Then she breathed a sort of

164

laugh, leaned back, her face averted, and said: 'Victor was no fool.'

Lucy boiled water, mesmerised by the rage becoming steam. It vanished in the air, to reappear upon the window, water once more, streaming down the pane, to be wiped away by Agnes.

2

Anselm returned to a sunny day in England. The sight of Larkwood pierced him. In a flash he longed to hear the bells and find himself in the psalms that named everything when he could not. At the entrance to the Priory, Father Andrew said, 'Schwermann's grandson, Max, wants to see me tomorrow afternoon. I'd like you to be there.'

'Of course.'

'Are you all right?' The Prior glanced briefly sideways.

'Yes, thanks.'

Funny, Anselm thought wistfully, watching the Prior's square back as he slipped through a side door, this is want I'd wanted all along, to be involved in the fray, to be called upon, and now it's happening it has somehow lost its savour.

Max Nightingale was a painter. By which he meant, he said, someone who paints pictures that few people buy but who continues to forsake career and financial security in order to paint more pictures that might never be sold. He made regular money working as a waiter or, when things became unbearable, smiling over a cash till at McDonald's. Anselm placed him at about twenty-seven. He had close-cropped hair and held his head ever so slightly to one side, as if anticipating a sudden slap. They were taking tea by Anselm's favoured spot

165

on the south transept lawn. Warm sunshine fell over them.

Max spoke as if language was a clumsy tool, hesitating occasionally, his eye on a mental image that defied representation in a sentence. But when he did name something it stood out starkly, because of the unexpected angle of his observation.

'I said to my grandfather – look, hundreds of thousands of Jews are being transported across Europe to a small village in Poland. They won't fit in.'

'What did he say to that?' asked Father Andrew.

'He said, "Go to King's Cross. Stay there for an hour or two, watching the trains leave, one after the other. Then go outside and look at the people in the street, buying their newspaper, getting a taxi. Do you think they know the ones on the trains will all be killed? Day after day?"' Max raised his hands as if there was nothing else to say, knowing the explanation was somehow wanting.

Anselm thought of London occupied by foreign troops, the city cordoned off into sections while one ethnic group was arrested, packed into requisitioned buses and taken to a railway station. What would he have thought in time of war, watching the trains pull away into the night, always to the same destination? A bee drifted lightly over untouched tea and sandwiches, while paper serviettes fluttered in the breeze: the lazy motions of peacetime.

Max seemed to be weighed down by an old confusion. He said, 'Look, I never knew my father . . . so I grew up with this man who's now hiding. I'm not suggesting he didn't know about the killing . . . I just find it incredible, unimaginable.'

'The incredible has a habit of disrupting the parts of our lives to which we're most attached,' said Father Andrew simply, adding, almost under his breath, 'it's why I became a monk.'

'Did that make it credible?' asked Max.

'Not quite, but the old life became unimaginable.' Father Andrew took off his glasses, revealing small red footprints on the sides of his nose. He polished the lenses and put them back on. 'All I'm saying is this: you have to be very careful before you dismiss the unbelievable, if it taps you on the shoulder or kicks you in the face.'

Max beetled his brow and his eyes flickered. He said: 'I've asked to see you because he mentioned something else that I think you should know, which is all the more unimaginable. It's another kick in the face.'

He looked frankly at Father Andrew, having caught him with his own words. Involuntarily, Anselm saw the face of Monsignor Renaldi at the Cardinal's shoulder, expressionless, non-committal, but waiting, eternally waiting.

'He says he did the *opposite* of what's alleged against him. But he won't say any more. He wants someone else to explain, someone who was there.'

'Who?' asked the Prior.

'A Frenchman called Victor Brionne, though he's now called something else. We've got a private detective on to it.' He glanced from monk to monk. 'Apparently it's fairly easy if you know the name. And we do . . . it's Berkeley.'

'Max,' said Anselm, confidentially, 'do you mind telling us if and when he's found? Anything touching on the conduct of your grandfather is likely to have an effect on the Priory in due course.'

'Yes . . . I'll let you know.'

3

Agnes and Lucy sat in the gathering dusk, two bowls lying empty upon the table.

167

'When will Wilma move in?' asked Lucy, sleepily.

'When she's ready.'

They could just about hear each other breathing if they cared to listen.

'How will she know when to come?'

'She'll just know. People like Wilma have a very different sense of time. Appointments, arrangements don't mean anything. She doesn't follow clocks. She just lives in each day.'

Lucy rose and cleared the table. Agnes spoke out of the shade:

'Forget Victor.'

'What do you mean?' asked Lucy, stopping and looking down at her.

'Nothing. It's all right.'

Lucy put out her arm and Agnes took it with both hands, as if it were a railing. With a nod she dismissed further help, making her way towards the bathroom to get ready for bed. She walked deliberately, touching now to the right and then to the left, finding objects placed in position for the purpose. Lucy remained in the kitchen, hearing the click of a switch and the faint run of water, simple noises that begin and end the day; and, presumably, a life.

Lucy looked up. Agnes stood motionless, like an apparition, framed by the doorway in a long dressing gown and red furry slippers, a hand on each jamb. Evening light, all but gone, traced out her nose, a parted lip; and to Lucy it was as though Agnes had died and this was a final, wilful resurgence of flesh, a last insistent request to see Lucy just one more time before she fluttered into memory.

At that moment the hall clock struck the hour. Brass wheels turned, meshing intricately. Time, no longer suspended, seemed to ground itself and move. They looked at one another across a divide, hearing the slow, brutal counting from afar taking slices off all that remained between them. Lucy and Agnes stood helpless, waiting.

'Gran, please don't go,' said Lucy, in a voice from their quiet days in the back room when everyone else had left them to it.

'I have to, Lucy. Death is like the past. We can't change either of them. We have to make friends with them both.'

Tears filled Lucy's eyes to overflowing. Thunder groaned far off to the east and the room darkened abruptly, as though a great hand had fallen over the sun.

4

Storm clouds had quickly gathered over Larkwood and by late evening large drops of rain threw themselves in heavy snatches upon its walls. A wind was gathering strength, threatening to wrestle old trees through the night.

Anselm and Father Andrew sat either side of a great round window overlooking the cloister. Anselm gave a précis of all he'd learned since departing for Rome, situating the nature of the task that had been entrusted to him – the finding of Victor Brionne. The Prior listened intently.

'A pattern of sorts emerges,' said Anselm in conclusion. 'Monsignor Renaldi can only look to logic – the Priory must have known something of great importance, outweighing whatever Schwermann and Brionne may have done, otherwise they would never have helped them. And that is broadly supported by the oral tradition of the Priory, which remembers Schwermann was hidden because of some undisclosed noble conduct – something effectively repeated this afternoon by his grandson, who got it from the mouth of the person most intimately concerned.'

Father Andrew slowly repeated the troubling words, '"He risked his life in order to save life" . . . it's a crafted phrase, a jingle . . . it disguises as much as it displays.'

'At least it gives us some idea as to why the monks at Les Moineaux helped him escape,' said Anselm.

'But why does he want the secret brought out into the open by Victor Brionne? Why not speak up for himself?'

'The two of them belong together—'

'As if they are two parts of the same, torn ticket,' interjected the Prior. He added, 'That was quick footwork, by the way, to get Max Nightingale to tell us when they've found him.'

Anselm wasn't sure if that was a compliment. The Prior went on: 'So what do you do now – wait?'

'Not quite. A private detective can only open so many doors. Max's candour is just one string to my bow.'

'You have another?'

'Yes. I think so.'

Father Andrew fell into an abstraction and said, 'Maybe one day they'll make you a Cardinal.'

Later that night Anselm heard the bells for which he had longed; he sang psalms that named the motions of his soul; but, to his faint alarm, he did not find himself in quite the same place that he had left. Or rather, a slightly different person had come back to Larkwood, not entirely known, even to himself, and he didn't know why.

5

Lucy sat in the warm darkness of her flat wrestling with two emotions, each getting stronger, each slipping out of control.

She was losing her grandmother: the foundations of grief were being hewn out of rock. But at the same time, in another part of her soul she was gaining something. The fundamentals were already in place and she hadn't noticed them in the making. Perhaps they'd been built years and years ago. But the result was that Lucy found herself intrinsically and terrifyingly receptive to Pascal Fougères.

The phone rang. Reluctantly, she lifted the receiver.

'It's me, Cathy.'

'Hi . . .'

'Well, do you regret missing the Turkish bath?'

'No.'

'Ah.'

'Honestly, he's just an acquaintance.'

'Where did you go?'

'For a meal.'

'Where?'

'In a crypt.'

'Sounds like my sort. How did you meet him?'

'I'm too tired to explain,' Lucy said, laughing for the first time that day.

'I'll sweat it out of you. Give me a call.'

They said goodnight and Lucy put the phone down with a sigh. As with all misunderstandings, Cathy was on to something. Since meeting Pascal Lucy wasn't quite her old self, and she didn't fully recognise who she was becoming.

171

Chapter Nineteen

1

'Apollo adored the Sibyl so he offered her anything she wished,' said Pascal, turning a beer mat round in circles. A gathering of other conversations drifted from the debating room out to where they sat on the veranda. Putney Bridge lay black against a scattering of white and orange evening lights.

'And?' said Lucy.

'She asked to live for as many years as she had grains of sand in her hand. He granted her wish but she refused to satisfy his passion.'

'Sounds like a good deal to me.'

'Not entirely.'

'Why?'

'She forgot to ask for health and youth.'

'Ah.'

'So she grew old and hideous and lived for hundreds of years.'

'Doing what?'

'Her old job, writing riddles on leaves, left at the mouth of her cave.' He sipped his drink. 'That's the part of the myth I like, the fragility of what she had to say; words written on leaves, easily made incomprehensible if disturbed by a careless wind.'

Lucy could only think of Agnes, the sand all but gone. She

said, 'I understand her, though, wanting to live so much.'

'Yes, but life pushed on is always death pulled back. It comes. In a way there's something dismal about wanting to postpone what you can't avoid.'

'But it can come too soon.'

'That's what the Sibyl thought.'

Lucy admired his lack of complication – but with nostalgia: her own simplicity had been mislaid. She had seen death at work, its industrious regard for detail, and, like the men who dug up the roads, its preference for doing the job slowly.

'I think you'd get on with my grandmother,' she said.

They had met at Pascal's suggestion. He gave no reason; he just asked. So they sat down with no purpose other than a shared inclination to know one another better. Leaving the Sibyl behind, Lucy raised the key question:

'What do your family think of you dropping journalism for all this?'

'Not pleased at all.'

'Do you mind if I ask why?' She had the sparkling enthusiasm of a specialist.

Settling back, like a long-distance driver who knows the road, Pascal said, 'It's all about guilt, really' – he flipped the beer mat – 'even though none of us were around at the time. To put it bluntly, the whole family ran off to the south, leaving my great-uncle Jacques behind in Paris. Okay, it was his choice, but it's an unpleasant fact. If they'd stayed with him, maybe they could have done something after he was arrested.' He sipped his beer, thinking. 'That's probably not true, but it's one of those peculiar notions. Once thought, it won't go away. They settled on the Swiss border and Jacques was deported to

Mauthausen. They survived. He didn't. The lack of symmetry says it all. After the war they made sure Jacques was remembered. It was all they could do. Schwermann and the rest had vanished. So I grew up with a complex memory of remorse, pride and what you might call unfinished business.'

But, as Pascal explained, the family memory had become complicated by the political career of his father, Etienne, and the complex mood in France during the 1960s. Myths assembled after the war to smooth out the realities of Occupation – the mix of resistance and cooperation – had come under attack. Heroes were denounced, villains rehabilitated. And it was within this public struggle that Pascal's father had deftly trodden the political stage. He'd had considerable ambition and a considerable problem: his father, Claude, had been a supporter of Vichy and he couldn't refer to Jacques' exploits without placing a spotlight on collaboration and plunging his name into the maelstrom of conflicting views about the past. So while Pascal had grown up with a memory of stolen retribution, the official family line on war crimes had become one of merciful forgetfulness. Let the past bury itself. Thus, when Paul Touvier was arrested in the late eighties, Etienne had been for understanding the moral complexity of the time, but the high-minded Pascal, then seventeen, had advocated judicial retribution. After all, he'd been a French servant of the Reich. That row had caused no lasting harm. For his parents it had been just one of the more extensive entries in the Register of Differences filled out by Pascal as he defined himself against them, made colourful by adolescence and by that fact destined to fade back into unanimity once he'd grown up and seen things as he should.

Pascal did grow up, and things did fade, but, as always happens, far less than his parents expected. He became a political journalist with a side-interest in Vichy, producing one or two scoops about notorious figures who had lived comfortable lives in post-war France undisturbed by their past. This was closer to the family bone, and, looking back, it was only a matter of time before Pascal's research touched upon Jacques' life and, by default, upon his father's understanding of his prospects. It was Pascal's career, however, that flourished. Appointed as the Washington correspondent for *Le Monde*, he moved to the United States, and that was when the door to his present life opened. By chance he found the memo referring to Schwermann and Brionne. He said, 'After reading that I knew there was a good chance of finding them. It was a moment of crisis, believe me.'

That moment took Pascal home to a bright Paris morning, the sort that could generate a song. His mother was happily moving in and out of the salon, relieved to have her boy at home again; father and son were enjoying the bashful pleasure of shared manhood come too soon. Pascal spoke, knowing the coming cost, the loss of amity: 'I want to find him.'

Etienne put down *Le Monde*, read with a new enthusiasm since his son's elevation, and stubbed out a cigar. Monique came in, buoyantly suggesting a walk in the park. She withdrew, uneasily, at a signal from her husband.

'You can't,' he said.

That command had a peculiar effect on Pascal, pushing him down the road. 'I can.'

'You mustn't.'

'What about must?'

Another silence.

'Pascal, France has suffered enough.'

'That's not the test.'

More silence, with a chasm opening wide. Pascal's father

175

reached over, with both hands: 'I beg you,' he said with barely suppressed panic, 'look at things with older eyes, just for a moment, with the wounds of those who endured the Occupation. Why do you think de Gaulle, of all people, reprieved the death sentence on Vasseur and Jean Barbier in the sixties? Why do you think d'Estaing honoured Pétain at Douaumont in the seventies? Why did Mitterrand shake Kohl's hand at Verdun in the eighties? Because sometimes we cannot make a synthesis of the past, and there comes a time when we have to *forgive* what we can, when it is *better* to forget what cannot be forgiven. Your generation is obsessed with the failures of your forefathers. Let them judge themselves. You wouldn't have done any better.'

'I'm sure I wouldn't, but that's why an obligation rests on the next generation – to expose the past for what it was. This is not just about Jacques. It's about *history*. Getting it right. The same year Barbie was convicted, Le Pen said the gas chambers were a minor detail of the war. There's a kind of forgetting we have to stop.'

His father, exasperated, said: 'Pascal, I'm asking you to leave it be. Leave the past alone.' Etienne went angrily to his study without waiting for a reply, as if parental censure was sufficient to deflect a disobedient son.

As with most adult passions, they are born in childhood. The strength of Pascal's conviction had not come from his family as such but from their butler, Mr Snyman. He'd known Jacques and had told Pascal all about The Round Table. For Pascal he was a patriarch, the only survivor of the times. After his father left the room, Mr Snyman slipped in.

'Did you hear all of that?' asked Pascal.

'Yes.'

176

'What would you do?'

'It's not what I'd do that matters; it's what Jacques would do. If he could.'

'And what's that?'

Mr Snyman took a step closer, his hands raised as if what he had to say was so fragile it might break if not physically handed over. 'He'd hunt him down. Schwermann is one of those few people responsible for something that lies on the other side of forgiveness.'

Pascal went upstairs and knocked on the study door.

'Papa, I'm sorry. I have to do this.'

'You'll regret ignoring my advice.' His father stood with his back to his son. With profound disappointment he said, 'You care more for the dead than the living.'

Monique stood at the door, wavering between husband and son. She was crying.

Then Pascal said something untrue, something he did not mean and which he bitterly regretted afterwards. But it sounded good. 'And you care more for political preferment than the truth.'

They had, of course, spoken since; and Pascal had said sorry, and his father had said it didn't matter, and his mother had run out to the patisserie. But it was too late. Certain things, once said, can change at a stroke the interior workings of love, leaving the outside architecture untouched. Perhaps, thought Lucy, that was why Agnes had taken such deep refuge in silence.

Pascal made contact with Jewish groups and Resistance organisations in Paris who formed a consortium: the laborious process of gathering evidence began. The anxiety of the investigators was that Schwermann had kept a low profile as far as the paperwork was concerned. His name rarely appeared in

177

print even though sources demonstrated he must have been at certain meetings and received particular memos. And no one knew the name under which he was hiding. Then Pascal received an anonymous letter posted from Paris. He said, 'It contained one line: "The name you seek is Nightingale." I thought it was a hoax but I passed it on.'

The problem of building a case strong enough to secure a conviction, however, remained a concern. It was while discussing this matter with Mr Snyman that Pascal had been urged to find Victor. Mr Snyman had said:

'I knew Victor. He was like a brother to Jacques. Things became difficult between them when they fell in love with the same woman – I forget her name . . . the war split them further . . . but now, after so many years, when Jacques is dead . . . I am sure he would speak out.'

Lucy studied Pascal's animated face with concealed horror: he seemed to know nothing of Agnes. The narrative moved on, leaving Lucy stunned by the omission. The allegations were formally laid with the Home Office. And, life being what it is, no political discomfort came to trouble Pascal's father. The lesion between them lay open, through a fear that was never, in fact, realised.

A bell rang, urgent and frantic, for last orders. Pascal and Lucy decided to leave. On their way out Lucy caught the eye of The Don – as she'd named him – that warming fusion of Gandalf and Father Christmas. As before, he bestowed a nod.

Standing outside, Lucy said, 'Brionne is not going to walk into a police station. It's a fond hope, nothing else.'

'I know,' said Pascal with resignation. 'We need a miracle.'

'I thought you said we couldn't mention God?'

'In certain circumstances God has a habit of mentioning himself.'

2

Anselm's confidence in finding Victor Brionne lay not in his investigative powers, for he had none, but in one of the more prosaic features of modern life: the proliferation of countless documents with lists of names and addresses. The Inland Revenue, the Department of Social Security, National Insurance, the National Health Service Central Register, the Drivers Register, and more, beyond imagination. Three things only were needed by an amateur in Anselm's curious position: the name of the person concerned; a contact in the police involved in the investigation of a serious crime (which opened many closed doors); and a good reason why that contact would reveal what they learned to the amateur.

Anselm was relatively sure he possessed all three conditions. He knew the name; instinct suggested DI Armstrong could be the contact; and her cooperation might be forthcoming if its basis was the finding of a key witness for a major trial, Anselm's only request being to have the first interview. The plan crystallised almost by itself while he was still in Rome. And as it did so, Anselm's recognition of his own importance in the scheme of things expanded proportionately, producing a sense of power that he tried to suppress but which he acknowledged with a dark flush of pleasure.

3

Ordinarily Anselm had two periods of manual work – one in

the morning before Mass, the other in the afternoon until Vespers. However, the Prior had agreed to release Anselm whenever necessary to pursue anything to do with the task he had received from Cardinal Vincenzi. That broad principle was stretched to encompass games of chess with Salomon Lachaise at the guesthouse. But since his trip to Rome Anselm had found it difficult to look his companion in the face — for he was now burdened with a riddle: 'Schwermann had risked his life to save life.' And his task of finding Victor Brionne now set them apart, for it was this man who would reveal the meaning of the words.

They sat either side of a table, black against white.

'No talking,' said Anselm as they were about to start.

'But in the beginning was the Word,' replied Salomon Lachaise.

'Indeed,' said Anselm.

Salomon Lachaise then sprinkled the early stages of play with abstract enticements — an unworthy attempt, thought Anselm, to distract his opponent: 'A violation of language is a violation of God.' ('Mmm', said Anselm.) '. . . in hell there are no words.' ('Mmm.') '. . . and yet the silence of the Priory brings forth words of praise.' ('And other things,' murmured Anselm.) '. . . the world will be redeemed by words.' Anselm marked that one for future use.

'Is it not strange,' continued Salomon Lachaise on a fresh tack, 'that God, on one reading of Exodus, refused to disclose his name to Moses when he first revealed himself?'

'Yes,' said Anselm. He eyed the tight configuration of pieces. Each move seemed to spell trouble but there had to be a way out.

'And is it not stranger still that God should change the name of his servants to mark a new beginning?'

Anselm looked up sharply into a face of restrained curiosity. 'What do you mean?'

'God made the covenant with Abram and he became Abraham. Simon the fisherman became Peter the rock. There are lots of examples.'

'I see,' said Anselm, returning his attention to the battle.

'The change of name obliterates their past, bestowing a blessed future.'

'That's a good point. I might use that one Sunday.'

'And when the Amsterdam synagogue expelled Spinoza for his ideas, they invoked God to blot out his name under heaven.'

'That's interesting,' said Anselm genuinely.

'So who was it that dared to take the place of God and give that man across the lake a new name, a new life?'

The two men faced each other. A sensation of rapid foreshortening brought the gentle gaze of Salomon Lachaise unbearably close to Anselm's secret. They sat as friends: one of them waiting patiently for judgement, the other, Anselm, engaged in an enterprise that might absolve the need for a trial – hope and its adversary at one table.

'That's another good point.'They were the only words Anselm could assemble that did not require him to lie.

Salomon Lachaise reviewed the state of play upon the board and, with a look of quiet amusement, toppled his king. 'Anselm of Canterbury, I resign.'

Chapter Twenty

1

It was a sensible arrangement. At the back of the flat were two bedrooms, side by side, one of which had French windows opening out on to the garden. That was where Agnes slept. The other was for Wilma. They left their doors ajar at night.

Lucy was staggered at Wilma's cleanliness. For fifteen years she'd bustled from Hammersmith to Shepherd's Bush, to a drop-in centre by a church. There she showered, took her breakfast and then came back to feed the birds in Ravenscourt Park. She'd met Agnes while tailing a pigeon. A friendship had grown, unknown to anyone in the family, including Lucy. It was always that way with Agnes. She had small, secret spaces in her life which were only discovered by accident. Surprise questions were an act of trespass, so the family got used to stumbling upon things and pretending nothing had been uncovered. And so it was here. Wilma's intimacy with Agnes passed without comment, even though a first, brief association was sufficient to confirm that Wilma was pleasantly and ever so slightly mad.

Agnes now had a wheelchair but she would not sit in it. She pushed it round the flat, moving slowly and with relaxed deliberation as if negotiating an obstacle course, smiling at little victories and wincing at scuffs upon the furniture. The frontiers of her world were contracting and she rubbed against them. She no longer went to the park, or along the river to watch the boats, but moved from room to room, from chair to bed, and, whenever possible, out to the garden among fresh green things.

Wilma was tidying her room again when Lucy decided to mention the gun. She had been foraging in a cupboard for something Wilma had put away when she'd touched the barrel. She'd left it there, wrapped in a duster, with four corroded rounds of ammunition. The incongruity of Agnes with a revolver could not pass without comment. This was a secret space that had to be invaded, tactfully, as they sat in the back garden.

'A French officer gave that to Arthur,' explained Agnes. 'He brought it back, along with his clock. They were his only souvenirs. I'd forgotten all about it.'

'But it's illegal. It should have been handed in.'

'Take it to the police after I'm dead,' said Agnes.

The word struck Lucy like a back-handed slap. But to Agnes it was just another sound. She said, 'I'd like to go inside now.'

They returned slowly to the flat. For a long while Agnes jiggled her wheelchair at the French windows, trying to get it over a ridge. Lucy watched from behind, detesting her impulse to push past and move things along, to get away from this constant, slow pageant of illness.

'I expect you see rather a lot of young Fougères,' said Agnes, leaning forward to push.

'Not really.'

'I suspect he rather likes you.'

'Stop it, Gran.'

As they passed Agnes' bureau by the door Lucy saw a sheet of cardboard. 'What's that?'

183

'An alphabet card.'

The letters were written very neatly in lines of four, forming six columns.

Agnes stopped and turned, her blue eyes alarmed as by the heavy approach of a new and threatening machine. 'When I can't talk any more, I'll point.'

They looked at each other, helpless.

Every time Lucy saw Agnes something happened to wound her memory. A gallery of imprints hung in perpetuity. That evening joined the rest. She would for ever be able to see her grandmother standing by a door, thin arms on a wheelchair, her eyes resting on the alphabet.

2

Anselm was reading Athanasius' *Life of Anthony* when the Prior knocked on his door. Anselm had always enjoyed all that wrestling with demons for it struck him as a powerful metaphor for aspects of his own inner life whose battles were fought with fiends less easily discerned.

The Prior had come to say that DI Armstrong had dropped by and, since it related to Schwermann, would he deal with it. Anselm closed his book and went to the parlour entrance. She was walking to and fro, preoccupied. After greetings were exchanged, she said, 'Father, there's a couple of things I'd like to mention. First, we're going to interview Schwermann, I expect over several days. If the community doesn't mind, we'd prefer to bring all the kit and do it here rather than take him to a station. Here's a list of dates. We might not need them all. It depends on what he says.'

'Of course, I'll raise it with the Prior,' said Anselm, taking the sheet of paper.

DI Armstrong hesitated. In Anselm's experience, the point mentioned last in a series was always the most important, and, if of a sensitive character, usually introduced with reticence. 'Would you like a short stroll in the grounds?' he asked. 'It's quite reviving to look at someone else's work.'

They passed through an iron gate still swinging on one hinge since heaven knew when and entered the majestic wilderness of a wet, half-kept garden.

'So when are you going to take him off our hands?' invited Anselm, pointing the question at the source of presumed discomfort.

'That's the second thing. It's why I'm really here, as you've probably guessed. I could have sent the interview dates by letter.'

'Yes,' said Anselm knowingly, not having thought of it.

'Can I speak in absolute confidence?'

'Yes.'

'Schwermann is here to stay. I know you were told it was only for the short term but nothing is being planned to move him. I also know you were told it was unlikely any charges would be laid but that was and is nonsense. Once the interviews are over a decision will be taken, but the idea that he'll just go home is fanciful.'

'So if and when he's charged,' said Anselm, 'the media will have another field day at our expense.'

'I expect so, which brings me to what I really wanted to say.'

They walked in silence towards a bench by an open sloping shed. Finches and sparrows skipped across the grass, their small heads jerking left and right, alert to every movement of the wind.

Sitting down, DI Armstrong said heavily, 'I can't prove this, but I suspect the Priory has been set up for a fall and I don't know why.'

'How?'

'Let me put the whole thing in a wider context. If there is a trial, there will be a colossal embarrassment factor for the government. Schwermann was interviewed in 1945 by a young British Intelligence officer, Captain Austin Lawson. As you know, he went on to a life in politics and is now a Labour Peer. There is something alarming and mystifying about the record of interrogation. Hardly anything was written down. In fact, it contains no more than was repeated in the memo found by Pascal Fougères — I get the feeling Lawson only filled out a report because he had to.'

'Maybe he didn't know what Schwermann had done.'

'That's possible. Not very much was known in the aftermath of the war, and Lawson was young, twenty-four, so he could have been a bit naïve. But I seriously doubt it.'

'Why?'

'Because he deliberately left out vital information . . . like the false names of Schwermann and Brionne, where they got them from . . . and there's no record of an interview with Brionne at all, although he must have spoken to him. It's as though Lawson knew something and let them go. He wouldn't have made the decision, but it would have been upon his recommendation.'

'Is he a Catholic?' asked Anselm suddenly.

'As it happens, he is. How did you know?'

'His first name . . . it's short for Augustine . . . just a guess.'

'Why ask?' said DI Armstrong. The voice contained stealth, patience, the tip of a claw.

186

'Nothing,' said Anselm, shrinking, clasping at levity. 'Idle, irrelevant curiosity. A particularly Catholic sin. Sorry.'

DI Armstrong seemed to wrestle with an unwelcome confusion. She cast an eye of longing around the peaceful enclosure. Checking herself, she said, 'The problem for the Home Office is that they have no control. We do the investigation and if there's enough evidence there's a trial. They couldn't stop it if they wanted to. So there's a risk the whole mess will be brought out into the open. And Schwermann wasn't the only one. There were others.'

'Why do you think that Larkwood is being set up for a fall?'

'Milby has to brief the Chief Constable every couple of weeks, and together they have meetings with the Home Office because of the sensitivity of the case. Of course the politicians can't bring influence to bear, blah, blah, but I'm sure they're the ones who make "suggestions" about what is best for national security, public relations and so on. And without wishing to smear my boss too much, he's rather susceptible to fixing things if there's no other way.'

'Drug squad realism?'

'Yes, he's never quite left the back alleys. Anyway, right from the outset he was encouraged, shall we say, to let Schwermann know we were on to him. Milby's got a few tame journalists – you know what it's like, favours for favours – so he tipped one of them off, a local hack. Then for some reason Schwermann came here. Once we were informed, Milby let one of the nationals know.'

'What on earth for?'

'It's not his agenda. It must be the Home Office, and it seems to me they've done what they can to make it look as though Schwermann enjoys the support of the Church. It's as though they have something on you that could be relevant to the trial, but for political reasons they're keeping it under wraps.'

DI Armstrong paused. A fraction too long, thought Anselm, and he saw the ploy. He thought: she senses the Church may be involved but doesn't know how, and she's hoping I'll offer the answer. This was the true reason for her visit: she had her own question and she'd slipped it in while making a disclosure, trying to get a monk to open up when he was probably most vulnerable. Anselm approved enormously of the technique and would have liked to crown it with success. But he would have to dissemble, for he now understood completely why the government were preparing to compromise Larkwood.

Schwermann was bound to disclose during the trial that a French monastery had protected him after the war and that British Intelligence had interviewed him and released him, and that this would never have happened unless he'd been believed to be innocent. And it was this very argument the government would adopt, with a twist, should a conviction nonetheless ensue. The Home Secretary would say those dealing with the matter at the time had been influenced, in great part, by the moral authority of the Church, who, as it happens, had protected Schwermann once more when his accusers named his crimes.

DI Armstrong had finished what she had to say; but her finishing was expectant. She looked at Anselm and he began his dissembling, impressed and saddened by his own adroit paring of the truth.

'It sounds as though the government would like a companion if, in the end, there's a public outcry, and who better than the Church. They would be the real target of interest.'

'That's what I thought,' said DI Armstrong as if closing a line of enquiry. Anselm sickened a little because her satisfaction presumed his honesty, and because he was now going to exploit her trust of him.

'How strong is the case?' he asked lightly, by way of preamble.

'Difficult to say. I've interviewed the former Captain Lawson and he says he can't remember a thing, which I don't believe. Most of the witnesses are elderly and susceptible. The bulk of the case rests on documents and the interpretation of what they mean . . . so it's pretty finely balanced. If we could find Brionne, assuming he's still alive, then we might have some direct evidence, but he's vanished.'

Anselm said, 'When you came here, you asked if you could speak with absolute confidence.'

'Yes?'

'Can I now do the same?'

DI Armstrong scrutinised Anselm's face. 'Yes . . .'

'First, don't ask me any questions, because I am bound not to answer them. Second, I promise that what I now ask can only serve the interests of justice, in its widest sense.'

DI Armstrong frowned, but nodded.

'I know Victor Brionne's new name. This is what I ask. If I give you the name, and you find him, will you tell me where he is before you do anything and allow me to talk to him first? After that he is all yours.'

DI Armstrong stood and moved away. Anselm followed her gaze towards the bare window arches of the old nave. Tangled streamers of vermilion creeper drifted lazily where fragments of glass had once conspired to trap the sun for praise. The swish of the leaves was like a faint pulse, or distant water on a beach of stones. Turning back to Anselm she said, 'All right. What's he called?'

'Berkeley, Victor Berkeley.'

Anselm's bargain had come at a price he had not foreseen. She was taking not only him on trust but also the world he represented, its history, its old stones, once considered sacred without question.

Anselm walked DI Armstrong to her car. He said, 'Thank you for the warning.'

'It's nothing.'

They walked a little further and Anselm, suspicious, said, 'One other thing. Have you any idea how Father Andrew knew in advance of our first meeting that Milby had slipped a word to the Press about Schwermann?'

She stopped, smiling broadly, suddenly young and no longer a police officer, simply herself: 'Yes. I told him.'

Chapter Twenty-One

Anselm frequently observed that the fears he entertained turned out, in the end, to be groundless; but he'd never learned the trick of disregarding new ones at their inception. Like the man in the Parable of the Sower, Anselm invariably found himself unable to protect the seeds from the rocks. A case in point was Victor Brionne, the mention of whose name had only ever caused him to stumble.

Yet again someone had come to Larkwood with something to say; yet again Father Andrew had summoned Anselm to deal with it; and yet again the person concerned had been brushed by the past, only this time it was simple. Delightfully simple.

'He's in his mid-fifties, I'd say,' said the Prior. 'Altogether engaging. I've put him in the parlour.'

They walked down the spiral stairs leading from Anselm's room to the ground floor. Shafts of sunlight cut through slender windows like a blade. The monks passed through light and dark in silence, to the low patter of their steps.

'He wants to talk about Victor Brionne. I didn't get his name.'

He had the poise of a relaxed subject before a sculptor. His short hair was silvered throughout, contrasting with vital and arresting eyes. He sat with one arm resting midway upon a crossed leg.

'Father, for reasons that will become clear, I'd rather not

191

introduce myself. I'm in a delicate situation which forces me to sneak around on tiptoe.'

Returning a smile, Anselm said, 'I'm intrigued.'

'What I have to say is not particularly exhilarating, but it's probably worth knowing. You see, my mother knew Victor Brionne.'

Anselm's eyes widened. He focused afresh on the clean features, not unduly marked by life's capricious tricks, the black roll-neck pullover, the soft suede shoes.

'They were very good friends. From what she said I think he would have liked to marry her, otherwise I can't think why she would have kept his name in mind.' He laughed lightly, easily. 'It's one of our quirks, I suppose, that we all remember the people we might have married.'

'Yes, I know what you mean,' said Anselm.

'But it wasn't to be. He became a casualty of the war after all, through sheer bad luck. He was struck by a falling chimney stack weakened by the Blitz. I can't understand the divine arrangement of things whereby a man could survive a world war and then be killed by bricks tumbling out of the sky.'

'I know,' mused Anselm sombrely. 'I've never yet been able to reconcile providence with experience. But I keep trying.' He moved on, 'Your mother met someone else?'

'Yes, but she never forgot Victor. She can't have imagined what his past involved. It's strange to think that my father could have been Victor Brionne, a man who worked alongside a Nazi war criminal. Even so, none of us really know our parents.'

Anselm warmed to the reflective modesty of his guest and said, 'Except, perhaps, when they've gone.'

'Yes, and then it's too late.'

They smiled at one another as through opposite windows in parallel buildings.

The visitor said, 'I've told you this because I expect there must be plenty of people who would like to find Victor, and, to speak plainly, neither I nor anyone in my family particularly want to get involved. We live a peaceful life far away from those times. My mother's dead, so she can't make a statement to the police, and I wouldn't relish tabloid attention on the little we know made into a feast for the curious. Our link with the man was a very long time ago and we'd like to leave it like that.'

'That's most understandable.'

'I realise that keeping my name back must be unattractive,' said the visitor, 'but it's as an excess of caution, not distrust. Should anyone ever knock on our door, and that's possible, I'd like to know in advance that the Priory played no part in the finding, however accidental it might be.'

'Yes, I see what you mean,' said Anselm, thinking of Brother Sylvester whose progress towards sanctity had left the discretion of the serpent well behind.

'As long as you are obliged to house your guest, if I can put it like that—'

'You may; that's exactly the situation—'

'Then this could be the place where those with a legitimate concern will come. So do feel free to repeat what I've said, but I'd rather it was left unattributed.'

'I understand.'

In certain circumstances Anselm had a fondness for death. It tended to resolve all manner of complications for the living, especially in families, though few were prepared to admit it. But this was an example of the principle's wider application. The death of Victor Brionne might have caused grief elsewhere but it simplified things enormously.

193

The visitor stayed for Vespers and afterwards Anselm walked him to his car.

'I've a long drive ahead.'

'I won't ask where to,' replied Anselm. At that moment his eye latched on to the distinctive red lettering of *The Tablet*, a Catholic weekly, lying by the back window. Anselm always read it cover to cover, after which he feigned intimate knowledge of world and religious affairs. As the visitor slammed the car door, Anselm, unable to restrain his curiosity, stepped closer – he'd noticed the small white address label. He just caught Mr Robert B . . . and then the vehicle crunched away across the gravel.

Anselm waved farewell. It had been one of those encounters, all too short, that could only end with pages left unturned. In the withdrawn life of a monk it wasn't every day that Anselm met someone like Mr Robert B. The vehicle moved slowly and Anselm noted the stickers on the rear screen: 'National Trust', 'Whitley Bay Jazz Festival', 'Cullercoats RNLI' – each a snapshot of a life's enthusiasms.

Walking back to the Priory, Anselm thought he wouldn't say anything to DI Armstrong just yet. Her research would confirm what he'd been told. The death of Victor Berkeley would become public knowledge and he could write to Rome and let them know that the old collaborator had been struck by bricks from heaven.

And while he was smiling to himself, the one peculiarity of his conversation with Robert B struck him. At no point had they mentioned the identifying feature of the dead renegade: his false name, the name by which he must have been known.

Chapter Twenty-Two

1

The idea of going to Larkwood Priory came to Lucy late at night after she had been grilled by Cathy about 'the Frenchman' – an expression that, for Lucy, included Victor Brionne. The next morning Lucy forsook a lecture on the Romantic era and rang Pascal.

'I've had an idea. It's a one-off, but it might yield something.'

'Go on.'

'Wherever Brionne might be, he is bound to know that Schwermann has claimed sanctuary at Larkwood Priory. There's a chance he, too, might contact the monks. Either he's looking for somewhere to hide, or he may want to speak out but doesn't want to go to the police . . . there are all sorts of possibilities.'

The line hummed lightly. Pascal said, 'It's worth a shot.'

'I'll pick you up in the Duchess, a Morris Minor built and bought before we were born.'

A monk called Father Anselm led them to an unkempt herb garden and a table beneath an ancient wellingtonia tree, talking of his schooldays in Paris. At the first natural break Pascal said, 'Father, let me say, I for one haven't swallowed the story that the Priory has any sympathy for "Schwermann's predicament"

– I think that was the phrase. I used to be a journalist so I recognise the musings of a hack when I see them.'

'I'm very grateful for that,' said Father Anselm, not, it seemed, entirely at ease. 'It would appear we live in a time when any swipe at the Church sounds credible, which is probably the Church's fault as much as anyone else's.'

'Maybe, but one of the first things I learned as a journalist was that if you set anything down in print, however bizarre, it looks plausible.'

The monk said, 'Unfortunately some stories about the Church are both bizarre and true.'

Turning to the subject of their visit, Pascal said, 'Father, Eduard Schwermann is one of those alarming people who diligently went to work within a system of killing as if it was a Peugeot factory. After that, someone hid him.'

The monk seemed unsurprised at something that had always struck Lucy as astonishing.

Pascal continued, 'There will be a trial, but it doesn't follow that justice will be done. Turning over the past is a bit like waking Leviathan. Anything can happen, and sometimes it's the innocent that get devoured.'

'I've seen the devastation many times.'

'To stop that happening we need someone who knew him and saw him at work.'

'Who?' The question seemed artificial.

'A man called Victor Brionne. That's why we're here. I know it's unlikely, but if he makes contact with the Priory for any reason, will you urge him to come forward? I'm not asking him to go to the police, just to talk with me and my colleague in private.' Pascal nodded his head towards Lucy.

The monk leaned forward, his expression a miniature of

regret and slight confusion. 'I used to be a lawyer,' he said, as if disclosing a forgiven sin, 'so I know how important a witness like Victor Brionne could be in a case such as this. And, as it happens, someone did come here to talk about him, a man whose mother had known him. But he came only to say that Brionne had died in an accident. The man kept his anonymity because he didn't want to get involved.'

'How did he die?'

'He was hit by a falling chimney stack.' The monk seemed to find his own reply transparently unsatisfactory.

Pascal frowned. 'A falling chimney stack? Didn't that strike you as convenient?'

'I had no reason to doubt him.'

Lucy sensed growing discomfort.

Pascal said, sharply, 'Did he know the name, the name he hid behind?'

The monk paled.

'Did the person mention the name?'

'I'm afraid not.'

'So there's no way of confirming what you were told? Death produces more paper than anything else.'

Lucy glanced from Pascal to the monk, who now seemed slightly adrift from the conversation. He looked up, as though to speak, when his mouth froze. Lucy turned in the direction of his gaze and saw an elderly monk walking across the grass with a young man about the same age as herself.

'Brother Sylvester,' said Father Anselm weakly.

'I knew I'd find you hiding here,' said the old monk, waving over his companion. 'This is Max Nightingale. Used to be in the Scouts, you know.'

197

Brother Sylvester's distinctive contribution to community life inspired two extreme reactions: protective affection and a desire to kill. The ground in between was narrow and easily traversed. Watching Sylvester potter back to the reception, halting here and there to rub and smell herbs along the way, Anselm stepped swiftly from the first to the second.

As Porter, it was one of Sylvester's tasks to answer the telephone and take messages. The considered view of all was that about half got through. Therefore, Anselm had no idea Max Nightingale was coming, and Sylvester had now airily brought him into contact with the man who had exposed his grandfather.

Pascal rose stiffly, saying, 'Thank you for your time, Father. We'd better be going. If the nameless visitor calls again, I'd ask him some more questions.' He walked quickly after Brother Sylvester, followed by Miss Embleton.

'Is that Pascal Fougères?' asked Max.

'Yes,' replied Anselm resignedly.

Max took a step, halted and then called out, 'Hold on . . . just a second . . . tell me about Agnes . . . and a child . . .'

The young woman who'd said hardly anything throughout their short meeting turned abruptly, showing an involuntary flash of pain. She hurried past Fougères and out through the gate.

'I showed my grandfather a cutting last week,' said Max, watching them part. 'It was about him, Pascal Fougères. My grandfather hadn't realised he was involved in the group that had exposed him . . .' He blinked rapidly, half squinting, 'The next thing I know he's walking back and forth . . . mumbling

. . . and out spills that name . . . as though he could see her there, in the room . . . I barely heard him after that . . . but he said "child" as if he'd seen flesh and blood.'

They were alone, now, in a scented garden.

Max said, 'I asked him today what he meant and all he'd say was that Victor Brionne knew the answer.'

Anselm felt a sudden affiliation with the young man. They were both relying on the missing Frenchman to make sense of strained loyalties.

'You know, Father,' said Max, 'I think we are in much the same position. My grandfather planted himself here, behind these walls, and I sometimes wonder if he took refuge in my childhood . . . another secluded place where questions don't have to be answered.' He looked blankly at traces of paint beneath his nails. 'But now I've grown up.'

'Unfortunately,' said Anselm, 'that is never more apparent than when we ask the first forbidden question. Maybe that's when we really cease to be children.' Thinking of the young woman with the haunted eyes, Anselm went on, 'I wonder who Agnes might be?'

Max said, 'I get the feeling Pascal Fougères doesn't know . . . but the girl does.' He made to go, saying with a tinge of disinterest, 'I just came to let you know there's no sign of Victor Brionne as yet.'

'There's still time,' said Anselm hopefully. 'Something will have found its way on to paper.'

After Max had gone Anselm devoted half an hour to John Cassian's Sixteenth Conference, *On Friendship*. Putting down the text at the bell for Vespers, Anselm was struck by an answer, on the face of things, unrelated to his reading, even before he'd formulated the question. Did Agnes know Victor? Yes, she did; she most certainly did. And they had both known Jacques – an interesting fact that had escaped the family education of Pascal Fougères.

Anselm shook his head, ruing the scheme of things that only allowed him to discover great truths by accident.

3

They travelled in silence for a mile or so. The roads were empty and the evening sun was beginning to dip behind the darkening trees.

'Who's Agnes?' Pascal said.

A cold, crawling sensation spread over Lucy's scalp: it's a fact, he's never even heard of her. Proudly, vehemently, she said, 'My grandmother.'

'And the child?'

'Her son.'

'The father?' He'd guessed the answer: his own history, the redactor's script, had been torn in two.

Lucy checked her mirror and pulled into a lay-by near a farm gate. The sun slipped further down, a dying blaze. She said, 'Jacques Fougères, your great-uncle.'

'What happened to the boy?'

Lucy couldn't read his expression. Resentment and despair choked the words.

The whole story would now tumble forth. Pascal wound down his window, pulling in a slap of cold fresh air, and Lucy broke her promise to Agnes.

The late evening sky had acquired a faint glamour, like the

surface of the sea, deep but impenetrable. Lucy drove into the advancing night, the obstacles that had lain between her and Pascal floating all around — broken words on a rising wave, a swell made of two rivers suddenly joined.

Chapter Twenty-Three

1

Pascal rang Lucy on her mobile while she was having lunch with her parents. Her father sat at the head of the table; her mother had just left the dining room for the kitchen. The opening bars of Beethoven's Fifth, electrified and appalling, blared out from Lucy's pocket.

'Destiny, I presume?' asked Freddie woodenly.

Lucy took the call.

'I think a little miracle happened when we were at Larkwood Priory.'

'It passed me by.'

'Meeting Max Nightingale.'

'You're joking.' She thought of him with revulsion. 'I call that unfortunate.'

A long moan of hopes betrayed floated out from the kitchen. As usual her mother was battling with milk and powder, strong adversaries that would not be reconciled.

Pascal said, 'I don't know why he threw that question in about your grandmother but he hadn't the faintest idea who she was.'

'That's not a miracle.'

'But if he knows of her, he may well know of Victor Brionne . . . and his name.'

Her father realigned his plate, clinking it against a neatly laid dessert spoon.

Lucy said, 'But he's not going to tell you, is he?'

'I'd like to find out.'

'You're joking again.' Lucy sensed the future, predatory and inevitable.

'I'm not. In a way he's no different to you or me—'

Lucy spat, 'How?'

'He's part of the aftermath. He's not a criminal. I'd like to meet him, it's just . . . right . . . and I couldn't be bothered to work out why.'

'I have to go,' said Lucy. The approval of her father flowered in a smile. Phone calls during meals were not encouraged. It had been one of Darren's specialities, done on purpose.

The call ended, and Lucy's father said, 'Dreadful things those. Who was that?'

'Just a friend.' The barricade on her private life appeared. Her father scouted around for an opening, looking for light between the slats: 'How's your study getting along?'

'Not so bad.' The phrase sealed a gap. Lucy had detected the true meaning beneath her father's question: 'You made a hash of Cambridge so please don't fail again.' She thought: fail who? You or me? Who do you really think lost out in my growing up? Shocked by her own charity she answered: we both did, terribly, and she suddenly wanted to touch him. She took her father's empty plate and laid it on hers. When were they ever going to forget the past? Why were they cursed to remember everything?

Her mother came into the room, hands on her hips, her face fallen: 'I'm afraid there's lots of lumps in the custard.'

'Oh God, not again,' said her father as he reached out for Susan's hand.

Anselm drove Salomon Lachaise to Long Melford, a town of Suffolk pink not far from Larkwood. Having parked they walked into Holy Trinity Church, a huge construction more like a cathedral, its magnificence built upon medieval piety and the wool trade. Salomon Lachaise removed his heavy glasses, squinting with wonder at the windows and the empty stone niches in the chantry, once the home of solemn apostles. They passed through a churchyard to the Lady Chapel.

'This was a school after the Reformation,' said Anselm, pointing to a children's multiplication table on the wall. Salomon Lachaise quietly studied the enduring markings of long, long ago. He said, 'It is a kind of mockery, but one cannot survive without shame.' He pressed small hands deep into cardigan pockets, making them bulge. 'It is something I could never tell my mother.'

'Why?'

'Her peace grew out of my being an ordinary boy, doing his sums at school like all the others.'

Anselm said, 'But why shame?'

'Because you cannot escape the sensation that you have taken someone else's place.' He looked closely at the wall. 'It's like a debt to heaven.'

They stepped outside, back into the churchyard. Salomon Lachaise said, 'When I was a boy my mother used to say that hell was the painless place where everything has been forgotten.'

'That doesn't sound so bad.'

'It couldn't be worse.'

'Why?'

'Because there's no love. That's why there is no pain.'

They walked beneath a milky sky shot with patches of insistent blue. Anselm looked up and asked, 'Then what's heaven?'

'An inferno where you burn remembering all that should be remembered.'

3

Cathy and Lucy finally made it to the Turkish baths. There were three rooms linked by arches. Each got smaller and hotter than the one before. For twenty minutes they sat upon the white-tiled seats of the first chamber. Steam swirled around them. Their heads slowly fell under the weight of bone as strength drained away. At a nod from Cathy they moved into the next phase of affliction; when Lucy thought she could bear it no more, Cathy gestured towards a small, empty compartment. None of the other users had been in there. The heat was overpowering. Lucy slumped in a corner, blinded by sweat, until she was so weak she could barely lift her limbs. Cathy leaned against the wall, her eyes tightly closed. Through the burning fog Lucy could just see the small scar upon the flushed cheek. It kept the lead, always a fraction redder.

Cathy slowly raised an arm, pointing to a swing-door adjacent to the entrance. 'You first,' she breathed.

Lucy staggered back, blinking rapidly, her eyes swimming from the sting of salt. She pushed through the door into a bright room by a small pool. Somehow she lay on a table.

'That was hell,' she said. 'I'm never coming back as long as I live.'

'It's not over yet, love,' said a deep voice. A woman with thick muscles appeared, armed with a huge lathered sponge. At

205

its touch upon her toes Lucy howled. It was too much. The lightest contact was like merciless tickling. Lucy shrieked until she was hauled off and pushed towards a warm, gentle shower. When she emerged, the woman with the muscles gave her a shove and Lucy toppled into the pool of freezing water. When she surfaced she was ready to die. Death had lost its sting.

Lying on a padded leather divan, wrapped in a warm towel, Lucy had her first experience of transcendence. By her side on a small table was a mug of hot, sweet tea and a bacon sandwich. Cathy lay upon a parallel couch.

'I believe in God,' said Lucy.

'I'm told a bishop died of a heart attack in a place like this.'

'No better surroundings.'

'I don't think he made it to the pool.'

'He coughed it on the table?'

'So it seems.'

'What a way to go.'

Cathy reached for her sandwich and said, 'Did you take my advice and invite the Frenchman out?'

'I did, actually,' replied Lucy.

'Where did you go?'

'A monastery.'

Cathy chewed thoughtfully. 'Before that you had a meal in a crypt.' She licked melted butter off a finger. 'Where to next time?'

'A pub, I suspect.'

Chapter Twenty-Four

1

Lucy met Pascal on a wet pavement outside Sibyl's Cave on a Friday night. She said, 'It's seething.'

'We'll be all right.' He rubbed his hands confidently, as if about to spin a couple of dice down the felt. He winked and Lucy bridled. She couldn't split the gesture from scaffolds and whistling beery cheek. He said, 'I have a good feeling about this.'

Pascal had obtained Max Nightingale's phone number from Father Anselm. The meeting was set up. Apparently he'd been keen. When Pascal had told Lucy she'd felt a sharp, churning disgust. 'Good,' she'd said.

Lucy yanked at the pub door, releasing from the bright hallway a gasp of heat and noise. The lounge was packed with competition, professionals loudly shedding the pressures of work. They glanced into a small smoking room. Thick blue swirls hung above the tables like belchings from so many garden fires. Empty glasses stood in tight crowds. A young girl in a short black skirt pushed past gripping a damp cloth. They forced their way towards the veranda entrance. Pinned to a jamb was a forbidding notice: Private Party. Through the window panel Lucy saw suits, legs crossed while standing, wine glasses pressed to the chest: the boss was leaving. Pascal pulled her by the arm towards the debating room.

The appetite for argument was on the wane – young bloods were heading for the bar or home, leaving disparate clusters of older men. Where were the women? thought Lucy. Her gaze shifted and she saw Max Nightingale sitting in a corner. On the table was a black motorcycle helmet. It stared at Lucy and she thought of an empty, severed head. They joined him, pulling up chairs.

'Who's Sibyl?' asked Max Nightingale. Lucy noticed dark grime beneath his nails: a trace of his grandfather's dirt. Catching her glance he said, 'Paint. I've been painting.'

'Papered cracks?'

'No, pictures.'

'Oh.'

'Sibyl?' he repeated.

Pascal said, 'She's the main player in a tragic myth, a mystic who pushed off death and spent centuries in a cave. She wrote out riddles on leaves but left them to the mercy of the wind.'

Max Nightingale stared back blankly. 'I thought she was the landlord.'

Lucy laughed, against the will to scoff . . . she who hadn't known either.

Pascal said, 'You asked a question at the Priory – about Agnes and a child. Where did you get the name from?'

'My grandfather.' He spoke frankly, quickly.

'Do you know who she is?'

'No.'

Pascal seemed to see suspicion and caution peeling away. 'I'd like to ask you a question, but first I just want to say something.'

Max Nightingale removed the helmet from the table. A space opened up, flat, ready to be crossed. Lucy regarded it with horror.

Pascal said, 'We've been born on different sides of a night-mare, but it's worth saying . . . I've got nothing against you.'

Max Nightingale flinched. Then, recovered, he said, 'Ask me your question.'

Lucy heard a shuffle: standing almost over them was the man she called The Don.

2

Brother Sylvester must have enjoyed one of his flashes of competence, for he managed to transfer a telephone call from the switchboard to the extension where Anselm was to be found. The shock of the feat momentarily distracted Anselm's attention from DI Armstrong's words:

'We've put all the evidence to Schwermann during the interviews. He said only one thing, a quotation: "*Zwei Seelen wohnen, ach! in meiner Brust.*"'

'I'm sorry, I can't help you there.'

'I don't need help, thank you. It's from Goethe's *Faust.* Translates as "Two souls dwell, alas, within my breast." I think it's an admission of sorts.'

'But it won't get you very far with a jury.'

'I realise that. Anyway, the investigation is over. We're going to charge him tomorrow with murder.'

'Joint enterprise?'

'Yes.'

Anselm had a premonition of what was to follow.

'As for Victor Brionne, or Berkeley, nothing has turned up. There are no records to show that he ever lived or died, not under those names.'

Anselm thought back to the charming Robert B, legs crossed,

confiding the little he knew; coming to Vespers and taking his time in parting.

DI Armstrong said, 'Brionne has been a very cautious man. He must have changed his name again – perhaps by deed poll, or simply by claiming his papers had been destroyed: that would have been fairly easy for a refugee after the war. Either way, there's little chance of finding him. It is as though he never existed.'

3

'May I join you?' A warm smile lit The Don's face, among a shock of white hair, from his scalp down to the beard. In his hand was a pint of beer. Without waiting for a reply he drew up a chair and sat down.

'I recognise you, actually,' he said, nodding to Pascal, 'from the television.'

Max Nightingale opened his mouth to speak but the stranger said, 'Well, well, here we are, four open minds round one table. There's nothing we cannot question and, as so often happens in the dialogues of Plato, our combined ignorance can lead us to the truth. The blind can lead the blind after all.' He smiled cheerily.

'Look,' said Max Nightingale, 'we're in the middle of something.'

'I'll join in.'

'I'm sorry, but—'

Pascal interrupted: 'Max, this is the debating room. I should have said . . . anyone can participate . . .'

'So,' said the man with the white beard, looking amiably round the table, 'what's the subject?'

Pascal said, with strained patience, 'We haven't got one.'

'Then let me oblige,' and rather too quickly he said: 'My thesis is that getting hold of the truth requires us to distinguish different kinds of narrative – symbol, allegory, parable and the like. Now, one of the main problems is when one form of discourse pretends to be another . . . myth or fable masquerading as fact. Story dressed up as history.'

Max Nightingale looked deeply bored.

The stranger said, 'Have any of you read the Narnia books?'

While Pascal and Max Nightingale seemed irritated at the interruption, Lucy was relieved. It was an interlude in a difficult meeting, that was all. Pascal could ask about Brionne's name after the discussion was over. There was no rush. She said, 'I've read them, several times.'

He smiled winningly and cried, 'But you haven't tried talking to a lion, have you? It's just a myth about good and evil and the lion wins.'

Lucy noticed Pascal's face darkening with a sort of expectation.

The stranger said, 'There's no difficulty in that instance because there are no facts, it's just fiction. But what happens when fact and fiction mix?' He raised his glass. 'Let's take the Holocaust, for example.'

Lucy shivered at his serene manner, the use of charged language without reverence.

He smiled, saying, 'How much is fact and how much is fiction?'

'Let's go,' said Pascal, standing up.

'Am I the voice of temptation in your wilderness?' he pouted.

Lucy glanced at Max. He had paled and seemed unable to respond. She rose, picking up her coat. The straps of her rucksack were tangled round her feet. Her purse fell out, coins rolling under the table. A number of people close to them turned at the noise. An old man nearby grimaced and pulled himself up, his head inclined towards Pascal and his tormentor.

'Come on,' snapped Pascal.

'Let's take the Schwermann trial,' said The Don, supremely relaxed. 'He might be convicted. But who'll question the old fairy tales?'

'Lucy, please, come on,' said Pascal.

The old man lumbered over and grabbed The Don's shoulder, tugging at the cloth. He shouted, 'I've had enough of you, clear off. Go on, get out.'

The Don stumbled to his feet, his smile suddenly twisted with suppressed rage. 'Get your hands off me, you ignorant—'

'I'm not scared of y-your sort,' the old man stuttered, raising a shaking fist.

From the other side of the room someone yelled, 'Dad? What the hell . . . ?'

Max and Pascal rose quickly, moving round the table. The old man pulled harder, his fist drawing back. Suddenly, with a look of ecstasy, The Don swung his arm in a sweeping, imperious arc and struck the old man across the face. At the same time Pascal lunged forward, trying to come between the two men. Then Lucy gasped. Pascal slipped and tumbled over. He spun to one side, falling. His left arm caught the edge of a table, his body twisted and there was a sickening thud. Pascal groaned, like one asleep, rolling his head from side to side. Both arms lay limp upon the floor. Lucy covered her face, staring at him through shaking fingers. A thin wail broke out of her that wouldn't stop. She could only see one of Pascal's feet, the rest

212

of him now surrounded by people on their knees while others pushed tables and chairs to one side.

An ambulance came. All Lucy could remember afterwards were the colours. Green sheets, a red blanket, shiny chrome bars on the stretcher, yellow jackets and pale, white faces. Someone took her hand. An arm went around her shoulder. There was no sound any more, either from her or all around. It was as though she was wrapped in great puffs of cotton wool, and she floated in a vacuum, deep inside her head.

The last thing she saw before being led outside into the night air was the place where Pascal's head had come to rest. A small but thick smudge of blood shone at the base of a rather vulgar table leg, ornate metalwork curving down to a small iron globe.

Lucy was brought home by a woman police officer at three in the morning. Alone in her flat, still surrounded by a heavy, numbing insulation, she saw a flashing light on her answer machine. Her body moved towards it and pressed a button.

'It's me, Cathy,' drawled a voice into the darkness. 'I tried you on your mobile without success and I now confidently entertain certain suspicions. So, what did you do this time? Bell-ringing? Call me sometime.'

4

Morning light danced across the hills around Larkwood. Captivated, Anselm opened the windows of his cell. He sat quietly, preparing himself for Lectio Divina, but started at a distraction: footsteps moved swiftly on the corridor outside, growing louder. It was peculiar because monastic comportment

213

forbade anything that might disturb the spirit of recollection, and it was unheard of at that hour, even in the breach. A knock struck his door. Anselm rose, turning the handle with apprehension.

Brother Jerome had a clutch of newspapers under his arm. It was his task to read diverse reports and opinions from Left and Right and distil them into a balanced news bulletin to be read out during lunch. He had evidently just collected the papers from reception. Without saying anything he pointed to a passage on the front page of a national. Pascal Fougères had been taken to Charing Cross Hospital, Hammersmith. He had died shortly afterwards from a brain haemorrhage sustained during a fall. The accident had occurred, it seemed, when he intervened in a quarrel about the last war. Police sources said an investigation was under way.

Anselm shut his door and slumped on to a chair. With his mind's eye he described Leviathan rising out of a boiling sea, arching high into a red sky, dripping water like rain.

Chapter Twenty-Five

The cottage on Holy Island was more of a manor, having many rooms and a large, windswept garden leading down to a stone wall built by hands that knew a craft fast becoming scarce. Immediately beyond lay an intimate, curved shoreline of green and black boulders, some round but others angulated despite the endless blandishments of the sea. From the bathroom Victor could see the deep pink sandstone ruins of a Priory, hollowed by wind and rain; from where he slept he looked out upon Lindisfarne Castle, cut against a pale sky, joined as one to the high crag from which it rose, reaching out to the Northern Lights. Beyond lay Broad Stones and, further, Plough Rock, and then the bare, flat, silent sea.

'You should be safe here,' said Robert. They had walked to the north end of the island, overlooking Emmanuel Head.

Victor nodded.

'I told him what you told me, that Victor Brionne died after the war; and I told him what I told you, that someone else married my mother. I told him the truth. If anyone comes asking questions about you, they'll be told you're dead.'

Victor stood once more upon the lip of an abyss. There could be no further discussion. It would have been better if Robert had not gone to the Priory, for he had become a tiny link between Victor and whoever might still want to find him. But he was trying to help his father and that was all that mattered. Robert wasn't to know that Victor had changed his name a second time. No one knew that, so the chances of anyone looking for Victor Berkeley being led to Victor Brownlow were remote. Perhaps he had been precipitate in disclosing anything to Robert at all. Maybe he should have taken the risk and carried on as if nothing had happened, living his life on the ground he'd laid over the past. But with Schwermann unmasked, the desire to hide had been irresistible; and, despite the burden of secrecy, he'd wanted to tell Robert at least who he had been, to let Robert in, ever so slightly, on the scourge that had laid waste to his father.

Brownlow: Victor liked the name and always had done. It had been an inspired choice.

They turned and walked back, arm in arm, to 'Pilgrim's Rest', Robert's holiday cottage. A cold sea wind, wet with spray, hustled them along. And, with a sadness first born when he was a boy, Victor thought of Jacques, and now Pascal Fougères, whom he had never met and who had wanted to find him. They should have been able to meet as friends and bridge the years, but a great gulf had been fixed between them. Victor followed Robert through the garden gate and thought angrily: I could never have helped Pascal Fougères, even if he'd found me – that would only have been possible if Agnes was alive. But she's dead, as if by my own hand.

216

Part Three

'Now is the time for stripping the spirit bare,
Time for the burning of days ended and done . . .'
(Laurence Binyon, 'The Burning of the Leaves', 1942)

Third Prologue

6th January 1996.

The slow, physical destruction was matched by an increased mental clarity, a loosening between flesh and spirit. Agnes often felt a fluttering in her stomach, as though something roped to a ground peg was trying to take off. She wondered if she was going to be sick.

Agnes had lain day after day and night after night upon her back, or on one side and then the other, Wilma doing the dutiful, turning her this way and that. And then came the ointment, and the jokes, for the bedsores. The job done, she was left alone.

Agnes never realised there was so much to contemplate in one room: the paint lifting ever so slightly on the window frame, soon to be a soft curl pulling away from the wood; the pattern of faint shadows changing imperceptibly with the movement of the cloud, lighting little things with a barely noticeable difference. But once Agnes had seen all there was to see she got very bored. And then, for no apparent reason, she remembered how Merlin had taught Wart, the future King Arthur, the art of seeing – by changing him into another animal. So Agnes imagined herself as a bird, looking down from on high at the intricate mingling of things, like a hunting kestrel afloat on a bearing wind.

She saw the boat upon the Channel, bound for France, and her father staring anxiously out to sea with a little girl by his side – a beautiful girl, standing on the first rail, her hair adrift and her red coat about to be thrown leeward before he could stop her or see the abandon upon her face. She saw Father Rochet holding her boy in a parlour, just after the baptism, staring bravely through those infant eyes to another place and another child. She saw Madame Klein by the split boards of a cattle truck, pushing other mouths away from a thin stream of air, standing on a fallen, wheezing mound. Agnes turned into her pillow with a low moan and rose higher still, above the gathering wind. Through the first swirls of evening mist she saw a light upon the Champs-Elysées and a young man behind a desk, checking address lists and the timings of the next day's work. His face was set hard. Down she swooped, faster and faster, over the chestnut trees heavy with leaves, and into the room, through the slate-blue iris and into his shivering optic nerve.

And Agnes understood. She finally saw into Victor Brionne, the traitor. Slowly she raised her hands, frail fingers extended and shaking. She could not speak. It was too late to write anything now. And she could no longer dictate.

Wilma bustled through the door with a cup of ice cubes, a saucer and a teaspoon.

Chapter Twenty-Six

1

The trial of Eduard Walter Schwermann opened on a warm morning in the second week after Easter. Queues for the public gallery stretched from the Old Bailey towards Ludgate. The Body Public sat on canvas chairs nibbling sandwiches. Flasks of tea stood like skittles on the pavement. Many in due course would be turned away when the Porters informed them there were no storage facilities for their hampers. Anselm, on his way to meet Roddy, was forced off the kerb. He crossed the street and looked back at the noble inscription high upon the court wall: 'Defend the children of the poor and punish the wrong-doer.' Anselm gazed upon the crowds and moved on, discomposed by the faint hint of carnival always attendant upon the airing of other people's tragedy.

Two weeks beforehand, Schwermann had moved out of Larkwood at six in the morning, hidden among a loud convoy of vehicles and motorbikes. He would be held on remand for the duration, Milby had said with yawning indifference. Schwermann's stay at the Priory had lasted a year. That same afternoon, Anselm and Salomon Lachaise met at The Hermitage for a glass of port over a game of chess. Reviewing their many matches, Anselm had been judged the overall winner, although that did not reflect the distribution of talent between them. Luck, it seemed, had played the better part. The ensuing match was a draw, each not truly wanting to win. Salomon Lachaise had left the next day for London. He would be staying in a small flat above Anselm's former chambers, overlooking the main square of Gray's Inn and a short walking distance from the Old Bailey. The offer had come from Roddy on his last visit to Larkwood (while he didn't believe in God, he often came to the Priory just to 'peep over the rim'). Such an offer, from the old rogue's mouth, meant no expenses would accrue. And thus the subject of remuneration, always delicate for the recipient of kindness, was quietly and happily dismissed.

Walking briskly, Anselm turned his thoughts to what lay ahead. First, he'd arranged to meet Roddy at chambers for a low-down on the principal players in the trial – a taste of old times. Afterwards, however, Anselm would catch a train to Paris to see the Fougères family – for a more unpalatable task. Milby, through DI Armstrong, had suggested he might go on their behalf, given the unpleasant legal realities that required sensitive explanation.

'I think the boss is right,' DI Armstrong had said. 'It would be better coming from someone like you.'

Anselm had agreed, but had found himself seizing the opportunity to request another favour, made tawdry by a hint of bargaining: 'I have something to ask of you. It relates to Victor Brionne.'

'He's gone, I'm afraid.'

'Can I have the same assurance as last time? If I tell you what more I know, will you allow me a first interview?'

DI Armstrong had looked Anselm directly in the face. 'I don't know what you're doing, Father, but you must have crossed a line, morally and legally. I think you should step back. Go home.'

'I'd like to, but I can't. I haven't yet worked out where the line was.'

'No, Father, we all know where it is.'

'I've said something very similar to other people in the confessional. I'll never say it again.'

'I can't forgive sins, you know that.'

'I give you the same assurance as I did last time. What I am doing is in the interests of justice.'

'All right, go on.'

'A man came to see me. He told me Brionne died after the war. In a peculiar way everything he said struck me as true — and it still does, even though I am sure now it was false. Intuition tells me he's related to Victor Brionne.' He'd given the signposts he had remembered: Robert B, the *Tablet* subscription and the rest. She'd written them down in a notebook, saying, 'Father, you really don't have to make a deal with me. I'd do this even if you refused to go and see the Fougères family.'

Anselm had reddened under the reprimand, all the more so because he sensed DI Armstrong no longer saw him in quite the same light. The monk wasn't that different after all.

Roddy was languidly smoking a cigarette while studying a wall of closed files as if they were strange objects uncovered by the Natural History Museum. He was dutifully engaged in that old internal debate, the outcome of which was already decided: to read or not to read?

'VAT fraud,' he said by way of explanation. 'I find the facts tend to get in the way of a good defence. Good to see you.'

He turned away, chortling, and reached for Anselm's hand. After covering gossip about the latest string of inexplicable judicial appointments, Roddy moved on to the Schwermann trial.

The judge was a safe pair of hands: Mr Justice Pollbrook, known as Shere-Khan because of his patrician vowels and his tendency to strangle weak arguments while scratching his nose. Leading Counsel for the Crown was Oliver Penshaw. 'Terribly nice chap, rather solemn, engaging bedside manner – which is probably why he's got the brief – but he's far too decent. Has a tendency to let the witness go, just when he should finish 'em off.' Roddy turned to Anselm, adding, 'That's why they've given him Victoria Matthews as a Junior.'

'What's she like?'

'Young, charming and, to the unsuspecting witness, apparently harmless. But that just hides the knife. They're a good team. Balanced. If Oliver has any sense he'll keep her wrapped up for any witness who might wreck his case.'

'What about the Defence?'

'Henry Bartlett, without a Junior. A small man with vast talent. He'll choose two or three cracking points and admit everything else. Short cross-examinations. By the time the jury retire there's a good chance they'll only remember what Henry chose to demolish.' Roddy drew deeply on his cigarette. 'It'll be an interesting match. Have you got a ticket?'

'No,' said Anselm from afar. The hunt, the chase, going in for the kill, the runners and riders, hitting the crossbar, caught behind, nose-enders. It all sounded rather distasteful now: the understandable levity of soldiers on the front line.

Roddy looked at his VAT files as one nudged by a conscience often ignored by more astute experience. 'I do hope your life of abstinence can be suspended for two hours. We haven't had lunch in years.'

'It can, Roddy. But keep it simple. I've a train to catch.'

'What on earth are you expecting, old son?' said the Head of Chambers, his reputation for moderation sorely offended.

2

A section of the court had been set aside for survivors and their relatives. Old and young were side by side. Lucy could not look upon them for long. Here, in this place, at this time, they had a majesty at once subdued and harrowing. She wondered if there was anyone else like her who could not take their proper place because of the tangled weave of history.

With that thought she found a seat beside a small man in his mid-fifties. He wore an old cardigan with the stem of a pipe poking out of a side pocket and heavy, thick-set glasses. He gave a nod of greeting as she sat down. Further along she noticed Max Nightingale. She had not seen him since Pascal's death, although he had left his number with the police should she want to speak to him. She didn't. She felt she should, but could not do it. And she was too weary of spirit to work out whether or not it was fair. Who cared what was fair after what had happened? Fairness was a word for children, to ensure everyone got a turn. Life, she had learned, was no playground.

The Defendant chose not to be present while the submissions on Abuse of Process were advanced on his behalf. The court was not occupied for long. Mr Justice Pollbrook slashed his way through anticipated arguments and contrived courtesies with languorous ease.

'Let's get on, shall we?' he said lazily, surveying the field of slain propositions.

225

The jury were empanelled. The Defendant was summoned. Doors opened and banged. He emerged flanked by guards, as if he had been drawn up from a hole in the ground. His appearance astonished Lucy: she had expected to glimpse the shape of evil but this man was no different from any other pensioner she had seen. A dark grey suit and a slight stoop produced an effect of respectful vulnerability. He stood, thumbing the hem of his jacket, while the indictment was read out.

The Defendant faced various counts of murder between 1942 and 1943. After each charge was put to him he entered a plea, his eyes fixed above the judge to the Crown Court emblem with its dictum: 'Dieu et mon Droit.'

'Not guilty.' The lingering guttural intonation had not quite been spent.

'Louder, please.'

'Not guilty.'

'Thank you, Mr Schwermann. You may sit down,' said the judge in scarlet and black, seated higher than all others among worn leather and panels of oak. From the Bar below, paper rustled and bewigged heads turned and leaned, whispering among themselves. Outstretched arms passed folded notes back and forth. The judge opened a notebook and lifted his pen.

Amid a silence the like of which Lucy had never heard before, Mr Penshaw rose to his feet.

'Ladies and gentlemen, my name is Penshaw. I prosecute in this case, assisted by the lady behind me, Miss Matthews. The gentleman on my left, nearest to you, is Mr Bartlett. He represents the Defendant. My first task is to give you a summary of the case against the accused.' Mr Penshaw rested his arms upon a small stand in front of him, referring now and then to a sheaf of notes. 'You are about to try an ordinary man charged with an extraordinary crime. The state calls upon you for one purpose: to decide his innocence or guilt. The Crown says he devoted the best years of his early manhood to the systematic deportation of Jews from Paris to Auschwitz. A three-day journey to the East in cattle wagons, where they were gassed upon arrival or worked to death. You will listen to the voices of those who survived. They will tell you of the terrible things they saw, from which you will instinctively wish to turn away. But you must not. You will have to listen and look dispassionately upon the actions of this man, whose crimes occupy one of the darkest chapters of history. And I'm afraid I must tell you now it is with the massacre of innocent children that you will be most concerned.'

Lucy was lost to her surroundings. No one seemed to breathe or move. There was just the calm evocation of a time long past, strangely alive to her as though it were part of her own memory.

'SS-Unterscharführer Eduard Schwermann was posted to Paris in July 1940, a month after the city fell into German hands and the Occupation began. He was twenty-three years of age and a volunteer. For one of low rank, he was astonishingly close to the highest echelons of his masters. Based in the Jewish Affairs Service of the Gestapo, he was an aide to its chief, the personal representative of Adolf Eichmann. The latter was Head of the Jewish Affairs office at Gestapo headquarters in Berlin, eventually captured, tried and executed by the State of Israel in 1962. By the end of the war, this small department had presided over the deportation of seventy-five thousand, seven hundred Jews from France, most of them to Auschwitz.'

For economy the Crown had restricted the evidence against Schwermann to operations in Paris during 1942. The case would focus on his participation in the notorious 'Vél d'Hiv' round-up (code-named 'Vent Printanier', or 'Spring Wind'), and the destruction of a smuggling ring whose purpose had been to save some of the children likely to be arrested.

Mr Penshaw went on to explain that at 4 a.m. on 16th July 1942, 888 arrest squads broke into Jewish homes throughout the city. For two days, amid screams and shouts, young and old were hauled through the streets to collection points. Coaches, once used for public transport, took them away – either to the Vélodrome d'Hiver, or to Drancy, an unfinished housing complex on the edge of the city. Time and again these squads returned to the old Jewish quarter, whose history stretched back to the Middle Ages and whose winding streets had been a refuge since the Revolution. News of the round-up spread like fire. Panic set in. Over a hundred people committed suicide. Paris watched, dumbstruck. No one could have foreseen this aspect of Occupation – 12,884 people vanished, including 4051 children.

In due course, as the Defence formally admitted, families taken in the Vél d'Hiv round-up were first sent to other internment centres in the Loiret, either Pithiviers or Beaune-la-Rolande (known as the 'Loiret Camps'), or Compiègne. There, the children were separated from their families before being transferred to Drancy. The parents were deported to Auschwitz. The children, all under sixteen, later made the same journey and suffered the same fate. It was thought 300 or so may have survived.

In the months prior to 'Spring Wind', rumours of a massive round-up spread throughout Paris. A group of young French students, all roughly Schwermann's age, decided to act. Led by Jacques Fougères, a smuggling ring known as The Round Table was formed, linked to Jewish and other Resistance groups in the city. The aim was to collect Jewish children from various 'drop off' points in Paris and hide them in monasteries outside the city. From there they would be taken to Switzerland. It was an heroic and tragic effort. Heroic because they could never have protected the thousands at risk; tragic because they were all captured in the days before the round-up began.

So what bearing did these events have upon the young German officer now brought before the court in the autumn of his life? He was a member of the team that planned 'Spring Wind'; he stalked the rue des Rosiers and the rue des Blancs-Manteaux, overseeing wave after wave of arrests; he supervised the final departure of children from Drancy to Auschwitz. And as for The Round Table, he managed to infiltrate its ranks and secured the arrest of each member, before they could save any more children from the coming storm. The students were later transported to Mauthausen concentration camp where they met their deaths. The Jury would see the personal commendation Schwermann received from Eichmann, congratulating him on this 'achievement'.

Mr Penshaw emphasised the importance of viewing these events in the harsh light of the times. Hundreds of thousands of Jews had fled Germany during the 1930s, driven out by violence and the repressive legal machinery of the State. Many had sought refuge in France. But France fell, and within months of the Germans setting up their administration in Paris, they moved against the Jews. A census was ordered; businesses were seized; the first arrests took place in May 1941, with further round-ups in August and December. Then, on 20th January 1942, at a villa on the shore of the Wannsee, near Berlin, the Nazi government formally decided the fate of all European Jews. A 'Final Solution' was under way which required the urgent 'evacuation' of Jews 'to the East'. Two months later, on 27th March 1942, the first trainload of victims left Paris for Auschwitz. The 'evacuations' had begun, and the mass killing of Jews deported from France would now get under way.

Mr Penshaw concluded:

'The Prosecution case against Schwermann is simply this: he was inextricably involved in the machinery of death. And he must have known that execution or serious harm awaited those who were deported to the camps. If you, the jury, are sure this man was part of that enterprise then you must find him guilty of murder in relation to each of the charges laid against him.'

Lucy covered her face with her shawl and mumbled a sort of prayer to the ether: that Victor Brionne would come forward; that Schwermann would be convicted; and that Agnes would die in peace. Raising her head she looked to the man in the cardigan beside her, and saw the thin tears streaming down his face.

Chapter Twenty-Seven

1

Anselm left Mr Roderick Kemble QC prostrate in a cab at Waterloo and hurried through the Eurostar terminal, finding his seat a matter of minutes before the train lurched forward.

He gloomily skimmed a cutting on The Round Table Wilf had given to him. He'd shown the text to Roddy, who'd glanced over it while he ate, raising an aimless question as to why Jacques was interrogated in the June when the ring was not broken until the July. With affection, Anselm had filled the Master's glass. As expected Roddy appeared not to have read the cutting. The June arrest had had nothing to do with the events of the following month. Only a Silk of Roddy's standing could get away with that sort of blunder – and he did, frequently, with breathtaking aplomb.

Once in Paris, Anselm took a room in a cheap hotel near Sacré Coeur. The next morning he set off for the Boulevard de Courcelles, near Parc Monceau, to the Fougères home, wondering how he was going to phrase the application of the law to the death of their son.

All the witnesses were agreed on the basic facts: the pensioner, Mr Ogden, had grabbed the man with the white beard (Milby never named him. Instead he used a rather coarse term of art). The man with the beard had told him to let go, but Mr Ogden had then drawn back his fist. So the other had struck out. At that point Pascal Fougères had slipped and fallen, banging his

231

head. The terms of the conversation prior to the altercation had also been agreed. But, as the investigating officer repeatedly pointed out to the outraged witnesses, nothing said by the man with the beard constituted a criminal offence. Milby told Anselm that the police would have liked to nail him, ideally with a manslaughter charge under the doctrine of transferred malice – on the understanding that the backhand slap directed at Mr Ogden technically 'shifted' to Pascal. But that ignored the only compelling legal analysis: Mr Ogden was the aggressor and the response of his victim was not an unlawful act. The brute fact was that the terms of every other potential charge could not be stretched to accommodate the offensiveness of the victim.

After it became known that Pascal had died, the man with the white beard informed the police that he would not insist on charges being laid against Mr Ogden.

2

Etienne was the son of Claude Fougères and the nephew of Jacques, the Resistance hero. After the war the family had remained in the South – until the eighties when Etienne's political career rose from local to national level. That prompted the return to Paris. The house had been rented out for nearly forty years, so it was a real homecoming.

'And then, just when things got back to where they were before the war, Pascal was taken away.'

Anselm gleaned this and more from the mumbling old butler who opened the great black front door and took him slowly to a drawing room on the third floor.

Monsieur and Madame Fougères were subdued elegance

232

itself, sitting apart on either end of a pink chaise longue, their faces darkened by grief. Anselm moved gently over the terrain of sympathy, explaining the predicament faced by the police enquiry. To his surprise, they understood perfectly. They made no complaint: no sallies against the Law; no plea for a fairer world. They did not expect the legal system to give them something it was not designed, and could not be designed, to produce: a civic response proportionate to their loss. But while he spoke Anselm observed, painfully, the cleft that had opened between mother and father. It was freshly cut.

'I begged him not to go after that man. Begged him. But he would not listen,' said Etienne.

Monique Fougères closed her eyes slowly, her hands cupped upon her lap.

'I wish he'd left the past alone,' said Etienne. 'It's not a safe place while it touches on the living.'

Madame Fougères lowered her head, speaking quietly. 'Tell me anything he said, Father, anything at all. I want to imagine his voice.'

'We only spoke about Schwermann . . . and someone called Agnes.'

Anselm threw in the last half-truth as the door opened and the butler brought forth tea. Etienne's facial muscles had seized. The butler poured. Etienne reached for a small cup.

'Agnes?' he said, enquiringly.

'Yes. I got the impression she was once known to the family.'

'No, I'm afraid not.'

Anselm thought: you're lying. He said, 'Apparently she had a child.'

'Pardon?' said Etienne, an eyebrow raised, offering milk for the English palate.

233

'A child.'

'I'm sorry, no. As far as I know, Jacques never knew anyone called Agnes.'

Anselm felt the warm trembling of success: we were talking about Pascal, not Jacques . . .

Monique Fougères looked at her husband across a void. The butler softly closed the doors and the cleft between mother and father fell open wide.

3

By the great entrance cars chased each other down the Boulevard de Courcelles. The butler stepped outside with Anselm, his eyes towards the ornate gates of Parc Monceau. He said, 'I knew Agnes Aubret.'

Anselm only just caught the words.

'I held her child.'

The raucous sound of children spilled out from the park, scattering through the passing cars.

'Is she alive?' The butler spoke as though he would die.

'I'm not sure, but I think so. I've met a young woman who knows her.'

The butler pushed his hand deep into his pocket and produced a tattered envelope.

'Father, please, find out if she's alive. Give her this. It's from Jacques. He asked me to get it to her after the war, if he was caught and she survived.'

Anselm took the envelope.

'Say Mr Snyman has borne it for fifty years.'

The butler stepped back and the door swung shut. Anselm stood still, slightly stunned. He took another walk through the park to calm himself. It was crawling with children on their lunch break, arriving in cohorts from a nearby school. He paused by the gates into Avenue Hoche. A group entered two by two, each child wearing a white sash. And on the sash was the name of the school and a telephone number so that not one of them could be lost.

Chapter Twenty-Eight

The stout figure in the witness box was dressed in black and wore round bottle-end glasses. She did not require the interpreter and answered Mr Penshaw's questions with a disturbingly loud and deep voice.

'Your name, please, Madame?' said Mr Penshaw.

'Collette Beaussart.'

'You were born in Paris on 4th October 1918?'

'Yes.'

'You are now seventy-seven years of age?'

'I am.'

'You are a Knight of the Legion of Honour?'

'I am.'

'You were decorated by General de Gaulle at the Invalides in 1946?'

'I was.'

'Please confirm the following. You were a journalist and condemned the Nazi leadership prior to the fall of France and afterwards. You were arrested on 18th February 1942. You were deported. You are a survivor of Drancy, Auschwitz and Ravensbrück.'

'I am.'

Before calling any evidence, Mr Penshaw told the jury he intended to present the first witness, Madame Beaussart, out of chronological order so as to give them a constant reminder of what the case was really about. 'And so, ladies and gentlemen, in the coming days when you are listening to bare, lifeless facts about train timetables or the method used to fill in a deportation record, remember well what Madame Beaussart will now relate.'

Lucy listened with a sort of proprietorial desperation. She had recognised the name. Collette Beaussart was the political prisoner Agnes had written about. They'd both got typhus and saved one another through talking . . . about jam. This was the woman who'd claimed Agnes was part of the group to which she belonged, the politicals who were transferred to Ravensbrück. Lucy wanted to stand up, to claim the witness as her friend. But a wall had been built. She would listen, like everyone else; and watch her go, like everyone else.

Madame Beaussart was twenty-four when the gates of Drancy closed behind her. She witnessed the arrival of children taken in the Vél d'Hiv round-up, after separation from their parents. She saw them depart for the East. 'I saw them come. I saw them go.'

The courtroom was utterly quiet, save for Madame Beaussart and the soft scuffle of pen upon paper. Lucy was on the edge of her seat.

'They came in boxcars, all of them under thirteen or fourteen years, the youngest just over a year or so. They were filthy, their bodies covered with sores. Many had dysentery. Attempts to clean them were futile. Some were seriously ill with diphtheria . . . scarlet fever. One of them, naked, asked me why her mother had left her behind. I said she'd only gone away for a while . . .'

Madame Beaussart's voice, loud, wavering, uncompromising, described the horrors of trying to care for the abandoned.

237

'Like the rest of the prisoners, they slept on dirty straw mattresses until their time came to move on. Then their heads were shaved.'

At dawn, Madame Beaussart and other internees brought the children from where they lay, to the courtyard. Some didn't even have shoes. In groups of fifty they were packed on to buses. Each bore the number of a freight carriage. A thousand left at a time for the station at Bourget.

It was Schwermann who, with others, supervised their departure.

'He paced back and forth, impatiently, lists in hand, his face like stone, barking orders. I can still see the children . . . and I hear now the engines that took them away.'

Mr Penshaw sat down.

'Madame Beaussart,' said a yielding, compassionate voice. It was Mr Bartlett. He stood perfectly still, rotating a pencil between his fingers. 'Should you wish to sit down at any time, please do not hesitate to ask his Lordship.'

'Thank you, but no.'

'Could you please describe what you can recall about the appearance of the camp at Drancy?'

'I can remember it all.'

'Then choose the details which you remember best.'

'I said I can remember everything, sir. I cannot forget.'

'You remember the armed guards?'

'They were French, my own countrymen.'

'The provision of electricity?'

'Almost entirely lacking.'

'How many prisoners to a room?'

'About fifty.'

'Sleeping on what?'

238

'Bunk beds, planks. Many slept on plain straw.'

'If I may say so, Madame Beaussart, your memory is without fault.'

Lucy glanced at the judge, his head still, his hand writing down every word as it fell.

Mr Bartlett picked up a sheet of paper. He seemed to hover over its contents, then spoke in the same even, encouraging voice.

'Do you recollect anything in particular about Mr Schwermann's appearance?'

'He was very handsome, with blond hair standing out against his black uniform.'

'Let me test your memory again, Madame.' Mr Bartlett was smiling winsomely. 'Do you recall the leather riding breeches?'

'Yes, I do. They shone.'

Mr Bartlett paused to look at the sheet of paper.

'You would agree this form of dress was distinctive?'

'Oh yes.'

'Idiosyncratic?'

'Yes.'

'Utterly memorable?'

'Yes.'

'Almost a caricature of a German officer, the sort of thing you've seen in the films?'

'No, not in films. I don't watch them. I can't bear to. I have pictures of my own and they've never gone away. I cannot forget that man and what he did. Never, never, never.'

Madame Beaussart covered her mouth.

'Would you like a glass of water, Madame?'

She nodded. And with shaking hands she tried to drink, spilling water over her fingers.

The judge put down his pen, saying, 'Do take your time.'

'I'm sorry,' she mumbled, 'I've waited all my life for this moment.'

'We all understand,' said the judge.

Mr Bartlett waited until Madame Beaussart was ready to continue and then he handed the sheet of paper to the usher, to be passed on to the witness.

'Would you be so kind as to look at this photograph?'

The witness took off her glasses and produced another pair from a small pouch.

'That is the man you have been describing, isn't it?'

Without hesitation she replied, 'Yes, that is him. Schwermann.'

'And of that you are sure?'

'Yes.'

'His appearance is etched in your memory?'

'Yes.'

'Look again, Madame. Is there nothing that causes you to doubt your judgment? It was, after all, over fifty years ago.'

'I will never forget the man who forced those children on to the buses.'

Inching towards the jury, Mr Bartlett said: 'Madame Beaussart, you have been right about everything you have told the court today. Except in one important detail. But let me make it plain, I do not challenge your candour. The man in the photograph did supervise deportations from Drancy. He has already been convicted by a German court, in a trial you were unable to attend because of a serious illness from which, thankfully, you have recovered.'

Madame Beaussart, bewildered, could not speak.

'You have correctly identified someone else, not Mr Schwermann. I will supply the details to the court in due course.'

He sat down, the flap of his silk gown disturbing loose papers laid out neatly on the table before him.

Chapter Twenty-Nine

1

Anselm got back to Larkwood just after Vespers, in time for a brief conference with Father Andrew before supper. They sat in the Prior's study, looking out over the cloister garth. It was a calm evening and long shadows lay on the neat grass like canvas sheets of scenery fallen flat.

Father Andrew asked, 'How did they respond when you said the police were powerless?'

'With inspiring equanimity. I'd prepared myself for bewildered anger.'

'Those close to politics often understand better than most the limits of the law.'

'There was something between them though, coming I think from the mother, something like an accusation. That is where the anger lay, the confusion. And by accident I think I trespassed upon it.'

'Anselm,' said the Prior dryly, 'most of your accidents stem from intuition let loose. What did you say?'

'We were talking about Pascal and I mentioned Agnes, that she had had a child, and I asked if she'd ever been known to the family.'

'And?'

'The mother said absolutely nothing but the father said

241

Jacques never knew anyone called Agnes ... we weren't talking about Jacques but he made the link.'

'And you call that an accident?'

Anselm remonstrated, 'Not far off. My best cross-examinations were always by mistake. I didn't realise how clever it looked until it was done.'

The Prior smiled with faint indulgence. Anselm continued, 'Anyway, I then had a most peculiar encounter with the butler. Throughout he pours the tea, sidles in, says nothing, sidles out ... but when he shows me the door he tells me he knew Agnes and held her child. He then gives me a letter to deliver to Agnes from Jacques, a letter he'd guarded since the war on the off-chance she survived.'

The two monks pondered in silence. Frowning, Father Andrew said, 'It is clear from what Max Nightingale said to you that his grandfather, somehow, knew both Jacques and Agnes. In this whole tragic business they seem to be the only ones to have reduced him to a state of panic. So they must have come across each other during the war ...' He rounded on Anselm: 'What was that riddle you were told about Schwermann at Les Moineaux?'

'That he had risked his life to save life.'

The Prior tilted his head as though straining to catch distant voices. His glittering eyes vanished behind long creases ... but whatever he'd sensed was slipping out of reach.

The bell rang for supper. Anselm said, 'The strange thing is, how do Etienne Fougères and his wife come to know about Agnes and her child?'

They rose and entered the corridor. The busy sound of other feet heading down to the refectory echoed from a stairwell. The Prior replied, 'Jacques' family must have passed it on after his death' – he followed his insight through – 'and in due course Etienne told his wife . . . but they did not tell their son, Pascal . . . a secret known by a paid servant, a butler . . . now, why's that?'

Intuition failed them both and they went into the refectory.

2

The evening meal was the usual emetic blend of leftovers from the guesthouse. Anselm pushed something purple around his plate. There would be no knowing what it had been in its many previous lives. Afterwards, the community filed into the common room for recreation, where Anselm joined Wilf in his usual corner by the aspidistra that no one watered but yet miraculously never died. It was one of Wilf's greatest attributes that he used events in his life as a prompt for research into things about which he knew nothing. After Schwermann's arrival he had quietly buried himself in reading about the Occupation and its aftermath. He liked to share his findings and Anselm enjoyed his reported forays, marked as they were by the wonder of David Bellamy having found a new snail in the garden.

'Wartime creates its own unique moral dilemmas,' uttered Wilf with Delphic calm, inviting a request for more disclosure.

'Why's that?' obliged Anselm.

'Well,' said Wilf, gratified and settling back, 'there's the strange case of Paul Touvier. A traditionalist Catholic but in the Vichy Milice. Pushed into it by his father and a priest. So he's French, policing the French for the Germans.'

'A collaborator,' contributed Anselm obviously.

'Indeed. And his job was to combat the Resistance.'

'Not a very devout thing to do.'

'Bear with me, Father. For therein lies an interesting conundrum. The Resistance assassinated the Vichy minister of information in 1944. The Germans wanted reprisals. According to Touvier, they demanded the execution of a hundred Jews. He says he bargained them down to thirty, and ordered the deaths of seven, at Rillieux-la-Pape, as an appeasement to save the remaining twenty-three.'

'Where's the devotion in that?'

'Well, there isn't any, of course. Only it set me thinking. Here is a man who will, in due course, be convicted in absentia of treason. I don't know any more about him, and what he said was probably nonsense, but it occurred to me that it was only those who collaborated who were in a position to bargain with the Nazis if the opportunity arose. That is not, of course, a reason for collaborating. But it suggests an interesting abstract principle: in certain situations, only someone who's lost himself can do the good deed, even though he can never make atonement for what he has done.'

A shared pause of reflection ensued. Wilf picked up a newspaper, found the crossword and said: 'Even so, I can't for the life of me understand why Touvier was hidden in a monastery.'

'Pardon?' said Anselm.

Wilf repeated his observation, frowning gravely at the first clue. 'Fundamentalists, apparently. *Intégristes*. Not our cup of tea.' A touch complicated, he added, because Touvier had been pardoned by Pompidou. Ten years later he went into hiding when it transpired he could still be prosecuted. He was eventually convicted of the Rillieux murders in 1994, the first Frenchman to go down for war-related crimes against humanity.

'Hideously embarrassing for the Church when they caught him, of course,' pursued Wilf, laying the paper on his lap, 'if only because it dredged up the ecclesiastical compromises of the past.' During the war, he said, the Church had been in a very difficult position. Pétain and Vichy reintroduced support that had been previously withdrawn by a viciously anti-clerical state. An alliance grew that was far too cosy. 'It was all rather complicated.'

Slightly uneasy, Anselm left Wilf to his crossword. As he got ready to clean the refectory floor he all but heard another voice, whispering, and he saw the luminous eyes of Cardinal Vincenzi: 'It's all rather complicated.'

Chapter Thirty

1

The court rose for the day after Mr Bartlett had made his surprising announcement that followed the completion of Madame Beaussart's evidence.

'That seems a good place to stop, gentlemen,' said Mr Justice Pollbrook.

Bile stung Lucy's gut and she thought bitterly: You're right. There's no point in going on. It's a mess; a bloody, senseless mess. Max Nightingale hurriedly brushed by, his mouth set tight. The man in the cardigan beside her stood to make way, his features relaxed as if by an expectation painfully fulfilled. Lucy left the court in a sort of panic, as though the air had swollen with a stench. She ran to St Paul's tube station and shoved herself into the doorway of a heaving train. Elbows, staking their claim, stiffened. The carriage door slid shut, scraping across her back. I endure this, she thought, so that I can give my grandmother a summary of 'the day's play'. That's what one barrister had called it.

The opening of the trial had brought focus to Lucy's life, lost since the death of Pascal. Struggling to attend lectures, she had confided in her tutor, a man who seemed to apprehend a fear she had not even mentioned: the prospect of dropping out of the course, a second failure from which she might not recover.

He referred Lucy to a college counsellor called Myriam Anderson. Talking helped to a degree; but death, of all experiences, could only be accommodated through further suffering, and entangled with that prospect was the certain death of Agnes. These two events, one past, the other to come, lay like a frame on either side of the trial, giving it shape. Myriam had said: 'It's tempting to separate life's problems into miniatures — that's when the trouble starts. Your greatest asset is that you see the single canvas.' Myriam watched Lucy closely before saying, 'Don't rule out another death.'

'Sorry?'

'Another death — an outcome to this trial that defeats your hope.'

By the time Lucy reached Hammersmith, the long shadows of evening lay as still as paint, losing depth and shape as the light withdrew. She pushed her key into Agnes' front door lock and stepped inside, slipping on the wet tiles and crashing into the wall. Bloody Wilma.

Agnes could no longer speak or walk. A nurse came twice a week. Susan paid a visit every other day. As for Freddie, the monumental unease that had once kept him apart from Agnes seemed to be crumbling, not at the edges but deep down in its foundations. Lucy saw a pallor spread across his face whenever he came to Chiswick Mall: he simply could not bear to witness the slow, tortured decline that was received by Agnes with such shattering calm.

Lucy crept down the dark corridor towards the thin band of orange light across the floor. She stood at the door, pushing it silently ajar. Agnes lay completely still. So still Lucy thought she had gone. Her heart raced. And then Agnes lifted one arm,

247

like an ailing Caesar at the games. Lucy approached and sat by
the bed.

'The trial's under way.'

A nod.

'We heard from Madame Beaussart today, the journalist you
met in Auschwitz, the one who dreamed about making jam
and you dreamed about eating it. You wrote about her.'

A nod.

'She remembers almost everything.'

Lucy could go no further.

Agnes didn't respond. Her face could not be read; only her
eyes, and they were turned to one side. Had she already heard
the news – about the first witness for the Crown abandoning
the stand, exclaiming through her tears that she *did* remember
Schwermann? Had she heard about Mr Bartlett's surprise
announcement to the court? These were things Lucy would
not say, not to Schwermann's most secret victim, lying here
unable to reply. Agnes would discover them soon enough when
Wilma declaimed from *The Times* report next morning.

Agnes moved her head towards the bedside table and her
alphabet card. She had a simple method. After pointing out the
letters of a word, she paused and rested her hand. Then she
spelled out the next word. It was the lightness of her wrist,
moving like a conductor, and that pause, still fingers upon her
breast between measures, that broke Lucy down.

P-A-S-C-A-L

A long pause followed: this introduced the subject she wanted
to talk about, like a heading.

T-R-Y

Pause.

T-O

248

Pause.

C-A-L-M

Pause.

T-H-E

Pause.

F-I-R-E

Pause.

W-I-T-H-O-U-T

Pause.

P-U-T-T-I-N-G

Pause.

I-T

Pause.

O-U-T

Pause.

Lucy nodded gratefully, reaching out to meet the anxiety, the entreaty deep within her grandmother's blue eyes. Sensing the question that was trapped in Agnes' head she added, 'The college are being enormously helpful. They've told me to take a few weeks off. They're sure I can catch up.'

Agnes touched Lucy's arm, and then continued:

I-F

Pause.

V-I-C-T-O-R

Pause.

A-P-P-E-A-R-S

Pause.

I

Pause.

M-U-S-T

Pause.

S-E-E

Pause.

H-I-M

Pause.

B-E-F-O-R-E

Pause.

I

Pause.

D-I-E

Lucy stroked her grandmother's shaking hand. Agnes couldn't point for long. Anguish pulled down the corners of her mouth.

'Gran, I think he's gone for good.'

Agnes shook her head.

H-E

Pause.

W-I-L-L

Pause.

T-U-R-N

Pause.

U-P

Lucy lifted her grandmother's hand again and smoothed the skin, as if to ease a deep bruise, the wound that still believed an old friend might yet turn up to redeem himself. So much of their relating had now been transferred to a meeting of hands. It replaced the voluntary silence that had once been a communion. Lucy reached over and took the alphabet card. She had something to say that had never been said:

I

Pause.

L-O-V-E

Pause.

250

The handle of the door turned and Wilma came in with the bowl of ice cubes, a saucer and a teaspoon.

The vestibule floor was dry and safe to walk upon when Lucy left. On the way out she walked past the front room. It was no longer used. Agnes had left it for ever. The piano, the television and the furniture stood waiting for joking removal men in white overalls.

2

The morning after his return from Paris, Anselm went to the library to write some letters, mindful of Johnson's observation that a man should keep his friendships in constant repair. He had just sealed an envelope when Father Bernard, the cellarer, put his head round the door. There was a telephone call for Anselm that had been transferred by Sylvester to the kitchen. There was no point in trying to get him to re-direct it. They both hurried down the stairs, habits flapping like wide streamers on a kite that refused to get off the ground.

The call was from Detective Superintendent Milby, enquiring how the visit to the Fougères family had transpired. Anselm explained, concluding with the ambiguous remark, 'I'm very glad I went.' Milby then transferred the line to DI Armstrong's extension.

'I think we've found Victor Brionne,' were her first words.

'Good God.'

'Not exactly, others were involved. The person who came to see you was almost certainly Robert Brownlow. He's fifty-five and lives on the north-east coast in a place called Cullercoats.

251

His father, Victor Brownlow, lives in London – Stamford Hill. The place looks shut up and has been for months according to the postman. The son, however, pays rates on a property on Holy Island, "Pilgrim's Rest". We've had local police drive around in civvies and it looks like that's where he's gone to ground.'

'I'll give you a ring as soon as I have spoken to him.'

'You may as well tell him to contact me. He can't go on running, not at his age.'

'I will.'

Anselm fished out a pencil from his habit pocket and said, 'I've another favour to ask.'

'I hope you're not going to surprise me again, Father.'

'No, this is different. Can I have Lucy Embleton's telephone number? I've got a letter for someone she knows.'

'Father, since I came to Larkwood Priory I've met nothing but mysteries.'

Anselm walked back to the library deep in thought and collected his correspondence, before strolling into the village to post them. On the way he glimpsed a flaming red Fiat Punto with a foreign number plate turning towards Larkwood. It was oddly familiar, but Anselm applied himself to another pressing distraction. Something was nagging at the back of his mind and he could not entice it forward. But he was absolutely certain of one thing: the name Brownlow was familiar, and it went back to his schooldays.

3

Lucy broke her journey home by calling unannounced upon

252

Cathy Glenton. They'd only spoken to each other once since Pascal's death, when Lucy rang to tell her what had happened. After that Lucy had slipped out of circulation. A couple of messages on her answer machine from Cathy had not been returned. But on leaving Chiswick Mall, Lucy suddenly felt the urge to see her old friend.

The door opened narrowly and Cathy peeped over a lock-chain. Lucy saw the white cotton bathrobe and the towel turban around her head. 'Is it too late?'

'Nope.'

They shuffled into the kitchen. 'So, what are you up to?' asked Cathy, producing two bottles of beer from the fridge.

'Attending a war crimes trial.'

'Why?'

'Long, long story. I don't want to talk about it.'

'Fine. How's your grandmother?'

'Dying slowly. I don't want to talk about that either.'

'Fine.'

Cathy sat in the corner of the settee, her legs tucked beneath her. She stared into the narrow green neck of the bottle and said, 'I'm sorry, so sorry, for being such a fool.'

'What do you mean?' asked Lucy, kicking off her shoes. She sat against a wall.

'About you and Pascal.'

'Oh,' sighed Lucy with surprise, 'forget it.'

'When you didn't call back I thought you were angry with me.'

'No, no,' replied Lucy with feeling, apologetic. 'I just wanted to be morose on my own. Now I want to be morose with you.'

'Fine.'

253

They drank their beer. 'It's always the same,' said Cathy after a while. 'You get to our age and every now and then you recover the enthusiasm of childhood, but you just get another slap across the face.'

Lucy glanced over to Cathy and said, 'You once told me you never think about the past. That's rubbish, isn't it?'

'Yes.'

Suddenly, without brutality, Lucy asked, 'What happened with Vincent?'

'I screwed up. Monumentally.'

'How?'

'It's astounding, looking back. I mean, he was really different. No interest in a career, money, all that stuff; did lots of charity work, quietly; said great things I wanted to write down . . . and I ended it.'

'Why?'

'One day he got really, really smashed. We had a row about nothing — a wet towel left on the floor — but he called me an ugly bitch.' She put her bottle carefully on the floor. 'The next day I started covering up the scar. He said sorry, didn't mean it, and so on . . . and then I realised what had happened: I'd changed, just like that.' She clicked a thumb and finger. 'I hadn't realised my self-confidence was so fragile. We sort of made up, but I steadily edged him away. All rather self-indulgent, really. I heard the siren call of existential meltdown, thinking it might give me added depths. I suppose I wanted him to chase after me. But he took me at my word. I should have hung on to him.'

'Where is he now?'

'Married to some other divinity.'

'Cathy, I'm sorry.' Lucy felt strangely ashamed of her own appearance.

254

'Don't be. The artwork's only an interim measure. Inside I'm becoming a goddess that soars over all flesh. There. Are you morose now?'

'Yes.'

'So am I. Let's play Snap.'

Chapter Thirty-One

1

Anselm got back from the post office in time for lunch, which proved to be an unspeakable combination of cold pasta and beetroot without any other benediction to hold them together. Brother Jerome's news bulletin was a helpful distraction, containing an interesting item on the trial. Anselm determined to read the whole report once he'd escaped from the refectory. Meanwhile, an agenda fell into place: he would see Lucy Embleton and Salomon Lachaise the next day, before heading north to confront Victor Brionne at the weekend – another cold prospect that now filled him with dread. By Sunday night, after sending a fax to Cardinal Vincenzi, his involvement in the whole affair would be over. After lunch Anselm spoke to the Prior and received the necessary permissions. He then pinched the newspaper from the library and made for his bench by the Priory ruins.

After Bartlett had cross-examined Madame Beaussart, he'd surprised the court by volunteering to disclose his client's defence. As the judge had observed, Schwermann was under no obligation to do so, but Bartlett had said he deemed it right since 'it could only assist the jury in this particularly difficult case'. Not quite, thought Anselm. It was a ploy to get round the fact Schwermann had not cooperated with the police. A 'No Reply' interview always looked suspicious, even if it did pay homage to Goethe. So Bartlett was making Schwermann look as helpful as possible to the jury. And he must have chosen his moment, having got the answers he needed from the witness. Showing Madame Beaussart the photograph was a risky shot, but Bartlett must have noticed the prosecution didn't formally prove *how* she knew Schwermann. In the absence of that foundation Bartlett had crept upon her warily, his instinct for the kill growing warm.

Bartlett had said that Schwermann had occupied a minor clerical post in the SS; had never visited a concentration camp; and had never 'witnessed any of the horrific sights so forcefully described by the courageous lady whose testimony we have just heard'. Schwermann admitted he knew the deportees were going to Auschwitz but he believed this was a staging post on the way to Palestine, part of a wider policy of forced emigration. And as for the smuggling ring, he accepted that he brought to the attention of his superiors information that had come into his possession, but he had no influence or insight into what would happen to them afterwards. While there was no burden on the Defendant to prove his innocence, in this particular case the Prosecution would be shown to flounder without particulars, clutching at circumstantial evidence.

So that was the strategy: four big points, just as Roddy had predicted – three overt and one concealed. The first, a complete denial of ever having seen the machinery of a death camp. Second, a sincere belief that 'evacuation' meant just what it said. And third, the fate of the smuggling ring had been handed over to others. Technically, this meant Schwermann denied being part of a joint enterprise whose object or possible outcome was death or serious harm. Bartlett sensibly avoided stating his fourth argument because its inherently comic properties

257

undermined its force: the 'I was only obeying orders' defence. But Anselm knew the jurors would be led along by frequent references to Schwermann's youth, his lowly rank and the power of others. There would be no laughter and the point would be forcibly made. It might even coalesce into pity.

Bartlett's disclosure, however, was alarming in other respects: there was no reference to Les Moineaux and no mention of Schwermann having saved life rather than taken it away. The riddle remained an unexplained secret. Anselm had just turned to the obituary pages in search of light entertainment when he heard a sober voice at his elbow.

'Father, if we hadn't shared the cup of plenty I'd think you were hiding from me.'

Anselm blenched.

'I thought I'd give my legs a big stretch, before hitting São Paulo. And I have a few answers from the realm of Sticky Fingers.'

2

Lucy left the court half an hour before the end of the morning session in order to meet Father Anselm, the monk. She had been surprised to hear his voice on the telephone the night before. He was coming to London and had an important matter to discuss with her. He'd told her not to worry. They met outside St Paul's Cathedral and sat on the steps. Apparently it was something he'd often done when he'd been at the Bar, taking a breather from a savaging at the Old Bailey. 'That court,' he said, 'was the scene of some of my more spectacular failures.'

After a moment's reflection the monk said, 'Lucy, I have a

258

letter from a man who knew Agnes Aubret. It was written during the war by Jacques Fougères, the father of her child, and given to this man for safe-keeping, to be delivered to Agnes if she survived the war. He has asked me to deliver it to her. I believe you know the Agnes I seek.'

'I do, she's my grandmother.' The rapid mix of nausea and wonder acted for the moment like a sedative. She spoke with a calculation she did not possess. 'She has motor neurone disease. She can't walk or talk but she understands everything. Her inner life is all she has left. Can I ask who gave you the letter?'

'Mr Snyman. I'm sorry, the name means nothing to me.'

'He was a Jewish refugee, from country after country. He played the cello, with my grandmother at the piano. I've never heard her play but you can tell, once you know, by the look of her hands . . . the fingers are long and beautiful and they're always reaching out for something.' Completely without warning she started to cry, not tragic sobs, cracked cheeks and hissing valves, just free-flowing water upon smooth ivory skin; water that would not stop, that she did not want to stop, that she wanted to run for ever, down her face, her body, and into the sea. 'She was a member of The Round Table. She saved children but lost her own. She survived Auschwitz and Ravensbrück and saved two other children; one, my aunt, who died without being told, and the other, my father, who still doesn't know. Now she lies dying, unable to speak, unable to move; she's lost everything, everything, except her breath. Tell me, if you know, because I don't, why can't *she* be given something, just this once, before she dies?'

'I suspect this won't surprise you,' said the monk, 'but there aren't any satisfactory answers to questions like that. In a funny way all we can do is listen. Can I give you some consolation?'

259

'Please do.'

'The best people I have ever met are the ones who've carried on listening.'

Lucy thought of Agnes, often silent, always attentive in a way that was foreign to all those around her.

'And another is this,' said the monk. 'If you keep listening, you still don't get any answers but more often than not the questions slip out of reach and cease to be questions. The bad news is that it takes about ten years.'

'Thanks. And what about the ones that stay?'

'We've a choice – either the whole shebang's absurd . . . or it's a mystery.'

Again Lucy thought of Agnes, absurd to none, a mystery to anyone who knew her. Rummaging for a handkerchief, her eyes swollen and smarting, she said, 'I'll arrange a meeting for you with my grandmother, but it will have to be after the trial. She's entirely focused on its outcome. A letter from Jacques, now, could overwhelm her.'

The monk shuffled on the step. He said, 'This weekend I hope to meet Victor Brionne.'

A suffocating exhilaration rose and pressed against Lucy's chest as she spoke: 'I must talk to him.'

'That would be most unwise. If it became known that someone who had been observing the trial had spoken to a key witness, all hell would let loose . . . or, indeed, if I said anything to him on your behalf. You will have to let things run their course.'

Lucy could only laugh. The trial itself had now silenced whatever she could have said on Agnes' behalf. The displacement of Agnes was complete. She said, still laughing hoarsely, 'I had hoped to make sure Brionne told the truth about Schwermann.'

The monk's face darkened. 'Perhaps he will.'

'Take it from me,' said Lucy miserably, 'he won't.'

Strangely sad, and with compassion, the monk said, 'If Victor Brionne gives evidence at the trial, I hope he doesn't disappoint you.'

Before Lucy could remonstrate he changed the subject. 'You must have found the death of Pascal an awful shock.'

'I did. I still do.' Lucy watched the busy pedestrians walking criss-cross on the pavement below. They'd finish work tonight and go for a drink, unwind and complain about the boss or their mortgage; then they'd go home. 'One of the reasons he met Max Nightingale was to say he had nothing against him. Frankly, I couldn't see the point.'

Father Anselm mused a little and said, 'When I first became a monk, there was an old member of the community, a dreadful chap, always cross, murmuring a lot as we say in our way of life. When he was dying I went to see him and he said, "Anselm, all that matters are tiny reconciliations. Be reconciled whenever you get the chance." At the time it struck me as rather sad, but later I wondered if he'd made a discovery bigger than himself.'

Lucy thought Pascal would have agreed. Herself? Yes, but not yet, some other time. She said, 'Have you any consolations for the grief-stricken?'

'No. Terrible business. Nothing to recommend it whatsoever.'

'We're agreed.'

They stood. 'I have to go,' said the monk, 'I've another appointment. You're always welcome to spend some time at Larkwood.'

'I'm not sure I believe anything.'

'You don't have to.'

With that he held out his hand, suddenly reserved. They

261

shook, and then she watched him disappear among the suits and briefcases.

3

Anselm slipped down a side street to an Italian restaurant from which Roddy had been banned in 1975. Salomon Lachaise was waiting for him. Anselm apologised for being late.

'How's the trial progressing?'

'This morning we've had a specialist on Resistance operations in Paris telling us about The Round Table. She's thirty-eight, authoritative in relation to the many documents of the period, but she wasn't there. It is as I anticipated. There are so few left from that time. Now is the era of the expert.'

Anselm poured them each a glass of wine from a carafe. Salomon Lachaise said, 'She finished with an account of how Father Rochet and Jacques Fougères died at Mauthausen. It wasn't, as for so many others, through the weight of stones in the quarry, or by hanging, or by having the dogs set upon them. A guard beat Father Rochet with a lash. Fougères intervened. At gunpoint they were forced onto the electric fencing. They walked arm in arm, watched by a silent, starving crowd.'

The delightful ritual of shared eating suddenly lost its simplicity.

'The Defendant brought about the end of The Round Table,' said Salomon Lachaise, 'although we are not told how he learned of its work. His subsequent diligence attracted a personal commendation from Eichmann; not, I think, an accolade I would send home to my mother.'

'No,' said Anselm.

'The evidence is given with due ceremony,' said Salomon Lachaise. 'The scribes bend over their pages, writing down what is said as though nothing should be lost.'

The waiter came with bread and then vanished, as if his job were done.

'But at times I wonder if the evidence is just a palimpsest, and we'll never find out what's lying beneath the words.'

A kind of resentment burned Anselm's stomach. He didn't want to play a part in the devastation of other people's hope by being the one who forced Victor Brionne into court. Unable to bear that thought he said, by way of distraction, 'Have you spoken to any of the other observers?'

'No.'

'There are two young people, a man and a woman, who go every day.' Anselm described them.

'Yes, I know who you mean. They sometimes sit either side of me.'

'You sit between two extremes. They've even met privately, on the day Pascal Fougères was killed. The man is Max Nightingale, a grandson of the Defendant.'

Salomon Lachaise stiffened and snapped his fingers. 'I thought I recognised him. The lad was there in the woods, by the lake when you and I first met . . .' He seemed caught off-guard by a kind of wonder.

'The woman is the granddaughter of Agnes Embleton. She was a member of The Round Table. She's dying. Why no statement was taken from her defeats me.'

'The names of the smuggling ring were read out this morning. That one was not among them.'

'At that time she was called Aubret.'

Before Salomon Lachaise could reply the raddled waiter reappeared, his eyes fixed on the passing world outside the window. He delivered, in something approaching a song, what seemed like the entire contents of the menu. They listened with awe, like a claque. When he'd finished Salomon Lachaise said, 'Thank you very much indeed, but I have to leave.' Turning to Anselm he said, regretfully, 'The court reconvenes in ten minutes.'

'It's my fault, I'm so sorry.'

'No, no. We will do this another time.' He bowed slightly and left, running as if the building were on fire. Anselm surveyed the table, his appetite gone. He'd chosen this restaurant because it had been a favoured place in his days at the Bar when blessed by an accidental victory. He'd now brought to it a subtle type of failure. That was not something to celebrate. With due ceremony he ate the bread and drank the wine, and quietly slipped out.

4

Lucy sat in the public gallery, absorbed by Father Anselm's words. They repeated themselves in a jumble, as though she were swiftly scanning radio stations, catching partial transmissions. A letter from Jacques Fougères . . . Mr Snyman . . . Victor Brionne . . . Agnes . . . Pascal . . . death . . . reconciliation . . . and that the evidence to come might disappoint her. It was an unusual thing to say, reminiscent of what Myriam Anderson had said about another possible grieving, over the death of a final hope. Her reflection was disturbed by a quiet cough.

264

'May I introduce myself? We sit here every day, and we don't even know each other's names. I am Salomon Lachaise.'

The remark was addressed to both herself and Max Nightingale.

'I thought you might like to join me for tea one afternoon.'

Chapter Thirty-Two

It struck Anselm as a rather peculiar request, though not unprecedented. A guest had arrived unannounced while he had been in London. He'd asked, in broken English, if Anselm, and only Anselm, would hear his confession. He'd said he'd say who he was afterwards. Brother Wilfred had left a note on Anselm's door giving the time arranged – 8.15 p.m., forty-five minutes before Compline.

Anselm sat in the dark of the confessional, slightly uneasy. He didn't notice when the faint grating noise began. It was dispersed by the vast, empty nave and seemed to come from all around, but quietly, without definition, and yet coming closer. The sound of feet moved swiftly over the polished tiles. The door to the confessional opened. A man swore, stumbling on to the kneeler by the grille. A fluid heaving of breath, curiously familiar, rose and fell. The French voice jolted Anselm out of Larkwood on to a landing without a light:

'I haven't been in a confession box for nigh on fifty years.'

'We never got rid of them.'

'That's not what I meant.'

'Sorry. Rather silly of me.'

'I'm not here to confess my sins.'

'There aren't any others you can confess.'

'I've come to reveal the sins of my church, and yours. And if you can still raise your hands in absolution after I'm done,

266

you're a braver monk than me. I'd rather leave it to God himself.'

'Father Chambray,' exclaimed Anselm. 'How on earth did you get here?'

'It took a lot of planning, at my age and in my condition. I could not leave it any longer. I've been following the trial and nothing of what I know has come out. I'll stay for a few days and then I'll go home. First, I've got a question for you. On your life, tell me: have they told you what happened in forty-four?'

'They?'

'Rome.'

'No.'

'Is that why you came banging on my door?'

'Yes.'

Chambray stopped to think. He mumbled, 'Just as I thought . . .'

Anselm leaned towards the grille. 'What are you here to say?'

'They know, and they've kept it quiet, even as the trial has opened up what that bastard did. But I told them. Everything. In forty-five.' Chambray pulled himself off the kneeler and slumped back on a chair. Anselm squinted at the grill. There was nothing but shadow, black as a pit. The breathing grew calmer.

'Now I'll tell you. Because you, too, have been duped.'

'How?'

'Wait,' he snapped, coughing. He paused, settling back. 'They came in the middle of the night, towards the end of August 1944. We didn't find out until the morning Chapter. The Prior, Father Pleyon, said we were going to hide them both until their escape from France was arranged. No explanations given.

A Nazi and a collaborator. Imagine that. In a place that smuggled Jewish children away from their grasping hands.'

A shadow seemed to move in the darkness towards the grille. Chambray, closer, rasped, 'To understand anything you have to look back . . . it's the same here . . .' The presence withdrew, leaving the harsh inflection of the last words.

'It probably begins about 1930 with the election of a Prior, well before my time.' He was tapping his fingers slowly against wood. 'Priory lore had it down as a spat between Father Pleyon and a dark horse, Father Rochet. One an old aristocrat, the other a republican. Pleyon was known as "Le Comte" because he was a popular confessor with a few well-known royalists, and Rochet was "Le Sans-culotte" because he was always banging on about the Revolution, Rights of Man and all that. It was a Priory tradition to have nicknames.'

Anselm, sensing a softening with the opening of memory, asked, 'What was yours?'

Chambray chuckled. '"Le Parieur", because I took bets on decisions made by the Prior.'

The thinning laughter turned to rumbling breath, in and out, in time to the soft tapping of old fingers. He found his thread:

'There were two candidates: Le Comte was the favourite, with a simple but clever chap called Morel as a rank outsider.'

Anselm knew the name. It lay engraved on a plaque on a Priory wall, commemorating an execution yet to come.

'Things turned nasty. Rochet took against Le Comte, which surprised no one because he was from the other end of the pond. The shock was what he did. Everyone said you had to be careful with Rochet.' The voice in the dark was confiding, educating. 'He had some wild ideas, but there was always something in what he said. He saw connections in things most people missed. Read too much. So I'm told, anyway. And looking back on his opposition to Le Comte, he had a crazy suspicion that could never have mattered. But then, ten years later, he was shown to have been right. At the time they just thought Rochet had gone one step too far.'

'What did he do?'

'He disclosed that Le Comte had connections with Action Française and the Camelots du Roi,' Father Chambray replied significantly.

'I see,' breathed Anselm appropriately.

'Does that mean anything to you?' His voice sharpened.

'Sorry, no.'

'Lord . . .' Chambray waited, gathering what patience he could find. 'Extremists, wanting a restoration of the monarchy, with Jews and Freemasons shown the door. Rochet's objection was that they represented the worst aspects of the Middle Ages.'

'What did he mean?'

'Well, I wasn't there, but he meant antagonism to the Jews. The story goes that in the Chapter before the election Rochet said something like, "The Round Table of Christ cannot have a man in the seat of honour who is not a brother to the Jews." And remember, the violence and the desecrations had already begun in Germany. Within a couple of years Hitler would be Chancellor. As I've said, Rochet had a way of seeing things . . .'

'What happened?' asked Anselm.

'Le Comte became Prior. Rochet had gone too far . . . and Pleyon got his revenge.'

Anselm frowned in disbelief. Priors didn't do things like that. But he listened.

'Within the year a young girl from a nearby village died in childbirth. She never named the father. Rumour said it was Rochet, and on the strength of that, so I was told, Pleyon threw him out. He was sent to a parish in the capital.'

'Was there anything to the rumour?'

'Well, it seems he'd applied to leave the priesthood, but then changed his mind after the death . . . Anyway, Pleyon got rid of Rochet . . . and the community ousted Pleyon because a lot of monks thought the removal of Rochet was a settling of scores. That's when I came, under the new Prior, Father Morel.'

'So what happened to Rochet?'

'We next heard from him just before the fall of France, in early 1940. He addressed us all in Chapter. I was only in simple vows but I was allowed to attend because of what he intended to say. That was the only time I met him. He wanted to know if the Priory would join a smuggling ring to get Jewish children out of Paris if the need arose. Who do you think had doubts?'

'Pleyon?'

'Exactly. All dressed up as reasonable enquiry, but there was little enthusiasm. Rochet had foreseen that and he came prepared. Pleyon asked if the ring had a name. It has, Rochet replied. What is it? asked le Comte. "The Round Table," said Rochet. It was a slap across the face from old Sans-culotte. Le Comte didn't have much to say after that. Prior Morel decided to join the scheme, we were all bound to silence and the children began to arrive. And then, in 1942, the pigs turned up and shot the Prior.'

'How did they find out?'

'Wait, I'm coming to that. After Morel's death, Pleyon took over once more; it was a crisis, he was a strong man. And I

270

have to say,' the voice became lighter, searching, as if assailed by unwelcome generosity, 'he led the community with enormous sensitivity. He was a changed man.'

'And he was in place when Schwermann and Brionne arrived in 1944?'

'Yes.'

Chambray had stopped his finger-drumming. He was tiring under the weight of memory. He continued:

'After the execution there was nothing we could do to find out what had happened. We were in the Occupied Zone in the north; we had to wait until the war was over before we could make any enquiries. The opportunity arose the day Schwermann and Brionne turned up. We knew then that the Germans had fled Paris. I asked Pleyon if I could go as a visiting curate to Rochet's parish, to see what I could find out. To my surprise he agreed. Arrangements were made with the Bishop and I left a few days later. By the time I got back Schwermann and his dog had gone, with new names taken from a song. This is what I found out.'

Chambray shuffled in his seat, leaning closer to the grille.

'Rochet was a loner. No one knew of his past as a monk. Adored by his parish. Some said he drank – you know what I mean?'

'I do.'

'Many of his friends were Jews, though none survived the war. The Resistance knew he was up to something but had no idea what it was, so they distrusted him. A Communist, they said. According to the Resistance, The Round Table was broken in one day. Most of the arrests took place simultaneously in the early afternoon of fourteenth July. Rochet was picked up in the evening, drunk. One of the ring, Jacques Fougères, was

271

taken that night at his own home, even though his family had already escaped. For some reason he stayed in Paris, as if waiting for something or someone. No one knows.'

Anselm did. He must have been waiting for Agnes Aubret.

'The Resistance believed Rochet was the traitor. You see, he'd known Brionne from before the war. So the thinking was: Rochet told Brionne, who told Schwermann, and the Germans then arrested Rochet once they'd swept the floor.'

'But why would he do it? He had no reason.'

'Maybe he lost his grip when drunk. Destroying everything around him, good and bad. It happens.'

'Yes, but I'm not persuaded. And I get the impression you're not either.'

'I'm just telling you what everybody else thought. I'll tell you what I think in a minute. I came back to Les Moineaux and told Pleyon everything. Oh, he was ill at ease, especially when I told him I didn't swallow the Resistance line on Rochet. I said it must have been someone else. All he did was nod. He told me he'd used diplomatic family connections to get Schwermann and Brionne into England. But then, and mark this well, I was bound to secrecy. I was not to discuss what I knew or thought with anyone. He said he didn't want speculation about Rochet to divide the community again.'

'So if it wasn't Rochet, who was it?'

The thick breathing rumbled as if it were far off, deep in a cave.

'Who else could have sent them down the river?' asked Anselm quietly.

The reply came, drawn out, inexorably detached. 'Pleyon. He betrayed The Round Table.'

'That's too convenient,' replied Anselm instinctively.

'Think about it.' Chambray's voice rose, harder. 'Why else would Schwermann and Brionne come to Les Moineaux? None of us knew them. How did they know that they would be safe, that the Prior would protect them? They came because they *already knew* he was the one who had betrayed the ring. He was in their power. If he did not do what they asked, they could reveal what he had done. And it was in his interests to help them. He got them out of the country before the reprisals got under way. Don't you see? Pleyon was a collaborator as well. He was saving his own skin.'

Anselm was captivated by the neatness of an argument he had failed to see. Chambray continued:

'It all makes sense. Pleyon was the one who showed Rochet the door all those years ago; he was the one who had doubts about The Round Table scheme in the first place, and when I got back to the Priory after my stint in Paris, he bound me to secrecy . . .'

'But why should he bring about such a catastrophe?'

'He didn't want to. He didn't realise what would happen. He thought they'd just get a warning. But he was wrong. And after the shooting of Prior Morel he was a changed man. Why?'

'Remorse?' asked Anselm.

'Absolutely.'

Chambray was right. Anselm sensed the hardening of loose data into an intractable judgment.

'So it's obvious now, isn't it: Pleyon betrays the ring, thinking it will simply end the scheme – but he hasn't foreseen the firing squad. He becomes a humbled, penitent man. But then, the war over, the two of them arrive, ghosts from his past, reminding him of what he did, claiming him as their brother. He's trapped by what he's done, and he uses his authority and influence to ensure they escape justice.'

He's right, thought Anselm. That is the one explanation that meets all the questions. But now there was another enquiry.

'You said that Rome knew everything?'

'The lot. I wrote it down in 1945, despite Pleyon's order, and sent it to the Prior General. He wrote back saying my report had been passed on to the Vatican. They did nothing. Absolutely nothing. And then Pleyon died of a heart attack a year or so later. I left the Priory in 1948 and haven't been back since. I've never left the Church but I sit on the edge, neither in nor outside. They'll find my body in the porch.'

Anselm groaned, those last words having struck him a blow he so fully understood, for there were many living on that line whom he would reach if he could.

Chambray struggled to his feet and pushed his way out of the box.

'I'll leave you a copy of what I sent to Rome. You can read it for yourself.'

Anselm called out, 'Father, was it you who sent Schwermann's false name to Pascal Fougères?'

The old man rasped, 'No . . . I never learned what it was . . . but I remember the song – "A nightingale sang in Berkeley Square."'

The breathing and shuffling moved slowly away, like that of a wounded animal, until the nave echoed to the sound of its parting. Then there came the opening of a great door, an implacable slamming from the in-rush of wind, and a silence reaching out to the one who had gone.

Chapter Thirty-Three

1

Having spent the afternoon listening to an historian recount the exploits of The Round Table, Lucy left the court and made her way to Chiswick Mall for a conference organised by her father. On the tube she rehearsed the various interventions of Mr Bartlett, most of which seemed to be largely insignificant. But they left the impression of a man who cared about the detail, regardless of whether or not it helped his client's case. He was fair, judicious and yielding. He helped his opponent. He helped the court. And no doubt the jury thought he was helping them in all his little ways. Turning her mind from that, Lucy anxiously thought of the other meeting proposed with such enthusiasm by Mr Lachaise as they had left the court. Upon enquiry, Max Nightingale had said he was a painter. Mr Lachaise had instantly suggested the three of them go together to see 'Max's work' on Saturday afternoon. Lucy had been so completely unsettled by the innocence of his manner that she could not bring herself to refuse. But that was another day. Tonight had to be endured first.

They all sat in the front room. Doctor Scott, the Senior Social Worker, a Regional Care Adviser from the Motor Neurone Disease Association, Freddie, Susan, Lucy and Wilma.

'The reason why we're all here,' said Pam from Social Services, 'is to discuss Agnes' future.'

'She hasn't got one,' said Wilma.

Pam blinked uncomfortably. 'We need to coordinate a care plan, to make sure Agnes is empowered to face the future in her own way.'

Doctor Scott winced. Freddie didn't like it either, although probably for different reasons. He had his own scheme and Lucy saw it at once, before he spilled out his demands. He wanted professionals in (and, by implication, Wilma out). He wanted volunteer visitors from the MND Association to come round every day. He wanted equipment loaned or bought. Anything and everything that would clean up the messiness of dying, although that word was studiously avoided. Freddie preferred to use convoluted expressions which, by their abstraction, focused all the more sharply on the reality he could not bring himself to name.

A potential structure of care (Pam's phrase) was constructed. Freddie enthusiastically endorsed all the proposals, perhaps not quite understanding Pam's reverent doxology that 'empowerment was to do with having choices'.

The package (Pam's phrase) was taken through to Agnes. She listened as Pam explained the options, Freddie making confirmatory interjections as she went along. When she'd finished, Agnes nodded towards her bedside table. Wilma fetched the alphabet card.

T-H-A-N-K-Y-O-U

Pause.

V-E-R-Y

Pause.

M-U-C-H

Longer pause.

I

276

Pause.

O-N-L-Y

Pause.

W-A-N-T

Pause.

W-I-L-M-A

Freddie embarked upon an appeal for sense to prevail until professionally disengaged by Pam using low-key techniques. Back in the sitting room, she translated what 'empowerment for choice' actually meant. Exasperated, but in control, Pam said, 'It's her death, not yours. Let her go in her own way.' She was unrelenting and mercilessly firm.

Freddie, confused, said, 'You don't understand. I just don't want to see her suffer.' He couldn't stay to discuss it any further. Overwhelmed, he left brusquely, blinking quickly to mask the well of tears.

Pam gave her number to Lucy, saying she could call her at any time, night or day, 'given what was to come'.

2

Mr Lachaise was already at court when Lucy took her seat the next morning. So was Max, who now figured in her head by his first name, an alarming mental shift that had occurred without formal approval. Mr Lachaise offered them both a mint. Max took one; Lucy did not.

Miss Matthews, the Junior to Mr Penshaw, stood for the first time to 'take' a witness for the Crown. She called Doctor Pierre Vallon, an elderly French historian now resident in the United States who had previously been based at the Institut d'Histoire de Temps Présent in Paris. He was slightly stooped, with a kind,

277

enquiring face. His hands held the witness box as if he were upon the bridge of a ship. He wore a dark, limp suit and a fat bowtie.

Doctor Vallon explained that historians were largely divided on almost every question pertaining to the Occupation. After the armistice with Germany, he said, France had been divided into two regions: the 'Occupied Zone' in the north, under direct German control, and the Unoccupied Zone in the south which was managed by the new French government, based at Vichy. The latter operated all governmental institutions in both zones but were obviously subject to their German masters. And it was at this early point that scholarly opinion began to divide. The most sensitive issue was participation in the deportation of the Jews. Crucially (for the purposes of the trial), the key question was whether those involved knew that the Nazi project was murder on a massive scale. Doctor Vallon believed that by 1943 many Vichy officials must have known what was happening in the camps. As for someone in the Defendant's position, an SS officer based in Paris, there could be no significant doubt: such a one would have known precisely what happened to the victims when the freight carriages reached Auschwitz. SS memoranda expressly referred to the fact that the Jews were to be exterminated.

At the conclusion of Doctor Vallon's Evidence-in-Chief, the court rose for lunch. Cross-examination would begin at ten past two. Lucy quickly left the building and paced the streets for an hour. Then she came back to her seat beside Mr Lachaise, who again offered her a mint. Yes, please, she said.

'Doctor Vallon,' said Mr Bartlett as he stood up, 'are you familiar with the expression "strong words"?'

'Yes.' He looked puzzled by the curious question, as did the judge, as did the jury.

'I suggest it is false. Words are weak. Do you agree?'

278

'Possibly; I don't follow you.'

Mr Justice Pollbrook put down his pen, his baleful eyes resting on Mr Bartlett who said:

'In the mouth of one they disclose; in the mouth of another they disguise. Words cannot resist corruption. Those who hear them can be easily deceived. Do you agree?'

'Mr Bartlett,' interrupted Mr Justice Pollbrook indulgently, 'are you leading us to the pleasures of Wittgenstein?'

'Oh no, my Lord, I very much doubt if that would assist the jury.'

'They already look rather bemused, and I am among their number.'

'All will become clear, my Lord, if I may continue.'

'Please do.'

'I'm most grateful.'

Mr Bartlett then abruptly changed subject, the previous exchanges left suspended in the memory as a tidy, distinct cameo. 'Doctor Vallon, you told my learned friend that in June 1942 Eichmann summoned his representatives from France, Belgium and Holland to Berlin in order to plan the deportations. He wanted to begin with France, is that right?'

'Yes. It was to be a grand sweep across Europe, from West to East.' The academic leaned forward, a fearless, authoritative stare fixed upon his interrogator.

'And there had been a vast influx of Jews into France throughout the thirties, up to the spring of 1940?'

'Yes.'

'Driven out by Nazi terror?'

'Yes.'

'Doctor Vallon, is it right to say that the parlance of the day distinguished between "Israélites" and "Juifs"?'

279

'Yes.'

'"Israélite" was a relatively polite term describing French-born Jews who were "assimilated"?'

'Correct.'

'And "Juif" had a pejorative overtone, referring to foreign-born Jews?'

'That's right.'

'The distinction did not exist, of course, in the refined vocabulary of the German authorities?'

'Absolutely not.'

'That said, would it be right to say Eichmann effectively exploited the distinction in order to commence his programme of expulsion with as little protest as possible?'

'Yes, although I don't know if he thought in those terms. He wanted to use the French administrative machinery in the planned deportations, so he began with the stateless Jews, the émigrés, knowing that the relevant officials were reluctant to pay their resettlement cost in France.'

'That is a most unfortunate turn of phrase in the circumstances . . .'

'I meant no—'

'Of course, it was innocently used. However, Doctor Vallon, the innocence of language is a subject to which we shall heavily return.' Mr Bartlett frowned, looking at the jury. Then he said, 'However, let's stay with the word "resettlement". Do you accept that the cooperation of the Vichy authorities relied upon an understanding that these Jews were being resettled in the East?'

'That is too broad a question. At the highest level I don't think reliance upon an understanding came into it. Several Vichy officials were openly anti-Semitic, and for them the removal of Jews from France needed little encouragement or explanation.

280

Throughout the various government departments that carried out the orders, however, there were obviously shades of opinion and levels of knowledge.'

'Is it fair to say that a substantial number of people – officials and members of the public – were unaware of the killings, and believed that "resettlement" meant just what it said?'

'Many may have done so, yes, but only at the outset.'

'Subsequently, did French cooperation, if that is the word, proceed in an untroubled fashion?'

'No.'

'Why?'

'The general population were appalled by the mass arrests of 1942. Thereafter, State anti-Semitism, which had prevailed through indifference or agreement, was gradually undermined by civil resistance. Thus, when Eichmann wanted to move against the French Jews, the authorities refused, no doubt wary of how the public might respond. Official capitulation slowed down, under protest, and the deportation programme floundered. By this stage, rumours of what "resettlement" meant had begun to trickle through. Thousands went into hiding. By the end of the war there were still two hundred and fifty thousand Jews in France. But the scale of the killing was horrendous. A quarter of the Jewish population were murdered.'

'My Lord,' said Mr Bartlett, 'may I suggest a short break? These are not easy matters for the jury to hear.'

'Or indeed any of us,' said Mr Justice Pollbrook. 'Half an hour, ladies and gentlemen.'

3

Lucy stood with Mr Lachaise and Max outside the courtroom.

Max had his hands thrust deep into his pockets and was staring at the floor. Mr Lachaise said:

'What we are hearing is a prelude to the argument for ignorance. It is heartbreaking.'

Lucy glanced at the small man with the ever-gentle manner, still wearing the same cardigan. Who was he, beyond his name? She dared not ask. In a peculiar way he frightened her. He spoke with chilling authority.

'In 1941 Radio Moscow revealed that Soviet Jews were being massacred by advancing Nazi troops. In 1942 the BBC described large-scale transfers of Polish Jews from ghettos to camps. Reports of mass extermination in places like Chelmno got to London in May 1942. The Polish Resistance informed London about the gassings at Auschwitz in March 1943. You cannot annihilate a people without the world finding out.'

Max, with his eyes still fixed on the floor, his shoulders pressed inwards, folding into himself, suddenly whispered, harshly: 'The Defendant is my grandfather. I'm sorry. You can't possibly want me anywhere near you . . . or to come to my studio . . . I think it's best if—'

'I know exactly who you are,' said Mr Lachaise in the same dry, authoritative voice. 'And I want to see your paintings.'

The usher pushed open the door to the court and called everyone back. Mr Lachaise took Max by the arm and Lucy followed.

4

Within minutes Mr Bartlett had referred to the reports of killing described to Lucy during the adjournment, some of which had not been publicised at the time of receipt. He then said: 'As regards the population in France, they may have come across non-specific rumours that some people would not have believed?'

'Unfortunately.'

'For the rumours were incredible?'

'That is part of the tragedy. Yes.'

'Reasonably rejected by any right-minded person?'

'Not quite, Mr Bartlett. You appear to have missed the point I made before. Cooperation floundered because there were others who *did* believe the rumours.'

'But you do accept there was room for both positions – acceptance and rejection.'

'Of course.'

Mr Bartlett stopped asking questions. Lucy sensed the turning of a lens, a movement away from the last words to a sharpening of focus on what was about to come next. He said:

'Would you credit Mr Schwermann with the same beliefs and suspicions as a French policeman aged twenty-three based in Paris?'

Doctor Vallon all but laughed. 'The proposition is offensive. He was part of the machinery. He had daily contact with Eichmann in Berlin.'

'There is no room for doubt?'

'In my view, no.'

'None whatsoever?'

'None.'

Lucy felt deep unease. Doctor Vallon was only saying what Mr Bartlett expected him to say.

Mr Bartlett said, 'Would you be so kind as to consider Volume Seven, section A, page two.'

Doctor Vallon was handed a ring-binder. He found the page and gave a nod of recognition.

'This is a telex from Paris to Department IV B4 in Berlin, dated August 1942,' said Mr Bartlett.

'It is.'

'From Mr Schwermann?'

'Yes.'

'To Adolf Eichmann?'

'Correct.'

'Please tell the jury what this telex is all about.'

'It reports that a thousand Jews had been transported from Drancy to Auschwitz.'

'Turn the page, please. This is a memorandum referring to the same transport. What does it record?'

'That sufficient food for two weeks had been provided in separate trucks by the French government.'

'This was not an uncommon practice, Doctor Vallon, was it?'

'No, but—'

'Don't be grudging with the facts, Doctor Vallon; it is there in black and white. Provisions were being sent with these passengers.'

'I'm not being grudging with the facts—'

'This is entirely consistent with resettlement, rather than extermination?'

Doctor Vallon closed the folder and snapped, 'None of the food was distributed. It was taken by the guards at Auschwitz.'

Unperturbed, Mr Bartlett said mildly, 'Answer the question, please. The texts are consistent with a perceived policy of emigration, and wholly inconsistent with a policy of execution upon arrival, are they not?'

284

'As words on a page, possibly.'

'Don't scorn ordinary meaning, Doctor. These are words, not runes.'

'I'm well aware of that.'

'Anyone reading these documents could have understood them to reflect a policy of resettlement outside France. Yes?'

'An ignorant reader might think that fifty years after the event, but not the author. I keep stressing to you, he was a part of the machinery. There are other SS memoranda in these files which expressly state the Jews were to be *ausgerottet* – eradicated.'

'Yes, I know,' said Mr Bartlett in a measured, patient voice. 'And none of them were written by Mr Schwermann, were they?'

'No, but—'

'And there is not a shred of evidence that Mr Schwermann ever read them?'

'Well, we don't know.'

'There is no suggestion that he used such language himself?'

'Not as such, but it is an obvious inference that he—'

'Doctor Vallon, we'll leave the jury to do the inferring. Among this mass of documentation there is not a single sentence that demonstrates Mr Schwermann had explicit knowledge of extermination, is there?'

'There isn't a piece of paper that says so, no.'

'And there are lots of other pieces of paper that record very different terms to *ausgerottet*, terms that we know Mr Schwermann read and used.'

Doctor Vallon had guessed the next direction of attack. He said, 'Yes, and they're all *tarnung* – camouflage.'

Mr Bartlett opened a file. 'Indeed,' he said warmly. 'Perhaps

285

now is the time to consider the innocence of language, whose ordinary use can so easily trap the unwary, even the likes of yourself. Please turn to File Nine, page three hundred and sixty-seven, and consider the words on the schedule.'

A clerk brought the file to Doctor Vallon, who went on to agree that the German High Command were extraordinarily concerned about the vocabulary to be used when describing the process of deportation to Auschwitz. It was variously described as *Evakuierung* (evacuation), *Umsiedlung* (resettlement) and *Abwanderung* (emigration), or *Verschickung zur Zwangsarbeit* (sending away for forced labour). Even the architects and engineers at Auschwitz referred to the gas chambers as *Badeanstalte für Sonderaktionen* (bathhouses for special actions). Their memoranda recorded the phrase in quotation marks. And, of course, the entire apparatus of genocide was named *die Endlösung* (the Final Solution).

Mr Bartlett said, 'The whole point of the exercise is to deceive the reader or listener, is it not? Someone somewhere is expected to believe the surface meaning?'

'Yes, I accept that.'

'There were three meetings held in Paris to plan the Vél d'Hiv round-up. Mr Schwermann attended two of them. The understanding was that those arrested would be deported "for labour service" – is that right?'

'Yes – even though thousands of children would be taken.'

'Phraseology that Mr Schwermann could reasonably have taken at face value?' pressed Mr Bartlett.

'I have already told you, he is one of the deceivers, not one of the deceived. He will have seen other documents that refer to extermination.'

'Would he? Do you always read the notes of the meetings you miss or avoid?'

286

'As a matter of fact I do.'

'Do all your colleagues?'

'No. No, they don't, actually.'

'Thank you, Doctor Vallon.'

Mr Bartlett promptly sat down.

'That is enough for today,' said Mr Justice Pollbrook with a weariness of having seen it all before.

5

Lucy went to Chiswick Mall and listened to the news with Agnes. There was a lengthy report on the evidence of Doctor Vallon. Agnes listened impassively while Lucy broke ice cubes in a saucer, feeding the melting fragments to her on a spoon. Agnes turned them over in her mouth like boiled sweets, her eyes glazed as one hearing a dull story on a wet afternoon.

Time mocked the survivors, thought Lucy. Everyone who lasts long enough becomes an end point in history, and then they must listen to others pass judgment upon what they have not known. But even after all this time, could there be any serious doubt? Schwermann must have understood the circumlocutions of his masters, just as Pam had understood Freddie's.

Chapter Thirty-Four

1

In the natural course of things, Father Andrew made many decisions, passed off as 'suggestions', that Anselm was unable to fathom. One such was the proposal that Anselm 'might' show Father Conroy the North Country on the way to finding Victor Brionne. To Anselm's mind sightseeing did not blend with the task of confronting a fugitive collaborator. But the 'suggestion' had been made. There was some sense to the proposal: it transpired that Con was writing another book after all (only this time he intended to ignore its likely condemnation by Rome). Frequent travel to the library at Heythrop College, London, and hours of drafting at Larkwood had worn him out. He needed a break.

And so, on the day Lucy listened to the considered views of Doctor Pierre Vallon, the two men left Larkwood first thing after Lauds. With Conroy at the wheel they sped north, the skies getting wider and brighter, the horizon flatter and longer. Anselm's mind opened like a plain and he saw scattered here and there, like totems, the outline of those who had recently crossed his path; and Conroy sang wonderfully mournful songs to himself about a betrayed woman and her abandoned child, a young father on a British prison ship and a ditty on violent child abuse. You had to cry; you had to laugh.

Anselm turned his mind to the conversation with Father Chambray the night before, noting bitterly how apposite it was that the truth should finally have made its way out in a confessional. Father Pleyon, a monk of Les Moineaux, had betrayed The Round Table. Unforeseen executions had followed. And by an inexplicable, almost comic quirk of circumstance, Father Pleyon had become the new Prior. Why was it, thought Anselm, that chance so often assisted the wicked? Schwermann and Brionne had been handed a lifeline just when they might have been brought to justice: their accomplice had become the Prior and had lived long enough to secure their escape.

But Father Chambray had pieced together some fragments. He had read the signs. He had told Rome and they had done nothing. And, in dismay, he had left his Priory and his church, a priest for ever in a wilderness without sacraments.

'Con,' said Anselm, 'would you mind not singing for a moment?'

'All right, so.'

'Tell me again what Sticky Fingers told you.' Anselm had already been told, but he wanted to place the little Conroy had found out in context now that he had spoken to Chambray.

Conroy pursed his lips, thinking. 'The Vatican Secret Archive holds two reports from Les Moineaux, and both had been withdrawn by your man Renaldi in early April 1995.'

'Just after Schwermann was exposed.'

'Aye. The first was written by Chambray shortly after the end of the war.'

Anselm knew what it contained, and he would soon see a copy.

'The second was written a year or so afterwards by Pleyon, just before the Lord called him to Himself. It was sent on to

Rome by the new Prior with a note saying the old skin didn't get a chance to finish whatever he wanted to say.'

Anselm, like Father Chambray, could now read the signs that had fallen into his hands. He placed himself before an earnest, sincere Monsignor quietly watched by an attentive Cardinal, each knowing the whole narrative set out by Chambray. But they had only disclosed the incomplete report of Pleyon, knowing it was the beginnings of a self-preserving fiction. 'I'm trying to protect the future from the past,' the Cardinal had said.

Conroy returned to his singing and Anselm slept. They lunched and then pressed on, saying little. As late afternoon cloud gathered over the rolling Cheviot Hills, Conroy pointed to the signpost directing them to Victor Brionne's hideaway. After a few miles of empty, windswept road they reached a display board, informing the unwary that Lindisfarne was a tidal island. They were just in time to cross the narrow causeway before the cold, slate-blue sea crept over the sands and cut them off from the mainland. By the time they had found their bed and breakfast, booked by Wilf the night before, no one could reach or leave the island.

When night fell, Anselm left his companion in the bar and wandered outside, over to a cluster of solid monastic ruins, a fortress carved out of the sky. Standing alone with the wind in his face, he joined himself to the Celtic monks who had once gathered beneath brooding arches by a sea that ran to the ends of the earth; he said the psalms of Compline, as they had once done, while the sharp night enclosed him. Then he walked along a rocky shore towards a large house with its windows lit, the curtains left open. A wooden plaque on a gatepost bore the name 'Pilgrim's Rest'. Anselm leaned on the adjoining wall,

290

concealed by darkness, looking in upon a play of domestic contentment.

Robert Brownlow sat at a piano. Adults and children, seemingly endless in number, passed to and fro across the glass as if on a stage, each with a walk-on part. Most were laughing, cans or cups in their hands, little boys and girls with beakers spiked with straws, and no one seemed to notice the old man seated by the window, looking out into the night as if he were alone.

That must be Victor Brionne, thought Anselm, and none of his family realise he carries a secret, except perhaps Robert. All available generations had gathered for a bash, untouched by the trial in London that had never been more than words in a newspaper, remote but disturbing if read, destined to be thrown out with the cold leftovers within a day or so. Anselm suffered a stab of grief on their behalf. Was it really necessary to pull down what had been built over fifty years? Should the little boy with the beaker have to lose the grandfather he thought he had? Or go to school and hear whisperings or taunts? But then Agnes Embleton was approaching death, unknown to the judicial process, a forgotten victim. Lucy had once been a child with a beaker spiked by a straw but she had not been spared by ignorance. The vindication of one family entailed the destruction of another.

Anselm turned away heavily, wishing dearly that he did not have a part of his own to play: the awful role of the minor character who brings the news he does not understand, whose brief speech shatters unsuspecting lives, and who then walks off for a smoke in the dressing room. That would be Anselm's contribution to the Brownlow family history.

Brownlow. Again Anselm strained to recover a stirring at the back of his mind evoking a pleasant sensation. It was a name he'd known as a boy.

291

Max Nightingale's studio was a single room above a pet shop in Tooting. He said he lived elsewhere but a camp bed stood folded in the corner next to a small fridge, a Primus, a wobbly clothing rail and other innumerable signs of sustained habitation. Leaning against each wall were canvases stacked three or four deep. The walls themselves were covered with work in progress. Light swam among the colour. It was extraordinarily peaceful.

Max was self-conscious but seemed pleased to bring Lucy and Mr Lachaise into his private place. He glanced easily at the walls as if they represented a quiet gathering of his silent family, not one of whom had the capacity to cause acute embarrassment.

Mr Lachaise walked slowly past each canvas, his glasses off, his face peering at the fluid marks of the brush, once wet, now caught glistening in time. He took several steps back, replacing his glasses. 'Quite wonderful,' he said, almost to himself.

Max had withdrawn to one end where an easel was angled against the light, beside a table with jars and saucers huddled by a battered box. He kept away from Lucy, though not obviously, rearranging brushes and tubes of paint. Turning round she saw a painting hung upon the back of the door.

The picture described the hint of a face, perhaps an open mouth crying out, amongst swathes of gorgeous yellow and orange, breaking down in places to smatterings of diaphanous brown and gold, lifted up, as it were, like tiny hands. It was more a study in colour than shape, but the coincidence of lines suggested such a fragile purpose that the viewer was compelled to impose a reading upon it. Lucy understood its mood and wanted to run her fingers along the frail ridges of paint.

She said, 'Does it have a title?'

'"Sibyl's Cave".'

Lucy surveyed the vibrant, tragic beauty, unable to detach herself from its activity.

'Would you like it?' asked Max.

In her taut mind she clutched at a refusal, but she wanted it. Lucy nodded quickly, keeping her eyes on what she had seen.

3

Anselm rose at 5 a.m., having been unable to sleep. He tried to say Lauds but a strong, invasive melancholy scattered his powers of concentration. And yet his mind was deeply attuned to the important task of the day. He would neither eat nor drink nor rest until it was over.

Conroy emerged cheerily for breakfast, eating everything that was brought forth from the kitchen. His irrepressible gathering in of all life's moments – even eating – raised Anselm's spirits. The Prior had been right all along. It was a good idea to show Conroy the North Country . . . for Anselm's sake. He decided to bring his companion with him for the confrontation, as long as the great oaf didn't tell any jokes.

Shortly after ten, Anselm pushed open the gate to 'Pilgrim's Rest'. Conroy followed him to the stone porch. The door was ajar. Voices drifted warmly from an unseen room. Anselm immediately imagined a coffee pot, loaves of bread, jars and pots upon a table, mingled morning greetings, children opening the fridge. He knocked. A moment later the door swung back in the hands of a little girl with large, enquiring eyes. And then Robert Brownlow appeared.

'Ah,' he said lamely, the colour draining from his face. 'You've made it for my wife's birthday.'

Inside, they were introduced to Maggie, Robert's wife; and then two of their five children, Francis and Jenny (with their respective spouses); and then the three grandchildren. But not Victor. He was not in the room. Anselm and Conroy were described as friends of Robert, who, throughout the entire charade, masked his anxiety with near complete success. Only Maggie, with her tight folded arms, betrayed a suspicion of insight. Then Robert led his guests to an upstairs room and knocked on the door.

Is this what a major war criminal looks like? thought Anselm. He wore various shades of respectable green, with a tartan tie, the unmistakable appearance of good but ill-fitting finds from tatty high street charity shops. His shoes were well worn but neatly polished. Robert stood behind the armchair that swallowed up the runaway.

Now that he'd found him, Anselm had no idea what to say. Whatever enquiry Cardinal Vincenzi expected Anselm to undertake, and whatever insinuated pressure Renaldi hoped he would exert, was not going to happen. The meeting had its own agenda. Anselm introduced himself and said:

'Schwermann couldn't hide for ever and neither can you. The police already know that you're here. Even if you say nothing to them, and Schwermann's convicted, he'll begin an appeal. His legal representatives were looking for you and they'll not let you go once they know that you've been found. So if you're going to hide, it's for the rest of your life. Is that what you want?'

294

The gentle clunking of a trowel upon the rim of a plant pot rang from the garden. Anselm glanced out of the window. Maggie was helping one of the children plant a flower.

'Victor,' said Anselm, 'I don't know what happened in 1942 or 1944. Nobody does, except Eduard Schwermann and you.'

He was standing upon a worn rug, uncomfortably aware his calling in life transformed any public reflection into a sort of sermon. He stepped off the thread pedestal, saying, 'There's a jury empanelled in London to make a decision. They sit there, day in day out, hearing evidence, mostly from people who weren't there. It's a journey into memory with stumbling guides doing their best. But you, Victor, are different. You know the answers. Schwermann believes that if you enter the witness box, he'll be acquitted. There are others who believe the opposite; that you, and only you, can prove he is guilty. Only one side can be right. I'm afraid I'm going to sound like a priest now, but the truth will out. Hasn't the time come to give the past a proper burial?'

Victor Brionne's face became mobile but his lips did not part. Deep down, thought Anselm, he's holding tightly on to something. Anselm wrote down DI Armstrong's name and number and placed it upon a sideboard. As he reached the door he turned instinctively and said:

'You knew Jacques Fougères?'

'Yes.' It was the only word he had spoken. His voice, in that one brief sound, disclosed a grave, enduring ache.

'You know he had a blood relative, Pascal Fougères?'

He nodded.

'A young man who did everything possible to bring Schwermann to trial. Do you know he wanted to find you?'

There was no response. Robert looked down upon Victor.

'Do you know why?' Anselm pleaded. 'Not to expose you, or blame you. But because he had faith in the love of old friends. He believed that you would tell the truth.'

Victor closed his eyes, averting his head from Anselm's unrelenting words.

'He died on the very night he met some friends to discuss your importance. Not for himself, not for his own family, but for all those whose memories are being scattered to the wind.' Anselm opened the door, his voice suddenly raised, indignant and accusing: 'Did Pascal die for nothing . . . absolutely *nothing* at all?'

The house was empty when they got downstairs. Walking down the path they could see the family way ahead, ambling towards Lindisfarne Castle. Robert joined Anselm and Conroy at the gate. He said, trembling, 'Father, I meant what I said when we first met. Victor Brionne died in 1945 as far as I'm concerned. Is it right to dismantle their world?' He nodded over the wall, anxiously, at three generations becoming specks in the distance.

'Is it right to leave other lives in pieces?' replied Anselm. 'I don't pretend to have the answer, Robert. I doubt whether your father knows. But he's the one who has to choose.'

Chapter Thirty-Five

1

Lucy took 'Sibyl's Cave' home with her and placed it over the mantelpiece. For the rest of the weekend she kept re-entering the room to look at it. In that hint of a face drawn by the sweeping paint she saw Agnes, young and old, transcendent, aloft her disappointment.

When Lucy met Max and Mr Lachaise at court on Monday morning they all shook hands. Something like ease was growing between them. This was all the more remarkable because she (and presumably Max) had no idea as to who Mr Lachaise, their convener, might be. There was a disarming quality to his simplicity, like dealing with a child. Only he was nothing of the kind. He seemed older than anyone Lucy had ever known. And she recognised in his every move a type of empathy, something indefinable, that he held in common with her grandmother. She would have liked them to have met.

As was now common practice, the three of them sat in a row listening intently to the evidence presented before the court. For the next couple of days Mr Penshaw called a hotchpotch of witnesses to describe the nuts and bolts of organised murder. Mr Bartlett asked few questions, confining himself to small errors of detail.

297

'In fact, the first deportation from Le Bourget-Drancy comprised standard third-class railway carriages, did it not?'

'Yes, I'm sorry, you're quite right. If it matters.'

'Precision always matters,' said Mr Bartlett kindly.

Bartlett very occasionally gave a brief smile to the jury. After all, they'd been seeing each other every day, listening to the same witnesses. Lucy felt an atmosphere was developing between them. They were in this together, doing their level best. One or two had begun to smile back at him. Was it courtesy or empathy?

Lucy struggled to name a growing sensation. By some alchemy, Schwermann was almost detached from the proceedings. The link between the young SS officer and the elderly Defendant before them was peculiarly slender, the actions and attributes of fifty years ago having to be fixed on an older, much changed and hence different man. The passage of time itself had blurred not only the edges of responsibility but the consequences of the crime. Several newspapers had begun to question the propriety of the trial 'so long after the events in question', those being the fleshiness of killing, the smell of filth and the sound of fear. The younger man who'd been there was slipping out of reach; the older chap seemed crucially disconnected from his own past.

One radio programme debated 'the age-old problem of Personal Identity'. If Schwermann at seventy-six was not the *same* man he had been at twenty-three could he be punished at all? Several newspapers explored the reach of ethics within the law, proper and improper. And many perfectly reasonable people from both sides of the fence appeared on *Newsnight* and within ten minutes were fairly evenly savaged for their trouble. The Defendant had become a 'philosophico-legal' problem, as

298

well as an alleged killer. Lucy absorbed all the words, admiring the careful scrutiny of educated minds, but thinking all the time of leaves . . . thousands upon thousands of them, wafted helplessly into the air, no one knowing from where they had come or where they would go.

Watching Mr Bartlett at work, Lucy thought that someone had to bring the SS-Unterscharführer back into the present, through the tangle of reasonable civilised arguments, and put him in the dock – someone who had known him at the time. And, apart from Agnes, there was only one person left.

2

Anselm and Conroy got back to Larkwood late on Saturday night. They spoke in snatches on the way down, each of them preoccupied by a vision of what would soon befall the Brownlow family. No wonder the prophets were such a miserable lot, said Conroy. Glimpsing the fulfilment of history, even a tiny flowering of righteousness, was not a pleasant sight. It wasn't all slaked thirst, free corn, oil and new wine. And, unfortunately, getting the balance right between today's children and the wrongs of their parents was a task that went well beyond the remit of the Crown Court.

Anselm retired to his room on Sunday afternoon to write a report for Cardinal Vincenzi. The text he produced was brief to the point of insolence. He set down the facts: Brionne had been found; he might give evidence; its substance had not been revealed. The whole was extended modestly with a few connecting phrases. With a flourish of respectful obedience, Anselm signed his name.

Anselm went down to the Bursar's office, his report in hand.

A fax machine and photocopier stood side by side. On an opposite wall was a grid of pigeonholes, one for each monk, a private depository for mail and handouts. Anselm faxed his letter directly to Cardinal Vincenzi in Rome and the Papal Nuncio in London. He had been instructed not to send a hard copy, so he placed the actual text in a folder addressed to Father Andrew – for eventual lodging in the Priory archives.

Turning to leave, Anselm checked his mail. There was one envelope. It must have been put there in the last hour or so for the pigeonhole had been empty after lunch. Opening it, Anselm withdrew the report from Father Chambray. An attached note from the author said he had gone to London en route to Paris that night. He urged Anselm to visit him the next time he was in France. That was a welcome gesture from a man on the boundary of things, a man who had once slammed a door in his face.

It was a flimsy text, a carbon copy on tracing paper. Anselm sat and read. It was all as Chambray had recounted. The last page, however, went rather further than their previous discussion.

Father Pleyon secured the passage of Schwermann and Brionne to England through personal diplomatic connections in Paris and London. Contact was made with a new monastic foundation in Suffolk that had been established by a French motherhouse shortly before the war. Schwermann would stay with the monks for a month while alternative arrangements were made by the British authorities.

Anselm put the report back in the envelope and glanced at the fax machine, thinking of his own brief letter to Rome. Its readers would already know that Eduard Schwermann first came to Larkwood Priory in 1945.

300

Reading other people's letters without permission was the sort of thing that Freddie considered abhorrent. It was one of the many admonitions he had stressed when Lucy was a child and he was laying out the benchmarks for upright living. Which of course turned out to be ironic because he would dearly have loved to learn about his daughter if she would but tell him, and she wouldn't, and that left peeping at her mail, which he never did, not even when Darren's distinctive letters had fallen upon the doormat and Lucy had left them open in her unlocked room. She had done that on purpose, knowing he would want to look, and knowing that he would not.

So it was genuinely an accident when her father picked up a letter to Lucy from her college tutor referring her to Myriam Anderson, the counsellor, and giving her permission to miss lectures and tutorials for several weeks. It had fallen on the floor, out of a coat pocket, while she was visiting her parents, and Lucy had left for Brixton none the wiser. He gave it back to her, with an apology, a day or so later at Chiswick Mall. They were standing in the hallway, just as Lucy was about to leave. She took it, flushing, and answered the trapped question he would not ask:

'I've not dropped out.'

Freddie studied her face for a long while. 'But why, Lucy? What's wrong?' She'd expected anger, more of the old dashed expectations spilling forth like dirty water. But that didn't happen. For once, he seemed lost, unsure of how to keep hold of the threads that linked him to his daughter. He raised his hands and Lucy felt the lightest of pulls towards him. She said, quickly, 'I had a friend who died.'

The telling seemed to leave him winded. He didn't even know about the friend, never mind the death. To her astonishment he came forward and put an arm around her, drawing her head into his neck. Lucy could not remember when that had last happened. She started crying, not for Pascal, not for Agnes, but for herself . . . and for her father.

'I'm terribly sorry,' he said.

'So am I.'

And they both knew that their words went far deeper than a reference to recent grief. They reached back, further than either of them could ever have intended or imagined, deep into the unlit past.

As Lucy pulled herself away, she met her father's open gaze with dismay: how would it ever be possible to tell him about the trial, about Agnes' notebook, and about his very self?

Lucy attended court the next morning and took her seat. She asked Max what he'd done the night before. Waiting on tables, he said. How awful, she replied. Pays the rent, he responded. Mr Lachaise polished his glasses reflectively, listening to their quick, simple exchange.

The barristers filed into court but, unusually, the jury were not summoned. Mr Justice Pollbrook came on to the bench. Mr Penshaw rose to his feet:

'My Lord, owing to a rather surprising development in this case, I fear it may be necessary to have a substantial adjournment so that—'

'How long, Mr Penshaw?'

'At least the rest of the day.'

'You can have this morning.'

'My Lord, the development is significant, and I anticipate

the need to serve additional evidence upon my Learned Friend. He will need to consider it *most* carefully.'

There was a pause. Mr Penshaw had spoken in Bar-code. The judge quickly scanned the lawyers below.

'Very well. You can have until two-thirty tomorrow. That's a day and a half. Mr Bartlett, any objections?'

'No, my Lord, I've always enjoyed little surprises.'

'Court rise.'

Lucy thought, faster than she could order her mind: it's Victor Brionne. He must have decided to speak out. Why else would he have come out of hiding? Why else would the Crown so enjoy expressing their concern for Mr Bartlett? He comes to strike down his former master.

Suffused with exultation, Lucy turned on Schwermann in the dock, but was stunned to see his relief and the slight trembling of repressed emotion: the look of one who has heard the soft approach of his saviour.

Chapter Thirty-Six

1

Lucy returned to court unable to forget the look of hope that had smoothed the anxious face of Eduard Schwermann. But now, sitting in the dock, he looked to the public gallery with growing agitation, directly towards the empty seat of Max Nightingale.

Mr Lachaise was uncharacteristically wearied, like the front-runner who unexpectedly limps to one side, unable to continue with the race. Another man, roughly the same age as Mr Lachaise, caught Lucy's attention, being a new observer among what had become a familiar throng. He stood out not through that difference but through the imprint of tension. His short silvered hair, neatly cut and parted, suggested the boy as much as the man. She suspected that he was here with Victor Brionne, who was about to give evidence on behalf of the Prosecution.

When Counsel were all assembled, the judge came on to the bench in the absence of the jury.

'My Lord,' said Mr Penshaw, rising to his feet, 'the adjournment has been of considerable assistance. If I may briefly explain—'

'Please do.'

'An individual came forward from whom it was thought a contemporaneous account of events involving Mr Schwermann might be forthcoming. A statement was taken by the police which your Lordship has no doubt seen.'

'I have.'

'There is nothing deposed therein which adds anything of significance to the Prosecution case. I do not propose to call the witness.'

The judge languidly raised an eyebrow. 'Has Mr Bartlett seen the statement?'

'He has.'

'Good.'

'My Lord,' said Mr Penshaw. 'That completes the evidence for the Crown.'

'Mr Bartlett, are you ready to proceed?'

'I am.'

'Call the jury please,' said Mr Justice Pollbrook, turning a fresh page in his notebook.

Desperate and confused, Lucy grasped for an understanding of what had happened. How could the Prosecution case come to an end without evidence from Victor Brionne? What had he said to the police that was of so little value? As she threw the questions like flints around her mind the jury returned to their seats, the Crown closed their case and all eyes locked on to Schwermann who, at any moment, would make his way from the dock to the witness stand. Mr Bartlett made a few ponderous notes with his pencil. He sipped water. A collective apprehension rapidly spread throughout the court. The judge patiently waited and then, just as he opened his mouth to speak, Mr Bartlett suddenly rose, saying:

'My Lord, notwithstanding the usual practice of calling the Defendant first, in this particular case I call Victor Brionne.'

'What?' said Lucy, aghast.

Mr Lachaise leaned towards her and said in a low, strong voice, 'Do not worry.' With an affection tainted by anger she

305

thought: it's always the powerless who are most generous with their comfort.

Victor Brionne walked through the great doors. The appearance of the man who had haunted so many lives mocked expectation. He was wholly ordinary – shortish, with a wide, laboured gait; owlish eyes, his skin dark and deeply lined – the sort of man you'd meet in the market. He took the oath. His eyes avoided the dock, and he turned only once towards the handsome man three or four seats away from Mr Lachaise. Then he faced the jury.

Mr Bartlett constructed Brionne's Evidence-in-Chief like a master stonemason. Both hands held each question and every expected answer was pressed slowly into position. He halted work frequently, allowing facts to settle.

'Mr Brionne, you worked with Eduard Schwermann between 1941 and 1944?'

'Yes.'

'You are French by birth?'

'Yes.'

'You joined the Paris Prefecture of Police in June 1941, at the age of twenty-three?'

'Yes, I did.'

'You were, however, not an ordinary policeman, in the sense that you were based at the offices of the Gestapo.'

'That's right.'

'I shall spare the jury an argument as to your status. Your place of work made you a collaborator?'

There was no reply. Brionne's lower jaw was gently shaking.

'I asked if you were a collaborator. Please answer.'

Very quietly, Brionne replied, 'Yes.'

306

'Louder, please.'

'Yes. I was a collaborator.' The words seemed to burn his mouth.

'Please tell the ladies and gentlemen of the jury how you came to work with Mr Schwermann.'

'I spoke good German. I was transferred to an SS department within weeks because they required a translator.'

'And was that the extent of your "collaboration"?' queried Mr Bartlett, slightly stressing the last word.

'It was enough.'

'Mr Brionne, I am now going to ask you some questions about an organisation known as The Round Table. We understand Mr Schwermann was credited with uncovering the smuggling operation. Did he ever tell you how he did it?'

'Not exactly, no,' Brionne wavered. 'All he said was that a member of the group had told him everything.'

'Did he say who this person was?'

'No.'

'Did you enquire?'

'I didn't, no.'

Mr Bartlett's voice was growing imperceptibly louder, imposing a sort of moral force on to his questions. 'Having discovered, or perhaps I should say, having been presented with this information, what did Mr Schwermann do?'

'He made a report to his superior officer.'

'And the inevitable arrests followed?'

'Yes, they did.'

'Do you recollect the morning of the day the arrests took place?'

'I do.'

'Were you alone?'

307

'No. I was with Mr Schwermann.'

'Please describe his demeanour.'

'He was anxious, smoking cigarette after cigarette.'

Mr Bartlett contrived mild surprise. 'Let us be absolutely clear. Is this the day The Round Table was shattered?'

'It was.'

'A day for which he would later receive the praise of Eichmann?'

'Yes, that's right.'

'It should have been a time of excited apprehension for him, should it not?'

'Yes, I suppose so.'

'Have you any idea, then, as to why he was so anxious?'

'No.'

'Let's see if we can find an answer. You knew Jacques Fougères?' The barrister was speaking quietly now.

'We were the best of friends. The best . . .' He'd become a mourner in a dream.

'Mr Brionne, did Jacques Fougères have a child?'

Lucy sat forward.

'Yes.'

'A boy or a girl?'

'A little boy.'

'Did you know the mother?'

'Yes. Agnes Aubret.'

'By reference to the racial regulations implemented by the Nazis, to which ethnic group did she belong?'

'She was Jewish.'

'And the boy?'

'The same. He was Jewish.'

'Even though the father was a French Catholic?'

308

'Yes.'

'As far as Mr Schwermann's superior officers were concerned, the boy, if found, would unquestionably have been deported?'

'Yes, unless she had forged papers to conceal her Jewishness.'

'Where is Agnes Aubret now?' asked Mr Bartlett quietly.

'She perished. Auschwitz.'

Brionne was unable to continue. His face shuddered repeatedly with such violence that the judge suggested he might like to sit down, but Mr Bartlett pressed on urgently:

'And the boy, the boy; what happened to the boy?'

'He was saved,' mumbled Brionne, turning quickly to the dock. 'Mr Schwermann took the child, before the arrests were carried out, and hid him with a good family.'

Mr Bartlett followed through quickly and quietly, prompting fluid, hushed replies.

'How do you know this?'

'I saw it with my own eyes.'

'How often did the opportunity to act in this way arise?'

'Just this once.'

'He seized it?'

'He did.'

Lucy could not bear it any more. She sidled hurriedly out of her row towards the court doors as Mr Bartlett sat down and picked up his highlighter.

2

The folder was sealed as if it were meant to survive the rough handling of a prying child. Max stared at the unmarked surface, the bands of brown masking tape crossing each other like planks

309

in a garden fence. His fingers held the corners lightly, reluctantly, as if the whole might dirty him.

Anselm had brought Max to the table beneath the wellingtonia tree after he'd arrived at Larkwood unannounced. A thick stubble dirtied his neck and cheeks. He said: 'The day my grandfather came here, he gave me this.' Max placed it on the table and drew his hands away. 'He told me "You're the only person I can trust, you always have been, but now it matters more than ever before. Keep this safe. Show it to no one. If Victor Brionne is found then bring it to me immediately. If not, and I'm convicted, then I want you to burn it. But promise me this; do not open it."'

Anselm's mind tracked back to Genesis and the instruction of the Creator: not to eat the fruit of the tree that gave knowledge of good and evil. Schwermann had played God with the same rash confidence that obedience would be rendered. Max continued: 'Yesterday, the Prosecution asked for an adjournment. In my guts I knew it was because Brionne had turned up. I've just heard a news bulletin. I was right. The Prosecution have closed their case. As we sit here, Brionne is giving evidence on my grandfather's behalf. I'm meant to have brought this to court' – he pointed at the folder – 'but I can't, not without knowing what's inside.' He pushed it towards Anselm. 'I can't open it. I've brought the one part of him he did not bring to Larkwood.'

Somewhere out of sight, one of the brothers was at work making one of the songs of spring: the unhurried scrape of sandpaper on outdoor timber, a preparation before the laying of paint. Anselm took the folder and carefully pulled it apart. He withdrew three documents held neatly together by a paperclip. Laid on the table, their corners lifted lightly in the breeze.

310

The dull blue ink had the slight blurring characteristic of print from an old typewriter. Anselm signalled to Max to come closer, to see for himself.

The first was headed 'Drancy–Auschwitz'. It carried a list of numbered names and was evidently a deportation register. Before Anselm could scan the entire page his eyes alighted upon a single entry:

4. AUBRET, Agnes 23.3.1919 Française

The lower right-hand corner had been signed by Victor Brionne – representing, presumably, either the compilation of the list or confirmation of its execution. Anselm turned it over and saw the faded smudge of ink around the indentations of lettering: the list had been typed upon a carbon sheet. This was the original. Somewhere there was a duplicate. It was an irrelevant detail that nonetheless attached itself to Anselm's concentration.

Anselm turned to the second document. It was another Drancy–Auschwitz convoy list, a block of names. The dates of birth caught his eye. He stared at distant trees, carrying out a spontaneous horrified calculation. They were all children. Each was marked off as though safely accounted for on a last school trip. And there, near the top of the page, Anselm saw what he half expected to see: a boy called Aubret, aged fifteen months, French, and in the margin a broad, unwavering tick. Again, the paper was signed by Victor Brionne. Instinctively he glanced at its back. Curiously, the page was clean, without the marks of carbon.

Anselm turned quickly to the third sheet. It was an SS

memorandum dated 8th June 1942 and appeared to be an interrogation record. Although Anselm could not understand German, the term 'Judenkinder' was nauseatingly clear. There was a sub-heading in French within quotation marks, 'La Table Ronde'. Beneath it was a list of names, roughly a dozen, two of which he recognised: Agnes Aubret and Jacques Fougères. The bottom of the page carried the signature of Victor Brionne. He turned it over. Once more it was clean, an original text.

Anselm's pulse raced in disgust. He put the documents back in the folder. The questions sprang forward: why had Schwermann kept these at all . . . and why had he retained original records, leaving behind a duplicate only in the case of Agnes Aubret?

'Max,' said Anselm. 'Your grandfather has prepared for this trial, right from the start, even before he knew the outcome of the war. These show that Brionne was involved in the betrayal of The Round Table and the deportation system . . . with those papers you hold your grandfather's life in your hands.'

Max was blinking rapidly. He said in a detached, failing voice, 'He must be blackmailing Brionne. Whatever Brionne is saying to the court will be a fairy tale . . . agreed between them fifty years ago.'

'I'm afraid you're right.'

The soft song of spring played on: the scraping over dry, rough wood. Max bit his lip and said, 'Before I go to the police . . . I'll have to prepare my family, my mother . . .'

'Would you like me to come with you?' asked Anselm.

'Yes.' The word was barely spoken.

Anselm didn't want to say what was pressing upon his mind but he had no choice:

'Max, I don't want to make things worse but there isn't much time – you need to speak to the police as soon as possible. The Prosecution will need what you now possess.'

'Mr Brionne,' said Miss Matthews stonily, 'you have been very public-spirited, coming forward, it would seem, without any outside compulsion.'

Lucy had slipped back through the court doors to find Mr Penshaw seated and the young woman barrister on her feet.

'Tell me,' said Miss Matthews with curiosity, 'when did you first discover the Defendant had taken refuge in a monastery?'

'On the news.'

'That would be April of 1995, a year ago,' calculated the barrister. 'And you made no effort to contact the police?' She firmly drew out each word.

Brionne turned to the judge, as if for help. Mr Justice Pollbrook stared back dispassionately.

'When did you first discover the Defendant had been formally *arrested*?'

'I . . . I'm not sure, perhaps it was . . . er . . .'

'Let me help you. On the news?'

'Yes, that's right.'

'That was in mid-August 1995, four months later?'

'All right, yes.'

'Yet you made no effort to contact the police. Why?'

Once again Brionne floundered, like a man with a map he could not understand.

Miss Matthews pressed remorselessly forward.

'When did you learn the Defendant had actually been *charged* with murder?'

313

'I think it was the next month.'

'You are right. Yet you made no effort to contact the police. Why?'

'I can't explain . . .'

'Why not? It strikes me that you have closely followed this case from the day the Defendant fled his home to the day this trial commenced. Is that so?'

'I have, yes.'

'Yet it is only at the last hour you come riding into court to tell us what you know. Why now?'

Brionne lowered his head, unable or refusing to answer. Miss Matthews patiently leafed through some papers. She looked up and said without a trace of sympathy:

'Are you frightened of someone, Mr Brionne?'

Still there was no response.

'Mr Schwermann, perhaps?'

Brionne became totally still. He held on to the sides of the witness box, controlling his breathing. But he would not speak.

'All right, Mr Brionne, if you won't reply we'll move on,' said Miss Matthews contentedly. 'When you finally presented yourself to the police a few days ago, after the trial had begun, you related only one great incident of heroism on the part of the Defendant. Is that right?'

'Yes.'

'Nothing about round-ups, internment centres, deportations or death camps. Correct?'

'That's right.'

'Just one, brief, glittering moment when a boy's life was spared, like Moses against the orders of Pharaoh?'

Lucy wanted to cry out: pick up the convoy sheets in front of you. The boy's name must be there. Please, please, look now.

'I'm sorry but it's the truth,' Brionne said purposefully.

'Is it indeed?' Miss Matthews suddenly shifted direction to the dirty underside of the rescue story. Mr Bartlett showed no trace of surprise.

'You proclaim he saved a boy from certain death at Auschwitz?'

'That's what I've said.'

'Then tell me this. Can this jury safely conclude that SS-Unterscharführer Schwermann knew "deportation to the East" meant one thing, and one thing only: brutal execution?'

Brionne started, caught off-balance by the question.

She's trapped him, thought Lucy, as Miss Matthews said, with icy detachment:

'Either the Defendant separated a boy from his mother for no reason, or he knew about the machinery of death. Which is it?'

Without forcing a reply, the interrogator drew a slow line across a page, watching him all the while. Then she sat down, leaving Brionne with his head bowed.

Lucy smiled to herself, her heart racing. Miss Matthews had learned a neat ploy from Mr Bartlett: the strange power of a well-placed, otherwise empty gesture.

Chapter Thirty-Seven

1

The curved timber-frames and weatherboards of the cottage would have been simply captivating but for the wide splattering of red paint. It had soaked into the wood and plaster and would not be hidden, despite attempts to scrub it away. This was the home of Sylvia Nightingale, lying by the banks of a river that ran through Walsham-le-Willows, a village thirty miles or so from Larkwood. Anselm drove there on a Friday morning, the day after his meeting with Max, the folder of documents on the seat beside him.

Before leaving Anselm had thought of making photocopies but didn't. The notion of duplicating the names of the dead seemed somehow irreverent, an act of trespass. Listening to the radio during the short journey, Anselm learned the court would not be sitting until the afternoon owing to Bartlett having asked for time to confer with his client. That, thought Anselm, was an answer to a prayer he had not made. Once the ordeal of the morning was over, he, or the family, could call the police, and that would prompt another more significant adjournment.

Max had already arrived when Anselm was shown into the cluttered, homely sitting room. The daubing had occurred two nights ago, explained Mrs Nightingale. It didn't reflect the attitude of the community for it was almost certainly the act of an outsider. Probably drunk, just a one-off, the police had said, trying to bring reassurance to the terror thrown upon the victim. Their words had brought no comfort. Fear had settled into a rigid mask. She was heavily made up, a crafted brave face, displaying everything she wanted to hide. Rebuffing words of sympathy from Anselm, she was an absurd, pitiable folly of strength. Her hair, wound into a bun, had begun to slip free. The comfortable disarray of things in the lounge suggested the unexpected suspension of a busy life.

'Charity work,' she said, pointing towards a pile of leaflets, 'until they said it was better if I didn't help any more. I've become an embarrassment. Not for the first time. Go on, you can explain.'

Max said, 'It's not relevant, Mum.'

'It is, to me.'

Max turned to Anselm and said, 'When Mum fell pregnant with me she wasn't married. My grandfather didn't approve. Neither did my father: he didn't even wait for my birth.' Max looked at his mother with a kind of thankfulness and pleading. 'When he saw I was a boy, my grandfather relented . . . I'm told . . .'

Mrs Nightingale said evenly, 'And to think, *he* was disappointed in *me*.'

The three of them sat as a triangle, reminding Anselm of a parish visit after a death but before the funeral. He explained, as sensitively as he could, the issues faced by the court, concluding with the revelation that Max had been entrusted with a folder of crucially important documents. Mrs Nightingale looked at her son, astounded, becoming angry.

'Why didn't you say anything, to me at least?'

Max said, 'He made it sound as though the truth could only come out if no one knew anything about his secret.'

317

'Listen to yourself, that's utter nonsense.'

'I know.'

'Then why the hell did you . . . Oh Max.' She looked aside, away from her son, with a look of total understanding.

'Mrs Nightingale,' said Anselm. 'These papers demonstrate that your father prepared himself for this trial as soon as the war came to a close. He kept a record of one man's betrayal, a disclosure that was made to him. That man gave evidence yesterday in your father's defence. He must have done so under duress, to save himself. Nothing he said can be relied upon.'

Mrs Nightingale stared at the carpet, her eyes brightening with resentment.

'There are other records,' said Anselm reluctantly. She looked up. 'They list the names of adults and children sent to Auschwitz.'

'No,' she said, shortly. 'No.' She used the word as if it were a racket, knocking back what she had heard, a slam past her opponent.

'It's true, Mum, I've seen them,' said Max.

'Shut up, you,' she snapped. 'Let me see.' She threw out her hand aggressively towards Anselm.

Anselm withdrew the three sheets of paper and handed them to Mrs Nightingale. She looked over each of them erratically, scanning up and down, flipping from one to the other, incapable of measured scrutiny, her face becoming moist. 'What do you want me to do?' she asked, for the first time transparently unprotected, her anger subsiding into dread.

'Absolutely nothing,' replied Anselm reassuringly. 'The police will handle everything.'

'The police?' she said with the specific, tragic astonishment that is the last defence of those who cannot face the obvious. She sat rigid on the edge of her seat. 'Have you any idea what

318

this has meant for my family, for Max, for me?' Her voice rose eerily. 'How do you know what these mean anyway?' She flapped the papers in the air, like rags. 'Who the hell are you to tell me what has to be done? We're the ones who have to live afterwards, not you . . .' Standing up, she raised the flimsy sheets before her eyes, crumpling their edges in her grip. She shook the papers back and forth, as if they were the smooth, indifferent lapels of circumstance; she let her despair loose into her hands, a groan breaking out of her mouth.

Anselm, scared by the unravelling emotion, sprang forward to retrieve the documents, now slightly torn. In an instant he saw the dainty bracelet and rings: old gifts, keepsakes of a lifetime, intimating the vast expanse of all she held dear, brought down in public ruin without warning, without having done anything to deserve the advent of shame. She stepped back, pulling her arms apart. In the tearing that followed they all stood still, each suddenly horrified. She walked hastily out of the room. Anselm looked at the few remaining shreds on the floor, hearing the swift striking of a match.

Mrs Nightingale walked back into the room with the unsettling equanimity that might come after a righteous killing.

'I'm terribly sorry.' Her voice was light and fresh, as if from another woman. She sat down, smoothed her skirt and wept.

Anselm let himself out. As he walked away from the cottage he turned and saw the mother held in the arms of her son.

Anselm drove quickly back to Larkwood. He would have to see Father Andrew urgently, given what he had learned from the documents, and what had just happened to them in the hands of someone who could not face what they contained. Sylvester reminded him the Prior was away for two days at a

319

conference, but he'd mislaid the contact number. Anselm left him thumbing scraps of notepaper and sought out Gerald, the sub-Prior. Father Andrew was tracked down and he arranged to return to Larkwood the next night.

Anselm went to his room and tried to be still, knowing the trial was moving towards an ending but that he alone possessed all the keys to its resolution.

2

The court reconvened on Friday afternoon. Lucy greeted Mr Lachaise, who again seemed deeply tired. Both of them commented on the absence of Max. The light conversation was a foil to manage the strain of waiting. For that afternoon, without doubt, Schwermann would give evidence. Lucy felt like one of those Spartan warriors on the eve of Thermopylae, ambling up and down, naked, waiting for the onslaught to begin. According to Thucydides they intimidated their enemy by leisurely combing their long hair. She had done the same thing that morning. She would watch Schwermann's performance looking her best. He would not leave her beaten and dishevelled.

When all the main players were in position, the jury were summoned. Mr Bartlett bade them good afternoon and said, 'My Lord, the following is a statement that has been agreed by the Crown. It has been furnished this morning by the legal representatives of Etienne Fougères.'

Mr Bartlett read out the text: 'I confirm Agnes Aubret had a child by Jacques Fougères. As far as we know, both Aubret and the child met their deaths in Auschwitz. My family are ignorant of the conduct ascribed by Victor Brionne to Eduard Schwermann.'

'A model of brevity, if I may say so,' said Mr Justice Pollbrook with approval.

'Indeed it is.'

'Mr Bartlett, have you checked the deportation records?'

'I have.'

'Is there any reference to Agnes Aubret?'

'Yes. For your Lordship's note, she was deported on the twenty-fourth of August 1942. The text can be found in File Q, page one hundred and seventy-nine.'

'I'd like to see the original, please.'

The master file was retrieved by Mr Penshaw, who opened it at the relevant place. It was handed to an usher who gave it to Mr Justice Pollbrook. He leafed through pages on either side and then said, 'The actual text to which I have been referred is a carbon copy. What happened to the original?'

'No one knows, my Lord,' said Mr Bartlett with polished regret. 'Perhaps it was damaged in an accident.'

Mr Justice Pollbrook studied the file again. He said, 'All the names of the victims have been ticked off, to confirm they were accounted for, but there is a blank space at the bottom where the supervising officer's signature should be found. Why is that?'

'My Lord, I have no idea. What you have before you is the original file retrieved after the war. There is nothing else. The relevant text remains a contemporaneous document.'

'Thank you,' replied Mr Justice Pollbrook uneasily. Abruptly, suspiciously, he said, 'Did you look for the child as well?'

'I did. There is no mention of him whatsoever.' Quietly, his eye on the jury, Mr Bartlett added, 'It seems, my Lord, that the records confirm everything Victor Brionne recounted to the court. Aubret was deported. The child was not.'

The judge blinked slowly and, with an expression of profound disdain, said, 'I thought you might say that.'

Mr Bartlett bowed slightly with his head. He then said, 'My Lord, having had the benefit of a conference with my client this morning, and in the light of the document I have just read out, I do not propose to call Mr Schwermann to give any evidence in his own defence.'

A great sigh swept through the court. After its subsidence, Mr Bartlett continued, 'I am confident this jury already knows the direction in which their conscience must take them. The case for the Defence is closed.'

Lucy turned to Mr Lachaise who, throughout the trial, had become a quiet source of steadiness, especially when reason saw no room for hope. But for the first time he slumped forward, his gentle face pale and drained of emotion.

Mr Justice Pollbrook adjourned the case, allowing time for Counsel to prepare their speeches and him his Summing-Up. By the time the judge had finished his remarks to the jury Mr Lachaise had recovered his customary self-possession. He suggested they have a coffee and a biscuit. Sitting in a small café off Newgate Street Lucy said, 'Why isn't he going to defend himself?'

'It's far too dangerous,' said Mr Lachaise. 'If he was cross-examined, his present position, however precarious, could only be harmed. He is on a knife-edge, illustrated by the rather good point made by Miss Matthews – he either separated a boy from his mother for no reason or he knew what was going on at Auschwitz but managed to save a single life. I hadn't thought of that before.' He looked exhausted again, but continued, 'Of course, the second alternative is not a defence. If true, it's a plea

322

for sympathy against the enormity of what he must have done. With a jury, pity is a sticky sweet. It's often savoured over justice.'

Lucy asked, 'Are you a lawyer?'

'No, but I grew up alongside a wonderful man called Bremer – the family solicitor – and he passed on to me the maxims of his craft. I have made them my own.'

'Mr Lachaise,' said Lucy tentatively, probing the inscrutable expression on his face. 'My grandmother was a member of The Round Table, and that explains me. But can I ask, why are you here?'

His large eyes glistened behind the heavy spectacles. Lucy could only fractionally recognise the meaning of his smile: it had something to do with misfortune. Mr Lachaise said: 'You may ask me any question under the sun, but not that one.' His voice dwindled to a whisper: 'I do not know the answer.'

3

Lucy left the court and went straight to Chiswick Mall. She found Agnes apparently sleeping. Her arms lay by her side upon white sheets; her face was still, the mouth slightly drawn at the sides; she seemed not to breathe. Lucy watched, her heart beginning to beat hard upon her chest. She touched her grandmother's wrist: it was cool, the skin shockingly close to the bone. Lucy spoke, as hope fled, 'Gran . . .'

Agnes opened her eyes. Her face seemed to change, a minute animation suggesting pleasure. Lucy drew up a chair and sat down. Relief loosened her limbs and she wanted to sob. Holding her grandmother's hand she said, 'It's almost over.'

Agnes blinked deliberately. Lucy knew – she sensed it from

years of knowing her grandmother – that Agnes wanted to laugh. Yes, she would have said, it is almost over. Soon I'll be dead.

Wilma came through the door. It was the usual time for reading out loud, something Lucy had done years ago when she was much younger and they would sit together in the fading light. It was a pastime that had been resumed by Wilma and she sat down and opened a pamphlet of poems.

'"The Burning of the Leaves", by Laurence Binyon,' Wilma said.

Lucy turned away, unable to watch the intimacy that had once been hers being played out with someone else. She fixed a stare upon the wall, shutting off her ears to the sound. But Wilma's hushed voice gathered strength and pushed aside her defences:

'"Now is the time for stripping the spirit bare,
   Time for the burning of days ended and done,
   Idle solace of things that have gone before:
   Rootless hope and fruitless desire are there;
   Let them go to the fire, with never a look behind.
   The world that was ours is a world that is ours no more."'

Agnes raised her right hand off the counterpane. At the signal Wilma stopped. She closed the pamphlet and left the room. The clean net curtains fluttered. Agnes gestured with her fingers for Lucy to come nearer. She did. The fingers said closer. Lucy bent down, almost touching the skin of her grandmother's face. Agnes barely moved but Lucy received the faintest touch of a kiss.

324

Chapter Thirty-Eight

'Give me the whole mess in order,' said Father Andrew. It was a cold wet night and a fire had been lit in his study. The stubborn wood cracked and spat at the lick of the flames. Anselm and his Prior sat close to the grate on creaking chairs. Flashes of orange light danced upon their concentration.

'It began with resentment,' said Anselm. 'Perhaps it goes back earlier, to the sort of differences of background and opinion we have here at Larkwood. But it's simple enough: Pleyon had his nose put badly out of joint by Rochet on more than one occasion. Events conspired so that Pleyon got his chance to have the final swing back. If what I'm told is right, it seems Pleyon may have been an anti-Semite, and that spurred his attempt to pull down Rochet. He betrayed The Round Table to Victor Brionne, who then told Schwermann.'

Father Andrew listened, his bright eyes chasing the whirl of sparks. He said, 'How do you know Pleyon had any contact with Brionne?'

'I don't. It's just an assumption. There's no other explanation for the facts.'

'How did either or both of them know all the names?'

'I'm not sure. I've a suspicion Pleyon only knew of Rochet, and perhaps one or two others, but that Brionne already knew the rest from before the war.'

Father Andrew gazed into the fire and said playfully, 'What

a coincidence that they should meet, each with a reason of their own to bring down their former friends.'

'Tragedy often arises out of coincidence,' replied Anselm defensively, trying to be wise.

'I suppose the pieces fit.'

'The assumptions are confirmed by what happened next.'

'Proceed.' The Prior seemed not to be taking Anselm altogether seriously.

'When the war ended the two runaways knew where to turn – Les Moineaux, and fortune had conveniently lodged Pleyon in the Prior's seat. He arranged their escape, planning to tell Rome a fairy tale about deceptive appearances to cover his own misdemeanour. But he died before he could really sink his teeth into the lies. As it happens, Chambray had already told Rome the full story – which includes the fact that Schwermann was passed on to us' – Anselm glanced at his Prior: no emotion disturbed the attentive calm – 'and they did absolutely nothing.'

Father Andrew raised his hands to the flames and said, 'Tell me about the papers that were torn up by that poor woman.'

Anselm described what he had seen – the list setting out the knights of The Round Table and the two deportation records, all signed by the man Anselm had urged to give evidence. He said, 'It seems Schwermann was a forward thinker. In the event that Germany lost the war he kept those documents so he could blackmail Victor Brionne.'

'Compelling him to do precisely what?'

'To testify that Schwermann saved someone when he got the chance . . . to give a handle for doubt . . . for pity.'

The Prior reached for a poker and jabbed the embers. With a hiss flame rushed upon exposed wood. Shadows twisted and

326

shivered. He said, 'And what do you say Rome were doing when they sent you off to find Victor Brionne?'

'When Schwermann came back to Larkwood it was like a signal, a threat – he could expose Rome as he had been exposed. That would mean everything Chambray had told them would come out into the open. It appears Rome glimpsed a solution based upon simple cause and effect – if Schwermann was reprieved, the face of the Church would be saved.'

'It has to be said,' observed Father Andrew, raking with the poker once more, 'Rome is sometimes more concerned about her complexion than her conduct.'

'In this case, if you've seen both, it's pretty unattractive,' said Anselm. Dismay at the calculating betrayal of his trust had settled into a judgment. 'They seem to have thought that if Brionne gave evidence there was a good chance he would absolve his former master, if only to protect himself. All they needed was someone to prompt him to come forward. So they used me' – he remembered standing in the cold, looking into 'Pilgrim's Rest' at the children with their beakers – 'and there's a grim irony in all this—'

'Which is?'

'I suspect Brionne was hiding not just for his own sake but also to spare his family. There was no point in devastating them for the price of a lie. But I pushed him and now it's been told.'

The fire crackled quietly, sucking in the darkness of the room. Father Andrew said simply, 'You *have* been thinking hard.' The two monks sat joined in contemplation: Anselm rehearsing the future; the Prior . . . what was he doing? Anselm sensed he was listening to the past.

Anselm said, 'I will have to go to the police.'

'Perhaps.'

327

'And it will all come out.'

'Perhaps.'

'And Larkwood, Les Moineaux, Rome; contempt will fall upon us all like rain.'

'Perhaps.' Father Andrew's chair scraped across the flags and he moved thoughtfully to the window overlooking the cloister, the heart of the monastery, concealed by the wet night. The firelight flickered on the glass. Father Andrew raised an arm and wrote a name slowly upon the condensation. It read: 'Agnes'. Hairline streams of water faltered down the pane from each letter. He said, 'Something tells me you should first go back to Victor Brionne.'

'Why?' asked Anselm.

'Because I am struck by the one thing you have not mentioned tonight: he believes Agnes to be dead, but you know she's alive.'

Chapter Thirty-Nine

1

Lucy's parents had arranged to collect their daughter on Sunday morning on their way back from a short break in Canterbury. Father, mother and daughter would then go to Chiswick Mall for an afternoon with Agnes.

The doorbell tore through the air twice. It was a buzzer more suited to the requirements of the fire brigade. Lucy could not hear the electric shriek without thinking urgency stood panting on the street. Her mother peeped her head round the door, eyelids aflutter. She stepped inside, commenting on Grandpa Arthur's clock as if he were there, nodding, on the wall. Her father followed, handing Lucy a mug with a picture of a cathedral on its surface. 'From the gift shop,' he said.

'Lovely glass,' said Susan, turning round, 'makes you think.'

Lucy snipped the door shut. When she joined them a moment later her mother was discreetly checking for dust; her father stood before 'Sibyl's Cave'.

'It's absorbing,' he said. Lucy joined him; their eyes met and she understood. His daughter had a life of her own, choosing pictures, banging nails into walls, all the little things unknown to him.

'Where did you find it?' he asked cheerily.

'A friend gave it to me.' The first two words almost dried her mouth. She did not expect to describe Max Nightingale in those terms, but having done so it could not be withdrawn. Instantaneously she thought of Pascal, the last time they'd met, and the old monk, known to Father Anselm, who'd died saying all that mattered were insignificant reconciliations.

'He's very generous,' said Susan, adding, as if she'd peered inside an envelope, 'assuming he's a he.'

'You're right,' said Lucy, reaching for her coat. She moved into the hall, to a safe distance. 'He's a painter.'

'An artist,' called Susan encouragingly. 'How lovely.'

2

In times of joy or profound uncertainty Anselm always retreated to the small lake at the end of the bluebell walk, roughly halfway between the Priory and the Convent. He brought Conroy with him, who'd reached an impasse in the writing of his book. For a moment they looked across in silence towards the middle of the lake, where a stone statue of the Virgin Mary, smoothed by years of wind and rain, rose from the water, her arms open in endless submission. They climbed into a rowboat by a failing wooden landing stage and pushed off, to low groans from the black-green timbers.

The events of the previous year had increasingly brought to Anselm's mind Tennyson's 'Morte d'Arthur', large sections of which had been mercilessly thrust upon him at school. The lines often came back, like snippets of song, cuttings in the mind. Looking at the shining levels of the lake Anselm said, 'Sometimes I think of Sir Bedivere charged by his dying king to throw Excalibur into the place from whence it came.'

Conroy took his bearings and began a steady pulling of the oars.

'He can't obey. Twice he lies. First, because he's dazzled by its beauty. Next, because he asks a cracking good question: "Were it well to obey then, if a king demand an act unprofitable against himself?"'

Conroy nodded knowledgably.

'So he lies. "What did you see or hear?" asks Arthur. "Just ripples and lapping." But the king knows the answer isn't true. He's waiting anxiously for something outside the usual order of things.'

The oar-blades cut the surface of the lake.

'"I'll rise and kill you with my hands if you fail me this last time," the king says, and the well-trusted knight runs for his very life to the shore and, with eyes shut, flings Excalibur far into the night. He's obeyed but expects his old lie to come true. But something undreamed-of happens, at the very last moment.'

They were nearing the middle of the lake.

'When he looks again, an arm clothed in white samite rises from the water and catches the hilt. Thrice it's brandished, and drawn gently beneath the mere.'

Conroy rested and scratched his thick arms.

'Overwhelmed, Bedivere runs back to tell the king what he's seen. There the king lies, among the stones of a chapel ruin. He's lost everything he cared about in this life. The Round Table is no more; its knights, man by man, having fallen under the sword. But the dream for which he hoped and waited has happened. The hand that gave him the sword has taken it back. His life has meaning. He does not die bewildered.'

Conroy pulled the oars through their locks, letting the boat gently turn and drift as it pleased.

331

'I've always had a soft spot for Sir Bedivere,' said Anselm. 'He's a bemused English empiricist, ill at ease with mysticism. And, rather unfairly, he gets his head bitten off for keeping his feet on the ground.'

Conroy made a pillow from his jumper, lodged it in the prow and lay back.

Anselm said, 'As a boy, I often used to wonder how Arthur would have died if Bedivere had come back and said, honestly this time, "Truly, I saw nothing but water lapping on the crag. She did not come."'

A slight wind threw ripples upon the lake, chasing shadows and reflections into a dark shiver. The boat turned in circles. Conroy was lying back, legs outstretched and arms crossed upon his chest. Unnoticed, the oars quietly slipped from their locks and bobbed away.

'"And God fulfils himself in many ways",' cited Conroy.

'Where's that from?' asked Anselm.

'The same poem; part of the old king's final testament, just before he dies as I'd like to die.'

'How's that?'

Conroy sat up, his face alight, mischievous. 'In the arms of three beautiful weeping women.'

3

Lucy and her parents sat at a table playing Scrabble in the small courtyard garden of Chiswick Mall. Agnes, propped up, watched from her bed through the open French windows.

Susan glared at the row of letters on her stand. Lucy leaned back to sneak a look: Q, F, X, L, B . . . She turned away, gratified. Her mother was choking without vowels. The game produced in Lucy a ruthless competitive urge that permitted minor infractions of the rules. It was her father's turn. He put the small tablets carefully on the board:

Y-A-W

'That's not a word,' said Susan petulantly.

'Is that a challenge?' replied Freddie, his hand on the dictionary as if it were a gun.

'No.'

Lucy studied her own predicament: Z, Q, K, O, S, O, A. It was hopeless. 'Would anyone like some tea?'

Her mother nodded fiercely.

Lucy passed through the French windows and sat by her grandmother's side. She leaned forward and said, 'What do you make of this lot?' She recited her letters. Agnes thought for a moment while Lucy retrieved the alphabet card from the side of the bed. Agnes replied:

Z-O-O-K-S

Lucy said, doubtfully, 'Are you sure?'

Agnes nodded with her eyelids.

'Thanks.'

Lucy went into the kitchen and put the kettle on. A noise behind startled her. It was her father.

'Anything wrong?' she asked innocently

'Lucy,' he said gravely, 'I saw you on the news, in the background, coming out of a court . . .'

Lucy thrust both hands into her hair, disarranging the carefully placed grips and clips. Her father struggled to continue. 'It's to do with Gran, isn't it?'

'Yes,' said Lucy, not curtly or reluctantly but with mercy.

'She knows that Nazi bastard, doesn't she?'

'Yes, Dad, she does.'

'My God.' He arranged his tie and rubbed an eyebrow, saying, 'Will I ever know what happened?'

Without reflection but with something approaching passion, Lucy said, 'Yes, you will, I promise, but it can't be now.'

'All right.' He spoke like a beggar on the street promised a sandwich instead of money. The reversal of power stung. She filled the pot with steaming water.

Chapter Forty

1

Mr Penshaw began his speech on the Monday morning with an ordered but piecemeal presentation of bare facts, in themselves not particularly startling. But something unstated imperceptibly emerged which, once before the mind of the court, grew minute by minute until Mr Penshaw named it with contempt.

'It takes an effort of charity to concede a man could play his part within the apparatus of mass murder and not know the dreadful end towards which his efforts were engaged.'

Mr Penshaw turned quizzically to the dock, bringing the eyes of the jurors on to Schwermann.

'Is it conceivable that an impressionable young man could be left in any doubt as to the fate of the children that passed through his hands? Is it credible that an intelligent young man could grind out euphemisms without knowing the terrible truth they concealed?'

He paused, returning his gaze to those whose task it was to answer the questions.

'No, he could not. And how do we know? Because of Victor Brionne. The penitent collaborator, the knight errant, the best friend of Jacques Fougères.'

Two others were conjured into the courtroom. The jury would think of Agnes Aubret, who died at Auschwitz, and her

335

little boy who was held back from the pit. Lucy could have wept. It was literally the other way round.

'If the Defendant intervened then he did so for reasons we will never know, and to spare this child a dreadful killing which he knew was prepared for him, like so many others, at the end of a railway line.'

Mr Penshaw had almost finished. He put his text aside and spoke with growing anger. 'There is only one conclusion you can draw. With all his senses and faculties attuned, this man wilfully played his part in a scheme that was grand to the twisted dreams of its architects, unthinkable in its proportions, purpose, and consequences, and whose victims now call out for justice. Do not forget them when you retire to make your decision.'

Mr Justice Pollbrook thought that a good place to stop for twenty minutes.

2

Anselm tried several times to contact DI Armstrong. His calls were not returned, so he left a message – that she should phone him urgently regarding a personal matter. Immediately afterwards he left for London, driven by Conroy. It had been arranged that they would lodge at St Catherine's, an Augustinian house near the Old Bailey. As they passed through the gates of Larkwood, Anselm took a last glimpse of the monastery, its countless roofs folding in upon the other like so many russet wings, and he felt an aching as he'd only known when he used to depart for his old life at the Bar.

The Prior of St Catherine's provided large iron keys, fashioned, it seemed, in the Middle Ages, and the next morning Conroy set off for the library at Heythrop College. Anselm removed his habit and walked briskly to the court. The Press, burdened by large bags bulging with lenses, were already circling the entrance. The big kill would come after the verdict. For the moment they were taking pot shots at the herd with an intimidating langour. Anselm nipped past, unnoticed, and entered the ancient hall he'd known so well before he was a monk. At a reception desk enclosed in thick glass he asked for either Detective Inspector Armstrong or Detective Superintendent Milby. After a long wait a smartly dressed WPC came to see him. She said:

'I'm sorry, both of them are involved in another case. I don't think they'll be here until tomorrow. Can I take a message?'

'No, I really need their help now, it's urgent . . .' He'd forgotten that criminal activity was rarely adjourned during a trial.

'Can I help?'

'Well,' he faltered, 'I want the home address of Victor Brionne.'

The WPC's face hardened, as before a crude sham. 'That is not our job.' She began to walk away.

Anselm grabbed her arm. 'I'm not from the Press, really, I'm a monk, a priest . . .'

The WPC turned, casting a sceptical, tired eye over Anselm's cords and jumper. 'I'll take a message, that's all.' For a joke she added, 'All right, Father?'

Once more Anselm left his number for DI Armstrong, saying it was urgent. On his way out he stopped, arrested by the motto beneath a crest on the wall: 'Domine dirige nos' – Lord direct us. Dirige, reflected Anselm, the Latin root of 'dirge', a lament . . . and also the first word of Matins in the Office of the Dead.

The outstanding feature of Mr Bartlett's speech was as much its length as its content. He spoke for no more than a minute.

'Ladies and gentlemen, I think we know each other well enough by now for me to be brief. You've heard the evidence. You know it as well as I do. I shall say nothing about it whatsoever. But forgive me if I draw one small point to your attention. Many of you may already be troubled by its significance.'

Mr Bartlett had an unnerving posture, a mix of the ornithologist and hunter: very still, watching for hours at a time, fascinated by what he saw, but ready to kill. He moved a few steps along the Bar towards the jury, away from his 'hide', his body relaxed, becoming Henry the man, not Bartlett the Silk.

'You cannot convict this man of being involved in a joint enterprise of murder. The edifice constructed by the Crown will not stand. Against others, yes, but not him.' He leaned back against the bench, sitting on his hands. 'The cornerstone is missing, it belongs to a different building. And you possess it. It was retrieved by Victor Brionne. In August 1942, a young German officer got one chance to save one boy, a Jewish boy. A boy who became a man, and who, as we sit here, probably still lives and breathes, and will never know that he does so because of Eduard Schwermann.'

Lucy looked blankly at the line of files in front of Mr Bartlett. One of them should have contained the deportation records for Agnes' son, but for some reason it wasn't there. It was the final obliteration. He hadn't even survived on paper.

Mr Bartlett moved back to his usual place, back into the courtroom, into the contest.

'These were dark, unimaginable times, far from the comfort of this courtroom. Ask yourselves: if he saved one Jewish child, would he have chosen to harm a hair upon the head of any other?'

He looked at the jury with such a hard stare of enquiry that Lucy thought for an awful moment someone might answer out loud. Then he said, like a command, 'No, he would not. Eduard Schwermann was, in his own way, a member of The Round Table, only they never knew it. Ladies and gentlemen, set this man free.'

Mr Justice Pollbrook began his Summing-Up of the evidence, his voice crisp and dry. After a few sentences Lucy heard the deep whispering of Mr Lachaise close to her ear: 'I think we need a little drink.'

They found a wine bar and took two stools by the window. Mr Lachaise ordered half a bottle of Brouilly.

'I trust you are well?' he enquired paternally.

'No.'

'Neither am I.'

'Cheers.'

They sipped a disconsolate communion. Lucy said:

'I simply cannot understand Mr Bartlett's last remark – about saving one child and therefore not choosing to harm another. It's rubbish.'

Mr Lachaise turned his glass in small, tight circles, bringing the wine up to the rim. 'It is rhetoric, not logic. Words well used. It is also deliberately ambiguous. To save a child means opposition to the system of killing, at least in that one instance. But it also means knowledge of the system that claimed the lives of all the others – and, given his participation in what

339

happened, that should be enough to convict him. Mr Bartlett, however, is gambling that the ambiguity will tilt in his client's favour.'

'But why should it? If The Round Table knew what "resettlement" meant, so did Schwermann,' said Lucy.

'I know. And so does Mr Bartlett. That is why he has done what every advocate does with a strong point that can't be refuted.'

'What's that?'

'He's ignored it, as if it wasn't there. In its place he's planted a seed of pity for an unsung hero.'

'But the jury can't fall for that.'

Mr Lachaise shook his head. 'Sometimes, we all like to think the right answer can only be found by making the most difficult decision, the one we're at first inclined to reject. It shows we took the matter seriously. My dear old mentor, Mr Bremer, used to say nothing more than pity serves to tip the balance.'

'I hope he's wrong.'

'So do I.'

He expressed agreement with such feeling that Lucy looked up, and she was shocked to see the awesome distress upon his face.

4

By early evening DI Armstrong had still not returned Anselm's message. Idle waiting seemed an offence against the circumstances. He fidgeted anxiously in his room, rehearsing the future. What if Agnes' being alive made no difference to Victor Brionne . . . and he refused to go to the police voluntarily? A yawning hole seemed to open before him, all the more frightening because Anselm had already decided to fall into it. It was not helpful to see the expanding dimensions beforehand. Without thinking, Anselm picked up the telephone and rang Salomon Lachaise.

They met at the same restaurant as before, sat at the same table and were served by the same waiter. The repetition of the past had the mark of ceremony and under its weight Anselm disclosed to his companion everything he had concealed on the last occasion: including his own role in finding Victor Brionne.

'I am deeply sorry – I presented one person to you when in fact I was another.'

'That is true of all of us,' replied Salomon Lachaise. 'Sometimes it cannot be avoided. You do not need my forgiveness, but you have it.' He fixed Anselm with a piercing gaze and said, 'Are you really prepared to go to the police and bring down your own life, the reputation of your church, your community?'

'Yes.' He was embarrassed by the simplicity of his reply.

Salomon Lachaise removed his heavy framed spectacles, revealing the vulnerable skin kept behind thick glass. He said, 'Anselm, go to see Victor Brionne, by all means. And deliver the message to Agnes Aubret. But promise me two things.'

'Of course.'

'First do nothing else until after the case is over—'

'But—'

'Promise me.' His voice ground out the words.

'All right.'

'And secondly,' he said, 'please put your habit back on. To me you're a monk to the core . . . and appearances matter.'

Anselm got back to St Catherine's to find a message pinned

to his door: DI Armstrong had rung and would meet him on Thursday evening at 5 p.m. on the steps of St Paul's. She could see him no earlier because of a murder enquiry. Anselm entered his room and immediately lifted his habit off the bed and smuggled himself into its folds. He then tiptoed down to the oratory on the first floor. Sitting in the dark, he could not escape the sensation that Salomon Lachaise had already known a great deal of what he had said, but one question in particular returned again and again: why had he forbidden Anselm to act to his detriment when it was required by what he had done and what he knew? Anselm's imagination was perhaps too easily excited, but he sensed his mysterious friend was about to cast an appalling light upon the tragedy that had engulfed him.

Chapter Forty-One

1

Mr Lachaise rang Lucy and suggested they meet for lunch in Gray's Inn Gardens at half past one. He did not propose to attend the end of the Summing-Up. Neither did Lucy, at least not all of it. The slow treading-over of the evidence was an unbearable form of waiting.

The gardens lay off Theobald's Road, neatly circumscribed by mansions of the law, elegant screens of pale magenta brick with regular white-framed windows like rows of pictures. Lucy strolled along a narrow passage into Field Court, a tight enclosure adjacent to an ornate pair of wrought-iron gates, resting between two pillars. Surmounting each was a fabulous beast with the head and wings of an eagle. She paused to study the strange, seated guardians. They threatened to suddenly move, relinquishing stone; to slink, warm-breathed, off their pedestals and wreak wrath and mercy upon High Holborn. What did they protect? Nothing. Whom did they save? No one. When would the day of reckoning come? Never. What were they other than dismal protestations at the absence of angels?

Lucy passed between them into the gardens. A lane of polished gravel unrolled between short trees, plump courtiers on afternoon parade. Benches, set well apart, secured leisure with privacy. Upon one of them sat Mr Lachaise, talking earnestly to Max Nightingale.

343

They did not hear her approach. Lucy sidled to the edge of the path, in line with the bench, reducing the chance of being seen. She harboured a not altogether irrational suspicion that Mr Lachaise had met Max first on purpose. As she drew near, she heard his distinctive, appealing voice say:

'Regardless of what you have said, do as I ask. Do nothing. Rest assured, there is no need.'

Then, unfortunately, she was seen. However, the conversation ran on in an entirely innocent fashion, which rather disappointed Lucy. She had liked the idea of consecutive meetings, up-turned collars and secret conversations. Mr Lachaise continued talking as he beckoned Lucy with his hand:

'You might think your paintings are not especially good, but I'm confident my colleagues will come to another conclusion. As I have said, leave it all to me. The University will issue the invitation; after that it's all very simple. Ah, Lucy, do join us.'

Lucy shook Max's hand. Seeing him outside the courtroom lit his absence from the trial as a sort of failure, as though he'd left her and Mr Lachaise on the front line. How peculiar, she reflected. He's from the other side.

'I've brought along some very Jewish provisions,' said Mr Lachaise, opening a large plastic bag. 'It's always bitter or sweet . . . I'll explain as we go along.'

They ate sitting in a line, passing curious things from one to the other.

'It's rather like *Waiting for Godot*,' said Lucy.

'Except this time,' announced Mr Lachaise, 'he might come after all, just when he's not expected.'

344

At 2.30 p.m. the gardens closed and, politely expelled, they strolled back to Field Court. Mr Lachaise left them standing at the gates between the two indifferent protectors.

In the absence of their intermediary, Max shifted: not clumsily, but through a refined guilt. Lucy saw its trim, its shine, the self-loathing that came from an organic relation to evil. A giddy sense of authority unsettled her balance, like a rush of blood. She could leave him bound, if she wanted. A delicious splash of something wholly foreign touched her lips. Her tongue tasted malice. She recoiled from herself and said, 'Max, to me you are Nightingale, not Schwermann. There's a big difference.'

'It's just paper over cracks.'

Lucy winced at the deliberate use of her words. 'I should never have said that. I'm sorry.'

'Don't say that to me, of all people.'

'I mean it. We're all cracked, covered in paper. I'm no different. There's nothing wrong with being ordinary.'

As they walked out of Field Court, away from the ornate garden protected by myths, Max said, 'I won't be coming to the rest of the trial.'

'Why?'

'I know he's guilty.'

'How?'

'I suppose I've known all along,' he said, 'but I never suspected that he'd entrusted me with the proof of his guilt.'

Lucy understood that elaboration would not come and that it lay in the past – given to Mr Lachaise while she stood contemplating the avenging, lifeless stones.

'I'm glad you liked the picture,' he said, backing away.

'I love it,' replied Lucy.

A half-smile broke his face. Something had been achieved. Lucy held out her hand. 'I'll be off then,' said Max as they shook. It was as much goodbye as a settlement of the past. Lucy watched him leave, threading his way against a stream. Symbolically, self-consciously, as in the final cut of a film, she waved at the back of his head as he vanished among a multitude.

3

Lucy arrived at the Old Bailey, just in time to catch the learned judge's final remarks. There was standing room only.

'It should be noted,' said Mr Justice Pollbrook evenly, 'that for fifty years no student of the times knew that Jacques Fougères had a child. This is now admitted by the family, and perforce by the Crown. Why it should ever have been concealed in the first place escapes my imagination, but that need not trouble you. The important fact is that the detail came from Mr Brionne.' He examined the jurors dispassionately. 'If you are satisfied that having told one significant truth the rest of his evidence can also be believed, then you are entitled to infer the boy, in fact, survived solely because of the conduct of the Defendant. If that is your conclusion, then you are left with the anomaly upon which Mr Bartlett seeks to rely – that it would indeed be strange for the Defendant to have pledged himself to an enterprise that involved the death or serious harm of other children. However, ladies and gentlemen, let me say this.' Mr Justice Pollbrook stared hard at the jury. 'In my long experience, people can be very strange indeed. Look at your own families. How

346

many of them leave you baffled at every turn? No, you must ask yourselves a different type of question altogether: if you are sure of what the Prosecution allege, you must find the Defendant guilty. If you are not sure, you acquit.'

The judge then went through each count on the indictment, giving a series of questions designed to determine whether or not the Defendant was guilty – of the 'if you decide A, then B must follow' variety. When he had finished, the judge closed his red book and removed his glasses, saying, 'Down whichever avenues your reflections may lead you, please remember this. The ground of suspicion belongs to the Defendant.'

The jury then retired, bound by a promise to consider what justice was required according to the evidence. Mr Justice Pollbrook said at this stage he only wanted a verdict upon which they were all agreed.

There was no mistaking it, thought Lucy as she left the court. Whatever the judge had said about the abstract requirements of the law, Schwermann's innocence or guilt was going to turn on what the jury thought about the strange story of a child, believed by them all to be still alive, known by Lucy and Agnes to be dead.

4

As arranged, Anselm met DI Armstrong on the steps of St Paul's.

'Coffee?' asked Anselm.

'No, thanks. How can I help?'

Anselm could not but note the perfunctory, professional courtesy.

'I would like to speak to Victor Brionne.'

'So I'm told.'

347

'It's important.'

'You said as much last time. "In the interests of justice, in its widest sense", I think you said.'

'I did.'

'That's not what happened in the courtroom.'

'I know.'

'Father, don't you think your meddling has done enough damage? There's a chance that rubbish from Victor Brionne could lead to an acquittal. Are you aware of that?'

Anselm blazed with humiliation. 'I promise, I had no idea what he was going to say.'

'Your promises are not entirely straightforward, I'm afraid.'

'But this time I know what I'm doing. Before I was in the dark.'

'As was I, and still am. I don't want to be enlightened. Here's the address and telephone number.' She handed him a piece of paper. It had been written down in advance.

'Thank you.'

'Father, I'm sorry to say this but I'm giving it to you not because I trust you, but because it's a matter of public record. He's in the telephone book.'

Anselm put the note in his pocket, his head bent, unable to face his accuser. When he finally did so, DI Armstrong had already turned around. He stood, emptied, watching her walk down the steps away from him.

5

Anselm returned to St Catherine's and rang Victor Brionne.

'I think we ought to have another talk.'

'Why? As a result of our last conversation, I came to the

court. Now, after my performance, I have lost my son. I don't think you and I have anything else to say to one another.'

'I want to talk about Agnes Aubret.'

'What's the point? Your curiosity has too high a price.'

'She's alive.'

'No, she's not,' he barked. 'I should know.'

'Victor, I know her granddaughter. Agnes survived. She is here in London. I will be seeing her within the next few days with a message from Mr Snyman.'

The line went deathly quiet. Anselm could hear the intake of breath.

'Snyman?'

'Yes. Victor, listen to me. Agnes is seriously ill. She will soon die. Now is the time to let out what you've kept back for fifty years.'

349

Chapter Forty-Two

1

The jury reconvened at 9.30 a.m. on the Friday. Throughout the passing hours Lucy and Mr Lachaise sat on the bench as if awaiting the ministrations of a dentist. By way of distraction Lucy described the miniature glories of the Duchess who, at that moment, was probably holding her own court in Chiswick Mall. Lucy had parked the old girl there in anticipation of the verdict . . . a verdict Lucy would probably bring to Agnes that evening. No decision had been reached by lunchtime. Lucy walked the streets. She kept moving, tiring her limbs, until it was time to get back to the Old Bailey.

At 2.30 p.m. the jury indicated through the usher that they had a question. Counsel, solicitors and the Defendant were called into court. Mr Justice Pollbrook came on to the bench. The jury were summoned. The foreman passed a note to the usher who gave it to the judge. He opened a sheet of paper, read it and handed it down to Counsel. The note was passed back to the judge who read it out loud:

'We would like to hear some evidence from the person who took the child saved by the Defendant. Can this be arranged?'

Turning to the jury, Mr Justice Pollbrook said, 'Ladies and gentlemen, you must not allow yourselves to be distracted by speculation upon evidence that might have been presented to

350

you. Your task is simply this: to decide the case on the evidence you have heard and nothing else.'

As everyone traipsed out Lucy turned to Mr Lachaise and said, 'They've decided he saved a child and they think it matters.'

'Like I said, pity is a sticky sweet,' he replied. 'I've tasted it myself.'

2

Anselm stood facing the home of Victor Brionne. Through the window he could only see books, from floor to ceiling on every wall. He knocked on the door. It opened. A rounded back split by braces receded. Anselm stepped in, along a dark corridor. A small square of greasy daylight hung suspended at the top of the stairs, behind a half-closed toilet door.

'Take a seat,' said Victor Brionne, pointing.

They sat in worn, charity shop chairs. A faded burgundy carpet lay in rucks, its pattern now barely distinguishable. Anselm's eye caught the glint of glass, from a wine bottle, standing close to Victor's chair like a furtive intruder. Anselm's keys bit into his thigh. He fished them out and put them on the armrest.

'If Agnes survived, it's a miracle,' Brionne said.

'She survived.'

Brionne ran a finger along one of the deep creases spreading beneath his large dark eyes. Quietly, astonished, he said to himself, 'If only I had known . . . all these years . . .'

'What difference does it make?' asked Anselm.

'What difference?' Brionne laughed, pulling out a cigarette from a crumpled packet. He struck a match. The flame hissed, lit his face and died. 'I was there when Rochet asked us to be knights of a Round Table of forgotten chivalry, and they all said, "Yes, yes, bring us our bows of burning gold, our arrows of desire, our shields. . ."' He stopped, trying to make out lost faces in the middle distance. 'Except for me. I asked why.' He turned to Anselm. 'I could not see the poetry in self-destruction.' Blue smoke swirled over his face.

'I went to see Rochet after the first round-up. He said it was just the beginning. Soon, they'd all be swept away. It would be a Babylon the like of which the world had never seen. There would be no weeping by any rivers, no Exodus. I don't know what came over me. I said I'd join the police.'

Anselm felt heat in a room with no fire.

'They'd carried out the arrests, so where better place to go? We'd know in advance what the Germans were up to.'

'What?' exclaimed Anselm.

Brionne seemed not to hear. 'Why did I do it? I didn't think about it at the time, but it was for Agnes.' He drew deeply on his cigarette. 'I had entertained what nineteenth-century novelists call "hopes". They were dashed in nineteenth-century fashion when I learned she was carrying Jacques' child. She told me a few months before I went to see Rochet. Somehow the two are linked: the end of my great expectations and me doing something that I knew would command her undying admiration, if ever she found out. There was a poetic symmetry in the self-sacrifice.'

Brionne got up and walked out of the room. He came back with a small, foxed black and white photograph with creased corners. He handed it to Anselm.

'That's her. I took it in 1936.'

She had long, straight hair, and had been caught in time as she threw the lot over her shoulder. In the shadow beneath, her mouth was slightly open, her eyes creased with . . . what was it? Self-consciousness, confidence, suppressed exhilaration . . . it was all of them and more, the gifts that come just before the parting of youth. Behind stood a young man, serious, his gaze fixed on Agnes . . . possessive, and wanting to be possessed.

'That's Jacques.' Brionne held out his hand for the photograph. 'So I joined up and got transferred to Avenue Foch, because of my German. At the time I thought it was the hand of God. Now? I'm not so sure. That was where I met Schwermann.'

Brionne dragged the bottle a few inches across the carpet, into better reach, and poured wine into a stained mug.

'He was ordinary to look at. The evil ran through his mind. He poisoned himself with pseudo-scientific pamphlets against the Jews. He underlined phrases and ticked margins.' He drank, the cigarette locked between two fingers. 'Anyway, Rochet decided he would be my sole contact. My code name was "Bedivere", and it was known only to him and the Prior of Les Moineaux and his council. If I needed to run, they'd protect me. So, there I was, at the heart of things. I hadn't been there long when "Spring Wind" was planned, though nothing had been worked out for the children. I told Rochet.' Brionne grimaced. 'So many could have been saved if we hadn't been betrayed.'

'Who by?' asked Anselm quietly.

Brionne raised a hand, beseeching patience. 'The strange thing was that Schwermann changed after The Round Table was broken. He abandoned his pamphlets. To this day I don't know why, but I believe it had something to do with the arrest of Jacques in June 1942.'

Anselm's memory spun back to that lunch with Roddy, when the old sot had pointed out how odd it was that Jacques had

353

been arrested in the June but the smuggling ring hadn't been broken until the July. He asked, 'What happened?'

'He'd been demonstrating after the Jews had been forced to wear a star – outside the building where I worked. He was picked up and Schwermann was told to give him a scare, so a French speaker wasn't needed. Anyway, Jacques spoke reasonable German, thank God. If Schwermann had needed me my cover would have been blown – which nearly happened when Rochet rolled in, demanding to see Jacques. He was hauled off, slapped about a bit and thrown out. Ten minutes later Agnes turned up, asking for me . . . I couldn't believe it, I thought the game was up. So there we are in the corridor – will I help, she asks, for old times' sake? Then Schwermann appears out of nowhere. He's staring at me, and her, and I can't think why . . . he doesn't speak French . . . he's meant to be giving Jacques the once-over. So I try to say to her, with my eyes, "Not here, not now, I'll do what I can."' He gulped more wine. 'She didn't understand.'

Brionne reached down beside his chair and pulled up the bottle, resting it upon the arm of his chair. The cigarette, unsmoked, had grown to a long finger of ash.

'Schwermann went back to work, but afterwards he wanted to know about her. Who was she? Did she know Fougères? No, just an old tart, I said. But I was worried. I found her a few days later and told her to keep away from Rochet and Jacques, for which she gave me a smack across the face.' He filled the mug, spilling wine on to his wrist; the ash broke and fell.

'Then, one morning, a month later, Schwermann told me he was going to lift a Frenchwoman in the eleventh arrondissement that afternoon and he wanted me to be there. On his desk was a file. After he'd gone, I looked. There was a report to Eichmann and an interrogation record – a handwritten draft and a typed copy – with all the names of the ring set down, spilled within minutes of being slapped about. He'd told them everything.'

'Who had?' blurted out Anselm. Brionne stared ahead, smoke pricking his nostrils and eyes, the desperation of the moment fresh upon him.

'I took the handwritten draft, gambling it wouldn't be missed. I didn't have much time. I only had three travel passes, forged by Rochet's contacts. I dated them and set off. Rochet himself was out. So I went to Anton Fougères. He wouldn't see me because I was a collabo. So I handed the paperwork to Snyman, who'd answered the door, along with the passes so they could use the trains. There was nothing else I could do. By nightfall The Round Table was shattered.'

Brionne closed his eyes as a heavy silence cramped the room. 'I didn't know we were going to arrest Agnes until we got there, because I thought she was still at Parc Monceau. The flat door was broken open from when they'd come for Madame Klein. We sat there and waited. I can't describe the rest.' He smoked, repeatedly drawing in thick draughts. 'We took her child and she screamed at me, a scream that pierces time. Then Schwermann knew I was involved in The Round Table. I never saw Agnes again. That is my last memory of her. A nurse took the boy to an orphanage.'

Brionne became eerily still, as though he'd quietly died. He said, 'Three days later, he called me in. He placed the typed interrogation record on the left side of his desk, disclosing all the names of The Round Table. Then he produced two convoy deportation lists for Auschwitz, each with a string of names

. . . including Agnes and her child. At the bottom was a space to be signed by the supervising officer, the one who ticks them on to the cattle truck. He put those on the right-hand side. "Sit down," he said. "You have a choice."

'I sat down. "If you sign these documents," he said, "you may keep the child. If you refuse he will see Auschwitz, and you will be shot."' Victor stared at the bottle on the floor, now almost empty. 'I signed everything.' A thin laugh expelled a gust of smoke. 'The irony of it struck me at the time: by writing my name I became the one who had betrayed The Round Table, just after I'd removed the proof that it was someone else – remember? I'd just given the draft to Jacques' father, Anton Fougères.' He drained his mug in long gulps. 'One thing happened next that I have never forgotten – I heard him being sick in the toilet. I collected the boy from an orphanage that afternoon and took him home to my mother. He was one of nine. The other eight were deported the next day. I cannot tell you what it was like to walk away with one of them.'

'Robert?'

'Yes.'

'Robert is Agnes' son?'

'Yes.' Brionne placed a shaking hand over his face. 'Schwermann supervised the departure of the convoy that took Agnes away. Afterwards, he kept the original list signed by me and placed an unsigned duplicate on file. As for Robert, he did the same thing, covering the deportation himself so that no questions were asked as to the child's whereabouts. The only difference was that no duplicate list was made. To tie the knot, he got a friend at Auschwitz to mess about with their records to make them consistent.'

356

'Why?'

'He told me that if the Germans lost the war, the public records would confirm that he'd saved a child when he'd got the chance.'

'So what?'

'I said that . . . and he replied that if ever he had to fight for his life, it could be the one thing that might save him from the gallows.'

Brionne left the room. Anselm heard him swill his face in a rush of water. He spoke from the kitchen, coming back to his worn chair. 'He read a lot of Goethe. "*Du musst herrschen und gewinnen, oder dienen und verlieren*," he told me later. "You must either conquer and rule or lose and serve." A very German apology. For the rest of the time I knew him he sweated profusely.'

The enormity of Anselm's wilful credulity towered over him. He'd guessed Schwermann was blackmailing Brionne because of the documents given to Max, but that didn't mean Brionne had done anything to induce the blackmail. It was simple logic.

'From then on, he often used to say, "*Zwei Seelen wohnen, ach! in meiner Brust.*" I was part of him and he was part of me, two souls dwelling within one breast. I was the one who would have to tell the tale of his heroism. I was the one who could procure his escape, using The Round Table structure to his advantage. And, in due course, I did. When it became clear the war was over, I took him to Les Moineaux.'

'But neither of you were known to the community,' said Anselm.

'Father, just because they did not know me does not mean I did not know them. I told Father Pleyon, the Prior, that I was "Bedivere" and I was welcomed. And then I had to put

357

that saintly man in the same position Schwermann had put me, which was ghastly because he had been the monk responsible for running the operation at the Priory.'

'Father Pleyon?'

'Yes.'

Anselm remembered Chambray referring to the doubts raised by Father Pleyon when the smuggling operation was first put to the community, and he saw at once the wise stewardship of Prior Morel – he had given the main job to a man with his eyes on the risks, rather than the enthusiast. And then Anselm glimpsed something he had never considered . . . he remembered Father Pleyon's report to Rome . . . it was Pleyon who had ensured that Rochet met the Fougères family . . .

'I told him if he couldn't hide us, yes, a Nazi would be caught and hanged. But so would I. And the boy Schwermann had spared would learn the terrible truth about his own history. But if he assisted our escape, well, the child would be spared, a second, final time. The boy would grow, freed from the past, and some good would be salvaged from so much evil. And Schwermann? He would have been saved for the sake of a child, the least in this life but the greatest in the Kingdom. There was poetry in that. Father Rochet would have liked it.' Brionne lit another cigarette. He passed one to Anselm.

'Father Pleyon asked if he could write a report to Rome, explaining what had happened. I agreed. Robert was hidden in the convent as a refugee and I saw him every day until our passage was prepared for England.'

Anselm gave a moan of self-recrimination. Father Chambray had misunderstood every detail and Anselm had devoured the conclusions, principally because Rome had tried to hide them.

Brionne said, 'When Schwermann was recognised on a train,

as we were leaving Paris, he led them to me, one carriage further along. I was interviewed by a young officer, much the same age as me. I looked him in the eye and told him the same thing: Schwermann would hang, but what about the boy sitting on the bench outside? He was a brave man. He let us go.'

The young Captain Lawson who could not remember anything when pressed by DI Armstrong, thought Anselm.

'I built a new life for Robert,' said Brionne. 'He married, had children . . . but I was always waiting for Schwermann to be exposed, because I knew he'd come looking for me.'

'So you went into hiding when he turned up at Larkwood Priory?' asked Anselm.

'Yes. And I would have stayed there if you hadn't asked me if Pascal Fougères had died for nothing.'

'But Victor, why didn't you reveal what had happened?'

'I wanted to, but when I stood there, in the witness box, I couldn't do it. I looked at Schwermann. I looked at the survivors. And I looked at Robert. I hadn't been able to tell him anything before seeing the police. How could I explain to him that I'm not his father? How do I prove that I didn't put his mother on the train for Auschwitz? That I didn't betray all her friends, and my own? Only Father Rochet knew I'd been a secret member of The Round Table and he's dead.'

'But Robert knows you, loves you; he would have believed you.'

'Father, you forget something.' His voice was steady, uncompromising, detached. 'I was trapped as a collaborator for the rest of the war. It was the price for Robert's survival. I couldn't tell him that. So when I took the oath in court, I told the truth, even though no one understood the actual meaning of what I said. It's contemptible.'

359

The swift consumption of wine had taken its toll. Brionne licked his lips; his head began to loll, suddenly dropping now and again off its axis. He spoke as though about to weep. 'And the irony of it is that afterwards, when I stood with Robert in the street, I knew I'd lost him because he thought I'd lied.' He let out a great sigh. 'And all the while Agnes, his mother, my dear friend, was alive, here in London, and I could have condemned Schwermann in her name . . . It is too much, too much . . .'

Appalled by the plundering self-sacrifice, Anselm said, 'After all you have suffered, you can restore to Agnes her son. You have raised him from the dead. I will speak to Robert.' He walked over and knelt by Brionne's chair. Taking the wine bottle out of his hand he said, 'Victor, who betrayed The Round Table?'

'Oh Father,' he said mournfully, 'do I have to say it out loud?'

3

At 4.17 p.m. the waiting was over. Everyone returned to court: Counsel, solicitors, observers, the Press and, of course, Eduard Schwermann. When all were comfortably seated, Mr Justice Pollbrook came swiftly on to the Bench. Lucy, sitting beside Mr Lachaise, watched the string of jurors file into their seats. They all looked guilty. The clerk stood up with his litany of questions. The foreman stood up, ready to deliver her nervous replies. After each answer was given, the clerk repeated the words verbatim, to remove all possible doubt. The foreman confirmed the repetition.

They had reached unanimous verdicts on all counts.

Chapter Forty-Three

1

The foreman was a young woman in her mid-thirties, wearing narrow glasses that insinuated bookish gravity. She wore black but her skin was paper-white. Upon hearing the first verdict, Lucy lost all memory of the previous questions and replies; they were swallowed up by her final, irrevocable judgment:

'Not guilty.'

The tidy phrase was hardly spent before a most awful collective gasp arose from one side of the courtroom. The survivors and their relatives who had watched the whole process of the trial, mute but concentrated, broke out in an agony of protest. Lucy released a shuddering sound, horribly similar to a laugh. She turned to Mr Lachaise. He sat still, with a repose wholly alien to the moment. His hand reached out to Lucy's. They were joined like father and daughter.

The other counts on the indictment were read out. Each received the same verdict: 'Not guilty.'

Lucy sat in a trance out of time, hearing words but unable to link them coherently. She could not dispel the image of Agnes, lying absolutely still, defenceless, consumed by silence. Everyone stood as Mr Justice Pollbrook left the Bench. And then from all around came echoing shuffles and bangs as though the court was being dismantled by stagehands impatient for home. The clatter became erratic, less insistent, and then faded.

'Excuse me, it's time to go.'

'I'm sorry?' said Lucy, stirring. The court and public gallery were empty, except for herself and Mr Lachaise. She was still holding his hand.

'It's time to go. I have to lock up,' said the usher, pointing like a curator towards the door.

Lucy stood. Mr Lachaise withdrew his pipe and thumbed the bowl reflectively.

'You can't use that in here,' said the usher officiously.

'Indeed not. It's just an old habit to occupy the hands.' With a warm glance he said, 'Go now, Lucy.'

She had always liked his accent and the engaging depth of his voice, like churning wet gravel. As she pushed open the swing doors she heard him ask:

'Would you be so kind as to do me a small favour . . . ?'

Then they closed.

Standing in Newgate Street, the presence of Agnes all around, suffusing metal, stone and cloud, Lucy hailed a taxi. 'Hammersmith,' she said woozily.

2

Anselm left Victor Brionne, knowing he would continue to drink but knowing there was little he could do to hold him back. Victor − he could call him nothing else − had urged Anselm to tell Agnes about Robert. It was a secret that could not be withheld from the little time she had remaining.

Anselm left shortly before 5 p.m. He dropped into a newsagent, drawn by the blaring of a radio from behind a curtain over the back room. He leafed through a paper, waiting for the news on the hour. The shock verdict delivered in the trial led a series of other items, culminating in the shock transfer of a football player. Two shocks, one at either end.

Anselm walked out, dazed, and looked around. It was a lovely, dusty, sunny day, and there were children playing in the street.

3

The front door was slightly ajar. Wilma must have popped out. Lucy walked purposefully through to Agnes' room. She kissed her forehead. It was warm and smooth, scented by baby oil – one of Wilma's gentle ministrations. Lucy took both of her grandmother's hands and said, 'Gran, they've set him free. It's all over.'

For a while Agnes did not respond. Her eyelids blinked slowly. Then her head swung to one side, arching backwards. From her mouth, stretched open, came a thin squealing exhalation of air that Lucy thought would never end.

In one scalding flash Lucy saw the snapshots of a lifetime – the catastrophic loss of a child; the death camps; the rescue of Freddie and Elodie, crowned with failure; the cost of silence; a remorseless, stripping illness; exclusion from the trial; and finally, when there was little left to take away, the vindication of the man she could, but would not, condemn.

The front door snapped shut. Wilma was back.

Lucy, completely detached from her actions, not fully knowing what she was doing, opened the bedside cupboard, searching for the revolver wrapped in a duster. She placed it with the four rounds of ammunition in her rucksack. Agnes, still trapped in a silent howl, tried to clutch at Lucy, her head flopping from side to side.

'Don't worry, Gran. I know what I'm doing. This is for Victor

363

Brionne. I'm not going to get into any trouble,' said Lucy, calm and reassuring, like a nurse.

'Would you mind explaining what is going on, madam?' said Wilma from the wings.

Lucy ran out, sweeping up the keys for the Duchess.

4

The radio from the newsagent blasted out an old Elvis hit about a woman, impolitely called a hound dog, who cried incessantly. Anselm set off for Manor House tube station, the singer's name having reminded him of a confession he'd once heard. The unseen face behind the grille had leaned forward, saying darkly, fearfully, 'Do you realise, Father . . . Elvis is an anagram for "Lives" . . . but also . . . "Evils" . . . the fiend is everywhere.' Anselm had said 'God is "dog" spelt backwards . . . the hound of heaven will protect you.' And the man had gone away healed.

Upon an impulse, Anselm patted his right-hand pocket, perhaps because it was lighter than it had been. The iron keys to St Catherine's. He'd left them on the armrest. Irritated, he began to retrace his steps. But there was no rush: Victor was going nowhere.

5

Lucy had written down Victor Brionne's address as he gave it with wavering self-pity to the court. Holmleigh Road, Stamford Hill. The words had mesmerised her, for they signified a home and garden – providing a life free of care on the other side of escape. She parked a few doors down, her eye on the neatly painted window frames. Night settled upon her conscience. She opened her bag and unrolled the duster. She pushed open the chamber and fed in the cartridges. Her hands moved quickly, professionally. She watched them, marvelling at their adroit purposefulness, their separation from her. She walked at a pace, before the light came back and she lost her nerve. Reaching the door, she struck it hard three times. It swung slowly back. Brionne appeared, slightly swaying on his feet.

'Yes?'

'I am the adopted granddaughter of Agnes Aubret. I want to talk to you.'

He stared at her through maudlin tears. 'What's your name?'

'Lucy Embleton.'

'Come in, but ignore the mess. I'm just beginning a bad patch.'

She hated the lurching intimacy of drink, the promise of unwanted confidences. And she hated him. She said, 'That doesn't bother me.'

'You're very kind,' he replied, retreating into the gloom. 'Would you like some tea?'

'No, thank you,' said Lucy, shutting the door and flipping down the lock. 'I won't be staying that long.'

6

Anselm rounded the corner, back into Holmleigh Road. The verdict lay upon his mind, pressing down like a migraine. By a low wall a cluster of young Hasidic Jews, bearded men in black suits and wide hats, stood talking animatedly; inside a house, Anselm glimpsed a number of women gesticulating.

Passing quickly round them, not wanting to hear their conversation, Anselm moved on towards Victor's home, further up the road.

As he approached the gate through which he had passed only a short while before, Anselm heard a voice from behind:

'Excuse me, Father, but could you spare a word . . .'

7

'I know exactly what you did to Agnes,' said Lucy at length.

Brionne nodded.

'I know what you did to her child.'

He nodded again, his eyes widening.

'And I know what you did at the trial.'

He moved towards a bottle and back, seeing it was empty.

'Agnes will die within the month. I would like you to die first.'

'How would you like me to oblige?'

'I have a gun.'

'That was very thoughtful of you.'

Lucy opened her bag and took out Grandpa Arthur's revolver. She cocked the hammer. 'It's already loaded.'

'Do you propose to do it yourself?'

'No.' She stretched from her seat and handed it to Brionne. 'I intend to sit here telling you every detail I know about Agnes, everything I know about my father, and everything about myself – and I will go on until you either shoot me or yourself.'

Brionne held the gun with a look of dark, drunken fascination. Gingerly, he raised the barrel, his eyes glazed and black. He bit a cracked lip and a spurt of blood ran on to his chin.

'I suggest you go now.'

'Father,' said a thin woman, walking down the path from an open front door, 'I saw you passing and, well, I wondered if you could say a prayer for a special intention.' She wore a head-scarf and florid apron, the combination redolent of wartime courage: wives on their knees scrubbing doorsteps, despite the nightly visits of German bombers.

'Of course,' said Anselm, retracing a few steps. Every street was the same, he thought: hidden behind each small façade was a universe of disappointment and hope.

'We don't see *our kind* here very often,' she said, nodding significantly at Anselm's habit and tilting her head down the road towards the other kind.

'I see,' said Anselm. A bitter, foreign urge to slap the bony face warmed him like a flush of blood.

'I'm Catholic, of course, like your good self.'

'I'm sorry but I'm an Anglican,' lied Anselm, his hand rising, the palm open; he put it on the gate.

'Oh,' she replied, discomfited, pushing stray dyed hairs under the scarf's fold. 'That must be nice.'

'It is.'

'Lovely. Well, then.'

'You have a special intention?'

'Well, I won't trouble you, it's just one of the family playing up . . . won't go to Mass . . . not a problem for your sort . . .'

Anselm heard the clip of a gate and looked round. To his amazement there was Lucy, wavering on the pavement, her hands loose by her side. He ran, exclaiming, 'Are you all right? What are you doing here?'

Dreamily, Lucy looked aside to the bay window. Anselm swiftly followed her drugged gaze: towards Victor, swaying uncertainly, the barrel of a gun pointing at his face. Anselm rushed for the door, throwing his full bodyweight against the lock. He bounced back, mocked by strength. Wildly, he struck it again, as though its tongues and grooves had given out all the needless griefs he'd ever known. And then, across a pause in the hammering, came a deafening short crack. Lucy cried out, like at a birth. Anselm held his breath until the tightness in his chest pushed out an oath. The woman in the apron and scarf scampered indoors to ring the police.

Chapter Forty-Four

1

The provision of an ambulance for Victor Brionne struck Anselm as incongruous given the circumstances. Standard procedure, said Detective Superintendent Milby with disinterest, dropping the gun into a plastic sample bag. He handed it to a colleague who stored it with the damaged book. 'All in a day's work,' he added, surveying the waste of Victor Brionne's life. Empty bottles, scatterings of fag-ash and an open packet of broken biscuits lay upon the floor.

'Pig,' said Milby.

An officer bending over an armchair recovered a set of keys, holding them up like a fish at the market.

'Ah, they're mine actually,' said Anselm.

The Detective Superintendent scrutinised his old adversary but let the puzzle pass. He said, 'Any chance of a favour?'

'Depends.'

'The girl wants someone to explain to her grandmother what's happened. Bit unwell apparently. More your scene than mine.'

'What's going to happen to her?' asked Anselm flatly, gesturing towards Lucy.

'Firearms. You know the game.'

'Favours sometimes have a price.'

'You should have been in the Drug Squad.'

369

Anselm urged the arresting officer to contact DI Armstrong, to ask if she would visit Lucy at the station. And then he accepted the offer of a lift to Chiswick Mall in a Detective Superintendent's carriage.

Anselm spoke assurances to Agnes, trying to assuage her trapped anxiety. He pulled his chair closer to the bed so as to read the alphabet card, but then the housekeeper entered pushing a television on a small serving trolley.

'Vicar, now is not the time to speak of The Last Things,' she admonished. 'You may preach, but after the news.'

2

Lucy sat on a bench opposite the Custody Sergeant's desk, waiting to be processed. Beside her sat Father Conroy, summoned at Father Anselm's request.

'At least you didn't pull the trigger,' said the priest.

'Would it have made any difference?'

'I was never that good at moral theology. But I do know about people who send other people to prison, and they think there is a difference.'

The declaration carried a weight. With the peculiar acuity that comes with anxiety, Lucy asked, 'Have you been to prison?'

'Yes.' He scratched the hairs on his thick arms. 'Several times.'

A liberating curiosity surfaced over the panic. 'What for?'

'Working with street kids in São Paulo.'

'You got locked up for that?'

'It's a touch more involved, so, but you can't make a home for those little divils without upsetting people.'

The arresting officer summoned Lucy with a flick of his

finger. Her pockets were emptied and she signed forms that she didn't read.

'Now, get your dainty skates on,' said the Custody Sergeant.

A waiting WPC took Lucy firmly by the elbow and escorted her down a colourless corridor to a cell. The heavy blue door slammed into position. Keys turned and jangled. The square peephole opened and banged shut. And, to the echo of withdrawing footsteps, Lucy started to cry.

The lock rattled as iron turned on iron. The door opened and DI Armstrong entered the cell. She sat on a chair fixed to the wall and said: 'You have been extraordinarily stupid.'

Lucy lifted her hands helplessly, as if she didn't understand what she had done. She continued to cry, increasingly terrified by the working out of the legal process upon her.

DI Armstrong said, 'I'll do what I can to smooth things for you but my hands are tied. You are in serious trouble.'

Lucy nodded, grateful for the promise of a friend, however useless, within the system that would judge her.

'There's been a development in the Schwermann trial,' DI Armstrong said, letting compassion slip out – evidently divining Lucy's undisclosed interest in the verdict. 'I don't know what has happened but I expect it will be on the news. You can watch it with me. That *is* something I can do for you.'

3

After the fanfare of headlines and solemn bells, the picture shifted to live coverage of the lead story at the Old Bailey.

Lighting stands and trails of wiring flanked the court entrance. Banks of cameras and boom microphones like slender cranes arched over metal railings on either side. Police officers in fluorescent yellow safety jackets stood at prescribed intervals around a pool of harsh, consuming light. High above the doors was the inscription read by Anselm at the outset of the trial: 'Defend the children of the poor and punish the wrongdoer.'

A home affairs correspondent explained that after his sensational acquittal Schwermann had been escorted back to the cells, where a discreet exit had been planned. However, as he was about to depart an unidentified male had presented himself to court staff, seeking an urgent interview on what was understood to be a private matter. Upon hearing the name of the man concerned, Schwermann had consented to a meeting.

'One thing we do know is that the consultation is over,' said the reporter. 'We're expecting them to emerge through these doors behind me at any moment. We understand this individual may well be a survivor who . . . in fact, there's some movement . . .'

The reporter shifted to one side as the court entrance jolted and opened, casting black, cutting shadows across the walls. A small man stepped out, shielding his eyes.

Lucy recognised the gentleman who'd sat beside her in the public gallery day after day giving her encouragement when it had no rational foundation, the man who had become a friend, Mr Salomon Lachaise. He moved to one side as Schwermann made his way forward. Microphones on angled poles followed him, clawing through the air at his neck and back.

Schwermann stood on the pavement, transfixed by the light, one hand nervously feeling the lower hem of his jacket. The camera position shifted closer, revealing Max Nightingale behind a policeman, his fists pushed deep into the pockets of his jacket.

Questions shot out from all sides, making it impossible to

372

hear what was being said except for the constant repetition of Schwermann's name. Salomon Lachaise looked on from a step – to Anselm's eyes as if from a judgment seat; to Lucy all of a sudden a man in mourning. When Schwermann looked up from the floor to the cameras the questions abruptly ended.

Salomon Lachaise stepped back into shadow as Schwermann spoke:

'This court has released me and declared me innocent. Before the eyes of the whole world I committed no crime.' He started to laugh, his face contracted with pain as if gripped by a spreading cramp. 'I started the war as one person, came to Paris . . . and overnight I became someone else . . . but I carried on doing what I'd done before.' Small explosions of flashlight struck his face as though he were standing by a crackling, angry fire. 'I admit I didn't cry "stop" . . . but I did do something worthwhile . . . and it gave me a reason to live . . . a reason to escape . . . a reason to fight this trial. All I want to say is this . . .'

Max Nightingale shifted his stance from behind the policeman to get a clearer view of his grandfather.

'Victor Brionne told the truth . . . but even he didn't know what he was saying . . .' Schwermann fell into a menacing, private fascination. The fine, smooth clattering of the cameras grew faster and louder; sheets of instantaneous flame danced and died, one after the other. Quietly, remonstrating with the light, he said, 'A boy was saved.'

His right hand shakily fingered his jacket hem. Eyes wide, like a painted toy, he said, 'Hasn't that made a difference?'

Eduard Walter Schwermann suddenly fell to his knees. The face of Salomon Lachaise moved into the light. A policeman lunged a step and halted, confused, as Schwermann, lifting the lower flap of his jacket, pulled at the inside lining. He fished something out and put it in his mouth, closed his eyes, bit and dropped like a marionette whose strings had been severed with a single cut.

As the commotion unfurled, the discerning viewer could easily see the diminutive figure of Salomon Lachaise in the background, walking heavily away from the pandemonium, into the shadows and out of sight.

4

Wilma unplugged the television and left the bedroom. The door clipped shut. For a long while Anselm tried to read the motionless face of the woman waiting to die. Nothing moved. There was just a slow blinking and then a welling-up of tears that ran into the soft creases of her skin.

Now was as good a time as any, thought Anselm. On this day of death there should be powerful words about life. He cleared his throat. 'Agnes, I have something to tell you.'

She raised a finger off the bedspread.

'I know you had a son, Robert, and that he was taken away from you.'

She reached for his hand.

'You have lived as though he were dead.'

She turned her head, applying the lightest of pressure to Anselm's fingers.

'Victor did not betray you. He took your boy and protected him. I have met Robert. He is very much alive.'

Agnes suddenly raised herself from the bed, startling Anselm, and rasped out a thick sound of pain or wonder. She fell back, gripping Anselm's hand. Her mouth moved round the shape of words but nothing broke into sound.

374

Anselm said, 'He's tall.'

A squeeze.

'In comparison to me, moderately handsome.'

A squeeze.

'I understand he's a prodigy on the piano.'

A frail, lingering squeeze.

'He's married to a charming woman. She's called Maggie.'

Her strength had gone; her fingers lay warm and still within Anselm's hands.

'They have five children. Some of them are married and they, too, have children. Agnes, you are not only a mother . . . you are a grandmother and a great-grandmother.'

Her lips pursed into a loop, her eyes wide and swimming. Somehow the years were stripped back and Anselm sensed the ambiance of youth, captured by Victor Brionne in the photograph seen earlier that afternoon. He immediately recognised her for who she was, and who she had become; they were one and the same.

Wilma bustled in, carrying a teaspoon, a saucer and a bowl of ice cubes.

5

Lucy was taken back to her cell. Half an hour later the heavy door swung open with a bang. Lucy was waved out by an impatient hand and taken to the Custody Sergeant's desk. Father Conroy was still there, beside DI Armstrong, who said: 'The Detective Superintendent says you can go home. You're bailed for a week. When you come back there'll be an interview. After that you may be charged.'

Lucy collected her personal belongings, signed more forms

and Father Conroy led her outside. On the street he said, 'Come on, I'll drive you home.'

As he pulled away into a stream of traffic, Lucy said evenly: 'They both deserved to die.'

'Say that to Father Anselm.'

'Why?'

'He's always full of surprises.'

'About what?'

'Convincing appearances.'

They did not speak for the rest of the journey. Father Conroy dropped her in Acre Lane, near her flat. As Lucy stepped on to the pavement he said, 'Nothing's what it seems, you know. Don't worry.'

Out in the cold she walked hurriedly to her door, fighting a growing sense of having stained herself by wanting to savour revenge, because she hoped Agnes had seen the news and felt the same: that she too had sought pleasure in watching the keeper of the flame extinguish himself.

Part Four

'They will come again, the leaf and the flower, to arise
From squalor of rottenness into the old splendour . . .'
(Laurence Binyon, 'The Burning of the Leaves', 1942)

Fourth Prologue

Agnes could no longer lift her arms or head, but her fingers moved and she could still use the alphabet card if everything was held in place. There were still some things that had to be said.

She was fed by drip now, procured by Freddie when he insisted that his mother would not die in a hospital bed but in her own home. Everyone diligently fussed over her needs, not realising that Agnes didn't care, knowing nothing of the carnival that raged out of sight.

For within her the heavens were lit by repeated explosions of fireworks, with every shade of blue and green and yellow and red, splintering into trillions of gleaming particles against a vast stream of silver, dancing stars. They fell as a shower upon her raised head, on to her lashes, balancing precariously on each curved, counted hair before tumbling joyously over into the abyss beneath, where she would soon follow after the reunion with Robert that would surely come. She had entered upon a timeless, enduring, secret benediction.

Chapter Forty-Five

1

The reliability of a wartime revolver after decades in a cupboard was literally a hit and miss affair. Unlike capsules of potassium cyanide. Which struck Anselm as a happy imbalance in the scheme of things, given Lucy's misguided attempt to provoke Victor's suicide.

It transpired that Victor had had no intention of killing himself at all. Like all men who have known grave dependence on alcohol, he had a certain clarity of mind that was sharpened when drunk. And so, confronted with a young woman whose level of foolishness reflected the degree of her distress, he'd thought it prudent to accept the offered gun. After Lucy had gone he'd pointed the barrel at his face, looking into the dark, narrow hole. It had been, he said, a sort of playing, an acting out of the preliminary steps to an oblivion that had its attractions but which he would not choose. How could he? No matter what personal suffering he had endured, no matter the scale of moral compromise, there was Robert, the children and the grandchildren. They rose like flowers from the catastrophe of his life, and their splendour, however circumscribed, had a fragile, redemptive quality. He lived for them. And now, Victor had learned that they lived for Agnes.

And yet, but for the protecting hand of luck, Victor would have shot himself. Upon lowering the barrel, the hammer suddenly discharged, held back (it turned out) by a hairline trigger. The round went off, destroying a rare copy of Doctor Johnson's dictionary that had cost Victor most of his retirement lump sum.

Victor was kept in hospital overnight, on account of his bitten lip and presumed shock, and released the next morning, whereupon Anselm paid him a welcome visit at home.

'As I told you before,' said Victor, 'I had always seen the irony of my predicament – on paper, I was the one who had betrayed The Round Table. So when I came to England I decided to set the record straight, if you will forgive the expression. The idea came to me when I was wondering how I might conceal my identity still further. I decided to change my name a second time. What name? I thought.'

'Brownlow?' interjected Anselm with a faint, querying smile.

'The man who rescued Oliver Twist,' replied Victor. For him it was an old joke, lame but enduring, a sniff at adversity.

'Of course,' snapped Anselm. 'I knew I recognised it.'

Abandoning the advantages his education and talent would have brought him, Victor then chose factory work as a long-term hiding place. For most of his employed life he stood by a conveyor belt putting lids on jars of mustard. He saved what he could for Robert's precocious talent at the piano. He met Pauline, his wife-to-be, at a church fair bookstall. Nature ran its course and she became a mother to Robert, but he was old enough to remember her coming into his life.

'When he was old enough to understand, I told him his real mother had died during an air raid. Disasters are always convincing.'

For twenty-six years Pauline had been his strength, the woman to whom he confided all that had happened. When she knew

382

she was going to die from a rare kidney complaint she wrote Victor a letter, to help him after she had gone. But they were lifeless words, shapes in ink. He used to stare at them, trying to summon up the voice that had once spoken to him, her passion, her belief in him, her constant forgiveness for the wrongs of which he was a part. He'd been to confession.

'He gave me absolution,' Victor remembered, 'but he refused to give me a penance. Keep talking to Pauline, he said. And I did. But her kidneys packed up and she died. That's when I started drinking.'

All the family thought it was grief; which was true, but it was also the other burden he could no longer carry alone. He attended an expensive rehabilitation programme sorted out by Robert and found it completely humiliating – not because he was proud but because he could not disclose the reasons for his collapse.

'They thought I was "avoiding the pain required to face the truth about myself". I found that judgment distinctly unpalatable. It was, as with so much of my life, a hideous misunderstanding.'

They sat in silence until Anselm rose. He had a train to catch.

'Robert will have to be told everything,' Victor said, exhausted. 'Difficult as that might be, the thought of it done is like . . . an accomplishment.'

'I have already arranged to see him,' said Anselm.

Cautiously, reflectively, Victor said, 'It's all been an inexplicable mix of misfortune and luck. But since I'm a religious man, I look to Providence. Only that rather complicates things, don't you think? Because there's no accounting for the graces received, set against what went wrong, without hindrance, for so long.'

Anselm didn't have a reply for that particular observation.

Lucy met Father Anselm on the forecourt of Liverpool Street Station. She had wanted to see him before he went back to Larkwood Priory, to say thank you, and had duly rung him at St Catherine's the night before. The monk stood behind his suitcase like one of those carved statues on the front of a cathedral, observing the passing world on its busy way to somewhere important. He saw her and raised a hand.

Lucy said, 'I'm told it's because of you I'm not going to be charged.'

'That's not strictly true,' replied the monk. 'Detective Superintendent Milby and I go back a long way. He'd never have put you through the system if he could help it. But what you did was remarkably daft, wasn't it?'

'At the time I was watching myself,' said Lucy. 'It was as though the whole episode was part of a play, and once I'd started writing the script I couldn't stop. At last I was in control. I could choose the ending. But it was unreal. I just wanted to rehearse what it would be like and see it through to the end.' She felt again the queasy warmth of guilt passed by. 'Detective Inspector Armstrong told me that, once cocked, the trigger was so light it could have gone off in my hand without me even touching it.'

'And you would have killed the last knight of The Round Table,' said Father Anselm, 'the man who saved Robert. It doesn't bear thinking about.' The monk went on to give a short account of Victor's true position in the weave of events. Horrified at the magnitude of her error, humbled and ashamed, Lucy said, 'Someone must have been looking after me.'

'I know what you mean,' replied the monk pensively. 'That is a phrase upon which to ponder.' He glanced at the departure board. 'I'm afraid I have to go.'

Lucy walked with him along the platform. 'I must tell my father who he is.'

'Yes . . . and I must tell Robert Brownlow whose son he is.'

Lucy felt the first stirrings of an idea that she knew would fulfil itself. She had a sense of festival, streamers, a family outing. Father Anselm stopped by the train door and said: 'Did you know that Salomon Lachaise was saved by The Round Table?'

'No.' She thought of the gentleman who had become her friend, having at one definite point in the course of the trial sought her out, along with Max Nightingale. 'And yet he didn't sit with the other survivors.'

The monk looked at her curiously. 'How strange. I didn't realise that . . .'

Lucy's idea took a firm shape:

'I'd like to bring all these people together, before my grandmother dies. They all belong in the same room.'

Surprised agreement lit the monk's face.

She said, 'Would you come, Father?'

'Thank you, and remember . . . I'm also a messenger from the past.'

A messenger: somehow, despite the long, unrelenting conspiracy of misfortune, a letter had been passed on, as by runners at night, despite the guns, despite the wire. It would be brought to Agnes just before she died.

A man in a tired uniform appeared, urging stragglers to get on board. The one remaining question fell from her lips as the door began to swing on its dirty hinge: 'I wonder what Mr Lachaise said to Schwermann . . .'

'Yes, I wonder,' replied the monk.

The door banged shut. A loud whistle soared over the carriages. The train heaved forwards, clattering on the rails. The man in uniform walked quickly past, his job done. And Father Anselm, his face framed by a grimy square of glass, moved away.

Chapter Forty-Six

Salomon Lachaise said he wanted to come to Larkwood. He needed some time to be alone and asked if he might stay at The Hermitage. The Prior granted his permission. For three days the Priory's guest wandered in the woods, along the stream and round the lake. Then, one morning, Anselm found a note in his pigeonhole. Salomon Lachaise would welcome a visit.

Anselm walked quickly through the fields after lunch. About two hundred yards from The Hermitage was a narrow wooden footbridge, without railings, spanning the stream. The small man sat upon the timbers. Silently, Anselm joined him. Their legs hung loose over the edge.

Salomon Lachaise said, 'Do you remember, before the end of the trial, saying you had been one person with me while all the while you were another?'

'Yes. You replied that that was true of all of us.'

'Your memory serves you well.'

'I wondered what you meant.'

'I'm not sure I'll ever be able to explain. But I will try. You know that I learned early on in my life that I was one of the few who had escaped . . . that my whole family had been taken away. I kept the memory of their names alive. I told you that I found peace in scholarship, that I owed the outset of my academic life to a survivor.'

'Yes, I remember.'

For a short while Salomon Lachaise pondered the rush of water beneath his feet. He said, 'My life changed on a bright, cold morning just after a lecture on feudal iconography. I walked into the common room at the University and picked up a newspaper. A journalist had discovered that . . . that man . . . had found refuge in Britain after the war.'

'Pascal Fougères was the author?'

'Yes. I decided to contact him, and told my mother. No, she said, dear God, no. Leave the past alone. I turned to Mr Bremer – I told you about him when we first met – the lawyer who had become my guide. He, too, had seen the article. He, too, advised me to get on with my life . . . to forget what I had read.'

'Did you?'

'No.'

Salomon Lachaise proceeded in a low monotone. 'I went to see Mr Bremer. I told him my mind was made up; I was going to join myself to those who were seeking that man. I asked for his support before I told my mother.'

'You received it?'

'No. It would be right to say he lost his professional detachment.'

'Why?'

'The article we had both read gave the name of the small town that man had come from . . . Wissendorf . . . Mr Bremer recognised it from his dealings with the lawyer retained by my benefactor. He made what I think is called a reasonable assumption of fact. My refusal to heed his advice forced him to tell me that the German lawyer acting on behalf of the "survivor" was the family solicitor for . . . that man.'

'Schwermann was the . . . survivor?' asked Anselm, aghast at the appropriation of the word.

388

'Yes. And to think . . . I made my name in a field of learning that is known as the age of patronage.'

Salomon Lachaise watched his dangling feet, carefully trailing the soles of his shoes against the heavy pull of water. Blackened silver spurted either side at every sweeping touch.

Anselm said, tentatively, 'Why you?'

Very slowly, Salomon Lachaise said, 'I was the last child saved by The Round Table, taken to safety by Agnes Aubret just before her arrest.'

Anselm turned and scrutinised the face of his companion. It was a miracle of calm, a screen of chalk that would fall into powder if touched. Uncomprehending, Anselm said, 'He must have seen your existence as a salving of conscience.'

'My entire academic life rests upon contamination. Everything I have achieved rises from poison, bright flowers out of filth. I shall never practise my art again.'

Anselm struggled to remonstrate, 'But surely . . .' He floundered, lacking conviction, for he knew that the most costly decisions are often not made – they happen.

'I did not contact Fougères and my mother thought that I had taken her advice. Shortly afterwards she died, peacefully. And while that brought grief, it set me free.'

'To do what?' Anselm had sensed something specific . . . something crucial.

'Mr Bremer was a meticulous man, a keeper of detailed records which he never destroyed. By chance there had once been an error in the transfer of funds from the solicitor in Germany to him. In sorting out the tangle he'd learned the name of the client. At my request he dug out his old papers and there it was . . . Nightingale.'

'And you passed that on to Pascal Fougères?' asked Anselm.

'Yes. When that man claimed sanctuary, I took early retirement and followed his route of escape, from Paris to Les Moineaux. I had an inkling he'd somehow taken the same route as my mother. Then I came here, to Larkwood. After that it was a matter of waiting for the outcome of the trial.' He breathed deeply, like one bent over, preparing to heave a rock to one side. He said, 'I waited for him to speak, to hear what he had to say to those he had robbed. But in the end he said nothing, and they freed him. He was exactly what he appeared to be, only the jury had a doubt. The moment I'd waited for had come . . . and I did not want it. I told an usher I wanted to see him and I gave my name.'

Again he ran his feet upon the surface of the stream, watching the sweeping cuts in the silvery rush, opened up, now closed, then opened up again. Salomon Lachaise described how he was shown through to a room rather like a post office counter.

A window of thick glass lay seated in the wall. Beneath, on each side, was a wide sill – a table passing through the divide – and a chair.

'A door opened and suddenly there he was. For a long while I just looked at him, each line upon his face, the nails upon his fingers. He raised a hand, putting it against the glass.'

Schwermann had spoken first across the divide:

'I didn't realise it was you, in the woods . . .'

'Yes.'

'I can hardly believe that you are here, that you have come.' Gratitude and fearful wonder loosened his drawn features.

'Yes, I have come.'

'How did you find out?'

'I am here, that is all that matters.'

'I managed to save you, do you know that?'

390

'Yes, I do.'

'After I got away and had enough money, I had you traced, I gave what I could, I've followed your success . . .' The appeal sought recognition, appreciation.

'Yes, I understand that.'

'I've had a family . . . a daughter . . . a grandson, but through all these years I have never forgotten you . . . I have thought of you, wondering how you have grown.'

'Yes, I am sure.'

'You were one of the reasons my life was worth anything.'

'Yes.'

'And now, when all the others have gone, it is you that has come to see me . . . I am overwhelmed . . .'

Perhaps it was the crippling tension of the moment, perhaps it was his saturation in culture, but in a flash Salomon Lachaise suddenly remembered a devastating passage from Virgil's *Aeneid*, where Aeneas towers triumphant over the fallen Turnus, a man of great strength, having defeated him in single combat; Aeneas raises his sword to carry out the execution, but Turnus pleads for his life, for the sake of his father; Aeneas checks the fall of his arm and hesitates . . . but then his eye catches the belt of Pallas, a trophy upon the shoulder of Turnus . . . Pallas, his dearest friend, slain without mercy . . .

Salomon Lachaise said, his voice cracked and low: 'What of the others, my mother's family, the thousands, the sons and daughters—'

'There was nothing I could do.'

'You did a great deal.'

The old man wheedled, as if for the hundredth time, 'I had no choice.'

'Yes, you did. You have forgotten too much.'

391

'Please, Salomon, listen . . . can't you forgive . . .' The pleading became a wail.

'I do not have that power. And neither does God. It belongs to those you abandoned. Now hear me.'

Schwermann became instantly still, as though his heart had ceased to beat. He simply breathed, a functioning suddenly foreign to his waiting, expectant body. Salomon Lachaise stood up and said: 'I raise in my hands the dust from which you were made and I cast it to the wind. May you never be remembered, either under the sun or at its setting.'

He turned away from the dividing glass. And from the prisoner on the other side, soon to be freed, came the sound of a withered, resentful moan.

Salomon Lachaise had finished speaking. The wild chase of water beneath their feet grew loud. Anselm repeated what he'd read in the papers:

'The police found capsules in two of his jackets, sewn into the same corner below the left pocket, with a loose thread ready to be pulled when needed.'

'So I understand.'

'Presumably they were taken out and put back after every visit to the dry cleaner's.'

'Yes, I expect you are right.'

Anselm thought of the private ritual, the unpicking and the sewing up over the years, the constant preparedness to escape a judgment imposed by anyone other than himself. Before Anselm could pursue his reflections, Salomon Lachaise said, with closing authority: 'I shall never talk of him again.'

As at a signal, they both clambered on to their knees and stood, Anselm helping his companion gain balance. Strolling

392

back to The Hermitage, Anselm said, 'What will you do now?'

'Travel. I want to keep moving. I have no commitments, no dependants.'

'You'll remain in Geneva?'

'Yes. As much as I have left the University, it remains something of a home. Anyway' – he smiled brightly – 'I intend to arrange a small exhibition of young Max's paintings. Have you seen them?'

'No.'

'You should. They possess alarming innocence. I shall try to use the ignominy of his background to his advantage. Otherwise it will remain a curse.'

'That is kind.'

'Nothing done for pleasure is kind.'

They reached The Hermitage shack, and Anselm made to amble back to the Priory. Pointing at the open door, Salomon Lachaise said, 'Can you join me for a final glass of port? I never go anywhere without a bottle.'

They sat on wobbling wooden chairs, sipping in silence, until Anselm said, 'Would you like to meet Agnes Aubret?'

Salomon Lachaise, with tears in his eyes, could not reply.

Chapter Forty-Seven

1

Lucy met her father in the noble gardens of Gray's Inn. As they entered, she pointed at the stone beasts on the gate columns. 'Griffins,' said her father knowledgably. 'Protectors of paradise. Don't they teach you anything about myths these days?'

His suit was crafted to his body, immaculately creased and cut. In his own world, thought Lucy, he was powerful and successful and wore the uniform of esteemed competence. When they found a bench, he dusted off dry particles of nothing with the back of a hand. Sitting like two lone strays at a matinee, each with their legs crossed, Lucy began the stripping of her father.

'Dad, none of us are who we think we are.'

Her father, enjoying a tease, replied, 'And I suppose no one else is who we think they are.'

'No, quite right.' She cut through the smart cloth of known appearances to the soft epidermis. 'It's true of Gran' – he looked suddenly wary – 'and it is especially true of you.'

Lucy explained to her father how he had been saved from Ravensbrück by Agnes, that he was born of unknown, murdered parents, from an unknown place, that they were buried no one knew where. And she told him Agnes was the mother of a son whom she'd lost, a son who had been found. He listened, entranced and dismayed, fingering the constricting knot of his

394

tie. When Lucy had finished he sat stunned, as though waiting for the lights to come on in a theatre, the only one left in a curved, empty stall.

'Do you know,' he said faintly, 'I think she nearly told me once.'

'When?'

'Years and years ago . . . before the rot set in . . . I was fifteen or sixteen and I gave her a mouthful about her silence' – again he reached for his restricting collar – 'I said she'd never cared, not even when I'd fallen as a boy and cut my knee.'

'What did she say?' asked Lucy.

Her father sat upright, the movement of feet scuffing a gleaming shoe. He wiped his dry lips with a handkerchief and said, 'Nothing, actually, at first. But her face crumpled . . . in a way that I have never been able to forget . . . and just when I thought she was going to tell me something she was gone, into herself . . .'

'She didn't speak?'

He nodded, his face flushed and shining. 'She said, "Oh Freddie, say anything about me but not that, not that."' He joined his hands in hopeless, abject supplication. 'God, I have to see her . . . I have to tell her I'm sorry . . .'

The gardens of the Inn were due to close, their lunchtime access about to be withdrawn by edict of the Honourable Benchers. Like a stream of obedient refugees, young and old started threading their way towards the ornate gates. Lucy and Freddie followed suit. They walked back the way they had come, changed from who they were when they'd entered.

'I had always thought, in some obscure way, she did not want me.'

395

These were words Lucy could hardly bear to hear. She looked down, fastening her attention on the measured crunching of fine gravel.

'In one sense, I suppose that is true . . .'

Lucy lowered her head further, her chin discovering a necklace given to her by him on her tenth birthday. She pressed hard against the warm gold chain as he spoke:

'Isn't life bloody awful sometimes. She could never have told me when I most wanted to know because I would not have understood. And now that I am old enough to understand she can't tell me.'

Lucy forced the tiny links into the skin of her neck. He said:

'I'd give anything to go back to that moment when her face fell, to tell her I didn't mean it . . . but that is part of the hell – I did mean it . . . I did. I just wish I'd never said it. Unfortunately, we have to live with what we've said, as well as what we've done.'

Reaching the gates, Lucy looked up. It seemed her father had aged, but the lines through his skin were yielding, well drawn. He was like a man who'd been well treated by an indulgent parole board. Yes, they would recommend his release; but so many years of imprisonment had passed that the spout within for exhilaration had rusted, clogged. They all watched him in a line, waiting for the bursting forth. He could only smile, shake hands, bow . . . mutter thanks.

He faced Lucy and said plainly, 'There's still enough time left to make a difference, don't you think?'

'Yes.'

They walked out into Field Court and the gates of paradise politely closed. Her father kissed her goodbye. Strange, thought Lucy: it was only since she'd told her father about the death

396

of Pascal that intimacy, of the kind they each wanted, had been restored between them. Glancing up at a mute griffin, Lucy could have sworn she saw the little beast breathe.

2

Anselm left Salomon Lachaise to the solitude of Larkwood and took a train to Newcastle. From there he took the rattling Metro to the coast where Robert Brownlow lived.

Anselm had made the arrangement with Maggie, who opened the door before he could knock. She led him anxiously to the foot of the stairs. Anselm told her not to worry and went up to join Robert in the lounge.

They stood at the window, looking out on Cullercoats Bay. Down below on the beach was little Stephen, heaping sand with his father, Francis.

'Francis is my eldest,' said Robert. 'Over there is Caroline, his wife, with the recent addition, Ian. He's eleven months.' A woman, evidently not used to the rigours of a sunny North-East afternoon, sat wrapped in an overcoat by an outcrop of rocks. The round, covered head of an infant protruded between the raised lapels.

'I've got four other children. Two are married, both of them have kids. Altogether we come to thirteen. And now we're in pieces.'

They watched two generations shivering on the sand.

'Robert,' said Anselm, 'you told me when we first met that Victor had died after the war.'

'As far as I was concerned, he had. That man was not my father. Victor Brownlow was. At least, that is what I wanted to believe, for their sake,' he nodded towards the beach, 'and for mine. But now, after watching him in court defending that man, it's the other way round. My father has died and I find myself the son of Victor Brionne.'

Unseen by his father, little Stephen had begun to undress, his face set towards the frozen sea. Stephen's mother, permanently alert, shooed her husband away, back to his charge.

Anselm chose his words carefully. 'Part of what you have said is true. Your father is dead.'

Robert turned, his brown eyes puzzled, not quite meshing with the bite of the words.

Anselm continued, 'As you say, Victor Brionne is not your father. Nor is he now. He never was.'

'What do you mean?' asked Robert.

'You are the son of Jacques Fougères.'

Robert's mouth fell slightly apart; he roughly drew a hand across his short, neat hair. 'The man mentioned in the trial?'

'Yes.'

'Who had a child by Agnes Aubret?'

'Yes.'

'I am that child?'

'Yes, Robert, you are.'

He moved away from the light of the window, unsteadily, towards a chair. Sitting down cautiously, he said, 'Agnes Aubret . . . my mother?'

'Yes.'

'Who died in Auschwitz?' His eyes began to flicker. He coughed, lightly.

'No. Robert, she is alive. She survived. She lives in London. She is very ill and will soon die.'

'My God.'

'It is a long and involved story,' said Anselm, moving to

Robert's side, 'and Victor will tell you everything. All I want to say is this. You are alive today because he saved you. The price he paid was horrendous and he's been paying ever since.'

'Tell me a little more, anything . . .'

Anselm briefly gave the outline of Victor's chosen path, with its unforeseen penalty, and his further choices.

Fearful, like one trapped in the sand, the tide approaching, Robert said, 'I'll have to relive my whole life, right from the beginning, find myself . . . seek out . . . my father . . . seek out Victor.' He stumbled over the changing references within simple words.

Anselm replied quickly, with gentle insistence, 'Robert, begin that journey with your mother; she already knows . . . and let Victor be your guide.'

Robert walked to the door and called out faintly, 'Maggie, come here, please . . .'

She came running up the stairs. As she entered the room Robert weakly extended his arms. She clasped his neck, exclaiming, 'What's happened, Robert? Tell me, tell me.'

Anselm strode outside into a sudden blustering, the long exhalations of the sea. Beneath a cupola of unremitting light he passed through a gate and found a cliff trail skirting the bay. He walked, his face averted to the wind, until, at a midpoint, he turned, squinting, and looked back: there was the house, etched into hard, shapeless cloud, the windows punched small and black; and there, below, on the beach, was little Stephen with tousled blond hair, piling up the wet sand . . . the carefree, joyous great-grandson of Agnes Aubret and Jacques Fougères.

Chapter Forty-Eight

1

The day before Agnes' first and last reunion with her family it rained: a bombarding, cruel inundation that bled the sky. Bloated cloud hung low, shrouding high-rise flats and sharp steeples. For once Lucy didn't want to be on her own. She rang Cathy and asked if she could stay the night.

Lucy took the tube to Pimlico and dashed through the puddles, her head bent into her chest. By the time she got to Cathy's flat she was drenched. After a bath, she wrapped herself in a large, warmed towel. When she padded into the sitting room she saw takeaway cartons lined up on a tray. Cathy looked up and said, 'Mongolian. Honestly.'

Lucy noticed the absence of make-up. Cathy looked younger, like she'd been at Cambridge but without the confident aggression. Outside, the rain thumped upon dull, empty pavements; and, as the night fell, Lucy told Cathy what would happen the next day. Cathy listened, moving food around her plate with tiny flicks of a fork. It was in the telling that Lucy had another idea. While they were preparing for bed, she stuck her head around the bathroom door and said, 'Would you like to meet someone?'

'Who?'

'A man.'

'I need a bit more than that.'

'He knows how to use a pallet knife.'

'Set it up.'

Lucy lay awake, longing for the wind and rain to be reconciled, or at least to put off their fight for another day. The weather was going to wreck the plans for the morrow. While she worked out an alternative strategy sleep crept upon her by surprise. When Lucy woke the next morning, weak sunshine stole between a gap in the curtains and lit the wall with a shaft of subdued flame. Throwing open the window, she listened with gratitude to the silent work of heat upon water, a union that always recaptured the first freshness of things.

After breakfast, Lucy abandoned the trousers and top she'd bought the day before and dressed in one of Cathy's smart conversation-stoppers: a navy blue dress with hand-painted enamel buttons. Standing on the doorstep Cathy warned, 'If you stain that, I'll weep.'

Lucy caught a glint of tears.

'I hope everything goes fine,' Cathy said.

2

Freddie had organised the reception at Agnes' flat. A trellis table was set up in the back courtyard, covered with plates, laden trays, glasses, plastic cups, bottles of Bollinger, Manzanilla and ghastly fizzy drinks for children. It was lavish, and Wilma said he'd gone mad. The guests arrived for two o'clock: Salomon Lachaise; Victor Brionne; Robert and Maggie Brownlow, with their five children, and their children; Father Anselm; and Father Conroy, who moved round the living room quietly, spinning threads among them all.

Stepping slightly forward, Lucy gave words of welcome and

then abandoned everything she had planned to say. Instead she said, 'I would simply like to remember the names of those who, for reasons we all know, cannot join us.' She raised her glass, speaking with unaffected ceremony, 'Father Rochet and Madame Klein . . . Jacques Fougères and all the knights of The Round Table . . . Father Morel . . . Father Pleyon . . . Grandpa Arthur . . . Pascal Fougères . . .' Lucy turned instinctively to her father, willing him to take the torch.

'And I thank heaven,' said Freddie, moving towards the open door, within earshot of Agnes, 'that among us there is someone who almost lost herself saving others. Friends, to my mother.'

They all sipped in silence. Unseen by all save Lucy, Wilma deftly wiped a surface. After the toast, parents surreptitiously produced toys, strategically laying them on the ground like bait to trap wild beasts.

The plan was this: each guest, after seeing Agnes, would knock on the door through which they had come, as a signal to the next, and then go out into the back garden through the French windows. The drawing of a single curtain secured privacy for each meeting. When he was ready, Lucy took Salomon Lachaise to Agnes.

The small man was dressed in an elegant suit with new shoes. He walked stiffly, his hands meshed. Lucy led him through the open door and then withdrew, watching his reverent approach. She heard his deep, compassionate voice:

'Madame Embleton, we have met once before, when I was a boy . . .'

Lucy shut the door. For a moment she stood still, straining to catch a word, as Agnes had once done with Madame Klein and Father Rochet. Then she turned away, as his voice rose.

She came back to the living room exhausted, and marvelled

402

at the smooth ministrations of Father Conroy. After a while there came a faint knock, and Lucy threw a glance at Father Anselm.

Agnes was elevated by pillows with the alphabet card on her lap. The drip stood tall, like a hiding guard, its tubes and bags clothed by a flag of linen. She wore a green silk blouse and red cashmere cardigan. The colours threw a faint diaphanous sheen on to the skin around her neck. Illness, resplendent and spoiling, could not take away her radiance. There were two chairs by the bed, with a vase of flowers on the table. Beside the vase lay a small school notebook. A light breeze gently flapped the curtain upon the open French window like bunting on a seaside stall.

Agnes' blue eyes fixed on Anselm. Emotion pierced his throat and he swallowed hard against a blade. Deathbed scenes, he thought; the last chance to say something sensible, something honest, to wrap it all up. But not here, not now. He shuddered: this wasn't death; that had been and gone, long ago, routed; this was life. He sat down, shaking, and took out a brown, brittle envelope. Lucy sat beside him as he withdrew a single sheet of paper.

'Agnes,' he began, 'I was handed this by Mr Snyman. He told me Jacques had given it to him before he was arrested, hoping it might be brought to you if, by some unimaginable chance, you survived the coming night.'

Through a simple dilating movement of the eyes, Agnes told him to read. Her breathing began to catch hesitantly; fine, curved lashes slowly fell, remaining shut. At the raising of a single, trembling finger, Anselm began reading, in French:

'April's tiny hands once captured Paris
As you once captured me: infant Trojan
Fingers gently peeled away my resistance
To your charms. It was an epiphany,
I saw waving palms, rising dust, and yes,
I even heard the stones cry out your name,
Agnes.'

Anselm paused at the end of the first verse. He looked over
to Agnes. A faint pulse jerked behind her eyelids. Anselm resumed
reading:

'And then the light fell short.
I made a pact with the Devil when the
"Spring Wind" came, when Priam's son lay bleeding
On the ground. As morning broke the scattered
Stones whispered 'God, what have you done?' and yes,
I betrayed you both. Can you forgive me,
Agnes?'

At the words of confession she opened her eyes. Inflections
of shadow seemed to move beneath her skin like passing cloud.
Agnes lifted her hand to one side, exposing the white, soft palm.
She turned to Anselm, who understood. He placed the letter
on the bed and her hand lay tenderly upon it as though it were
flesh.

After a long moment Agnes looked to Lucy, who walked
around Anselm to pick up the second school notebook from
the bedside table; then she reached for the alphabet card and
placed it in position. Agnes said:

F-A-T-H-E-R

Pause.

P-L-E-A-S-E

Pause.

W-I-L-L

Pause.

Y-O-U

Pause.

G-I-V-E

Pause.

T-H-I-S

Pause.

T-O

Pause.

M-R

Pause.

S-N-Y-M-A-N

Anselm took the notebook offered to him by Lucy.

Agnes continued:

W-I-L-L

Pause.

Y-O-U

Pause.

B-U-R-Y

Pause.

M-E

Pause.

A-F-T-E-R

Pause.

I-M

Pause.

D-E-A-D

Through his teeth, Anselm said, 'Of course.'

A–N–D

Pause.

N–O–T

Pause.

B–E–F–O–R–E

There was something about the fall of light upon her lips that suggested a smile: with joy, sorrow, acquiescence, loss, gratitude and farewell: each transparent inflection inhabiting the other. Anselm moved to the French windows and stepped outside, all but overcome by a stifled impulse to shout. He faced a small lawn in a courtyard garden that trapped sunlight between high, brick-red walls. On the far side, like someone lost, stood Salomon Lachaise, distraught.

4

Lucy left Father Anselm and returned to the living room; then Robert and Victor followed her down the short, narrow passage back to the half-open door. She stood aside to let them pass. Victor walked closely behind Robert, one arm round his waist, a hand upon his shoulder: a faithful mentor guiding a nervous protégé on to the stage at prize-giving – a boy frightened of applause, its roar, its power to dismantle what had been built in secret.

The door swung open at Robert's touch. On entering, Victor covered his mouth, defeated, and said, 'Agnes, je te présent . . . ton fils . . .'

Lucy stood transfixed by a miracle greater than any of the old school stories – manna in the desert, water from a rock or the parting of any waves – Agnes slowly raised her head and neck fully off the pillow. In answer to the call, her face turned towards her son. As Lucy backed away, astounded, she heard what to many might have been a sigh, a sudden loud breathing, at most a gathering of soft vowels, but to her it carried the unmistakable shape of a name not uttered in fifty years: 'Robert!'

5

After all the family had passed through to Agnes, Lucy stood alone by her grandmother's bed, looking out through the open French windows. The thick, polished glass flashed in the sun, catching dark reflections of red brick; people, young and old, talked casually, a hand in a pocket, a schooner twinkling; and tumbling upon the grass were the children, dressed in yellow and blue and green. Agnes gazed out upon them all. Lucy took in the drip and its serpentine tubing, sliding along the starched sheets to the back of a hand, its teeth hidden by cotton wool and a clean strip of antiseptic plaster. She ran her eye up her grandmother's arm to her captivated face. Lucy tried to stamp down the heat of unassailable joy, the wild fingers of fire: surely, this was a time for kicking down the walls. But she couldn't summon the rage: it lay dead in a yesterday.

Lucy kissed her grandmother's forehead and then slipped outside towards the front garden, separated from the house by a quiet avenue. Crossing the road, she saw Father Anselm leaning on a wall, looking at the river. He must have nipped out the back way, from the courtyard. Lucy thought she saw faint blue spirals of smoke rising by his head. But no, she concluded, a monk would never have a cigarette.

*

They both leaned on the wall, watching boys pull oars out of time.

Lucy said, 'I've waited all my life for what's happening now, although I never knew it.'

Father Anselm flicked something from his fingers.

'I could never have planned it,' she continued, 'because so much was hidden . . . but even if I'd known all there was to know, there was still nothing I could do . . . nothing I could say. We're all so helpless.'

They were both quiet, listening to the tidal lapping of the river. Lucy went on:

'I've tried – several times – to talk through the mess I did know about, to unravel the misunderstandings, but that usually made things worse. And yet, now, the words work . . . as if they've come to life.'

The water rippled across the stones below, endlessly smoothing them.

Father Anselm said, 'There is a kind of silence that always prevails, but we have to wait.'

They both turned and walked back to the house. Lucy said, 'I'm going to introduce Max Nightingale to an old girlfriend of mine. I suspect they'll get on.'

'Someone did that to me once,' said the monk, smiling, 'and look what happened.'

Lucy laughed. 'It can't do any harm then.'

'No,' said the monk, 'I get the feeling we're all on the other side of harm.'

'For now.'

'That's good enough.'

By the front door they heard soft undulations with a gentle melody, rising like a song.

'That must be Robert,' said Father Anselm, stopping. 'Do you know what he's playing?'

'Yes, it's my Gran's favourite piece of Fauré,' replied Lucy, deeply moved. '"Romance sans parole".'

'"A love song without words",' said the monk.

'Oh God,' exclaimed Lucy, 'every time I see you I cry.'

And the reserved monk took her arm in his and held it tight.

Chapter Forty-Nine

1

Anselm stood awkwardly facing Conroy on the forecourt to the Priory. His sabbatical was over. He'd finished his book and found a publisher with an appetite for trouble, and now the big man was heading back to Rome. After handing the manuscript over to his Order's censors, he'd catch a flight home to São Paulo and his children.

They shook hands, Anselm wincing at the grip. Conroy compressed himself into the driving seat and wound down a window.

'I'll wend my way so.'

'Come back.'

'Sure, I'm taking something of the place with me.'

'And you're leaving something of you and your work behind.'

'Pray for my kids.'

Anselm waved and the chariot of fire left Larkwood.

After Compline that night, when the Great Silence was under way, Father Andrew led Anselm out of the cloister and into the grounds, suggesting a walk.

They talked over all that had happened under a fading sky, then idled down the bluebell path towards the Priory. The woods on either side lay deep in silence, restraining a cool, brooding presence. A solitary owl cried out somewhere near the lake.

'Almost without exception, I misunderstood everything,' said Anselm, his feet scuffing bracken and loose, dry twigs. 'The list of misjudgments is too long to enumerate . . . all from prejudice, loose-thinking, fancy. But I'm not altogether sure the Vatican helped me along my way.'

Father Andrew stepped into the woods, foraging among the undergrowth. He re-emerged with a long quirky branch that must have fallen in the winds. The Prior smiled and swung the stick at the raised heads of winsome dandelions, a boyhood pastime that had come back in older years. He said, 'She has a frail face, made up of the glorious and the twisted.'

Anselm said, 'I still don't know what Rome was really up to.'

The Prior, harvesting, made a heavy, sweeping swish with his stick.

Anselm continued, 'The Vatican had two reports about what happened at Les Moineaux, one of them, damning, from Chambray . . . the other, from Pleyon, apparently exculpatory – only it was never finished. So Rome couldn't have known what Brionne would do when I found him and pushed him into court. He might have filled out the exculpation – which happened to be true . . . or he might have lied to protect himself. Either way, the face of the Church would have been saved. It's not particularly inspiring.'

'Like I said' – the Prior looked around for something else to reap – 'at times the face we love takes a turn, so much so that we might not recognise what we see. And yet, there is another explanation.'

'Which is?'

'Rome trusted the reputation of Pleyon over the words of Chambray.'

411

Anselm frowned with concentration as the Prior continued, '. . . and remember, they went to Chambray first, before they spoke to you, and he told them to get lost. His mind had been made up fifty years earlier.'

The Prior and his disciple slowed to a standstill. The owl, high now in the sky, cried again. An early silver moon hung over the Priory in a weakening blue sky. Anselm sat on the stump of a tree, cut down by Benedict and Jerome after the last year's storms. The Prior, standing, looked at him directly and said, 'And what about you?'

It was a typical question from him. It was so wide in compass that anything could be caught in its net. The Prior always threw such things when he had something specific in mind. Anselm said, 'I lost myself, and I don't know when it happened . . . I lost my hold on Larkwood.'

'It usually happens that way,' said the Prior. 'There's rarely a signpost where the roads divide.' He lopped a clump of ferns. 'Have you found your way back?'

Anselm looked down the path to the monastery, barely discernible from the trees. 'No, I haven't.'

'Good,' said Father Andrew, delivering yet another whack.

The Prior, as was so often the case, seemed to see things not on view. Anselm said, 'I think in an obscure way I might have arrived' – he had a sudden thought – 'helped on my way by Salomon Lachaise . . . the scale of his suffering.'

The Prior rested both hands on his stick, looking quizzically at his son.

'I can't tell you the route. But I've arrived with something like . . . tears in my soul.'

The Prior's gaze grew penetrating. Anselm said, 'Millions died from hatred, beneath a blue sky like the one over Larkwood

412

this afternoon . . . almost by chance, someone like Pascal is trodden underfoot like an ant, along with countless others. And yet, against that, the life of Agnes Embleton is resolved, as if there is a healing hand at work that cannot be deflected from its purpose. I just can't make sense of it, other than to cry.'

The Prior said, 'You never will understand, fully; and in a way, you mustn't. If you do, you'll be trotting out formulas. That will bring you very close to superstition. It can be comforting' − he struck out at the air − 'but it won't last.'

Walking over to Anselm, the Prior thought for a while, leaning his back against a tree. His silver eyebrows, thick and untrimmed, for once looked incongruous on a face so devoid of guile. He said, 'Those tears are part of what it is to be a monk. Out there, in the world, it can be very cold. It seems to be about luck, good and bad, and the distribution is absurd. We have to be candles, burning between hope and despair, faith and doubt, life and death, all the opposites. That is the disquieting place where people must always find us. And if our life means anything, if what we are goes beyond the monastery walls and does some good, it is that somehow, by being here, at peace, we help the world cope with what it cannot understand.'

Father Andrew touched Anselm's shoulder and together they headed down the last quarter mile to the Priory. It had suddenly turned cold, and the glittering lights in the distant windows carried a summons to warmth. Their feet fell softly on the path. The evening light slipped further behind the trees and the moon grew strong. Slightly to the east was the lake, like a black pool, and out of sight the Old Foundry.

Anselm said, 'Schwermann just stood there, before the world, saying he'd done something good among all the evil. He waved

413

it in the air as if it were the winning number in the lottery, a ticket to absolution.'

Father Andrew replied, quietly, 'There might just have been a trace of love in it.'

'Is that enough to redeem a man?'

'God knows.'

'It's terrifying, but do you think a man could so blot out his own life that he can't be saved?'

'No, I don't –' he flung the branch into a pool of shadow – 'but something frightens me far more. There might come a point where someone could choose hell rather than acknowledge fault and accept the forgiveness of God.'

They reached Larkwood Priory and the two monks pushed open the great gate, leaving the breathing woods to the coming night.

2

Lying in bed that night, waiting for *Sailing By*, Anselm involuntarily returned to his earlier reflections. He thought of Pascal and a brutal irony: an accidental consequence of his death was that Agnes was eventually reunited with her son. If Pascal hadn't died, Victor might never have come forward to give evidence . . . if he hadn't given any evidence, Anselm would never have discovered that Victor believed Agnes was dead . . . it was only when Victor realised she was alive that the whole truth came out . . .

And, going back further, if Pascal hadn't died then Anselm would never have gone to France and mentioned the name of Agnes to Etienne Fougères as the butler poured the tea, and discovered that Etienne knew about her, and Robert, and that his family had kept a secret for fifty years . . . That jarred on him now, as it had jarred on him then, but suddenly *Sailing By* began.

Instantly Anselm was in the crow's-nest of a great dipping schooner, high above the decks, with the scurrying crew in black and white below. The spars creaked and groaned and the sails strained against their ropes. Sunlight flashed upon cerulean waves and in the distance thick green foliage burst from the pale sands of a small island. It was a vision that suggested itself every time the music came on and Anselm blissfully surrendered himself to its charms, shutting down the engine of his thinking. However, with his thoughts attuned to the past, a window to his mind was left ajar. Just before he sank beneath the waves he heard a small voice, a little idea. He woke, knocking his radio on to the floor in excitement. This was one thing he had got right.

Chapter Fifty

The old butler led Anselm across the Boulevard de Courcelles towards a side entrance to Parc Monceau. They walked along a path until they reached one corner, near a monument to Chopin. Beside it was a play area with climbing frames and a sandpit, reserved for the under-threes. Stray fallen leaves skipped with each flick of the wind.

'That is where Madame Klein used to live,' said Mr Snyman, pointing to an elegant apartment building directly overlooking the grounds. Defined in those terms, the place appeared instantly hollow, its walls damp. 'That is where Agnes learned the piano . . . it is where I first met her.'

They sat down on a bench near a flourishing lime tree. The grounds were deserted, as if the usual strollers had been carted off. Within the hour, at lunchtime, it would fill up again and then the noisy play would rattle over the ornate fencing and fight with the rumble of the traffic.

'She's dead?' asked Mr Snyman.

'Yes.'

'Peacefully?' There was almost a prayer in his voice.

'Very much so.'

Eventually Agnes had been taken to hospital. The final stages of life could not be handled very well so an ambulance was called. Death popped by while Agnes was lying on a trolley in a corridor, her hand held reassuringly by a nurse. Lucy had run

416

to a pay phone to tell her father. When she'd got back Agnes had gone. The nurse had said she'd smiled. A few days later, Anselm had buried Agnes beneath sleet and rain in the presence of her family.

'I would dearly have liked to have been there,' said the old butler.

'I remembered you.'

'That is something.' After a subdued pause he asked, 'How did you find out about me?'

'It came as I was falling asleep,' Anselm replied. 'But there are reasons. I just didn't join them together properly. It was you who needed to escape, not your family. And yet they fled without you. There were other marks in the sand, like not coming back to Paris until no one could recognise you, and prodding Pascal to find Victor. And more. I didn't understand them until I'd already guessed what they meant.'

Anselm regarded the broken man with compassion. He would be a servant to the past until the day he died. It was his only home, and he was not welcome there.

The old butler stared deep into memory. 'I got back to the house after Victor had gone,' he said. 'My father showed me the record of betrayal. I sometimes think he must have slapped me across the face. But he didn't. I had condemned them all to death. But he understood. He knew I didn't mean to be so weak.' He paused. 'Please, can we walk? My limbs stiffen up unless I move. I may as well tell you what I've kept to myself since Agnes was taken away from me, with my only son.'

They walked side by side as Jacques Fougères spoke. Anselm listened, appalled.

'There were only three passes. We had minutes to decide what to do. "Go!" shouted Snyman, "use my papers." They'd

417

been forged by some friends of Father Rochet, making him a Fougères, my brother. "When they come, I'll say I'm you. At least it will buy time. For God's sake, go now! I've nothing to live for but you have a son, you have Agnes.'''

Jacques' voice grew strong. 'I said it wouldn't work, because our identity cards had a photograph. He shouted again, "Go! Forget the detail . . . take all my other papers . . . if you have to, produce my birth certificate . . . but take the chance, go, now!" I have thought of Franz . . . that was his first name . . . every night since . . . sitting in our house, alone, waiting for them to come, knowing that he would die and I would live.'

And Anselm thought of Mr Snyman at Mauthausen, defending Father Rochet from the brutality of the guards, another honour that had devolved on to Jacques Fougères, the Resistance hero.

'We rushed out of Paris. At one point a Gestapo official checked my father's papers, then my mother's, and when it came to me a distraction occurred and he waved us on. I didn't care about my luck, I just hoped that Agnes would be safe, that Schwermann would keep to his side of the bargain.'

Dense clouds over Anselm's mind began to lift, pushed by a quiet breeze. 'Bargain?'

'Yes. I trusted him. I had to, once he put forward his proposal.'

'What proposal?'

'It all happened on the day I was arrested for wearing the Star. I walked up and down Avenue Foch, wanting to goad Victor. If they picked me up I expected a few days' detention, nothing more. They dragged me in after fifteen minutes and threw me into a room with no windows. The walls were stained with blood that had hit the plaster and dried in thick clumps, with long streams running to the ground. There were bits of skin and hair trapped in the mess. It stank. I couldn't stop myself shaking, my arms, my legs, the lot. I started to cry. Then Schwermann came in with two others. They took down my trousers and tied me to a chair. The other two left and it was just him and me. There were screams echoing down the corridor.'

Jacques pulled air through his nose in slow heaves, as though labouring up a great slope. They turned past a kiosk selling fresh ground coffee, the aroma warm on the air. In front of them stood a delicate colonnade skirting a small lake. Its grace stung Anselm's eyes.

'Schwermann took out his pistol and forced open my mouth, resting the end of the barrel on my front teeth. I was so scared I wet myself and started blabbing nonsense about The Round Table, as if the disclosure of anything would save me. He put his gun away and listened with wide, hard eyes. I calmed, spilling everything out . . . even Robert's existence. He asked lots of questions, telling me not to worry. He was elated. Then he left the room for about half an hour. When he came back he had a proposal.

'Schwermann told me he wanted to smuggle a mother and child out of France. If I helped him, he would spare Agnes and me and Robert. The others would be arrested, of course, but they'd only get hard labour. So I agreed. But I told him I could only guarantee the child, because I didn't have false papers for the mother, but that if she could get to Les Moineaux the monks would sort everything out.'

Through the corner of his eye, Anselm caught sight of a grotto, and flowerbeds, immaculately kept. He turned away to Jacques and asked, 'Did Father Rochet help?'

'I couldn't involve him because he'd ask too many questions'

419

– he cleared his throat – 'so I thought Agnes could be the courier, using her own papers for the child.'

'Why her?'

He spoke the scalding words: 'Because she was the only one who wouldn't ask me why.'

They paused at the water's edge. The sound of children at play floated high on a light wind.

Jacques said, simply, 'Looking back, he was planning how to save the mother. It was obvious and I never guessed . . . and I set the run up . . . just for the child.'

Their footsteps crunched on the tiny stones underfoot as they jointly meditated on the simple anatomy of betrayal. And Anselm reflected once more upon his capacity to misunderstand. Schwermann, when speaking to the cameras, had not been talking about Robert Fougères and his blackmail of Victor. There had been someone else.

'He'd fallen for a French girl and had had a child,' said Jacques dryly. 'Only she turned out to be Jewish when the regulations were looked at more closely. He knew that in time she and her son would be finished. And then, by chance, I cropped up with an unexpected lifeline. So he saved them, leaving the remainder of her family to rot. The rest, Father, I think you know. He did not keep his word.'

'What happened to the boy's mother?' asked Anselm gravely.

'I thought you knew. That was part of the proposal Schwermann kept to himself. When Agnes was arrested he took her papers, all of them. That enabled his girlfriend to obtain a new identity card in Agnes' name. How do I know? On leaving Paris we went to my brother Claude's home near the Swiss border. He still had links with the Resistance around Fernay-Voltaire and Gex because he'd been part of The Round Table network – although he concealed it by vocal support for Vichy. So, my parents assumed a new role, finding placements for Jewish refugees and helping them to cross over. One day a woman claiming to be Agnes Aubret arrived. She'd made it to Les Moineaux, where the monks had arranged her journey to Gex. She stayed with us for three days. I made an excuse and stayed away until she was gone – it was unbearable. As far as I know, she was reunited with her child. I'd like to go home now.'

Bringing together what he had learned from Victor and Jacques, Anselm now finally understood what had happened in 1942.

Schwermann had fallen in love and had a child; a child that would be caught by the net – a net he would throw. Then, by chance, he learned about The Round Table . . . and the existence of another mother and child – Agnes and Robert. That was in June 1942. By July Schwermann had planned with pitiless calculation the resolution of his dilemma: he forced Jacques to arrange the smuggling of his own child to safety, through Agnes, and only then was The Round Table broken. He arrested Agnes himself – having planned all along to take her identification papers so that the mother of his child could also escape. But that left Robert abandoned . . . so Schwermann allowed Victor to keep the child on the condition he incriminated himself to such an extent that he was trapped, and if the need ever arose for Schwermann himself to avoid capture he could compel Victor to use his connections at Les Moineaux. And then Anselm remembered: when the Gestapo came to Les Moineaux only Prior Morel was shot. There had been no search of the convent, where Schwermann's child lay concealed. The infrastructure of escape had been left intact for the woman he loved.

Anselm and Jacques turned and retraced their steps back to the Fougères residence. Jacques explained how the Resistance in Paris, mindful of his parents' service to the cause, concealed suspicions of Jacques' treachery when Father Chambray came asking too many questions. They were content to point the finger at Father Rochet since they'd despised him as a drunkard communist. Jacques' identity as Mr Snyman became a form of exile, which his father, to his dying day, eased with compassion. Thereafter it was a secret, binding those in the family who had to know. After the death of his father he lived with Claude, and when Claude died he joined Etienne – shortly before Pascal was born.

The myth of Jacques' death at Mauthausen had bountiful consequences for the public reputation of his descendants. Keeping the story going led to accidental and conscious elaboration. By the early seventies, when Pascal was asking questions, Jacques had become the founder of The Round Table. Father Rochet, Madame Klein and all the others became bit-players in someone else's drama.

'You know, I think Mr Snyman . . . Franz . . . secretly loved Agnes, and he saved me for her sake. They played a lot of duets together, her at the piano and him with a cello.' He paused, as if slipping back to that candle-lit drawing room, the darkness hard upon the windows. 'You had to be there to know what it was like, listening to them in a room full of people who were all hunted and homeless. The melodies have got louder as I have got older, all of them now a single, crushing lamentation.'

They reached the great black door and Jacques inserted his key. 'There's often not much forgiveness in this life, you know, Father.'

'Yes, I know.'

422

With his rounded back to Anselm, the old man said, 'Robert has a family?'

'Yes.'

'Children?'

'Yes, and grandchildren.'

Jacques Fougères did not turn; he laid his head upon the door. Anselm said, 'I'm sure I could arrange a meeting . . .'

The quiet voice said in reply, 'No, Father, leave them in peace. To them I'm a dead man. It's better that way.'

Anselm drew out the school notebook from his plastic bag and handed it to Jacques. 'Agnes wanted Mr Snyman to have this. She gave it to me after I'd read out your poem. I'm deeply sorry it's not for you.'

The old butler pushed at the door as though it were made of lead.

'Perhaps it doesn't matter why,' said Anselm desperately, 'but you still helped save a boy, Schwermann's son.'

Alert with melancholy, the butler said, 'I've often thought of him . . . growing into a man . . . while I believed Robert had been thrown away.'

Anselm prickled with apprehension. He pictured a small man with haunted, penetrating eyes . . . the centre of a trinity . . . on his left, Lucy, the adopted granddaughter of the woman who saved him; to the right, Max, his own blood. 'Do you remember his name?'

'Oh yes . . . Lachaise . . . Salomon Lachaise.'

The butler stepped inside, extending his hand. Anselm grasped it and said, 'Jacques, that boy grew to be the man who avenged you.'

The butler smiled a farewell and the door snipped into its lock.

*

423

Beneath a pale sun without heat, Anselm wandered back into Parc Monceau, back to the quiet spot opposite the former home of Madame Klein, and sat on a bench just beneath what was once her window.

He thought of Salomon Lachaise: had he known that Schwermann was his father? His mother hadn't told him. It was a secret too painful to disclose. Involuntarily, Anselm suddenly recalled their first meeting, when he'd seen the small dark figure by the lake, cut out against the sky. Salomon Lachaise had said, 'I've come to look upon the father of my grief,' and then, moments later, he'd fallen on his knees before a man, a first meeting with a stranger, exclaiming, 'I am the son of the Sixth Lamentation.' Then Anselm remembered his friend's description of his mother, poring over the photographs of their lost family by candlelight with never a passing reference to the father he'd never known . . . the man whose name he'd never once mentioned in Anselm's presence. She had kept her secret, somehow, but Salomon Lachaise had eventually divined its shape . . . perhaps when she, struck with terror, had begged her son to leave the past alone after he'd announced his intention to help track down the man whom she knew to be his father. Yes . . . for sure . . . Salomon Lachaise had known . . . and he'd waited until the final moment before issuing a condemnation that only he could give.

Anselm looked around, ready to cry. The calm of Parc Monceau had been chased away by children; irrepressible, joyful, not yet hating school. Two or three darted past him, trails of sand falling from cupped fingers. His eye picked out the approach of a young woman aged about twenty-three or four. She glanced at her watch and lifted high a small bell, the kind Anselm had once seen round the necks of goats in Provence. She rang it

424

vigorously, releasing a thin tinkling heard more by its pitch than its volume. At the signal, other teachers casually appeared and ushered their urchins into a line of twos. Each child held the tail of the coat in front, forming a train. When the counting was over they were led off, singing a song that vanished on the wind.

After they had gone, Anselm rose and walked slowly after them, out through the ornamental gates and into the empty street.

Epilogue

'I saw the Sibyl at Cumae'
(One said) 'with mine own eye.
She hung in a cage, and read her rune
To all the passers-by.
Said the boys, "What wouldst thou, Sibyl?"
She answered, "I would die."'

(*Petronius*: 'Satyricon', translated by
Dante Gabriel Rossetti)

The second notebook of Agnes Embleton.
Written out by Miss Wilma Harbottle.

Dear Jacques
'Night and day I have lived among the tombs, cutting myself on stones.'

Do you remember that? Father Rochet said it, laughing, and he added, 'No, I'm not afraid of dying.'

It was the day we were all called together to set The Round Table in motion. Father Rochet said if anyone was caught they were to blame him. I was worried on his account, about what they might do, and he just laughed. And afterwards you said he was the sort of chap who would cave in under pressure. Do you remember?

Now that I'm dying, I can see lots of things far more clearly than I ever did before. When all the faces of my youth started coming back, I looked for yours. You didn't come. That's what first set me thinking. And something tells me you're still alive.

I have spent over half my life revisiting July 1942, always believing you and I, and our oldest friends, were betrayed by Victor. But, as I've said, I started seeing things differently. It wasn't Father Rochet who caved in, was it? It was you.

Did it happen when you were picked up for wearing that Star of David? I never sensed the link before, between your arrest that June and the breaking of The Table in July. But as this note

429

is being written, they're preparing to put Schwermann on trial. Everything I hear moves from your arrest to the betrayal a month later as if they were unconnected, yet it's obvious to me now that they were. I've looked back again. As usual, you organised the run. All the others were picked up in the afternoon, except for you. When I got out of Ravensbrück I was told you stayed at home after your family had gone. Why? Not for me. I was already in La Santé prison. Did you hang around so the Germans could find you easily? I don't think so. No, something went badly wrong on that terrible day and it has something to do with that last run. So, Jacques, if anyone waited patiently for the knock upon the door that night it wasn't you. Surely it wasn't Franz . . . Mr Snyman?

You had a hand in my dying, and our little Robert's. You didn't mean to, or want to. And if you have lived, as I believe you have, it has been no life. If I could see you again I'd kiss you and tell you what you must desperately want to hear. Instead, I raise these old hands of mine: may God protect you, always; and forgive you, as I do now.

Agnes

430

Author's Note

This novel weaves fact and fiction. The historical framework of the trial and the details of life in Paris during the Occupation are all (I hope) accurate. The Vél d'Hiv round-up occurred as described but I could not replicate the horror of what actually transpired.

The progress of judicial retribution after the war causes pause for thought. It was not until 1980 that Herbert Hagen, Kurt Lischka and Ernst Heinrichsohn, three Nazis closely involved in the deportation of Jews from France, were brought before a court in Cologne. Only two out of the thirty or so convicted in their absence by the French authorities had served a sentence (Karl Oberg and Helmut Knochen). Numerous alleged war criminals settled in Britain, but legislation enabling prosecutions to take place was not passed until 1991 (the War Crimes Act). Three hundred and seventy-six suspects were investigated. A third of them were dead, and twenty-five were innocent. The first trial took place in 1995 after a £5.4m investigation and collapsed due to the defendant's ill health. A second (and probably the last) prosecution was concluded in 1999. Anthony Sawoniuk was convicted of murdering two Jewish women in 1942. The name of one was unknown.

The reader wanting to better understand the previous paragraph, and the purging of Nazi Germany in general, could profitably consult *Blind Eye to Murder* by Tom Bower, cited below.

The Round Table did not exist, although monasteries throughout France were involved in similar activities. The idea was prompted by an event in the life of my mother, Margaretha Duyker. As part of a smuggling operation she took an infant by train out of Amsterdam to Arnhem but was arrested by the Gestapo. The child was taken away. She was imprisoned and eventually released. She died of motor neurone disease in 1989.

The Gilbertines never came to France. That is an invasion of my own making. They were the only English-born religious order and did not survive the Dissolution. At their foundation, the monks (canons, to be precise) followed The Rule of Saint Augustine and the nuns that of Saint Benedict. For simplicity I have opted for the latter.

For the purposes of the plot I have taken small liberties with the manner in which deportation records and other formal documents were compiled during the Occupation of France. I have rather ignored the security arrangements of the Old Bailey.

The facts in this novel were harvested from a variety of sources that traverse this tragic period of French history. It would be impractical to list them all but I record my debt to the following:

Blind Eye to Murder, Tom Bower (Warner Books, 1995)
Die Endlösung der Judenfrage in Frankreich, (Dokumentationszentrum für Jüdische Zeitgeschichte CDJC Paris, Deutsche Dokumente 1941–1944), Herausgegeben von Serge Klarsfeld, Rechtsanwalt (Published 1977)
France: The Dark Years, 1940–1944, Julian Jackson (OUP, 2001)
French Children of the Holocaust: A Memorial, Serge Klarsfeld,

(New York University Press, 1977)

The Holocaust, The French, and the Jews, Susan Zuccotti (BasicBooks, HarperCollins, 1993)

Le Syndrome de Vichy: De 1944 a nos jours, Henri Rousso, (Editions du Seuil, 1990)

Occupation, The Ordeal of France, 1940–1944, Ian Ousby (John Murray (Publishers) Ltd, 1997)

Paris after the Liberation: 1944–1949, Antony Beevor and Artemis Cooper (Hamish Hamilton, 1994)

Pope Pius XII and the Holocaust, edited by Carol Rittner and John K. Roth (Continuum by arrangement with University of Leicester, 2002)

The Sacred Chain: A History of the Jews, Norman F. Cantor (HarperCollins, 1995)

The evidence of Mme Marie-Claude Vaillant-Couturier, given at Nuremburg, 28th January 1946

About the Author

William Brodrick was in religious life but left before his final vows. He worked with homeless people and then became a barrister.

ABACUS

To buy any of our books and to find out
more about Abacus and Little, Brown, our authors
and titles, as well as events and book clubs,
visit our website

www.littlebrown.co.uk

and follow us on Twitter

@AbacusBooks
@LittleBrownUK

To order any Abacus titles p & p free in the UK,
please contact our mail order supplier on:

+ 44 (0)1832 737525

Customers not based in the UK should contact
the same number for appropriate postage
and packing costs.